I0716134

# Kaleidoscope
## Box Set

MIA LONDON

# Contents

# Black Tie

# Chapter One

♥

Dane sipped his iced tea, narrowing his eyes toward a brunette, in her early thirties, chatting with her friend over a salad lunch. She looked oddly familiar, but he couldn't place the face. Dane was generally good with faces.

She'd slung her jacket over the back of her chair, wearing only a pale pink shell. He'd learned that term from his ex-wife, Johanna.

*Ugh!* Just the thought of her made his gut churn.

The brunette's shoulders were strong and shapely, and the column of her neck delicate. When she smiled, her entire face lit up, and her posture smacked of confidence.

Then it hit him. She worked in the west building. *On the Dragon Project*, he thought.

*Damn!* That whole product line was getting sold. As CEO, he'd told only a few of his lieutenants, demanding they keep it under wraps until the ink was dry on the deal.

Dane had no idea what personnel the acquiring company would keep on.

*Shit!* No ring on her finger. That likely meant no financial assistance from a husband and possibly no savings.

Dane swirled the ice in his glass, watching as she crossed her shapely legs.

The waitress approached. "Can I get you anything else, sir?"

"The check, please. And…" he glanced at her name tag, "Roxy, I want you to bring me the check from that table too." He discreetly pointed toward the brunette and her friend.

Roxy smiled. "Yes, sir."

The waitress returned a short time later, and he placed some cash on the table. Then, he pulled out a business card and headed for the woman he had to learn more about.

"Excuse me."

Both women looked up at him. "Oh, Mr. Taylor." The brunette rose, her eyes widened.

He offered a hand. "I'm sorry. I know you work for me, but I don't know your name."

She took his hand and answered. "I'm Sophie St. Charles. I work data entry on the Dragon Project."

*Data entry? What the hell?* She looked too smart to be doing data entry.

"Yes. Well, I have a personal assistant getting ready to retire, and I'd like to talk to you about the position."

Her mouth gaped.

"Here's my card. Please send me your resume as soon as possible, Sophie."

She glanced down at the card. "Yes, sir. Thank you, sir."

He nodded to her and her friend, and then headed toward the exit.

*Sir.* He couldn't decide if he liked her referring to him in such a formal way. Made him feel like his father. But damn if the wheels hadn't started turning the moment her warm hand slipped into his.

He'd never done anything like this before. Almost everyone he'd hired had gone through HR first, but since she already worked for him...

Oh, who was he kidding? He wanted her. It was that fucking simple. He'd come up with a plan to parlay his open PA position with a way to get fucking Johanna out of his life. Well, at least, out of his mind.

*Yeah.* The gears were turning. He couldn't wait to hold her interview.

***

Sophie was nervous. The prior week at lunch with Anne, Mr. Dane Taylor—*The* Dane Taylor—approached her. She'd studied his theory on conducting business in China and was enthralled. He was a freakin' prodigy.

He'd asked for her resume, and it was all she could do to at least spit out *thank you*. He was a brilliant man who also happened to be attractive—intense blue-gray eyes, broad shoulders that tapered to a flat stomach, and a drop-dead gorgeous smile.

She'd gone back to her desk, finessed her resume, and sent it to his email. The following morning, she had a personal message from him asking her to meet in his office on the thirtieth floor for an interview.

Sophie'd told her boss, who couldn't believe it either.

Now she stood, waiting for the elevator with half a dozen other people. She smoothed her navy suit, her best suit. She'd paid extra attention that morning to everything—her skin, her makeup, her hair. She polished her heels and pressed her blouse, even though it hardly needed it.

Walking off the elevator, the entire floor opened before her. Rich hardwood floors led to the large reception desk. All the executives had offices on this floor. The receptionist steered her to the left where she met the eyes of an older woman, maybe sixty. The flooring transitioned to a plush, low-pile carpet.

"You must be Sophie St. Charles."

"Yes. Here to see Mr. Taylor."

"Please have a seat. He'll be right with you."

She sat fidgeting with her purse strap, for about ten minutes. The wait was about to kill her. She reviewed what she knew. Dane Taylor had graduated from Stanford and quickly rose up the ranks of IBM. He'd started an internet business and sold it for a few million. That funded his current business, Fortitude Technologies, which was now a Fortune 1000 company. He'd been married, but divorced two years ago and had no kids. She knew he worked a lot, and barely had a social life. Sophie figured he was ten years older than her.

Finally, a balding man in a tan suit opened the door and walked past the admin and down the hall. Shortly after, Mr. Taylor strode out his office toward her. He smiled, and she almost lost her footing as she rose from the sofa.

"Sophie, good to see you."

"Mr. Taylor, you too. Thanks for meeting me." Standing so close to him, she could smell his rich cologne. He wore a lightweight charcoal suit, crisp white shirt, and red striped tie.

He shook her hand, then with an outstretched arm led her to his office. He motioned for her to take the seat at his small conference table. Her resume, two glasses, and a water pitcher already appeared there.

He slipped off his jacket, hanging it in a closet along a rich wood paneled wall. Naturally, he had a corner office with a view of downtown Dallas. From here, she could see for miles. The space also held a heavy mahogany desk, a long leather Chesterfield sofa, and two tall plants by the windows.

"I hope you don't mind if I get a little comfortable. Already, I want the day to end and it's only ten a.m.," he joked.

She smiled as he slipped off his tie and unfastened his first two shirt buttons. The shirt was so fitted on his muscular physique, tapering close to the waist, it had to be custom-made.

He poured them each some water and took a seat.

"As I mentioned, I need a personal assistant. You will keep mostly regular hours, occasionally I will need some evening and weekend work completed. But we will be spending a lot of time together. We'll get to know each other very well. You will have access to my house and all my possessions. You'll come to learn all my likes and dislikes."

*Whoa!*

"What I'm trying to say, is that I will trust you implicitly. And in return, want you to trust me."

"Okay." That made sense.

"This may not be a typical interview for you, Sophie. My last PA was with me for nine years. I'm sad to see her go, but I am equally excited at the prospect of working with you."

*Double whoa!*

"In fact, I want to tell you right now, Sophie, that I want to hire you. I've seen your resume and can't believe you are just doing data entry."

"Yes, well—"

He held up his palm. "It's okay. I don't care. In this position, you will learn almost everything about Fortitude. I will teach you the business so that in two to three years, you can move to any department you want as a manager."

Her jaw unhinged, and she quickly slammed it shut. Relief and excitement flooded her body. She quietly exhaled. She'd hardly said two words to the man, and he wanted to hire her.

He smiled. "But I found myself in a bit of a quandary. I need someone to attend events with me. Plus, some additional things. As I mentioned, some nights and weekends, but I promise not to make a habit of it."

She nodded slowly. Why did she feel a *but* coming on?

His gaze locked onto hers as he slid her resume aside and opened a file folder. He lifted a single sheet of paper over to her. It was an employment contract. The salary was almost twice what she was making now.

She glanced up at him as if to see a joking expression. There was none.

Her duties were outlined, some menial, some looked incredibly top secret. She blinked. Again, it stated that she could move anywhere in the company after a minimum of two years as his PA.

"Wow. Mr. Taylor, this is very generous."

He nodded. "Now, that is one option for your employment."

"One option?" She parroted.

He pursed his lips, like he was searching for his next words. "There is another option." He leaned in slightly. "I would ask you not to discuss this second contract with anyone."

She swallowed as confusion swirled in her brain. What was he asking?

He slid the three-page document to her.

The second contract included overtime pay and a salary for a nanny. If he needed her at a special event that required formal dress, she would be granted access to shop on an expense account at select upper-end clothiers. Again, he would include her in projects with other departments so she could work her way up after the two-year commitment.

The second page of this contract outlined her *Additional Duties*. She skimmed the list and warmth crept up her neck filling her cheeks. He wanted sex, whenever and wherever he pleased. He would only have sex with her, and she with him during the two years. She would be on birth control so he wouldn't have to use a condom. The third page showed the test results of STDs. Everything negative.

*Oh my God.*

She looked up at him. Unknowingly, her fingers went to her parted lips. Her heart threatened to beat out of her chest.

"I know this is a lot to take in. The second contract has several more... requirements to it. Please look it over. We can discuss any questions you may have tomorrow."

*Holy crap!* He was serious. She sipped her water.

"Has anyone else ever been given this contract?"

"No. You would be the first. I have never had a need for such requirements of my personal assistants before. Like I said, I find myself in a precarious position, and I would rather not discuss the details."

She nodded.

After a moment, he spoke. "Take them home, read them. Let's meet tomorrow," he glanced at his phone screen, "at four. Alright?"

She shook her head.

His eyebrows lifted. "No?"

"I don't understand. You're rich, handsome, and I dare say, sexy." His facial features softened. "Why do you need me?"

He scratched his jawbone. "In my position, I have to be careful. The wrong woman could take advantage of me, possibly ruin me. Ruin everything I've worked hard to build." He shrugged a shoulder. "I can't risk it."

She could understand that. And he picked *her*. He didn't want anyone else. She wanted to ask why her, but she didn't have the guts. Hell, what if he changed his mind? God help her.

She swallowed hard. "I don't need to meet tomorrow. I've made my decision."

"You have?"

# Chapter Two

❤

Dane didn't bother to keep the surprise off his face. But it scared the shit out of him that she'd already made up her mind. He knew that likely meant she was out. And fuck him for not playing it right. He had to have her. *All of her.*

"Yes, and I think I would like to take the second contract."

Silence filled the enormous room. The blood roared behind his eardrums. He didn't know if he heard her right, so he processed it. "You would like to take the second contract?"

"Yes. When do I start?"

That made him smile. *Fuck me!*

"Well, thank you, Sophie."

"Thank you, Mr. Taylor."

"As far as your start date, I'll talk with your manager and get that arranged. I would like it to be as soon as possible, but that may not be feasible."

She blushed a beautiful pink color. How far did that blush go?

"Sophie, since you've already made your decision, I would love to take a look at what I'm getting."

Her eyes rounded like saucers.

He leaned closer, breathing in her lovely scent. He wasn't completely sure, but she might already be turned on. His dick grew another inch.

"Don't worry," he said in a low tone, "I won't fuck you now. I would love if you could stand up and undress to your bra and panties. Would you do that for me?"

She worked her precious red lips and rose. First, the jacket slid off her shoulders, then her blouse, and lastly she reached behind to unzip her skirt. She laid them over the back of her chair.

She stood in her heels, black bra and panties. She was exquisite.

He swallowed hard and motioned for her to step closer.

He separated his legs so she could move between them, not bothering to hide the raging hard-on trapped behind his silk suit pants.

"You're beautiful," he whispered. "Please turn around."

She slowly spun and presented her backside. He reached a fingertip to her spine. She jumped.

His fingertips roamed up her back, slowly savoring her silky smooth skin, then slid down to her voluptuous ass and hips. She had an elegant, hour-glass shape, full breasts, and hips that flared from her waist.

He continued his caresses and spoke. "I assume since you accepted my offer that you aren't dating anyone right now, correct?"

"No, sir." Her voice breathy.

"Sophie, turn around." He waited. "When we're alone, I want you to call me Dane. Can you do that?"

She nodded.

His fingers touched her thigh just above her kneecap and moved upward over her lace thong to her stomach. Goosebumps broke out, and he loved it.

"Sophie, you can say *no* to me. It's not in the contract because I hope you never do. But know that you can. Know that I won't be mad.

I don't mind fucking you while you're on your period. I'll want to fuck you as much as possible to curb my ache."

She fell speechless, her full lips parted with her accelerated breathing.

"You are simply gorgeous." He pushed forward in his chair, his face inches from her tits. "Let's test your comfort level, okay."

"Okay."

"I'm going to put my mouth on you. Can you put your hands behind your back?"

She did as he bid.

He'd admit, he softened his commanding style for her. Asking questions was only because he didn't want to scare her off. Soon enough, she would learn what he liked and how he liked it.

Leisurely caressing her arms, he stopped at her bra straps, meeting her eyes, gauging her response.

She didn't flinch.

*Good girl.*

He lowered the straps, watching her full breasts spill from their binding.

"Fuck me."

He hadn't planned to go this far, but he couldn't stop now. A thumb played over a nipple, bringing it to a point. His mouth claimed her nipple, hardening it even more.

She moaned.

Her scent wafted to his nose, and his dick flexed. Like a magnet to freshly mined nickel, his mouth clasped onto her other nipple.

His hands slid south, glossing over the lace of her thong. "Sophie, do you want to widen your stance?"

She was smart, she knew what he was asking. She probably needed to come right about now, and he wanted to be the one to give her a much-deserved orgasm. He didn't want to send her back to her regular job distracted and slippery.

She spread her legs before him, the scent came at him stronger.

He continued the gentle petting over her sex and allowed himself a little dip in her cleft.

Her clit poked against the fabric.

He massaged and circled her little bud, watching her expression.

Her head fell back as she moaned.

*Fuck!* She was so ripe. When was the last time she was with a man?

He'd done his research. He knew Sophie had a five-year old daughter and an ex-husband of four years. But he couldn't get much information on her personal life. Probably because she didn't have one.

He continued to stimulate her with his right finger and held her steady with his left hand. His mouth sucked the full fruit of her breasts.

Her hips pushed into his hand, and another moan escaped.

He wanted to rip those panties off her, but it wasn't necessary. Her clit twitched under his touch, and she writhed at his touch.

"Oh." Her voice wasn't loud. But some nights, maybe away from the office, he would have her screaming.

He held her steady through her climax.

Coming down, she panted and looked down at him, her eyes glassy with lust.

"Perfect. If you'd like to clean up, that door is my private bathroom. Help yourself."

She grabbed her clothes and scampered to the washroom.

She returned a few short minutes later.

He needed her gone before he did anything else. He offered a hand. "Thank you so much, Sophie. I'll be in touch."

"Thank you, Mr. Taylor." She followed him to the door and smiled one last time.

*Oh yeah.* One of the best decisions he ever made.

***

The last week had been a bit of a whirlwind. Sophie spoke to her boss, who was still completely dumbfounded about her moving to "The Tower"—that was what everyone called it—to work directly for the CEO, Dane Taylor. Her boss had pumped her for information, not that she had any to give.

Frankly, Sophie was just as dumbfounded. One minute, she'd been eating lunch with one of her best friends. The next, she'd stripped for a delicious tall drink of water and let him bring her to orgasm in his huge office, some thirty stories up.

It was the craziest, most erotic thing she'd ever done.

She hadn't told Anne or Tori *all* the details of her "employment contract" yet. She was pretty sure she wasn't allowed to, so that was fine. All her friends knew was she was Dane Taylor's newest PA, and they were excited for her.

She'd finished most everything she was working on with the Dragon Project, did some shopping after reevaluating her wardrobe, and started searching for a babysitter with flexibility.

She reported at nine a.m. Monday to the thirtieth floor, and his admin, Dorothy, gave her a tour of the place—bathrooms, coffee room, executive lunchroom, 'and of course, her very own oversized cubicle.

Mr. Taylor had a meeting in the north building and wouldn't be in until eleven, and had left Sophie a list of some things to take care.

She felt like such a nuisance, constantly asking Dorothy where to find things or people. Time flew.

Shortly before noon, Mr. Taylor stood at her cubicle. "Hello, Sophie."

She jumped and spun around. "Mr. Taylor. I didn't hear you."

He grinned. "Can you meet for a few minutes?"

Dorothy had just slung her bag over her shoulder. "The calls will roll to voicemail," she called as she made her way down the hall.

"Thanks," he replied and followed Sophie into his office.

"Please sit." He motioned to the same chair she sat in the week prior.

A warmth crept up her neck and cheeks.

"How is it going so far? Any questions?"

"Um." She tried to think of at least a few of the millions of questions she had, but damn, this man was so distracting.

He'd removed his jacket again, this time he rolled up his sleeves a few times before sitting.

"I can't seem to get a hold of Jessica at Elite Star Spa."

"That's okay. She's very busy and will probably call you back tomorrow."

"Okay. I also wonder if I could get a sort of corporate directory so I can find out who's who and how to get a hold of them."

A smiled tugged at his lips. "Certainly. I'll get you one." He eyed her with curiosity. "Anything else?"

"Um, not that I can think of."

"C'mere." He rose and offered her a hand to lead her to the windows. He pressed a button or something under his desk and walked up behind her.

"Sophie, you look wonderful today. I particularly like you in these kinds of skirts," he whispered at her ear.

She wore a dark gray pencil skirt with a tangerine blouse belted at the waist and black high heels.

He started kissing her neck, and she couldn't think of a reply. "I love looking out this window. It's almost like I'm up above the world, untouchable," he whispered into her neck.

"Mm."

His glorious kisses continued, and her breathing hitched.

"Sophie, were you able to get on birth control?"

"Yes, sir."

"That's good news because I desperately need to fuck you right now."

She moaned as his hands crept to her breasts.

"May I?"

"Yes, sir."

"Uh-uh."

"Yes, Dane."

"I love to hear my name come from your lips." He worked free her belt, the buttons on her blouse, and her skirt, letting it all pile on the floor.

*Oh God!* She was almost naked in front of the window, the huge window facing downtown Dallas and other high-rises.

"Sophie, I can feel you tense. Don't worry. Remember, the glass of this building is mirrored. No one can see you."

She exhaled. "Yes, sir—Dane."

His hands and lips combed her body. Soon, her bra fell to the floor. "Hands on the glass, baby."

She complied and his long fingers played over and around her sex, then with two fingers hooked on her panties, he slid them to the floor, leaving her naked save for her high heels.

"Fuck, you feel so good." He toyed with her nipples and caressed her skin, not yet touching her eager clit. How she needed to come. The slickness gathered between her legs.

"Turn around."

She did as she was told, standing in front of him for his sole viewing.

His lips instantly went to her breasts, sucking, licking, and nipping. Her head fell back against the window.

"Spread your legs wide, Sophie."

She moved her legs and watched as he undid his belt and pants, allowing his cock to spring free. Her mouth gaped. He had to have the biggest she'd ever seen—purple-tipped, eager, and standing at attention.

His gaze roamed her body as he went to his knees. "Hands on the glass, baby."

*Right.*

Thumbs gently glossed over her labia, and she quivered.

He blew across her clit, and she moaned.

*Touch me. Please, touch me.*

"Your clit is gorgeous. So willing." He leaned forward and lightly licked her.

Her hips pitched forward.

He slammed his forearm across her mid-section and licked her again, over and over, lapping her entirely.

She stifled a squeal.

The delightful torture brought on an orgasm faster than she'd ever experienced. The electricity shot through her, but Dane didn't stop. Another orgasm rolled through her, and a trickle slid down the inside of her right thigh.

He had her pinned to lick her still.

"Oh God. Oh God." She panted for breath as another orgasm started to build inside her.

"Dane. Dane." She was delirious with lust and passion. Her legs shook, and her third climax rocketed to the surface. She was light-headed, but before she could protest, Dane stood, lifted her leg to his thigh, and drove his huge cock into her.

She cried out, slamming a hand over her mouth that was too late to silence her outburst.

*Oh God, he feels so good.* She didn't want it to end, but she'd been so loud, he would probably fire her.

He came with a powerful thrust and a growl at her neck.

Slowly, the wave receded, and he pulled out. "Wait right here."

He crossed the room to the sink and turned on the hot water. He opened a drawer, took out a washcloth, and wetted it. He wiped himself, then rinsed the washcloth and brought it back to her, wiping the semen that had collected at her sex.

He put himself back together. Then, he collapsed in his chair and stared up at her, his chest rising slightly out of breath.

He was mad; she was sure of it. "I'm sorry I was so loud."

He blinked. "I don't care about that."

Another several beats passed. His silence confused her. Should she get dressed? "Are you mad at me?"

A small smile came to his lips. "No. Just the opposite." His gaze combed her again from head to toe. "You are a centerfold, Sophie."

He rose but didn't touch her. "I'll want you every day. Dorothy takes lunch about this time every day. When she goes, I want you to come in here so I can fuck you. If we have time, I'll fuck you twice. Do you understand?"

"Yes, s—Dane."

"Good. But know this, I will worship your body. You are not just some hole. Like today, I want you screaming out your orgasm. I want you in ecstasy. I want you to crave me filling you as much as I crave you. Do you understand?"

"Yes, Dane."

"Good. You can get dressed now and get some lunch." He spun away toward his desk and turned on his dual monitors.

And that was her first day at her new job.

# Chapter Three

♥

Dane had to be the fucking luckiest man on the planet. His company had posted its best quarterly numbers in history, his ex-wife was out of the country on some girls' trip, and he was fucking the sexiest damn woman he'd ever laid eyes on.

If Sophie could come to work naked…

*Ha!* He was crazy.

But fuck, she was incredible. So much built-up sexual tension. She hadn't been laid in years, he'd bet his last Benjamin on it. He'd taken her every lunch hour, as he promised. On the floor, against the glass, on the sofa, and once over his desk.

The last month since hiring Sophie had been unbelievable. And it was more than sex, at least it seemed that way, but he couldn't define it.

One Friday night, she stayed late. He'd cleared it with her when her child was at her father's house so she could "work late". He had some organizing to do, but nothing critical. He had arranged for the executive chef to bring them dinner before he'd left. Chef was always excited for special requests and the chance to try something new.

Dane and Sophie sat at the table and ate the scallops, asparagus, and rice with an expensive bottle of white he had stashed in his mini-fridge.

Her eyes lit up looking at the spread. And damn, if he didn't like that expression on her beautiful face.

When they finished, she started. "Dane?"

"Yeah."

"You said when I interviewed that we had to trust each other. That we would know just about everything about each other."

"That's right."

"So, can you tell me about your ex-wife?"

He exhaled long and slow. *Shit!* He hated talking about Johanna, the conniving bitch. That was the worst decision of his life. He swallowed the last of his wine and began. "We were married just over ten years. A few years in, something had changed. I denied it, but she wasn't the same woman I married. I think she was cheating on me, but I didn't want to believe it. I thought we were just in a slump. Well, she set me up. She hired a woman to seduce me. She has pictures, and right now she's bribing me with them. The kicker is, she waited until *after* we were divorced to bring it up. Now, she blackmails me anytime she wants something from me, threatening to spread the news to any tabloid *and* to Wall Street."

Sophie's lips formed a big shocking O. "So that's what you're dealing with right now?"

He nodded and rubbed the back of his neck.

She let a moment pass before she rose from her chair and came before him.

He swung his chair away from the table to look up at her.

In an unexpected move, she slowly, piece by piece, took off her clothes and dropped them in a pile on the floor. In just her high heels, she caressed her hands up and down her naked torso, over her breasts, and down to her sex.

*Fuck!* It was hot.

Then, she lowered herself to her knees and pushed his legs apart to crawl between them.

He was hard for her, and she knew he would be.

Keeping his gaze, she loosened this belt and pants. Pushing the fabric out of the way, she freed his stiff cock and wasted no time taking him into her warm, wet mouth.

"Oh fuck."

She worked him, and it was like heaven. She took him as deep as she could. No woman had done that to him before. Her gag reflex must have been incredibly low.

When he didn't think he could hold out anymore, he pulled her back by her hair and rose.

In one swift move, with his arm outstretched, he pushed all the plates, silverware, everything off the table onto the floor. He lifted her onto the table and flipped off her shoes, resting her feet wide on the round table.

"Time for dessert." And he devoured her dripping pussy.

Her musky scent had him wanting her thrashing beneath him, begging him to put her out of her misery. He licked and twirled, and when he thought she was close to coming, he'd pull back.

"Dane," she whimpered. "Dane." She writhed on his table, lifting her pussy closer to his mouth, but it did no good. Her beautiful milky sweetness dripped incessantly.

"Tell me you want my big cock inside you." He blew over her engorged red clit.

"I want it. Dane. Please."

"Uh-uh. Say 'Dane, please fuck me with your big hard cock.'"

She opened her eyes. "Dane, please fuck me with your big hard cock."

"Good girl." He pressed his tongue back onto her hard nub, playing and circling it until she bowed of the table and screamed out her orgasm. Her loudest scream yet. Before she completely came down, he stood and thrusted his hard spear into her slick cunt.

"Fuck," he called out, and in no time, she was coming again on the heels of his cataclysmic climax.

He collapsed over her, and her arms came around him. Normally, he had enough energy to stand and wrap it up. That was what he *had* done. He wouldn't linger. This wasn't some love connection. It was a relationship of convenience. A professional one with additional benefits negotiated.

But this time, he couldn't move. He was completely spent. She drained him of every ounce of thought and concern. For the briefest of moments, he hadn't a care in the world. All he knew was the exquisite warmth that filled his inside and wrapped around him on the outside. For the first time in a long time, he felt entirely sated.

He lifted on his forearms, taking the weight off her chest, and looked down at her luminous blue eyes. He could see the same peace in her eyes. It nearly took his breath away.

He gingerly slipped out of her and did his routine of cleaning them both up before she rose to put her clothes back on.

He walked to his computer and clicked open his calendar. "I have a black tie event in two Saturdays. I need you to be there." Then he stopped himself from sounding like an asshole. "I mean, would you like to come with me?"

The corners of her lips lifted slightly. "Yes, that would be lovely."

He typed something on his keyboard, then came to her. "I emailed you a list of places where I have a line of credit. You are on the approved list. Please go buy yourself a formal gown, and anything else you would like." He took her hand and gave it a little squeeze. "Sophie, you have been invaluable to me this last month. Thank you for everything." He didn't say thank you very often. Perhaps because he hadn't thought he ever needed to, but Sophie made him want to.

"You're welcome. Let me help you clean up this mess."

He shooed it away. "Don't bother. The cleaning crew will be in this weekend. I'll leave them a note to clean the carpet in my office, and it will be perfect by Monday morning."

She nodded and stood for a moment like she had something more to say. Instead, she smiled and said, "Okay, I'll see you Monday. Good night."

"Good night, Sophie."

She closed the door behind her.

***

Sophie lay in bed, staring up at the empty darkness of her bedroom. Images of Dane filled her thoughts as of late, and it was getting worse.

It was like he knew what she needed, when she needed it. Sometimes he'd sit with her for almost an hour, reviewing financial sheet data or getting her input on an investor call. He seemed pleasantly surprised when she knew certain things.

She'd graduated from Michigan and took a position with a small electronics firm as a production manager. It was an incredible learning ground. Things got off-track when she met Brice and accidentally got pregnant. They'd quickly gotten married, and it went downhill from there. Brice had an offer in Dallas and that's how they moved to Texas. Sophie was fortunate to at least have the kind of job that allowed her some time with her new baby. That was five years ago.

In one respect, she was disappointed she wasn't using her degree. In another, she was blessed to have Penny in her life. *Precocious Penny.* She smiled thinking about her precious baby.

Waking up an unused part of her brain now exhilarated her. She was learning so much under Dane's tutelage, it was exciting. Then there was the sex. *Holy Mother of God.*

She never knew sex could be so rousing. Her body reacted to his like it was made for him, made to please him. But he was oh-so-good at giving her pleasure too. He'd always made sure she came, at least once. Sometimes more, if there was time.

What didn't escape her was the fact that he never kissed her on the lips. *Never. Not once.*

Her throat tightened at the thought. She didn't know why and was too afraid to ask.

She wanted to kiss him. She wanted everything from him. Well, not everything. She knew better than to think they had any kind of future beyond these two years together. She'd fantasized about it—marrying him, moving in with him, waking up with him so he could make love to her before going to work. But she knew he was never getting into another serious relationship with a woman again. He'd gotten burned and had too much at risk.

That didn't stop her daydreaming.

Sophie knew there was a chance she was falling in love with him. She tried to rationalize that it was all the sex clouding her judgement, but that was a lie.

She sighed. It was nearly midnight, and she needed to get some rest. The following day she had to report to another building. She had an opportunity to shadow a manager in procurement for the day.

The next day flew by. Sophie wasn't as tired as she thought she would be, but it was odd not seeing Dane. Then a text came through. Dane.

*When you wrap up over there, I need to see you in my office.*

Her tummy flipped over. She had an idea what he needed. She texted the sitter asking her to stay later and possibly start dinner as well.

At five-ten, she walked into his office. Dorothy had already gone.

He looked up at her. A fire in his eyes shown that she'd never seen before. He reached beneath his desk and locked the door.

"Strip," he commanded.

He'd already removed his jacket and tie, and as she slipped off her jacket and blouse, she noticed the remains of a glass of liquor on his desk.

Something happened.

She stepped out of her skirt when he said, "Get over here."

Her heartbeat ratcheted higher. She crossed to his side of the desk.

He spun her to face the desk. "Hands on the desk."

She presented her ass to him, still wearing her heels, bra, and panties.

His hands went to her backside, sliding over her skin, then grabbing her panties, he ripped them in two.

She shrieked at the suddenness of his action. The scrap of fabric slid down one leg.

"Legs apart." She heard him unfasten his pants.

*Oh shit!*

She separated her legs, and with a hand at her hip, he dove into her barely wet channel, slamming into the end. She screamed.

He pumped into her like a madman, both hands gripping her hips, pulling her onto his cock so he could claim every bit of space her body would give.

He was fucking her. This time was not for her pleasure. It was all for him.

She bit down on her lip and clutched the edge of the desk for purchase. The building moisture slowly eased the discomfort for her.

In just a few short thrusts, he came into her with a growl. His hands crashed down onto the desktop around her, his bursts of breath blowing over her back.

Gee-zus! What just happened? He'd said he wouldn't use her like some hole, but this was evidence to the contrary.

He pulled out and walked to get a towel. After wiping himself, he tossed the towel on the desk for her. He moved in the front of the window, fixing his pants, and stared out into the nothingness.

She dressed and hid her torn panties inside her purse.

He muttered something she couldn't hear.

"What?"

He pivoted to meet her gaze head on, his eyes full of remorse. "I'm sorry."

She nodded. "Do you want to talk about it?"

"Not really." He let out a sigh and slammed back the last of his drink.

When he didn't start to speak, she mustered the courage. "I think you at least owe me an explanation."

The corner of his lip quirked. "You're right. I do." He inhaled deeply. "My ex-wife is making my life miserable. Making demands again. She spends money like water flows over Niagara."

"Didn't she get a settlement from the divorce?"

"Yes, a healthy one."

"Dane," she closed the distance between them, "have you thought of calling her bluff? I mean, how terrible would it be if the pictures came out?"

She held his gaze, witnessing them turn from sorrow to concern in a flash.

"It would be bad," he muttered and looked off in the distance.

She licked her lips. "I'm sorry."

His eyes returned to hers, and he shook his head. "You have nothing to be sorry for. I'm the one who's sorry. I should have never done that," he waved a hand toward his desk, "to you."

She gave him a smile of understanding.

"Go home. Please. Be with your daughter. Do you have a dress?"

She grinned. "Yes."

"Great. Then I'll pick you up Saturday at seven."

"Okay, good night, Dane." She lifted her purse and looped it through her arm.

"Good night, Sophie."

# Chapter Four

♥

This week had been hellacious. Johanna's shrill voice still resonated in Dane's ear.

*Dane, do you have my money? Money doesn't grow on trees you know, so make it happen.* Or the voicemail she'd left early in the week: *Dane, it seems that my trip to Bermuda cost more than I had expected. I'm gonna need another payment, just as much as last time, sent over ASAP.*

Regrettably, he'd taken his frustration out on Sophie. He hadn't seen her again the entire week as she was with Merlin in Procurement.

But the weekend was finally here. The thought had crossed his mind to skip the banquet. He didn't really need to attend, but it looked good for him to be there every year. And frankly, being with Sophie would be the highlight for him this year. He hadn't seen her since Monday. He missed her inquisitive nature, her contagious smile, and her curvy form cradled around him.

The limo stopped in front of Sophie's adorable, single-story house, and Dane climbed out. He rang the bell and was greeted by a tiny human with sparkling blue eyes and wavy light brown hair.

"Hi. Are you my mommy's boss?"

"Penny," he heard from deeper inside the house.

"Hi. Yes, I am. I'm Mr. Dane."

The nanny appeared and opened the door wider. "Hi. Sorry. Please come in."

Dane stepped into the great room and looked around at the comfy white sectional sofa, pale green walls, and the few toys scattered about. The room was warm and inviting—a reflection of Sophie's personality.

Sophie turned the corner and smiled at him.

"Wow." He scanned her from head to toe. She wore a deep rich, purple sleeveless gown with a high, kimono-style collar, a high side slit up her leg, and the fabric gathered at her waist only accentuated her breasts more.

She turned around. The back of the dress had a cut-out revealing some skin and hugged her ass.

"You look breathtaking."

She blushed as she stepped closer. "Thank you. You look very handsome too, Mr. Taylor." He wore his tux. Little thought was required for him to dress for an event like this.

He presented his arm. "Shall we go?"

She took a peek in her tiny black bag. "I'm ready." She took his arm.

"Bye, Mommy." Penny ran up to her.

Sophie leaned down to give her a kiss. "Be good tonight."

The girl grinned.

"See you later, Grace," Sophie called to the nanny.

"No rush tonight. I already have the guest room made up." Grace smiled and waved goodbye.

He walked Sophie to the limo and felt like a man on top of the world. He knew this was going to be a great night.


They strode through the doorway of the hotel's ballroom. The place looked like a palace in England—chandeliers, white clothed tables, floral bouquets, and an ice sculpture set in the center of the hors d'oeuvres bar. People meandered about dressed to the nines in tuxedoes and formal gowns. A four-piece band set up in the center of the side wall played a timeless number.

Quickly, Dane was greeted by Patrick Rodgers of CG&V and his wife, Shelia.

He pecked Shelia's cheek. "Great seeing you both. Allow me to introduce my date, Sophie St. Charles."

*What?! Where did that some from?*

Dane almost drew blood biting his tongue after he'd used the word "date." Sophie was an employee; this was *not* a romantic entanglement.

He schooled his features and reprimanded himself to be more cognizant for the remainder of the night.

Patrick and Shelia shook hands, both smiling at Sophie. "Nice to meet you."

They all chatted, and Patrick promised to call Dane the following week for a game of squash.

Dane retrieved two glasses of champagne from a passing waiter and handed one to Sophie. "Cheers. And thank you again for coming."

"Thank you for inviting me," she said with a coy smile.

She didn't say anything tasteless like *that's what you pay me for.* It might have been the truth, but something uneasy bubbled up in Dane's gut thinking she might only have come because it was in her employment contract.

"Hungry?" he asked.

"Yes. Famished."

"Okay, let's grab some appetizers since dinner won't be served for another hour."

They filled little plates with samplings of shrimp cocktail, bacon-wrapped water chestnuts, asparagus asiago spears, and more.

Dane pointed to a high table next to another couple, Herman and Blanche Parker of The Spine Team, and conversation ensued after the introductions.

Dane loved how Sophie held her own in every topic that came up. She was a natural, confident and easy-going, but not easily swayed. She might have an opinion but wasn't opinionated. He knew this about her from their time together in the office, but in this setting, he couldn't have been more pleased.

After a dinner of sea bass, potatoes au gratin, and field greens, Dane found himself mesmerized watching Sophie as she discussed Brexit with Tom Aldridge, CTO of DutchRoyal. She was positively fascinating.

As if sensing his attention on her, she glanced his way and smiled. They quickly wrapped their conversation as a singer came to the mic and announced the dancefloor was open.

Dane was so caught up in the conversation, so relaxed in enjoying his evening with Sophie, he hadn't even noticed Johanna was at the event. Across the ballroom, she had her hand rested on some poor sucker's arm as she put on a full-court press, flirting and teasing him.

Dane didn't know if she even knew he was there.

Sophie leaned in closer. "What's wrong?"

He peeled his eyes away from Johanna. "Dance with me."

Sophie's eyebrows crinkled, but she nodded.

Taking his hand, he led them to the dancefloor. He met Sophie's gaze—she at least deserved to know. Johanna was the only person on the planet who made Dane uneasy. Multi-million-dollar deals didn't affect him the way Johanna's mere presence set his teeth on edge.

"Johanna's here."

Sophie gasped lightly, and her eyes scanned the room. "Where?"

"She's the tall redhead over my right shoulder."

Sophie stared for several beats then looked back at him. "Do you want to leave?"

"It's all right." At least he would tell himself so. "Let's stay for dessert, then make a decision."

He held Sophie close, allowing himself a small respite with the gorgeous woman in his arms. Her scent and delicate feel when dancing evoked thoughts of laying her across his bed and feasting on her. He'd claim every inch of her with his hands, his mouth, his cock. He'd find every sacred spot that no man had discovered on her body—a path of discovery he knew would have her writhing and moaning for more.

He pushed the thoughts away. Too much longer, and even his tux jacket wouldn't hide his tented pants.

After a few songs, they returned to their table where a chocolate lava cake awaited each of them.

Sophie finished dessert, occasionally scanning the room. She watched as Johanna rose from her table, crossed the ballroom, and headed for the ladies room. This was Sophie's chance.

"Excuse me." She leaned in close to whisper, then stood to head in the direction Johanna took.

Walking into the restroom, a woman in a black, sequin gown washed then dried her hands before she walked out. Sophie saw only one stall door closed. That would be Johanna.

*Here goes.*

Setting her phone, she pushed her bag to the center of the vanity. Then she gripped the edge of the countertop and let out a sob. She sniffled a few times, made crying sounds, and soon the tears streamed down.

A few short minutes and Johanna walked out of a stall, her eyebrows trying to pull together.

"Oh." Sophie rose and blotted her cheeks. "I didn't know anyone was in here."

Johanna handed her a tissue. "Are you all right?"

Sophie sniffled and shook her head. "All men are pigs. They let their hands wander and take liberties, wherever and whenever they want," she muttered, looking down. "Sorry. My boss is a pig."

Johanna looked her way as she washed her hands. "What an asshole."

Sophie tapped her chest several times. "And I *love* my job. I hate the thought of leaving." Sophie gripped the edge of the counter, hiding the trembling of her hands.

"Why don't you go to HR?"

"I did. They said they'd 'look into it'. But I haven't heard a thing. I know they just want to keep their jobs, and they're not gonna risk anything for some two-bit secretary." She wiped away fake tears. "I just wanna...nail his ass but good. Who does he think he is?" She gritted her teeth for show.

"So, rake him across the coals."

"Sure, but how?" Giving her a look like she'd already thought of that.

"You could record him."

Sophie lifted her head in feign surprise. "Okaaay."

"If it's in his office, you have to be there before him to plant a camera."

Her eyes looked off to the side, pausing, as if working out the plan in her head. "Yeah."

"Cameras are cheap on the internet. Maybe get more than one." Johanna turned to face the mirror and reapply her lipstick. "Everything gets sent to your cell phone."

She nodded. "Right. This is brilliant. How do know all this?"

"I may have used this before," Johanna replied with a smug smile on her face.

She sent the woman a crocked smile. "You had to have used this... technique," she pretended like she was searching for an admirable word for the extortion, "once or twice on a boss?"

Johanna's shifty little eyes scanned the bathroom to make sure they were still alone. "Bosses, ex-husbands. All men are pigs, right?" She flapped her hand, her excessively long fingernails catching the light in the movement.

"I knew it. You're secretly smart. Like one of those people who look pretty on the outside and because so, everyone underestimates how brilliant they really are on the inside." Sophie embellished and could literally see the gleam in the woman's eyes grow.

"You're right. That's me exactly. When I had enough of my good-for-nothing husband, I recorded him with another woman. Best three hundred bucks I ever spent." She folded her arms over her enhanced boobs. "Now, anytime I need to tighten the screws on him, I just flash the tape of his cheating on me. Gets me what I want every time." She grinned like Cruella de Vil.

Sophie gasped lavishly and swung her arms around the woman. "Oh, thank you. Thank you. This could work. This could really work. And I'm free at last."

"Indeed." The woman waggled her over-plucked eyebrows. "Just remember to double check the angles, and you'll be good to go."

"I will. I promise." Turning on the little protégé act was easy with this woman. The woman was dying for attention and accolades anywhere she could get them.

The bitch spun around and headed out the door. Sophie let out a shaky breath.

# Chapter Five

♥

Dane glanced at his watch. Sophie had been gone for quite a while, and he was starting to worry.

Just as he'd decided to go hunt for her, his cell phone chimed with a text. It was from Sophie.

*Meet me in the lobby.*

He furrowed his brows but walked the stretch of the ballroom and out toward the lobby. Sophie stood like a wallflower hidden behind a Ficus tree.

"Sophie, what's going on?"

"Shh. Follow me."

He almost corrected her. He wasn't one who took the orders—he gave them. But he stopped himself, instead, following her down a hallway lined with conference room doors.

She opened the door to the "Shalimar" meeting room and flipped on the lights.

The door closed behind him.

She pulled her cell phone out of her bag. "I ran into Johanna."

His blood pressure instantly rose ten points.

She cupped her hand over his forearm. "It's okay. Really." Then she hit play on her cell phone.

At first it sounded like a woman crying, and quickly he realized it was Sophie. He stared at the phone trying to process. Then he heard Johanna's voice.

*What is going on?*

Sophie complained about men being pigs. *Him.*

His lips pursed, and he glanced her way.

She held up a finger as the recording continued.

He heard Johanna coach Sophie on videotaping him.

*Oh shit! This can't be happening.* He was being set up. His stomach dropped to the floor. Johanna continued, and then Sophie complimented her. The blood roared behind his eardrums. This might have been the second-worst day of his life.

The recording ended, and Dane took a step back.

Sophie's smile fell.

"What do you want?"

She stared at him for several beats, then asked, "What?"

"How much?"

Her eyes grew misty. She looked down at the phone, then up at him. "No," she squeaked out. "I don't want your money."

He took another half-step back, the anger mixing with betrayal, threatening to have him spill his dinner. "It's all right there, Sophie. Don't deny it. So, how much?" He crossed his arms over his chest.

Tears streamed down her cheeks.

*Oh, this woman is a pro.*

"Dane, I don't want your money. We got her. She's admitting to everything on tape. You may not be the only one she's blackmailing."

His brows pulled together, replaying the conversation he'd heard. "You set her up."

"Yes," she whispered, her eyebrows lifting.

It all started to make sense. Sophie baited her, and Johanna fell for it. "Oh my God."

"Right." The eagerness returned to Sophie's voice, and her tears dried. "You're free."

*Could this be true?*

He closed the space between them. "I'm sorry. I'm sorry I accused you—"

"Don't worry about it. What do we do with this?" She wiggled her phone in the air.

"Oh, that's easy." He retrieved his phone from his jacket pocket. "*Dane.*"

"Gary. I've got it. I've got Johanna on tape, confessing to the whole thing."

"*No shit! That's incredible. Can you send it to me?*"

"Sure." He looked at Sophie. "Try and send it to my attorney." He gave her the email address and waited. It took a solid minute to go through.

Gary spoke. "*I think I got it. Yup.*"

Dane heard the women's interaction coming through Gary's computer speakers.

"*Excellent. I'll take it from here. It sounds like you might not be the only one she's blackmailing.*"

"That's what Sophie said."

"*Yeah, well, you need to give that woman a raise. I'll take it from here. Let's talk Monday.*"

"Thanks, Gary." He disconnected the call.

Dane slipped his phone back in his pocket and stared at the woman beside him. How could he have thought so little of her? "Let's go."

Confusion crossed her face briefly before she replied, "Okay."

Dane gave instructions to the driver. After everything that had happened this evening, and how Sophie stuck her neck out for him, he had only one thing on his mind. Getting her in his bed. Showing her appreciation the best way he knew how when it came to Sophie.

She was gorgeous and smart, and for some reason, loyal to him.

When she'd played the recording for him, Sophie was confused by his reaction. He'd been taken advantage of too many times in the past, and he automatically thought she was doing it as well. It struck like a knife through the heart. She would *never* do anything like that. If something happened causing her to become unhappy with him or the job, she would just leave. She wouldn't resort something so slimy. She was *not* Johanna.

He held her hand as they rode in silence to his condo.

The driver pulled in front of his condo building, and he held open the car door for her.

Something was different. Dane was different. She knew he would be happy with the news of Johanna's confession, but this was a side she hadn't seen before in her boss.

Sophie had an idea he wanted to have sex, and a little thrill raced through her when they arrived at his place. They never had sex at his place. This would be a first.

The elevator ride was also silent. She didn't know if she should say something.

She walked into his spacious condo  a view of nighttime in Dallas beyond the great room which held a large, navy velvet sofa and white leather armchairs.

He pulled on his bow tie, loosened his top two buttons, and laid his jacket over one of the chairs. He approached her and cupped her cheeks, staring into her eyes. "Sophie, I'm sorry about earlier. I should have known you would never betray me like that."

The warmth from his hands spread through her entire being. "It's all right," she managed to squeak out.

He shook his head and stepped closer.

Her hands went to his upper arms. Was he going to kiss her?

He reached behind her neck and unfastened her dress, slowly pushing it off her shoulders to let it pool to the floor.

"God, you're so beautiful." His eyes scanned her body and landed on her lips. His thumb glossed over her lower lip. "Shit, Sophie. You make me want to do things I swore I'd never do."

Her lips parted. "Please do them."

He hesitated a fraction of a second and stepped closer, his shirt brushing against her hardened nipples. He lowered his lips to hers, testing at first then diving in.

Oh, God, his kiss. He pulled her closer—one arm around her waist, one hand clasping the back of her neck.

Her arms looped around him, sinking into the kiss, savoring his masculine taste and feel. Moisture gathered at the apex of her thighs.

His tongue reached her depths, tangling with hers. He growled into her mouth, then pulled back after several beats. "Come with me. I don't think I can't wait another minute."

She stepped out of her dress, and he led her to the bedroom.

He quickly stripped. His gorgeous, naked form was a view she didn't often get. They'd only had sex in his office, and he rarely shed his shirt and pants.

His muscles worked and flexed. Her fingers instantly skated over his sculpted abs.

He stepped back to grip her panties and slide them down her legs. He took her high heels with them. His kisses rained on her entire torso as his hands caressed her ass and thighs.

Rising, he yanked back the duvet. "On the bed, beautiful. I'm going to feast on you."

She settled down, and he wasted no time devouring her pussy. "Oh God, Dane." The sensations were exquisite for he always knew what to do and how to please her.

Shortly, he stopped, bracing one knee between her legs, his face mere inches from hers.

"You didn't have to do that." His words shown his disbelief.

Emotion poured from him that Sophie could only savor. This was the real Dane, not the powerful CEO she'd come to know the past month or so. She loved every side and facet of Dane, except for the side when he was stressed over Johanna.

He trailed kisses over her neck and down to her breasts, and his fingers gently stroked her sex.

She reached for him, taking free rein of his solid cock and smooth balls. He had no hair down there, and she loved it.

Her climb grew as he made love to her breasts and caressed her clit. "Dane, please." She tugged gently on him.

He lifted his head, and she shifted closer to the edge of the bed.

Seeing her shimmy to the side, Dane rose and stood beside her, mere inches from her face.

With a hand wrapped around him, she brought his hard cock to her mouth.

He groaned out loud. His hands continued to roam her body, returning to gently circle her clit, causing her muscles to clench.

Heat radiated off her skin. She was close, but she wanted him to come with her. She licked his smooth balls and then his length up and down.

"Fuck, baby," he rasped.

She sucked and licked, working his length with her fist and mouth. She tasted his salty precum, and he twitched over her tongue.

Dane slipped two fingers inside her as he slid his thumb over her clit. She released him as her body bowed off the mattress. She cried out when her orgasm exploded from within, and in just a few beats, he released on her chest, grunting and panting with the thrill and exertion.


Dane collapsed to the other side of Sophie, panting as he stared up at the ceiling. *Incredible.*

He should get up to get a towel and wipe his cum off her chest. But he couldn't move. A peace came over him he hadn't felt in years.

The room was now dark since he hadn't bothered to turn on any lights, but the moonlight illuminated the smooth skin of the woman beside him. God help him, he wanted more.

His erection barely relaxed. He rolled to his side to meet Sophie's gaze.

"Wow," she whispered.

He smirked.

Sophie spoke. "Can I ask you something? Will Johanna go to jail?"

"Probably not, but she won't be a problem anymore."

She sighed. "That's good. I'm glad."

After a moment of silence, he now had a burning desire to know why. He had to know where Sophie stood. "Did you do that because you work for me? Out of a sense of loyalty?"

She licked her lips. "Yes."

Her hesitation told him there was more.

"Was there another reason too?"

"Dane. I..." She glanced down, unable to face him.

He rose onto his forearm, resting on hand on her stomach, the other snaking up her neck and tangling in her hair.

She looked up at him, perhaps hoping he would drop the subject, but he couldn't.

Something happened tonight, and he was a changed man. Sophie somehow flipped a switch, and he, well, he couldn't go back to the way things were.

He placed small kiss on her lips. He'd held back kissing her for God knows why, and now he wanted to kiss her a million times over. She was the only woman he wanted to kiss.

He carefully shifted his weight over her, nudging his dick at her sweet pussy. He lifted her right leg to his side and caressed her thigh and hip.

He kissed her again. Not a voracious kiss, but a languid, sensual kiss, connecting them in a way he'd previously neglected. "Sophie, let me ask you this. If you took another job in the company, and didn't work for me directly, would you consider going out on a date with me?" His kisses moved to her neck, and he slowly pushed inside her. "Would you let me continue to fuck you?" he whispered over her skin.

"Oh, God."

His thrusts were gentle but the most sensual experience he'd had with a woman. "Would you spend the night in my bed? Tonight and other nights?"

Her eyes grew misty. She nodded wordlessly as he rocked them slowly in an erotic climb toward ecstasy.

She wrapped her arms around him.

"I want this, Sophie, even after you no longer work for me directly. I want you in my life." He wanted to say more, but it was too soon. Given more time, he would gain comfort in telling her how deeply he felt about her. How he wanted her to wear his ring. How he wanted her pregnant with his child.

A tear streamed down her cheek. "Yes. Yes to all of that."

He leaned down, claiming her sweet lips again, and never breaking their intimate connection. He'd make love to her all night, showing her, at least for now, how he felt about her, even if he couldn't say the words.

He was free to love again, and the perfect person for him was in his arms right now.

# Blue-Eyed Devil

# Chapter Six

♥

Brooke had no idea what she was looking for. All the laptops looked the same. Obviously, she knew some had more features, RAM, and whatever, but that still didn't give her a clear understanding of what *she* needed.

She combed the area again; all the sales reps were busy with customers.

She let out a sigh. If her computer could have just hung on a little while longer…

Brooke did freelance graphic design. She owned her own company. Prior to that, she'd been with a company that went under. Eight years she'd been with Schloop—a quirky, cutting-edge internet company that truly was ahead of its time. When she left, they gave her the laptop she'd been using for the past three years, and the prior night, it finally died.

She didn't know enough about technology to pick for herself. All she knew was she had one that had worked just fine and could do what she needed.

She stared at a laptop from a reputable company and rubbed her forehead.

"Looks like you're having trouble making a decision."

She lifted her head to the right to see a man standing beside her. He stood about six-two, had medium brown hair, and his dimples showed when he smiled. He didn't wear a nametag.

"Um, yeah. I was hoping for some help," she glanced the near-by area, "but everyone seems to be busy." That's what she got for shopping on the Friday of a holiday weekend, not that she had a choice.

"Maybe I can help. Do you know what you need?" He had a faint clean scent to him, like freshly showered, and he'd skipped the cologne.

She bit the inside of her cheek. "Not really."

"What are you using it for?"

"I do graphic design."

"Oh, cool. Well, then you'll definitely want a fast graphics card."

She didn't completely understand everything he was saying, but it certainly sounded good. And really at this point, she either needed to make a decision or come back another time. She'd hear this guy out.

He pointed to the left, stepping closer toward her as he spoke. "This one has a great graphics card with good storage too."

She nodded. "Okay. Is it fast?"

He tilted his head and straightened. "It's okay. But the best way to get a fast computer is to get one with a fast processor."

How did he know all this stuff?

"Okay."

He went around her to one with a larger screen and the price tag to follow.

"Wow." Could she spend that much?

"Right. The processor is one of the most expensive parts of the PC, but again, one of the best things you can do to get speed is invest in a fast processor."

Okay, that made sense. "How do you know all this?"

He grinned. "I'm sorta a computer geek."

This guy in fitted jeans and T-shirt with muscles pressing against the fabric was a computer nerd?

She turned back to the expensive PC. It wasn't that she didn't have the money; she worried she'd be buying more power than she needed.

"Oh, what the hell," she muttered.

He chuckled and the sound sent a nice little thrill through her body. She couldn't help but smile back.

"So, take this card to checkout. They'll get the computer for you there." He reached beside her for the identifying card and handed it to her.

"Okay." She could do this. Maybe she'd have to come back and see if they could save any of her data.

"Is there something wrong?" he asked.

"I, um, just have my old PC. It's dead, but I'm pretty sure all my stuff is still on the hard drive."

He glanced toward the back of the store at the help desk. There was a line of about twenty people. "Well, they can help you. Just looks like it might take a bit." His blue eyes met hers. "Did you bring your old PC?"

She nodded. "I guess I better get on it then. Thanks for all your help." She adjusted her purse strap and headed to the registers.

"You're welcome. Good luck."

She smiled, but she had the feeling this was gonna be a long damn day.

Standing in line at the checkout, she gazed one last time toward the help desk. The line hadn't budged. She also noticed her helper guy was two people behind her, holding a package of thumb drives.

She finally paid, fished out her car keys, and carried the large cardboard box. Her old PC was still in the car. If she'd thought this through, she would have brought it in with her.

Her helper guy walked up beside her just as she made it to the front door. "Need a hand?"

"I just... Yes, that would be great. I left my old PC in the car."

He lifted the box and walked beside her.

She popped the trunk of her six-year-old blue Mazda and reached for the box.

"So, what's your plan?"

She smirked. She didn't have a plan. "I guess go back inside and drop both of these off at the help desk. See if they can get me set up."


Curtis nodded slowly, watching the brunette struggle to get the old laptop into her bag. She looked so adorable nibbling her lips, trying to focus. So she thought she'd carry both laptops and her purse back inside and stand in line for assistance?

He shouldn't do this, but he couldn't let her go back inside and wait this out. Not to mention, she could be looking at another four or five days before she'd get it back.

"Why don't I help you with your data?"

She stopped and looked up at him, a little wrinkle formed between her eyebrows. "What?"

"I can help you transfer your data over. If your hard drive still works, it'll be pretty easy to move everything over. It'll take me four or five hours. These guys," he jerked his head toward the store, "will take four or five days."

Her full pink lips gaped. "You would do that for me?"

He nodded, then offered a hand. "Curtis Blankenship."

She smiled. "Brooke Fawn."

He pulled out a card from his wallet and handed it to her. "Do you have a card?"

Her eyes lit up. "Oh, yes. Of course." She dug into her purse and gave him her number.

"I'm over there." He pointed with his chin and lifted the box.

She followed him, carrying the old laptop.

He opened the back door of his late-model Ford pickup truck and set it inside.

She nibbled on her lower lip again. He thought she looked so cute, but her face still showed her concern.

"Here," he retrieved his wallet and pulled out his driver's license, "take a picture of my ID. I'll load your stuff and call you tomorrow morning."

She snapped a picture, and, based on her smile, she was feeling better that she wasn't just giving her brand new laptop to some complete stranger.

"Curtis, I can't thank you enough." Then she surprised the hell out of him. She leaned up on her tiptoes and hugged him.

Instinctively, he swung his arms around her and hugged her back. "You're very welcome. Enjoy your day off. Tomorrow you're back to work."

She gave him an exuberant smile and turned to head back to her car.

Curtis might have had a glance of her sweet, heart-shaped ass, but he turned his focus back to his truck and getting home to start work.

# Chapter Seven

♥

Brooke's cell phone rang around eleven o'clock Sunday morning. She knew it had to be Curtis. She was so thankful for his help, but equally nervous that he'd do something to screw it up. And if her bestie knew how easily she trusted this man, she'd never hear the end of it.

Secretly, Brooke looked forward to seeing him again. He had a nice face and a great body to go with it. And his sparkling, intoxicating blue eyes... It was serendipitous running into him at the electronics store because she'd likely *still* be there waiting for help.

"Hello?"

"Hey, Brooke. It's Curtis. I have your laptop done."

"Yay. That's great. How can I get it?"

"I don't mind dropping it off."

"Wait. I have a better idea. It's a little early, but let's meet for lunch. My treat. It's the least I can do."

He chuckled. "Okay." He mentioned a casual dining place midway between their two places. "How is thirty minutes?"

Fort Worth traffic on a Saturday? Shouldn't be a problem.

She double checked her clothes and freshened her makeup, not that she wore much. At thirty, she was blessed with clear skin, rosy cheeks, and nearly zero wrinkles.

Curtis grabbed a corner booth in a quaint, family-owned place and waited only two minutes before Brooke walked in. She looked even prettier than the day before in relaxed denim shorts, a pink floral tank top, and white sandals.

"Hi. I'm glad you called. How did it go?"

"Everything transferred pretty easily. Of course, none of your passwords are set up, so you'll have to do that." He pushed the laptop across the table.

She nodded and a few of her blonde locks fell around her face.

The waitress arrived, and they gave their orders for lunch.

"Your old laptop and all your new documentation are in my truck. We can get it when you leave."

"Perfect. I can't thank you enough. You're a lifesaver."

The sparkle in her green eyes was like nothing he'd seen before.

After a short time, his sandwich and her salad arrived. They chatted mostly about their jobs, his fascination with technology, and how she came to run her own graphic design company.

Brooke had this interesting mix of naïveté and business smarts. On one hand she was innocent and trusting, maybe too much so, and on another she was inquisitive and challenging.

He couldn't be sure if she was flirting with him or if that was just her style. He'd like to take her out on a date, but soon she seemed anxious to leave. Probably worried about being behind in her work.

They walked to his truck to retrieve the box holding the rest of her items. He placed them in her trunk.

She lifted on the tiptoes to hug and this time she lingered. Her warm, soft form felt incredible in his arms. She released and smiled. "Thanks again, Curtis."

He opened her car door. "You're welcome. Drive safely."

She drove off, and Curtis headed back to his truck with a semi. She was cute and sexy, and he scolded himself for not asking her out for dinner. He exhaled in exasperation.

***

Brooke was a fool. She kicked her apartment door closed and set everything down on the dining table. She should have asked Curtis out for a drink or something. He was not only good-looking but really nice.

She was scared; that's why she didn't ask. She had no idea if he had a girlfriend or was even interested in her.

*Dammit!*

But no time for beating herself up. She had work to do—her next deadline was four days away.

She booted up her PC—it was so sleek and shiny. All the icons on her desktop were moved or missing, but that wasn't anything to worry about. She systematically began opening and loading all her main work programs, including email. A few hours later, and most everything was in place. Now, to finish her project.

Brooke made great headway, when she stopped to make herself a little dinner and touch base with her bestie, Misty.

"Hey! Did you get your laptop back?"

"Yes, and I love it. It's like a hundred times faster than what I had before."

Misty chuckled over the phone. "Good to hear. So, I'm at David's right now, but I want to talk about this week."

"This week?" She shoved a bite of leftover spaghetti in her mouth.

"Yeah. The new movie with hottie Drake Baumer comes out this Thursday. We need to go."

"Okay, okay, we'll go."

"Good. I'll call you tomorrow. Love ya', mean it."

"Love ya', mean it." Brooke disconnected the line. In a way, Curtis reminded her of the actor Drake Baumer. Both were tall with medium brown hair, dimples, gorgeous blue eyes, and great muscles.

She sighed as she finished her dinner. Daydreaming about her own little hottie would not get her work done.

Darkness casted outside and another hour had passed when Brooke realized she needed another visual program. She rarely used it, but it came in handy on more than one occasion.

She scanned the desktop. *Nothing.* She perused the program list. *Nothing.*

*What the hell!*

Her heart rate kicked over as the anxiety rose.

*Oh no, it's lost!*

"Calm down," she told no one but herself. She routed around in her purse and pulled out Curtis' card.

It rang three times when he answered. "Hello?"

"Thank God. Hi, Curtis. It's me, Brooke. I need some help, please. Did you remember transferring over a program called GraphiXL?"

"Hey, Brooke. You did a search from Programs?"

"Yes." She tried not to sound stressed, but knew she was failing. "I looked everywhere."

"Okay, I got you. I added a screen sharing app on your PC for instances just like this."

"A screen sharing app?" Her stomach clenched. Her trust in him was unfounded, and now he'd installed some kind of PC hacking program. She should have known better.

"Yes. Don't worry. You have to initiate it for me to help you. Look on your desktop for the Powerof2 icon. It's blue and white."

She found it and clicked it open. He gave her a password to enter. She really had no choice; she needed his help, desperately. She was panicking.

From his home, she watched Curtis clicking here and there. He did a search which showed nothing, then he changed the text to something she didn't understand. The icon GraphiXL icon appeared at the top of his search results.

"Is this it?" he asked over the phone.

"Yes... It just looks different. The name's different."

"It looks like they now include the company name in the title. I'm not sure why. Why don't I save it to your desktop so you can find it easier next time?"

"Yes, please. That would be great." She could breathe again. Oh, thank goodness.

She double clicked on it, and the program opened. She needed to sign in, but it definitely looked like the app she was looking for.

"Thanks, Curtis. I'm sorry to bug you. I was really nervous there." She grinned, not that he could see it.

"I could hear it. Glad I could help. Call anytime."

"Thanks again. Talk to you later." She disconnected the line, and paused. She said "talk to you later" out of habit, but what if they *could* see each other again, talk to each other again.

She made up her mind. If he wasn't going to ask her out, she would do the asking. Heck yeah. He might say "no" but she had only one way to know for sure.

But first her deadline...

# Chapter Eight

♥

Curtis still smiled as he locked up and got ready to head to bed. Brooke had called in a panic, and frankly, he'd been a little dumbfounded. He could tell simply by the gigabytes that everything had transferred over to her new laptop. Ultimately, he found her program. Damn, he would have felt like shit if he hadn't.

He squinted his eyes at his PC, just about to shut it down. At eleven o'clock, he needed to call it a night; he had agreed to take his mom to church early the next morning.

He was still connected to Brooke. She hadn't shut down her PC yet. Was everything all right?

He furrowed his brow. After some hesitation, he made a few keystrokes to activate her camera. He had an overwhelming need to check in on her, to make sure everything was okay.

If she was stuck again, she might be hesitant to call him at this late hour.

The PC was in a dark room that was clear. He made some camera adjustments to bring the room into focus. He could see a bed and nightstand with an alarm clock on it. Something moved on the bed.

*Okay, great.* She was in bed. Curtis breathed a sigh of relief. He reached for the button to cut the connection when he heard a groan.

She sounded frustrated.

Curtis froze. He focused on his screen one last time.

She flipped back the sheet and laid on the mattress wearing an oversized T-shirt, staring at the ceiling.

If she was hot, why didn't she turn on the air conditioner? He reached again to shut down his PC when she sat up in bed and whipped off her T-shirt.

*Whoa!*

He should shut down, now. But God, she was gorgeous. He couldn't move. His sight glued to his screen and the beauty in lace panties.

She lay back down and slid her hands slowly over her body. Her right hand dipped beneath her panties.

*Fuck! What a beautiful sight.* Curtis adjusted himself to accommodate his growing hard-on.

She slipped off her panties and dropped them to the floor, then pulled open the top drawer of her nightstand.

*Oh crap!* She pulled out a vibrator. Her legs spread open wide as she made herself comfortable. The vibrator hummed in one hand, and the other hand gently toyed with her nipples.

*Holy fuck!* He should *not* be doing this. This was an invasion of privacy. But he couldn't stop himself. She looked so incredible, so real, so sensual.

Curtis' erection strained against the zipper on his jeans.

Her hips pulsed as she rocked her vibe. She moaned. Her panting increased as she dipped the vibe inside her channel then hovered over her clit again. She looked gorgeous.

Then she murmured something, but it was so low, he couldn't make out what she'd said. *Curtains* maybe, but the window wasn't in view of the camera.

Her next moan pitched higher. She was close. Her orgasm built until it finally released. She cried out, "Curtis," and he almost fell off his chair.

His jaw gaped as he watched her come down from her high. He could hardly think. He reached for the screen to his laptop and pushed it shut.

She'd called out his name. She'd been thinking about him.

He rose from his chair and strode to his bedroom. Without turning on a light, he stripped out of his clothes, leaving them in a pile on the floor. His erection stood at attention.

Brooke had masturbated to thoughts of *him*.

He took his dick in his hand, stroking it to the images of the gorgeous blonde from the electronics store. How she spread her legs and moved with the waves of ecstasy from her vibrator.

God, he shouldn't have watched her, but now he couldn't unsee what he saw.

He stroked himself harder and faster. He had to have her, he didn't know how, but he would have her. *He* would bring her to orgasm, not that battery-operated toy.

***

Sunday morning, Brooke filled her cup with more coffee and took the avocado toast to the table when her phone dinged with a text message. It was Curtis.

*Hi! I hope you got everything squared away last night. I was thinking we should go out for a drink Friday night. Are you free?*

Her chest pounded. He wanted to go out. Yes!

*Hi back! Yes, I'm free. What time?*

He replied quickly.

*Better yet, dinner and drinks. How about I pick you up around 7? Send me your address.*


She sent him her address and couldn't stop grinning long enough to eat her breakfast. She'd been thinking about him—his smile, his broad shoulders, even his hands were nice to look at. And last night, oh geez, she had so much pent up energy just thinking about those lips on her, and those hands caressing her.

She was getting wet already. *Stop! You have work to do.*

Friday couldn't come soon enough.

# Chapter Nine

♥

Sunday, Curtis had stayed away from his computer. His day had been packed with family stuff through dinner, then Randy came over to watch the game. He had nothing work-related to do, so the temptation to see if Brooke was still connected was gone.

Monday was a different story. Curtis worked like a fiend and before bed he decided to check in on Brooke. The need overpowered him. He knew better but promised just a minute. Just long enough to know that she was safe, and the place was safe.

The remote screen came alive, and it was in the same location in her bedroom on a dresser.

Her little light on the nightstand was on, but the bed was empty. Suddenly, her face came into view, inches in front of the laptop.

He knew she wouldn't know he was there. He wasn't proud of himself, but when she hadn't shut off the remote link, he made sure nothing on her PC had changed to show he was connected.

She was running some kind of program update. Looked like one of her work programs.

Then, she turned to walk toward the bed. She was completely naked.

Curtis' dick came to life.

Her sleek legs and her heart-shaped ass had him mesmerized. She flipped off the table lamp and pealed back the covers.

He adjusted the camera on her end to see in the dimly lit room.

She stretched like a cat, her legs bent and her feet sliding along the mattress. Her hands moved over her body, over her breasts, and down her stomach to her thighs. She pulled her right hand up an inch to move over her pussy.

"Mmm," he heard over his PC speaker.

Curtis opened his fly this time. He couldn't bring himself to shut off his PC, so he could join her in an orgasm.

As she stroked her glistening pussy, her back gently bowed off the bed. Her precious mouth gaping.

His grip worked up and down his shaft, the precum lubricating him. Watching her, he wondered how often she did this. Or was this a new thing? Something new since Friday—when they met? Or Saturday, when they had lunch together?

Fuck, he wanted to be there with her. It was crazy and ridiculous. He had to take her out on a few dates first. She didn't seem like a woman eager to hop into bed with a man, a near-stranger.

She reached for her vibrator but didn't turn it on. She simply slipped it inside her with one hand as the other circled over her clit.

"Mmm, Curtis."

*Fuck!* She called his name again.

His balls tightened, and her breathing came harder. He had to hold on for her. His sweet Brooke.

In a few short beats, she let loose and so did Curtis. Brooke moaned and writhed on the mattress, riding the waves of her stellar orgasm.

Curtis grabbed a towel and cleaned himself up. He closed the lid to his laptop.

*Fuck!* He had to stop doing this. This wasn't porn, this was head over heels fascination. He'd never met such a woman—an enigma—as Brooke, and if it were possible, he was already obsessed with her. In the very best way.

***

Brooke put the final touches on her project and sent it to her contact at seven p.m. Tuesday. A full day ahead of schedule. What had gotten into her this week, she had no idea.

Granted her PC was faster, but that didn't explain why she was thinking smarter or faster. She poured herself a glass of white wine and heated her skillet for a piece of fish she'd gotten Saturday at the market.

Ah, Saturday. What a glorious day. She met Curtis, and now they had a date planned for Friday. He was kind and attractive, and for some reason her hormones had gone into overdrive thinking about him.

Was it normal to masturbate every day?

Oh, well. She didn't want to dig into it too much. This infatuation with Curtis—or whatever it was—was in its infancy. She needed to take it one day at a time. Not to mention, she wasn't the type of girl to jump into bed with a man on the first date.

After dinner and two episodes of her Netflix show, she decided to wrap it up and take a bath before bed.

She moved her laptop into the bedroom and set it on the dresser like she'd done the last two nights. It made her feel better in case something sounded, she would hear it and address the issue instantly. Tonight's task, backing up her entire hard drive to the cloud. She had a service she wanted to use but needed to wait until after working hours. She didn't want anything slowing up her work.

With everything squared away, she walked to the bathroom with her Ereader. She stripped and stepped into the hot, bubbly tub of water.

This was her treat. Most days she would simply shower. When she had the time, she got to bathe. But this time her Ereader sat on the toilet lid. With her eyes closed, all she could think about was Curtis—his lips, his dimples, his easy-going style.

She wondered what his kiss would be like. Would he kiss her Friday? She hadn't been with a man in almost a year. If he'd offered something more than a kiss...well, she'd cross that bridge.

Geez, she needed another orgasm tonight.

She gently toweled off and smoothed on body moisturizer, glazing over her legs, her hips, her breasts. Her nipples peeked on contact.

She exhaled. Hanging up her towel, she flipped off all the lights and pulled back the covers on her bed.

She reclined and caressed her body, wishing those hands were Curtis'. She didn't want to make a habit of this, but having an orgasm at least meant no tossing and turning throughout the night.

A hand slipped to the apex of her thighs, finding it wet.

"It's wet for you, Curtis."

She giggled. Like he was able to hear her.

She stroked and circled her clit, sometimes dipping inside. Her free hand slid over her body, twisting and toying with her nipples.

She moaned. Her orgasm shot to the surface quicker than ever before. Her chest rose and fell, her breath returning to normal. Her hands hadn't moved. That wasn't enough, and she knew it. Her first orgasm was too quick. She needed more.

On their own volition, her hands moved slowly over her body.

Suddenly, a knock came at the door.

*What the hell?*

She panicked and raced to the closet to cover herself with a robe. Who could be knocking at—she glanced at the clock—ten-ten at night?

She stood in her bedroom—frozen, her heart racing.

Another knock, followed by, "Brooke. It's me, Curtis."

*Curtis? What's he doing here?*

She peeked through the peep hole to see him standing two feet from her door in faded jeans and a gray T-shirt.

She opened the door. "Curtis?"

"Hi. I'm sorry, I just... Can I come in?"

"Okay." She stepped back and closed the door behind him. She gripped her robe, looking up at him, her mind spinning with a thousand questions.

"I know it's late. I, um, couldn't wait for Friday." He stepped close, into her personal space, and raised his hand to cup her cheek.

The warmth permeated her face. She gazed into his eyes until the last moment when his lips met hers. The kiss was warm and tender, his lips firm over hers. She opened for him.

His free arm wrapped around her waist, pulling her into his hard body. Her arms pinned between their bodies.

He was here, and she didn't know why. And maybe she didn't care why.

She broke the kiss and blinked. "You're here. I was just thinking about you." The heat from her blush blossomed in her cheeks.

He looked down for the briefest moment, then met her gaze. "I know."

*What? That doesn't make any sense.*

He held her hand. "Follow me."

She didn't understand, but she let him lead the way to her bedroom.

He stood before her laptop and closed the lid.

"Hey, I was doing something."

"I know." His facial features softened, and he took her other hand. "I know."

He kept saying that, but she didn't understand. She stared at her PC when finally realization dawned. Her eyes rounded, and she pulled back. Her hand flew over her mouth.

"You saw me."

"Yes." His voice was quiet and full of remorse. "I was worried Saturday night. You were frantic about your program, and when I saw you were still connected... Well, I wanted to make sure you were all right."

"You were checking up on me?"

He nodded and closed the space between them, taking her hand in his. His warmth wrapped around hers.

She wanted to be furious, and embarrassed, and violated. So many emotions ran through her head. He *saw* her masturbate.

"I'm sorry I violated your privacy. Truly. Please forgive me. But when I saw you on the bed, you were so beautiful, *so* incredibly gorgeous, I couldn't turn away."

She swallowed. "How many times did you see me?"

"I saw you last night too. And I saw you go to your bed tonight."

She gasped and moved away.

"Please, Brooke. I heard you call my name. I was so turned on. And that's why I'm here now."

"Why? Why are you here now?" Her eyebrows furrowed.

"Because you called for me."

It was that simple. She called, and he answered her call. Oh God, this was either a dream come true or the beginning of a nightmare.

"You called me for a date because you saw me masturbate." It was more statement than question. She was mortified.

He shook his head, and his eyes read earnest. "I called you because I should have done it Saturday at lunch. I kicked myself for leaving you and not asking you out."

"You did?"

He moved close to her, so close she could smell his clean masculine scent. His finger smoothed a hair from her face and caressed her cheek. "I wanted to ask you out. I thought about you, and well, Friday is too long to wait."

*Friday is too long.* She nodded slowly.

He smiled. "I'm here now for you." His hand stroked down the lapel of her robe, his fingertips grazed the tiny area of exposed skin on her chest, and over her hand.

Her heart rate sped.

"I want to get to know you, Brooke. I want to learn your favorite movies, your favorite restaurants, what makes you mad, besides broken computers." He gave her a shy smile. "But I also know there are things you need right now, sweetheart, and I would love to help you. I would love to be the one to help you." His voice was so gentle, so sincere.

She couldn't believe he was here, and what he was asking.

He leaned down again to kiss her, sweetly, deeply. His arm wrapped around her, drawing her in, and his erection dug into her stomach. He broke the kiss and whispered over her lips, "Let me help you, Brooke. Let me make you feel good."

She was nearly panting now. She should tell him to go. This was not right. She didn't screw men she barely knew. But lordie, she wanted him to stay. She wanted him so bad.

# Chapter Ten

♥

Brooke looking up at him with those sweet innocent eyes made him weak in the knees. Curtis knew he shouldn't be there. He should have exercised some patience and waited for their date. But there he stood in her bedroom, asking her to let him pleasure her.

When he'd signed on to his PC to see her that night, and she'd walked naked from the bathroom to the bedroom, he knew what was going to happen. He didn't wait to see anymore. He'd shut his laptop and scolded himself. He had no right to invade her privacy.

Why his ethics completely went out the window, he couldn't say. He was ashamed of his behavior. He'd nearly scrubbed his face raw at the sink as he got ready for bed.

But his brain wouldn't shut up. As much as he chastised himself, he also thought; *If she needs to masturbate again, she has a burning desire inside that a third night of this won't fix.*

He'd said to hell with bed, and instead threw on jeans and a shirt and drove to her place. His erection ached the entire drive.

He might have been her fantasy, thinking about him as she fondled herself, but that didn't mean it didn't have an element of truth to it.

He almost broke out in a full sweat as he stood at her apartment door.

Thank the stars above, she hadn't thrown him out.

His fingers caressed her skin along the side of her robe.

She dropped her hands, silently giving him permission to touch her more.

His hand slid down her robe to the tie, loosening it from around her waist. His movements were slow and methodical, waiting for her to object.

She didn't.

"I should say no." She gazed up at him with such passion in her eyes, they looked almost black.

"And I should leave and wait until Friday. You can tell me to stop." His sight pinned to hers as he slid her robe open and gasped. "You're beautiful, Brooke. How is it you don't have a boyfriend to worship you like you deserve?"

She shrugged and gave him a shy smile.

Before he did anything more, he stripped out of his T-shirt and threw it aside. He resisted popping the button on his jeans to alleviate the strain pressing uncomfortably on his dick. This time was strictly for her; this was about her satisfaction, not his.

With his hands at her jaw, he leaned down to kiss her. He started slow and controlled, quickly building as he dove in. She tasted amazing.

Her hands gripped his shoulders, and she pulled her chest into his.

He nearly lost all control when her perfect, naked breasts collided with his bare chest.

Her hands reached between them and caressed him over his jeans.

Her touch was incredible. He didn't break the kiss. He couldn't. She was intoxicating. This beautiful, innocent woman let this bull into her sanctuary. He would not let her down. He would give all the pleasure she wanted and needed.

Her hand cupped him, and he groaned. He pulled back and looked again at her beautiful body.

Then he dropped to his knees before her. He kissed between her breasts and gazed up at her. "Brooke, I want to bring you pleasure. Pleasure you have been trying to get for yourself. Will you let me?"

She licked her lips and nodded. "Yes," she breathed out.

He peppered kisses over her breasts, languishing over her pink buds. Her sighs drove him.

His hands caressed her torso and thighs as his mouth traveled down her smooth soft skin, inhaling her womanly scent. Her pubic hair was short and just a shade darker than the blonde on her head.

His fingertips glossed over her mons, then dipped between her legs. His free hand cupped her rounded ass cheek.

She widened her stance.

God, she was so trusting of him. He would cherish that and honor her any way he could.

He slid a finger through her slit, loving the feel of her wetness sliding around. He caressed her pussy and over her clit as he made love to her breasts—sucking and licking them, bringing her closer to sweet ecstasy.

Her moans grew louder, and he knew she was close. He'd give her one orgasm, then lay her down and give her more. She shuddered in his clasp and moaned.

As she subsided, he rose and crushed his lips to hers. His tongue sought hers, coaxing her to dance with his.

Her kiss was eager and urgent; he knew she was not yet satisfied.

Wordlessly, he pushed off her robe and guided her to the bed. As she sat, he gently eased her down onto her back with his kisses and then spread her legs apart with his hand. "I want to taste you, beautiful."

She exhaled.

He trailed kisses down her neck, over her plump breasts, her smooth tummy to her pussy. Bracing her thighs apart with his hands, he devoured her pussy and clit, causing her to cry out.

"Curtis," she moaned.

He pushed against her thighs, farther than he'd seen when she masturbated. He licked, laved, and suckled her precious button. He loved going down on a woman, hearing their cries of ecstasy. But he especially loved bringing pleasure to this woman. This woman who had fantasized and masturbated to images of him. He imagined a thousand different ways he could please her. He only prayed she'd give him a chance after this one erotic escapade.

She came undone, shaking on the bed, she cried out, "Curtis!"

As her breathing calmed, he stayed kneeling in front of her. He lessened his grip on her and watched her in awe. He would do that again for her if two orgasms weren't enough.

She sat up to stand, and he quickly rose too.

Were they done?

His heart skipped a beat. With all his being, he hoped they weren't.

Brooke sunk to the floor in front of him and loosened the button on his jeans. His erection strained against the fabric. She freed his cock.

She looked up at him, her pink velvety tongue poked out. It was an offering.

"Fuck, Brooke."


Brooke gazed up at his impressive cock, then at his ocean-blue eyes, the intensity of which she'd never seen in a man before.

Curtis took his cock in hand slowly fed it into her open mouth. He groaned. God, she loved how everything she did fueled his passion—her masturbating, her wetness, her open mouth.

He pushed in and pulled back, increasingly working his way down her throat.

She relaxed her muscles and let him fuck her mouth. Tears streamed down her cheeks.

He quickly pulled out. "Oh God, Brooke, I'm so sorry. I didn't know I was hurting you."

She wiped her cheeks with her fingertips. "You didn't," she said softly. "It just happens when you hit the back of my throat. Do you want to stop?"

The fire in his sapphire eyes flared, and his lips parted. After a beat, he pushed out of his pants and shoes. He was an Adonis.

Her hands roamed his torso, feeling every ridge and chiseled muscle. She rose.

He wiped away a residue tear and cupped her cheek, bringing his sculpted lips to hers. He kissed better than any boyfriend she'd ever had. His tongue danced with hers; she sank further into his buff body.

He leaned back, meeting her gaze. "Lay on the bed, baby."

She shimmied to the center of her bed, her legs slightly apart. He leaned down to his jeans and donned a condom over his impressive length. She'd never been with someone so big.

He must have read her face. He leaned over her and cradled the back of her neck to peck her lips. "I'll take it slow, baby," he whispered over her lips.

She spread her legs wide and bent at her knees.

Curtis held himself at her pussy, making little circles before lining up at her entrance. His eyes returned to her face as he slowly pushed inside.

She let out a strangled moan.

He pulled back and took another inch. Each stroke gaining more room inside her.

She panted, and they'd hardly begun. "Curtis." Her fingernails gripped into his back. "Ah...so good." Her pussy was on fire with want.

His circumference stretched her pussy walls.

Another orgasm overtook her without any warning.

Curtis didn't relent.

She opened her eyes to see him staring down at her.

His gently thrusts never stopped. "Brooke, you're beautiful. And you feel so good. I want to please you. This won't be the only time I'm inside you, baby. You know that, right?"

"Yes...oh, God, Curtis." She had the workings of another orgasm, but it lingered.

He pulled out, his hands pushing against her thighs, his mouth quickly claimed her clit.

"Unh!" She bowed off the bed.

His tongue worked her and quickly tipped her over the edge. Her climax spiraling through her body like she hadn't just come moments before. She rarely had two orgasms at a time, and this was three! This man had fantastic hands *and* tongue.

After she'd calmed a bit, he positioned himself over her and drove in.

A wave of emotion came over her. "Curtis," was all she could muster.

"I know, baby. I feel it too." He claimed her lips again as he thrust into her more earnestly. His speed picked up, and her arms and legs circled around him.

Their bodies moving, connecting, like they had been made for one another.

He broke the kiss to flex his back and growl out his powerful orgasm, his cock twitching inside her.

He collapsed onto her, panting into her neck.

She held him, not wanting to let him go, not wanting the night to end.

He slipped out of her, and she missed the connection. He quickly dashed to the bathroom and dispose of the condom. When he returned, he yanked the sheet over them and pulled her close into him. He was warm and safe, and a feeling of peacefulness flowed over her.

"Can I stay here...tonight?"

She glanced up at him. "Stay as long as you want."

And she meant it.

He kissed her tenderly. After several minutes, he stopped and said, "I'm so glad your computer broke."

She smiled just as he rolled them over to start their love making all over again.

She sighed knowing he might be the last boyfriend she ever has.

# Firecracker
# Red

# Chapter Eleven

♥

Jeremy Bone stood before his vanity mirror when a knock came at his door. He wrapped a towel around his waist and glanced at the clock.

Seven at night. Trent wasn't due for another hour.

Jeremy answered the door, not prepared for what he saw. Valarie Mason. What the hell was she doing here?

"Hi, Jeremy. I'm sorry to bother you." Her eyes glanced down at his still shower-damp body and furrowed her brow. "Can I come in for just a minute?"

Valarie was once the love of his life. He could admit it. He fell ass over tin cups for her five years ago. And four years ago, he called it quits. "We're two different people," he'd told her.

Fact was she had control issues. He thought it stemmed from her OCD mother and demanding father. Jeremy just couldn't take it anymore. He called it off and never looked back. Well, *almost* never.

He sighed and stepped back.

She crossed the threshold, her arms tightly wrapped around her body. He knew that pose. That was an I'm-in-trouble-and-I-can't-stop-it pose.

"I'm in trouble."

He knew it! *Well, princess, you can't control everything.*

She walked toward the sliding glass doors out to his patio. Her near-perfect ass snuggly tucked in dark blue jeans. Her pink flats matched her pink sweater set that covered her insanely perfect tits.

*Don't think about that.*

"What's wrong?" He strode to the kitchen and grabbed a beer, silencing his exhale. He had a feeling he was gonna need it.

She nibbled on her plump lips. He wished she wouldn't do that.

"It's my business. I used a new manufacturer, and some things went wrong."

Valarie started a T-shirt company shortly before they'd met. She had unique designs and styles that were a particular favorite of women. Social media catapulted her online business, and she rode that wave of success. He knew business had been growing for her. He wasn't really stalking her... But the new manufacturer was news to him.

"What happened?" Jeremy leaned against his counter.

She stepped closer to meet his gaze. God bless her for having the balls to come to her ex-boyfriend to ask for help and still keep her head held high.

"He, the manufacturer, made some bad product," she shrugged her shoulders, "and I can't sell it. But since it was approved, I'm on the hook for it."

*Shit!* "How much?"

"Ten grand."

*Double shit!* "You don't have it?"

"No. For the last few years, I put everything I made back into the company, except for a small salary for me. Just enough to keep the lights on."

He nodded. He had the money. His stint with EPSN had set him up for a while; his rock star broker set him up for life.

"What's in it for me?" He thought he'd make her squirm for a bit.

She licked her lips. "Well, I can pay you back with interest. I already called my old manufacturer. They have a larger, recently modernized facility I can work with. My costs actually drop by going back to him, which means I can pay you back faster."

He nodded again. She had some smarts, this one. She saw the issue and devised a plan to fix it. "Okay." He took a swig from his bottle.

She made stepped closer, and her eyes widened. "Okay?"

The corner of his lip curved up. "Yes, I'll loan you the money."

She threw her arms around him and lifted onto her tiptoes to kiss his cheek.

The surprise affection shocked him. He wrapped an arm around her to stabilize them and set his bottle on the countertop.

"Thank you. Thank you so much, Jeremy."

*Fuck!* She smelled so good. And those tits. Valarie had the most amazing D-cups on the planet, and they were now pressing against his chest. He cursed the sweater she wore.

He circled her waist with his free arm, drawing her impossibly closer.

Her breath hitched in his ear.

His dick came alive at the memory of what he and Valarie had once shared—incredibly, hot sex, and lots of it. He had to let her go, but his arms simply wouldn't move. He leaned down and placed a kiss at the crux of her neck. One of the sweetest places on her whole body.

Her arms moved slightly around his neck, one hand weaving through his hair.

He kissed her again because he was stalling. His dick grew to its maximum size, and he hoped his brain would override it and make his arms go limp.

His arms seemed to be locked around this five-eight, blonde bombshell, taking up sides with his dick. Traitors, the lot of them.

He pulled on the neckline of her top, exposing more delicious skin to kiss and lick.

She whimpered and wiggled ever so slightly over his raging cock.

*Hell!* She wanted him to fuck her. Another traitor. Didn't they break up for a reason?

His brain was silent—an *Out of Order* sign swinging in the breeze.

"Valarie, do you want me to let go of you? I need to know now because otherwise I won't be responsible for my actions when I strip you out of your goddamn clothes."

She loosened her arms and stepped back.

Okay, at least someone was using their brain.

She slipped off her pink cardigan, folded it, and laid it over his kitchen chair.

His eyes narrowed.

Then she grabbed the hem of her sweater and yanked it over her head, revealing a lace and satin bra.

"Fuck," he exhaled.

Smoothing the sweater onto a neat pile, she returned to his orbit. "No. I don't want you to stop."

Maybe he was the luckiest bastard alive or maybe this was a train wreck in the making.

He could bury himself deep inside the woman who'd haunted his dreams for the past four years. Four long, hellacious years of the most beautiful, talented woman he'd ever met. How could he say no?

She ran her hands up his chest, laying kisses in their wake.

He didn't touch her. His dick was about to explode, but he couldn't lay his hands on her soft skin, her tits that begged for him, or her ass that his hands could barely cover half the area. Somehow, he was frozen in place.

"Jeremy, please. The past doesn't matter." She looked up at him with her pleading blue eyes. "We have the here and now. I want you. Tell me you don't want me too." She kissed his pec.

He groaned.

Then she did the unexpected. She dropped to her knees and tugged on the towel around his waist.

He sprang free an inch from her face.

Her tongue reached out and licked the tip, all while keeping her gaze up at him. *The little wench!*

She fisted him and covered the tip with her lips. Her made-for-sin lips he'd felt on his dick a million times. Every time better than the last.

She licked and sucked, working her fist in concert with her mouth.

He had enough. He hauled her to a standing position and crushed his lips to hers claiming her. At least for the night, she was his. And she goddamn knew it.

His tongue tangled with hers as her bra hit the floor. His hands cupped those gorgeous globes like they were magnets, pulling him in. Then he worked her jeans and yanked them down over her curvy hips. He dropped to the tile and kissed her belly and her mons. Her scent penetrated his nostrils. "Fuck, baby. I can smell your heat. You're ready for me, aren't you?"

Her face was flush with lust. She nodded and moaned as he licked her slit over her panties.

He yanked her panties out of the way and tasted her sweet pussy with the space her pants allowed. He should pull the damn things off, but he was too far gone. He spun her around and pushed her torso flat on his dining table. Yanking her panties to the side, he tested her pussy one last time, then aligned his cock and dove in deep.

"Unh," she cried.

"Fuck, baby, you feel so fucking good." It was like homecoming.

"My jeans, Jeremy. My panties are getting—"

He rammed clear to the end of her tight pussy. "Shut it, princess. You can't control this. What do you care about? Coming? And that's what I'll give you."

His thrusts were controlled because if he gave it his all, that would be over far quicker than he wanted.

He reached beneath her and caressed her full breasts—their weight pressing his hands against the kitchen table. How many times had they fucked in his place? On the sofa, the table, the balcony, the floor, and his bed? Countless times, and somehow this felt like the first.

"God, princess, you feel so incredible."

Her jeans just past her knees, her thong pulled to the side giving him access to her pussy, her pussy lips mushed together—she was the most-perfect wanton angel. His mouth trailed over her bare back, savoring the taste and feel of her soft skin.

"Ah." She was climbing. She could always come so easily. It was good to know nothing had changed. Well, that was precisely the crux of the issue...

"Come around me, baby. Then, I'll strip you down, lay you on my bed, and eat you until I'm ready to fuck you again."

She moaned, and her pussy muscles clenched his hard rod.

He increased his thrusts. Pulling apart her cheeks to see their joining, he would savor this for as long as he could.

Valarie's flutters started.

He gripped her hips and rode her until the orgasm crashed through her. She screamed, and when he was sure she was done, he pulled out and squirted his seed over her back.

Collapsing on his forearm, he panted into her neck. Her breathing as heavy as his.

# Chapter Twelve

♥

Valarie felt so incredible, she couldn't describe it.

When she'd showed up at Jeremy's, firstly, she didn't expect to find him in only a bath towel. Secondly, she had every finger crossed, toes too, that he would loan her the money to pay her supplier. When he said yes, she was ecstatic. Relief flowed through her. Without his loan, she didn't know what she would have done. She didn't exactly have the credit to go to her bank.

And then he held her close. Those strong arms wrapped around her. God, it was like all the memories from their time together came flooding back into every crevice and pore of her body. His hard, warm body pressed against hers was like a slice of heaven.

She didn't come to his place to seduce him. No. She wanted to secure a loan and leave. But then he'd laid his kisses on her, and she was lost. *Oh, that mouth!*

He'd taken her over his kitchen table, and then did just what he promised—laid her out on his bed for more. At one point, they were interrupted by a knock at the door, but he'd sent whoever it was away.

She hadn't asked for this. Honest. But now, God now, it was like an addict with a taste of what she couldn't have but wanted it anyway.

It was morning as she stared at her reflection and quietly brushed her teeth in Jeremy's bathroom. She had a glow to her skin she hadn't seen in years. Her body clearly never forgot what Jeremy could do to her. But what of her heart?

Jeremy had called it off after just a year of dating. He'd said he couldn't handle her controlling, OCD behavior.

It broke her heart when he walked out, but she couldn't change. She'd tried. Honestly, she tried. Some things had improved, but she'd guessed it wasn't enough for Jeremy.

Now what? She'd fallen back in his bed. If she were smart, she wouldn't expect anything to come from this.

"Valarie." She heard his voice from the bedroom.

She opened the door and walked through, still naked from the night before. "Yes?" She walked around to her side of the bed and climbed under the covers.

"Brushing your teeth, huh?"

"Yes," she replied hesitantly.

He lifted onto an elbow and stared down at her. "You know I don't care about that. I always wanted to feel you beside me when I slept, when I woke up. I wanted your naked body beside me, whether I fucked you or not."

Guilt flowed over her like a rushing waterfall. "I'm sorry." She glanced to the side. She couldn't meet his eyes.

He peeled away the sheet, revealing his hard-on close to her thigh. He stroked it as she watched him. "This. This, Valarie, is what you do to me," his voice was barely above a whisper. "What am I going to do about you?"

He used to say that years ago. He was talking like they were a couple again.

She didn't dare let herself think about that.

His fingertips caressed her nipples, bringing them to hard peaks. "Arms overhead." She complied. "I'm going to fuck you, then we're going into the kitchen, get some coffee, and talk about what happened."

*Talk about what?* But before she could ask, he tweaked her nipples harder, pulling her away from her thoughts.

His mouth claimed one nipple as his hand slid down her tummy to her thighs. He pulled them apart, then dragged his fingertips over her quickly lubricating sex.

Jeremy always did that to her. Made her wet fast. Made her come fast. Made her come hard. He was like no other man she'd ever dated. He knew how to make her body sing.

His finger glided through her slit, and up and over her burgeoning clit.

"Ahh, she bowed off the bed. She wanted to touch him. She craved him. But she didn't dare move.

Sometimes, this was what he wanted—her pliant, submissive, and willing to take whatever he'd give her. She recalled a few times he'd tied her up.

There was something so incredibly erotic about being at the whim of a man. A man whom you trusted whole-heartedly with your body, mind, and heart.

Her breath came shallower as he toyed with her sex, wetting her clit, making her ache with desire.

He shifted and stretched out between her legs, pushing them further apart, then he blew a hot breath over her.

"Jeremy, please." She would have begged if that's what it took. She didn't know what the rest of the day, week, or year held. All she had was this precise moment, and she wanted him inside her. She missed him every day he was gone.

Finally, he laid his tongue over her clit. The slightest touch coupled with his two fingers sliding deep inside her had her climbing fast.

"Uh-uh, princess. Wait."

*Wait?* She couldn't wait!

He pulled back, only twisting and stroking her wet channel as he waited for the urgency to pass. His tongue returned, and she thought she'd die. Sweat broke out over her lip. She needed to come.

More stroking. Slip-sliding in and out.

She writhed. She was close to bursting. "Please, Jeremy. Please."

Blessed be, he didn't stop. His tongue and fingers worked together, pushing her over the edge into wonderful oblivion. She screamed out his name.

Before she fully came down, he lifted her hips with his strong hands, aligned himself and dove in, slamming into the end of her. He pumped wildly, setting off another orgasm inside her.

She cried out.

"Fuck, Val. I can't hold on." He let out a throaty groan, and his hot semen shot inside her.

After a few short beats, he collapsed over her, both of them panting from the exertion. She swung her arms and legs around him, like she'd always done, pretending it had never stopped. That wasn't the truth, but for just another minute she could pretend he was still in her life.

After fucking Valarie in his bed that morning, he knew there was no turning back. He had to have her in his life. He'd already scolded himself for thinking about going back down that path. He knew he was crazy, but fuck! How crazy was he if he let some other man fuck her? Maybe marry her, or make her beautiful belly swollen with his baby?

*Oh fuck no,* he thought to himself.

Back then, he was an immature twenty-nine-year-old. Now, he knew how to manage his emotions, and his reaction to her little quirks, and that would be key to them getting together and staying together.

As he took down the mugs from the cabinet, he started, "So, what exactly happened with this new manufacturer?"

"Let me show you." She pivoted and walked into his bedroom. A minute later she returned with two of his T-shirts in hand. "Look at this shirt."

It was an old U2 concert shirt. "Yeah?"

"Now look at this one." She held up a red, department store tee he'd purchased last month.

"Now look the hems."

The concert tee had a single stitch-line, the red one had a double stitch-lines.

"This," she waved the old T-shirt, "was what I was going for. This kind of nostalgia is coming back. I wanted to do a one-time run of shirts like this and promote them as limited-edition."

She shook her head. "My manufacturer pushed back when I asked for this, saying his facility wasn't equipped to handle this kind of modification. And..."

"And he was right."

Valarie slumped into the chair beside him, biting her lips between her teeth. "Yeah."

When Val's tenacity crossed into control-mode, this was the result. What was he going to do with her?

Life just seemed easier for him. Not that there weren't bumps along the way, but sometimes going with the flow—not over-planning or overthinking everything—paid off. In Jeremy's opinion, life was too short to be stressed at every turn.

He sighed and sipped his coffee. They fell silent for a moment, when the idea hit him. *Oh, yeah.* This was how he could break her out of her stubborn, OCD nature. *Yeah, this just might work.*

"Okay, Val."

She glanced up from her coffee.

"I'm not going to bring this up again. What's done is done." He pursed his lips. "But I want you to think about how you can curtail this kind of freakish control and enjoy life going forward."

She opened her mouth, but he held up his hand.

"I know this was a business move, I get that. But if he couldn't do it, you find another way."

She nodded, and her shoulders dropped.

"If we're going to try this," his fingers swung back and forth between them, "we need to at least find some kind of compromise so that we can maximize fun and minimize you making me crazy." His voice was light, but sincere.

Her eyes glistened, and the corners of her lips raised. "We're gonna try?" Her breathy words escaped.

He clasped his hand over hers. "Yes. I probably gave up too soon. I think we could be good together."

"Oh God." She jumped up and leaned down, hugging him tight. "I missed you, Jeremy. Every day."

"I missed you too." He pecked her lips. If he did any more, he'd be late for work because he'd want her naked. "Are you free Saturday night?"

She nodded repeatedly.

He wanted to laugh. "We're going out for dinner and dancing. Now, we need to get our butts in gear because we have work to do."

In just under an hour, they'd grabbed a little breakfast, showered, and he handed her a check. She kissed him at the door, thanked him, and he watched her perfect heart-shaped ass stroll to her car.

He topped off his coffee, grabbed his car keys, and headed out. He suddenly had a lot he wanted to accomplish that day.

# Chapter Thirteen

T he next day, Valarie stared at her computer screen, unseeing. She was still in a daze about her and Jeremy getting back together. And they were going out Saturday, four days away. To her, it sounded like they were going to celebrate. She was so excited. She should go shopping and buy a new dress for the occasion.

Her phone dinged with a text. Jeremy.

*I'm coming over tonight.*

She lifted a brow. When did he get so bossy? *Really?*

He replied instantly. *Yes, I'm coming over so you can be cumming.*

Her muscles clenched down low. Oh God. They never could keep their hands of each other.

She texted back. *OK.*


An hour before she'd expected Jeremy, he called.

"Val, are you still on the pill?"

"Yes." Her hormones were too wild without it.

"Good. I have a lot of work to do tonight, so I can't stay."

"Okay." She knew this was going somewhere.

"When I arrive, I want you to answer the door naked."

She gasped. This sounded like a command. Didn't she have a say in the matter?

Before she could ask, he'd disconnected the call.

*Oh my.* She'd never done anything like that. She didn't like flaunting her body.

Valarie'd blossomed early and caught the attention of every boy in her class. She quickly learned how to cover up her "assets" and blend in with everyone else. The short time she was with Jeremy, he'd taught her to be proud of her curves and not to cover them up all the time.

After they broke up, she went right back to the way she liked it. The way she felt safe.

Keeping an eye out for his car, she waited, peeking through the blinds until she saw him pull up. She then stripped out of her clothes, folded them neatly on the coffee table, and waited by the door.

At his knock, she opened and hid her body behind the door, in case someone else might be out there.

He pushed the door closed and perused her body from head to toe. "That's my girl," he said right before he claimed her lips, dominating her mouth, owning every corner of it.

Her body crushed to his as she raised on tiptoes to circle her arms around his neck.

After a brief moment, he broke the kiss. With a hand still wrapped around her, he leaned down and ran a finger through her nether lips. "Are you wet for me, Valarie?"

She gasped.

"I think you need more before you can take my big cock into that pretty little cunt." He walked to the coffee table, and with a sweep of his arm, sent everything on the table flying—her clothes, a few magazines, the TV remote, and an unlit candle.

"I want you to lay right here, princess, and finger yourself. I want to see the wetness ooze from your body."

She swallowed hard. She'd never masturbated for Jeremy, for any man.

He stood by the table and waited. She wasn't going to be able to talk him out of it.

*Oh, God.* She walked to the table and took position on top of the hard wood, bending at the knees, her toes hung over the edge. Her right hand slid down her belly to her pussy. She stroked and dipped, allowing the pleasure to build inside.

Jeremy watched her with hooded eyes. "That's fucking gorgeous, princess." He took his time removing his clothes, leaving them in a pile on the floor—first his shirt, then his shoes, and on—all while his eyes were trained on her. His cock sprang free, and he wrapped his big fist around it, stroking. The precum shone on his tip.

He dropped to his knees, peering between her legs. God, she'd never seen Jeremy like this. It was scary and exhilarating at the same time. He licked his lips, then leaned close to blow a hot breath across her sex. With just a simple swipe of his tongue, she cried out unbidden.

Jeremy looped an arm under her leg and pinned it over her low belly before laying claim to her pussy with his entire focus.

"Unh." She was delirious with his sweet tongue doing so many wonderful things to her. Her orgasm climbed quickly, but then he pulled back.

He arched above her and whispered over her lips. "So eager." He stroked his palm across her throat down to a breast to twist and tug on a nipple.

The sensation shot southward. "Ah, Jeremy. Please."

His mouth covered hers, and she could taste herself on him. Without breaking the kiss, he aligned his cock at her entrance and thrust into her deeply.

He held the back of her neck so she couldn't break away. She screamed into his mouth as her walls of her vagina gave and stretched with the intrusion. He impaled her again and again, causing her orgasm to explode inside her.

She moaned as they rocked together, him finding his release and groaning into the crux of her neck.

"Fucking perfect, baby." He fought to catch his breath.

"Mmm," was all she could manage.

Making love to Jeremy was on a whole other level. She'd never had it this good, and she never would again. She had to make it work this time—for the sake of her body and her heart.

She wrapped her arms and legs around him for just a minute longer before he pushed himself up. He gave her lips a peck and whispered, "I need to get dressed. I have a present for you in the car."

Her heart skipped a beat. She loved presents, and Jeremy's were always the best. She nodded and released her hold on him. They both got dressed, and he left for his car.

Returning, he carried a large gold box with a big red bow around it.

"This is for our date Saturday night. I'm taking you to my club."

Ooh, that sounded special.

He placed the box in her lap and rested his hand over it. "This will be stepping out of your comfort zone. You will wear only three things—this dress, heels, and earrings. Nothing else. And I mean *nothing*. You can carry a bag if you want. I will *not* pick you up at the door. I won't be here to convince you to come with me. You'll have to walk to the car. From that point on, you are mine. Anything I say, you must do for the night." He tended closer and cupped her jaw. "But

I guarantee a night you will never forget. If you can do this, then we stand a shot. Then, Valarie, I'll take you back. If you'll have me."

Her heart stopped beating. She wanted him more than she needed air.

He stood tall and moved to the door, closing it silently behind him.

*What? Ohmigosh.* Her mouth gaped as she stared at the door, then down at the box.

He laid down an ultimatum. She couldn't blame him. She had issues that she'd been ignoring. She blamed him for the breakup, when really most of the blame rested on her shoulders. This wasn't some mild case of OCD.

She sighed and stared down at the box. She couldn't delay another minute. What was in this box that had him so excited?

She pulled loose the wide ribbon and lifted the lid. Inside lay a satiny, sleeveless dress, black strappy four-inch heels, and dangling, sparkly earrings. No lingerie? She took in a breath.

Lifting the dress from the box, she held it high. *Oh, God.*

The long firecracker red dress had loose, flowing deep Vs in the front and back, and a high slit up the side. It was simply gorgeous, but ohmigosh, she never showed that much skin. Even at the beach she had cover-ups. She couldn't handle people looking at her.

She quickly dashed to her bedroom, stripped out of her clothes, and slipped on the dress.

She gasped when she looked at the mirror. *No, no, no, no, no.*

It was worse than she thought.

The V was not only deep but wide, half her breasts were exposed. And the slit on the side was all the way up her left leg and stopped at her hip bone. One wrong move, one light breeze, and anyone would be getting a show.

She nearly broke out into a sweat. She couldn't do it. To wear this for him, she would love it. But to wear this out in public, never. Like never *ever*.

She wanted this date so badly. She glared at herself in the mirror and almost cried.

# Chapter Fourteen

♥

Jeremy sat with the driver in the limo outside of Valarie's apartment building. It was ten after seven. He knew she'd freak out about the dress, but with a body like hers, he knew she would look amazing. He only prayed she would find the inner strength to come out and join him. To hold her head high, and know that although this was out of her control, she could enjoy it. More than enjoy it...*thrive* in it.

Finally, her door opened. She locked up and turned his way.

Holy Mother of God! She was a knockout!

Her skin glowed from head to toe. Her walk was graceful and elegant. Her shoulders were pushed back, showing off her amazing breasts to the world. Her hair was pinned up in a stunning way, showing off the dangling earrings he'd bought her.

A quick glance at the driver and his mouth hung open.

Jeremy slipped out of the car and stood beside the car door as she approached.

He kissed her cheek and lingered. "You look absolutely amazing. You are sheer perfection."

"Thank you," she squeaked out.

His finger under her jaw lifted her chin. "You are exquisite. I am so proud of you. And I am so proud to have you on my arm. I know this was hard." He kissed her cheek again as she nodded. "But trust me, you look amazing. You will loosen up and enjoy yourself. I promise."

She carefully slid into the limo, holding the dress closed as she did.

Jeremy slid in after her and nodded to the driver. The driver already knew where they were going. Jeremy held her hand and let her adjust to being outside of her apartment in that dress.

Valarie was a knockout. She'd constantly tried covering herself, but that's the last thing he wanted. Tonight, she was going to learn how good it could feel to let her hair down and let someone else take the reins for a while.

The club they were going to was an occasional treat for Jeremy. He'd take a date, have dinner, dance, then go back to her place for dessert. They could have easily spent more time at the club, but he needed his date there just long enough to whet her appetite. She would be more than willing to let Jeremy indulge in any kinky fantasy by the time they'd made it back to her place.

Tonight would be different. He and Valarie would be there for hours—if that's what it took.

After a thirty-minute drive, they arrived at a tall, non-descript office building. The driver pulled the limo into the underground parking garage and stopped in front of an elevator with a red light illuminated over it and the letter W on the door.

They stepped inside, and Jeremy flashed his badge over the keypad, and the elevator ascended to the top floor.

"Wow. This seems pretty exclusive. I noticed we didn't take any of the other elevators."

He grinned. "It is exclusive. It's not like your typical club, but I assure you the food is excellent, as is the entertainment and the drinks."

She smiled. Her first smile of the night. *Progress.*

He laced his fingers through hers, and they strolled off the elevator, meeting the wall and the heavy wooden door in front of them with another W on it. Again, he used his keycard, and when the door clicked, he pulled it open for Valarie to walk through.

"What does the W stand for?" she asked.

"Wet."

They were greeted instantly at the hostess stand. "Welcome."

"Hello. Reservation for Bone."

"Yes, Mr. Bone. Right this way."

They followed the hostess—wearing a long sleek black dress, high in the front, low in the back—to a table between the room's center and the wall of windows.

"Wow," Valarie said.

The place had a warm, dark ambience. Most of the light came from the candles set on each table. The heavily tinted windows—facing downtown Dallas—gave the feeling of nighttime. In about an hour, the lights of the skyline would be visible.

Jeremy pulled out her chair, and she sat carefully to keep herself covered across the front.

He wanted to smile inside as she negotiated the gorgeous ensemble. He'd been half hard since she walked out the apartment door.

"Your server will be Felicia," the hostess announced, then she leaned down close to Valarie. "You look stunning in the dress." The back of her finger ran down Valarie's upper arm and grazed the side of her breast.

Valarie instantly turned beet red. She faced him with wide eyes. Jeremy simply lifted her hand and kissed the back of it.

Water was poured and a bread basket was placed in the center of the table. Then Felicia arrived. "Good evening, folks," she started with a smile. "Here are the selections for the evening. Any dish can be made gluten-free. Can I start you off with a drink?" She handed them the heavy cardstock menus.

*Absolutely.* His woman would need something to take the edge off. "Two Crown and Cokes, please."

"Yes, sir." Felicia also wore black—as did the entire staff—in the form of a short skirt and button-down top.

"This place is rather interesting," Valarie noted as she glanced around.

She probably noticed the pilasters separating tables in front of the windows. Or the semi-circular banquets that created privacy for the diners. Or the skimpy dress of the waiters, waitresses, and patrons.

He leaned forward, resting his forearms on the table. "Let me tell you a little about this place." He rubbed a thumb over the back of her hand. "As you can tell by the dated menus, they have one seating a night. Everyone arrives in time to order and is served at the same time. The selection is limited, but everything is fresh and prepared by world-class chefs. One of the things that makes this place unique is the overt sexuality."

Her cheeks tinted pink.

Drinks were set down before them, but Felicia didn't linger. They clinked glasses and drank.

"This isn't a sex club per se—"

She gasped, and he gripped her hand tighter.

"But the act of showing affection or appreciation for another isn't hidden."

She smoothed her lips together. "Like what...isn't hidden?"

"You may think you're the only one in sexy attire. Have you noticed the woman over my left shoulder?"

The woman in question wore a very sheer dark dress with a faint pattern and a skimpy thong underneath. Her areoles were clearly visible in that dress.

"Some waiters have their shirts opened beyond one or two buttons. And the waitresses are wearing either short skirts or skintight pants."

Her eyes moved, taking in the details of the space.

Felicia arrived. "Any questions about the menu?"

"Nope. I think we're ready."

They both ordered an appetizer and entrée but held off on the dessert for now.

Valarie caught sight of a couple in a curved booth where the man fondled his date's breast as she stroked his cock under the table. The pink flush deepened on Valarie's face, and she sipped her drink.

Jeremy decided that was enough disclosure for now and changed the subject to her work and life for the past four years. She'd done well for herself, and he was impressed.

Before dinner, Jeremy ordered a bottle of wine that would complement their dinners.

As they ate, the pianist played several instrumental pieces. The conversation flowed easily, as if they'd never broken up, and Jeremy was thankful.

When Valarie had shown up at his door this past Monday, he was surprised, but it also awakened a yearning inside. A yearning for this woman he'd loved, and now he recognized, probably never stopped loving.

The plates were cleared, and Valarie was on her second glass of wine. *Excellent.*

The female singer approached the corner of the dancefloor beside the piano and introduced herself. She invited patrons to the dancefloor which had a low-light chandelier hanging overhead. The singer started with a slow sexy number, and several couples wend through the tables to dance.

He held out a hand for Valarie. "Dance with me."

She smiled and let him lead her to the marble floor.

He wrapped an arm around her waist, drawing her near, as her arms circled his neck. Her breasts pressed against his chest was absolute heaven. He didn't realize how much he missed having her in his arms, and her sweet form molding to his.

"This is an interesting place," she murmured, looking at a couple to the right with the man's hand obviously under his woman's dress and cupped over her ass.

He grinned. *You ain't seen nothin' yet.*

She turned back to him. "So 'Wet' doesn't refer to the alcohol?" She asked the question but knew the answer.

He shook his head. With his free hand, he stroked her throat, descended her cleavage, resting it over a full breast.

She swallowed but didn't move to break the intimate contact.

"No, baby. It's not about the great drinks. It's about how a woman gets when she's aroused."

They barely moved in their dance, merely swaying to the beat. His hand slid underneath the dress, at the bottom of the V, gently cupping her breast from below. "You know how much I've dreamt about these breasts when you were gone. Your breasts are perfect, Val." A thumb toyed with her hard nipple. "I would wake up hard with your body on my mind."

She glanced around, witnessing a little canoodling from the other patrons.

He stroked her breast, allowing the fabric of the dress to pull off to the side. Only his hand hid her breast from view.

Her full red lips parted as her breathing sped.

"My body missed yours, Val. But my heart missed you too."

She trained her eyes on his; they showed a slight sheen.

He loosened the grip on her breast, drawing it away as his fingertips toyed with her nipple.

A throaty moan escaped her.

"Does this feel good, baby?"

"Yes," she breathed out.

He put her dress back in place and removed his hand. Her nipples poking against the fabric were breathtaking.

Her eyebrows furrowed, likely expecting him to continue.

*Good.* "Let's get some wine." He wanted it all with her, but she needed to be ready.

They sat and sipped their wine. She watched the dancers and the people around, and he watched her.

One man sat in an alcove by the window, but his partner wasn't visible. Only the bottoms of her shoes under the tablecloth as she was likely giving him a blowjob.

"Tell me something else about this club." She leaned in closer to whisper.

He held her hand and kissed the back and licked the sensitive spots in between her fingers. "The wait staff is available for those who would like any additional service."

Her eyes rounded.

He nodded. "I once saw a man who came alone, and his waitress sat on his lap, her skirt fanned around them. His hands were under her sweater, holding her breasts as she moved over him."

Valarie's mouth gaped. "No way."

He nodded. "You can do really whatever you want here; it just needs to be tasteful."

"Huh." She glanced around some more. She might be thinking how much they were going to do. Or maybe it was just that it was a great place for people watching.

A new song came over the speakers. "Take another sip, baby, and we'll dance."

She took a healthy drink and rose.

They found a cozy spot close to the wall that divided the entrance and hostess stand from the main room.

As her hands went to his neck and shoulder, he grabbed them and lowered them to his waist and under his jacket. "Keep these here for a while, baby."

She bit the inside of her cheek, assuming he had plans and it would do no good to argue.

He leaned down softly kissing her plump lips, then taking more as she opened for him. His right hand stroked her throat again and caressed her tit over her silky dress, not breaking their passionate kiss. He switched hands to love on the other breast. The ache was probably building pretty good in her.

"Baby, unbutton my shirt."

She met his gaze and did as he asked. All the while, his hand never left her breast. He slid the fabric aside, as he'd done earlier, revealing one breast.

Her breath hitched.

He held her gaze as he moved his hand to the other breast, peeling back the dress, leaving her chest bare.

She whimpered.

His look told her he would not be denied. "You can do this." He glanced around and a few eyes were on them.

Next, he pushed on her back so her bare breasts laid flush to his bare chest. He groaned in her ear, letting her know how amazing it was to have the skin-to-skin contact.

She was probably more comfortable having her nipples fully concealed now.

Jeremy swayed to the music, shuffling them on an angle to the crowd, instead of her back toward them. For this to work, she had to know what obstacles she was overcoming.

He sang in her ear with the singer, "Oh, I'd go anywhere with you."

She rested her head on his shoulder, slowly giving in to the moment.

He leaned down to pull away a strap from her dress, letting it fall down her arm, giving him access to kiss her neck and shoulder. "Did you miss me, Valarie?" He knew the answer.

"Yes." She panted lightly. "Yes, I did."

More kissing on her shoulder and neck. "Don't take your hands off me, baby." He tipped her head back, giving him unfettered access to the column of her neck, extending down to her partially revealed beasts.

Her breathing came faster.

Now, for the next test.

"Arch your back. Lean back, baby."

She tensed in his arms. When she didn't move, he cajoled her. "Let go, Valarie. You can do this. Give me what I've missed so much, baby."

"Here?" She whimpered, meeting his gaze.

"Yes. Here." His hand splayed across her back for support, waiting on her. He knew it wouldn't be easy, but he had to believe she wanted to make him happy.

Slowly, so slowly, she leaned back, as if a ballerina. She gripped his hips like her life depended on it, her mons pressed against his rock-hard dick. Her gorgeous full breasts were on display for anyone who cared to look.

He cupped one breast and laved at the other. He made love to her breasts, and for good measure, he pushed off the strap from her other shoulder.

She was staggeringly beautiful, bending back for his mouth to love on her, relishing the music and the gentle climb of ecstasy.

Of course, her eyes were closed.

That didn't surprise him, but it was enough to know anyone could see her, and she was giving up control, at least for a little while, to someone else. Someone she could trust, but with no say in how things would proceed.

He whispered over her skin. "You're gorgeous, Val."

She dared to lift her head and meet his eyes.

"Look around."

Several pairs of eyes were trained on her. One waiter even adjusted himself as he looked directly at her chest.

She turned back to him.

"They think you're beautiful. They see a woman letting go, taking in all the pleasure she can possibly absorb." He licked her nipple and lifted her back upright, but didn't adjust the dress. They weren't done yet.

He pulled her close, her rapid pants fluttered next to his ear.

One song flowed into the next, and he slowly moved his back inches from the wall. "Baby, I need relief. Unzip my fly and stroke me."

Again, her mouth gaped, but she didn't hesitate.

*Good girl.*

She stroked him, and to his surprise fished her way through his boxer briefs to connect with him.

"Fuck," he murmured in her ear when she cupped him.

He was on such a high, he could come in her hand if he wasn't careful. He kissed and suckled her neck, one hand reaching between them to play with her nipple.

His hand then slid along the side of her body to the top of the slit in her dress. "Are you wet, baby?"

He didn't wait for an answer just slipped a hand over her belly to her mons and dipped in between her lips.

She moaned. Her fucking clit was as big as he'd ever felt.

He massaged it lightly as he kissed her deeply. He didn't bother to glance up and see how many people were watching them now tucked in the back of the dancefloor. All he knew was he needed more. He would fuck her in the limousine, but he couldn't wait.

He broke the kiss to meet her gaze, then removed his fingertips to reach behind to squeeze her soft, full ass. Then slowly, he slid his hand down her thigh to lift her knee up the side of his leg.

Her hand stopped caressing his cock, and her jaw dropped. She knew what he wanted.

He nodded imperceptibly, but she saw it. "Take me, baby. Let me have you here, then we'll leave and I'll spend the rest of the night worshipping your body. Showing you how much I love you," he whispered over her lips.

Her breasts rose and fell as she cautiously leaned back, shifting her dress aside, and lined up his cock to her entrance. He bent his knees to gain better leverage and slowly pushed in.

She was wet and warm and swollen with anticipation.

Her head dropped back in a silent cry. *Fuck!* She was already coming around him.

After she came down, he leaned back. With his shoulder blades against the wall, he pulled her on an angle with him. His thrusts were short and leisurely as they found their place coupled together.

His feet in a secure position and his back wedged against the wall, he gained speed pumping into her. Then with his free hand, he glossed down the thigh of her standing leg.

"I've got you." He gently raised her thigh, effectively making her straddle him.

Sweat gathered on his brow. His strength wasn't a concern; he could hold her all night like this. He wasn't sure he could hold out for her to come again.

His thrusts continued. She gripped his shoulders, and her mouth hung open with her heavy breathing. One final barrier to knock down.

"Baby, hold this leg here for a second."

She bit her lip. "Okay."

He released his hold of the leg he'd just lifted and reached around her ass to the back side of the dress hanging straight down. Slowly, he dragged the fabric across her backside.

"Oh, God. Oh, God."

"Shh." He kissed her mouth, and after he had her ass cheeks completely exposed, he gripped her thighs and thrust with all his might.

She cried out into his mouth.

He let his thrusts get wild, the subtle coolness hitting the root of his wet cock and the edge of his sac.

The club might have never experienced such a blatant display of fornication before, but he fucking loved it. And based on the strength of Valarie's pussy muscles threatening to cut off the blood flow to his dick, she loved it too.

She clutched his shirt and jacket in her fists and screamed into his mouth as her desire exploded inside her.

He relaxed his muscles enough to let the lust and passion from days of pent-up anticipation finally release into her beautiful pink pussy.

The whole thing was heart-stoppingly beautiful.

He tore his mouth away from hers, her precious lips open to gasp for breath. He set down one leg and the back of her dress to retrieve a handkerchief. He pulled out of her, wiped himself, and gingerly wiped any semen that had begun to slip past her pussy lips.

Then he put himself back together and adjusted the front of her dress. She was once again fully covered.

He slipped his handkerchief into his jacket pocket and cupped her face. "Baby, that was the most beautiful thing I've ever done. Thank you for trusting me enough to give yourself over to me."

He placed sweet kisses over her mouth as she pulled herself closer to him. She was warm and soft with a heart of gold. Valarie was the last person he was ever going to date.

He raised his head. "Do you want to go home?"

She nodded.

Mad props to the waitress who'd already had his bill at the table, ready to sign. He saw a few eyes tracking their movements, but the fun was all theirs to have now. He was taking his woman home to his bed.

He texted the driver as they waited for the elevator.

She turned and looked up at him. "I thought you could do anything but it had to be *discrete*." Her voice rich in humor and amusement.

He chuckled and kissed the back of her hand. "Yeah. I'll probably get a three-month suspension for that."

They stepped onto the elevator, and he laced his fingers through hers.

She furrowed her brow. "Three months?"

"Yeah. Want me to call on the fourth month and get reservations?"

She smacked his chest, a twinkle in her eye, and he laughed. Laughed hard. The last time he'd felt this good was five years ago when he was dating the woman of his dreams.

And now she was back.

# Angel In White

# Chapter Fifteen

♥

Aidan hugged Vicki as she strode to their table at Ferrari's. "How are you, love?" He kissed her cheek.

Maurice wrapped his arms around her and kissed her cheek as well.

"I'm surviving. So glad it's Friday." She slid into the booth seat across from them.

Aiden and Victoria were best friends since middle school, and over the years he'd learned what every smile, frown, slouch, and snort meant. He could read her like a book. "Tough day or is this related to Daniel?"

She sent a sad smile. "No, no relation to Daniel. It's just been a long week. The state came in so everyone is on high alert."

Vicki worked in administration for a large nursing home group outside of Austin. Whenever the state came in to do an audit, Vicki's stress level went up.

"Wait a minute. What happened to Daniel?" Maurice's eyebrows pulled together.

He looked over at his boyfriend of two years. "Oh, I forgot to tell you. They broke up last week."

Maurice stretched a hand to Vicki's. "Nooo. I'm so sorry to hear that."

She gave him a half smile.

The waitress approached. "Can I get you anything to drink?"

"Yes, something strong," she replied.

Aidan grinned and ordered three cocktails and the calamari appetizer.

"So, what happened?" Maurice asked.

Over the years he'd gotten to know Vicki, his friend had come to adore her just as much as Aidan did. He could see it. They were like her older brothers, minus the arguing and bickering.

"Um, he sorta broke up with me."

Maurice tipped his head to the side. "What a loser."

"At first, I was surprised. He gave me no indication that he was unhappy."

"So, what's his deal?" Maurice did all the talking. Aidan already knew the story, and frankly he thought she was better off without Daniel. He couldn't put his finger on it, but Daniel wasn't right for her.

"He said he was bored. It's okay, really. He did me a favor. He kinda lies a lot."

Aidan's eyebrows shot up.

"I think it's a form of manipulation. I didn't see it at first—"

"Of course not. You can't always know when you're being lied to." Maurice leveled her with a look.

"Exactly. So, things started to reveal themselves over our eight months together. He would do it with other people too. So, you know," she shrugged her shoulder, "I'm good. It's for the best."

Aidan nodded.

Drinks came, followed shortly by the appetizer. Then they ordered their entrees. Aidan also ordered a bottle of red wine. Wine and Italian food went hand in hand.

The conversation flowed as easily as the alcohol. Vicki started to unwind and loosen up. She'd pulled the ponytail holder out of her hair and slipped it around her wrist. Whenever her long brown hair fell in her face, she'd just hook it behind an ear. In the restaurant's lighting, she almost looked like she had red highlights. She was a beautiful woman by any standard, and the lighting made her only more gorgeous.

Aidan remembered one time in high school at Danny Parker's party when he kissed her. He'd dated a few girls during that time, but nothing really serious. Of course, hindsight was twenty-twenty. With the handsome Italian stallion Maurice sitting beside him, it was obvious why.

But for a minute, a solid minute, he seriously questioned if he was gay when her soft lips, her warm tongue, sank into his. It might have been the best kiss he'd ever had, until he met Maurice.

At the time, they'd stared at each other for several moments after the kiss, but thankfully she'd broke out into laughter. She'd smacked his arm and chuckled. *You can't do that. I'm your best friend.*

They'd both had a big laugh over it, because she did him a favor. He never had a doubt that by graduation he was gay. And dating her, only to break up later? No way. He couldn't bear the thought of ripping her heart out. Thank the heavens above they stayed best friends, then added roommates into the mix after college graduation. They were like the line in the movie: "peas and carrots".

"So how was your day, Aidan?" Her voice brought him back to the present.

"Good. We have a new client in the firm, and I was given the account."

"A *big* client?" she asked.

He made a show of glancing around. "Let's just say he may or may not be CEO to the one of the largest smartphone companies on the planet."

Vicki and Maurice's eyes went wide. "Ooh. Sounds thrilling," Maurice said with a sly smile.

They all laughed out loud. The camaraderie between the three was easy, trusting, and unshakeable. Aidan wouldn't trade places with anyone. There had been trying moments, like when he needed to come out to his parents. But ultimately, they were accepting, and they positively loved Maurice.

"Where'd you go?" Maurice met his gaze.

"Sorry. Just thinking. I feel blessed." He reached for each of their hands. "To have you both in my life, I wouldn't change a thing. Life has been good, even when I came out and thought my life might be over."

"It helps that your parents love me," Maurice added, his self-aggrandizing smile stretching from ear to ear.

"What's not to love?" Vicki said, then leaned forward and planted a big smooch on his lips.

He smiled and winked at her. "Exactly."

"Wait. You can't just kiss him and not me."

She rolled her eyes but shifted her weight to lean forward and plant a loud kiss on his lips.

"Thank you," Aidan said, exaggerating the vindication he got from the kiss.

Maurice chuckled and soon they all were laughing.

Another hour, bellies were full, and the bill was paid. "Maybe we should leave our cars here and take a taxi home. We can just pick them up in the morning," he suggested.

"That works for me. Tomorrow's Saturday. I have zero plans, except scrub my bathtub and water my plants." She slurred a little on the final S. Maurice heard it too and smiled as he shifted out of his seat and offered her a hand.

She rose and then looped her arms around each man as they escorted her out the door. Soon, the taxi had them cruising down the dark highway toward home.

His mind raced ahead. He hoped Maurice would spend the night with him. Some nights Maurice stayed. The next morning they could lounge around naked drinking coffee in bed, talking about their ridiculous cases or politics or whatever. Some nights Maurice was too stressed and would go home.

Aidan knew not to take it personally. Maurice lived in his head so much. Thinking and rethinking. That was just how he was, and Aidan knew it. Working as an attorney, like Aidan, Maurice processed his stress internally, whereas Aidan was more of a talk-it-out kind of person. Maurice would tell him that was one reason they got along so well: opposites attract.

The cab stopped in front of their apartment building. An old building of stone with just a few units stacked close together, each apartment having several bedrooms, a back patio, vaulted ceilings, and stone fireplaces. It was a dream come true. If he and Maurice ever thought about living together, Aidan had no idea what he was going to do. He loved both his friends *and* the old apartment building.

Vicki opened her eyes and lifted her head off Maurice's shoulder and took Aidan's hand to stand on the curb.

"I'm beat, guys," she called out as she went to the kitchen for a glass of water. "I'll see y'all in the morning." She blew them a kiss and slowly made her way down the hall.

"Will you stay the night?" He turned and asked.

"Only if I get to fuck you," Maurice replied with a grin.

"I heard that," Vicki called from down the hall.

"Sorry," Maurice called back.

He turned toward his boyfriend and smiled.

# Chapter Sixteen

♥

The sun peeked through her drapes. Vicki slept like the dead and it felt so good. She must have needed—she glanced at her phone—ten hours of sleep. *Shit!*

She threw back the blanket and reached for her gray sweatpants and a plaid button-down shirt and dashed into her bathroom. She tried to make herself as presentable as possible as quickly as possible.

*What the hell. Who really cares?* They were just going to pick up the cars.

She heard voices coming from the kitchen. Making her way down the hall, she turned the corner to see Maurice leaning against the wall, sipping coffee, his back to her.

Shit, that man had a fine ass. Both men did. Vicki admitted to having more than one fantasy about Maurice after Aidan told her that he wasn't strictly gay, he was bi-sexual. She had a fantasy about Aidan once or twice too—the man was not only built, but he was so caring and funny, and would do anything for her. She was so freakin' happy that he finally found someone who was ying to his yang.

"Good morning, pumpkin," Aidan called, and Maurice spun around. Both men smiled at her.

"Oh, good, it's still morning." She reached for a coffee cup in the cabinet. "Sorry about that."

"No worries." Maurice toasted her in the air with his coffee.

"Y'all just say the word and we can head out of here."

"Super. My car's out front."

Aidan stepped closer to her and looked down with a grin. His bent finger glossed up the center of her cleavage.

At the sensation of his finger on her skin, she looked down. She'd missed a button and was damn-near flashing the girls for the world to see. "Oops." She set her cup down and clenched her shirt closed. "How about I put on a bra first, then we can head out."

The men chuckled, and she dashed back to her bedroom.

On the drive over to the restaurant's parking lot, Aidan started. "Hey, Maurice and I were thinking about heading to Zeek's tonight to see Cold Hard Cache. Wanna come?"

"No, that's okay. I'm staying in tonight. I have a date with the bathtub, white wine, and a new book boyfriend." Plus Aidan was so kind, he would invite her even if she was just going to be in the way. She had to watch how much she was a third-wheel in their relationship. "If I'm awake when y'all get in, we can watch a scary movie."

Maurice nodded.

"Deal." Aidan agreed.


That night she slid into the hot, sudsy water of her fresh scrubbed tub with a sigh. Perfect.

She sipped her wine and closed her eyes. Her mind wandered to earlier when Aidan teased her about her wardrobe malfunction. His finger gliding over her skin was surprising *and* decadent. He'd done something like that once before, and she never thought twice about it. They really didn't have much to hide between each other. But this time, there was a heat in his eyes. It all happened so fast, but she was sure she saw it.

It didn't make sense but that didn't stop her from having her little fantasy in the tub of his hands combing the landscape of her body.

Vicki had laughed it off, but damn if she didn't love it. Maurice was definitely a lucky man. Aidan had good fingers. She needed to find a straight version of her roommate, plain and simple.

***

Maurice slid onto a barstool next to Aidan, who had just ordered them a round of beers. The way the man smiled at the waitress was hypnotic. The waitress smiled back, no idea he had zero interest in women. But he had an easy strength and confidence, like a man comfortable in his own skin, and that was incredibly attractive.

Maurice wished he was more like Aidan.

Maurice was a classic A-type personality: work hard, play hard, laugh out loud. His relationship with Aidan was the longest he'd ever had. Sure, he thought about being with women, not a lot. Well, except for Aidan's roommate.

*Fuck!* Vicki was hot. He'd had a wet dream or two about the little firecracker. Her curvy body hidden under her stupid-ass work clothes was pure temptation. But he would never do anything behind Aidan's back. Nor would he risk a fantastic friendship with her. Maurice felt more at peace with Aidan—and Vicki too—than he had in a very long time.

Was there such a thing as having two soulmates?

The band came on and played some eighties rock. They weren't half bad. A few people danced. Maurice would dance, but generally he and Aidan kept their relationship discreet whenever they went out. People probably looked at them, thinking the two men were just good friends. Women would approach them occasionally and ask if they would dance. Sometimes they would ask for more. It was almost like a game with Maurice and Aidan, to act straight and wait for the propositions to roll in. It always made for a great night back at his place.

Maurice discreetly rested his hand on Aidan's thigh. No one was paying attention to what was going on under the table. Aidan looked his way, a twinkle in his eye. Maurice's hand crept higher to find the beginnings of a hard-on.

"Careful." Aidan muttered, the corner of his lip curled.

Maurice tended closer. "If I thought I could get away with it, I'd bend you over this table and take you fast and deep," he whispered close to his ear.

Aidan smiled and laced his fingers through his own. "If I thought we could get away with it, I'd let you."

The band took a break, so conversation was easier for a few minutes.

"So, is Vicki okay? I mean, with the Daniel thing?"

Aidan tilted his head. "I think so. It's like every day gets a little better. That tells me she wasn't as in love with him as much as she thought."

"Ah." Maurice wanted her happy, but he was secretly happy she was single again. "She, uh, looked pretty cute this morning—disheveled clothes, wild hair, still half-asleep."

"I know, right. She was another missing button from flashing us her tits."

Maurice laughed. "I wouldn't have minded. She's got a smokin' hot body, but I'm pretty sure she would have been mortified."

"Right. Thank God she has us."

They ordered more drinks and watched the band until about one o'clock.

"Babe, can you drive," he leaned in close to Aidan, "because otherwise we need a ride?"

Aidan smirked. "I noticed that. Yeah, I can drive. I've had less to drink."

They arrived safely back at his place. Before Aidan got out of the car, Maurice leaned over and gasped his shirt, pulling Aidan close. He pressed his lips to Aidan's, who opened for him. He cupped his jaw, diving into Aidan's warm mouth, tasting the masculine flavor. The fire that pulsed through his veins only Aidan could put out. Aidan was a balm on his heart and soul. His passion also matched Maurice's, and for that, Maurice felt blessed.

He broke the kiss long enough to say, "Let's go inside."

Maurice stumbled in a misstep up the curb and laughed. Aidan smiled and took his hand. "You got this, baby?"

He grinned.

Inside, Maurice slipped off his shoes. "I need to use the bathroom. I'll be right back."

As he came out, Aidan came down the hall. "Be right out. I'll meet you on the sofa," he whispered.

Maurice walked, following his hand along the wall for a little stability. When he came to Vicki's door, the last door before the great room, he noticed it was cracked open slightly. He couldn't resist. He pushed it open to peer inside.

Just as he suspected. She slept sprawled out in the center of her queen-size bed. The moonlight creeping in from the window made her look like an angel. He stepped closer, watching in awe as she slept on her stomach, draped in a white sheet, her brown hair cascading over her pillow.

"What are you doing in here?" Aidan whispered from over his shoulder.

"Look at her. She looks like an angel," he whispered back.

"C'mon. Let's not wake her."

Maurice heard the words but didn't let it register. Instead, he stepped closer, now inches from her bed.

Aidan looped a finger in his jeans waistband and tugged, wordlessly trying to get him to obey, but Maurice was rooted.

He watched the gentle rise and fall of her back as she breathed. *Beautiful.*

He reached for the white sheet, carefully peeling it back. Aidan tugged harder, but it didn't matter. He already saw her angelic body—face down, arms under her pillow, wearing nothing but a white lace thong.

Maurice looked up at Aidan whose mouth gaped at the vision before them. "She's beautiful."

# Chapter Seventeen

♥

V icki heard whispers, at least she thought she had. Maybe it was a dream. A lucid dream.

She laid there, comfortable on her pillowtop bed, aware of her semi-sleep state. She heard voices again. It sounded like her boys were back.

Then she heard Maurice's voice. It sounded like he said *She's our beautiful angel.*

Not bothering to open her eyes, she remained peacefully relaxed in her bed, accessing why the voices sounded so close. Then there was silence, only breathing, maybe kissing. She was also now vaguely aware that the sheet now longer covered her body. She was too damn relaxed to want to care.

She'd taken a long hot bath to do just that—relax.

"Vicki, you're so beautiful."

Now, she recognized that voice was Aidan, and he was definitely in her room.

So, both boys were in her room?

Should she get up?

A hand caressed the side of her leg, then she felt a kiss on her head. "Hello, precious angel." Maurice spoke this time.

She sighed. She didn't want to open her eyes; it was too much effort. And why would she bother? She trusted her men implicitly. They could do anything they wanted; they always put her interests before their own. They protected her to the ends of the earth.

Soon, two hands stroked her calves—maybe that was Maurice—because the kisses traveled to her neck as Aidan moved her hair out of the way.

Oh, God, this all felt so good. She prayed she wasn't dreaming.

Hands stroked her back and shoulders, while another set caressed up her legs to her ass.

*Oh, yes, this is incredible.* Warm hands and tender kisses soaking her in a sensual bath.

She couldn't quite wrap her brain around what was happening, and more importantly why. Aidan was gay. She knew that. Everyone knew that. And although Maurice was bi... Why wouldn't he—they—just go into Aidan's room?

She'd heard them some nights. The sounds of hot sex reaching Vicki in her room made her hot herself.

But they were in her room now, touching and kissing her.

She moaned.

"That's right, sweet angel. You lie there and let us take care of you. Would you like that?"

Would she like that? The two men most dear to her, her best friends, handsome as sin, somehow found her attractive and wanted to make her feel good. Was there even a question?

"Mmhm."

Kisses and licks gently peppered her entire backside, claiming every inch. The wetness at the apex of her thighs grew.

One of her men hooked his fingers under her panties, drawing them down her legs.

"Look at that gorgeous ass, Aidan," Maurice said in a low tone. Then his hands pushed her legs apart, and reached beneath her to raise her hips off the bed. He blew gently at her sex.

She moaned at the anticipation.

"You smell divine, angel. I bet you taste just as good."

Maurice's tongue—flat, wide, and long—swiped through her wet core, from her clit to her tiny back hole.

"Oh, God," she breathed out, and her eyes opened for the first time.

As Maurice made love to her with his mouth, Aidan kissed and suckled her back.

The sensations from her men were incredible—too much to handle and yet craving more.

"Sweet girl."

She opened her eyes to see Aidan before her, an amazing twinkle in his blue eyes. "I want to kiss you."

She lifted her head, and he cupped her face bringing his lips to hers. He dove in, possessing her like never before—better than their first time.

The climax bringing her out of sleepiness rose to the surface in full force. She broke the kiss and cried out. "Maurice."

*Oh, God, so good.* She wanted more.

Would it ruin everything if she wanted it all?

The titillating wave subsided. The sheet recovered her body.

*What?!*

She jolted, lifting on an elbow, facing them. "Are you leaving?"

"No, precious angel. You need to see what you're getting." Maurice spoke, the deep, dark glint in his eyes told her they were just getting started.

She covered her body with the sheet and pushed into a seated position.

Maurice reached for Aidan's shirt and lifted it overhead. Then Aidan did the same to him. Then they each worked on unfastening their jeans. Maurice squatted down before Aidan, pulling his jeans and briefs to the floor. His perfect erection sprang feel—hard and eager.

"Look, angel. See how hard he is for you."

Her mouth gaped. He was hard for *her*.

Maurice stroked him with his hand, then put his mouth on him, moving up and down. Aidan groaned and gripped Maurice's shoulder for purchase, then wove his fingers through his shiny dark hair. It was the most erotic thing she'd ever witnessed.

Shortly, Maurice stopped and rose, pushing off his pants as well. Both men stood before her completely naked, hers for the taking.

She lifted onto her knees and shimmied to the corner of the bed, facing them, forming a triangle. "You're both beautiful." She stroked a hand over Maurice's chest, then Aidan's. So mesmerized, she hadn't realized she still gripped the sheet over herself.

Aidan took her right hand, kissed the palm and the wrist. "Are you ready for more, angel?"

She nodded, looking up at both of her men.

Maurice took her other hand to rest on his chest. The sheet fell to the mattress.

"Oh, sweet Jesus."

"You're breathtaking, Vicki."

With their free hands, they caressed her like earlier, exploring her body like it was a fascinating new find. Soon, her men had lay claim to her breasts with their mouths.

"Oh, God. So good."

Maurice rose, clasping the back of her neck. "Head back, angel. Let Aidan love on your breasts. Yours are the only ones he wants."

Aidan sucked hard on a nipple, punctuating the statement.

Then Maurice claimed her mouth, his tongue diving deep, almost like he wanted to drown in her. It was their first tongue kiss, and she prayed more would follow.

As their hands roamed her body, she lowered hers to their beautiful cocks. Both men bigger than she'd ever had before, but somehow she knew, it would be perfect for her.

Aidan returned to her lips, both men huddling close. She felt them spread her knees farther apart and caress her thighs, so close to her sex.

"Angel, are we overwhelming you? We want you completely, wholly."

"When we take you, you will be ours. Can you handle that?" Maurice added.

"Oh, God, yes. This is what I want...what I've dreamed of."

Maurice smiled before claiming her lips again, his firm and demanding but laced with lust, like he couldn't get enough. As one hand gripped her jaw, the other roamed her backside. He reached under her, gathered moisture, to smooth over her tiny hole.

"Mmm." Her eyes fluttered at the new, foreign sensation.

Aidan's fingers roamed closer to her clit, exploring her tender flesh. "You're beautiful, Vicki." He stared into her eyes like he could see her soul. "I think I've always loved you."

Emotion welled inside her. She was surrounded by love, and it never felt so good, so real, so all-consuming. A tear slid down her cheek. "I love you too, Aidan." She kissed him, pulling him closer, and yet desperate for even more.

She broke the kiss and turned to Maurice. "I love you too, Maurice."

He smiled. "I know you do, and I love you too, angel." Holding her gaze, another finger entered her backside. He kissed her neck and suckled. "It will be a great honor to take you here, my love, while Aidan takes your pussy."

"Oh, God," she breathed out. The sensations grew stronger. Aidan's fingers played with her clit and pussy while Maurice's fingers prepared her backside.

More kissing, sucking, whispering accolades. Her sex had never been slicker. She ached for release. She felt dizzy with need. "Angel, when Maurice said you will be ours, he didn't just mean for the night. You know that right?"

She nodded. One night would never be enough.

"We will love you and worship you. You will have no other lovers and neither shall we. If you want babies, we will give you babies. You will want for nothing as long as we're here."

Tears streamed down her cheeks unbidden. She'd yearned to hear those words, and she prayed she could believe them.

Maurice added another finger.

"Ah," she cried out. She wanted them so fiercely. "I want it, I want it all. I am yours forever. But... will I be enough?"

Aidan drew her chin to face him. "You are always enough. And you were always ours, we just only now realized it."

The men continued stroking her, bringing her to the brink of ecstasy, but not enough to spill her over.

"Oh, God," her chest heaved, "I'm ready. Please. Please, fuck me. I need you both. I need you now."

Aidan looked at Maurice. "Let's make our girl feel good." He shifted closer and kissed his boyfriend deeply.

Maurice stood between her legs, wetting his cock with her essence. Maurice's arm wrapped around her from behind, and Aidan braced her hip. With their cocks in their hands, they aligned themselves at her entrances and slowly pushed.

"Ah," she cried out. "More. More."

They gently pushed in another inch.

Her arms overhead, one cupped the back of Maurice's neck, the other hand cupped Aidan's. "Yes. Please." She couldn't describe the intensity and raw lust coursing through her veins. She'd fantasized about two men—these two men—taking her, loving her, fulfilling her every wild dream.

They finally had pushed into her completely, and the orgasm hovering just beneath the surface clawed its way to the surface. They pumped just once and detonated her climax. She screamed, and they didn't stop pumping into her.

"Oh, God, so full, so full."

Another orgasm rocketed through her, making her head spin.

Her men held her tighter, kissed her body, sucked her nipples, raining compliments over her.

She felt like she could float away. Another orgasm was bubbling from deep inside. Like she had a lifetime of orgasms to have. "I'm going to come again."

Aidan spoke. "So will we, angel."

They pushed in and pulled back fervently, pumping until all three of them were coming together. Screams, grunts, growls could be heard for maybe a solid minute until the wave of ecstasy ebbed.

Maurice pulled out first and went to the en suite bathroom. Aidan wrapped his arms around her, shifting her back to the center of the bed and lay beside her. Maurice returned with a warm washcloth to wipe her personal areas gently.

He lay down beside her and covered them all with the sheet and blanket.

"You are amazing, baby." Aidan stroked her hip.

"Everything I had hoped and more," Maurice whispered in her ear.

They spoke almost reverently, taking turns kissing her, more sweetly this time.

"Rest, baby. We have so much more to share with you. So much we want to give. Sleep now. We'll be right here."

She was exhausted. She'd never come by penetration alone, she'd always needed external stimulation. Well, perhaps she just needed the right man, or men in this case.

"I love you," she sighed and within seconds she was sound asleep.

# Chapter Eighteen

A idan felt a high no drug in the world could provide, not that he was looking for one.

No, in fact, he'd been happy just the way things were. He had a great job, making good money. A boyfriend he loved and who loved him. A best friend and roommate whom he would do anything for.

But last night, the perfect picture got better. He could almost ache inside at the beauty they'd created. He was missing something in his life and never even knew it.

When his tipsy, adventurous boyfriend had stumbled into Vicki's room, he could have laughed. But Maurice hadn't budged, and Aidan'd panicked that they would waken her.

When Maurice pulled back the sheet to reveal Vicki's heavenly form, Aidan couldn't retreat. No, in fact he moved closer, like he was drawn to a priceless work of art.

God, she'd been so beautiful lying there with barely any clothing on. She should sleep naked, for nothing was worthy of touching that precious body.

Maurice had kissed him and told him she was theirs. Just hearing those simple words, Aidan knew it was true. She *was* theirs; always had been.

He had no interest in women; he'd known that for years. But maybe this was why he'd never forgotten their kiss back in high school. She was like a missing puzzle piece that fit so perfectly with them.

Aidan shifted on the bed carefully and gazed down at his male and female lovers. The missing parts of him that now made him whole.

Maurice sighed and opened his eyes, turning to smile at Aidan.

Without saying a word, he lifted on an elbow and Maurice mirrored his actions, meeting him in the middle for a kiss. "Thank you," he whispered over his lover's lips. "I didn't know how much I needed this."

"I know. Me too. She's now a part of us."

Aidan nodded and kissed him again. They broke the kiss and stared down at their angel. Wordlessly, they both took a hold of the sheet and peeled it away. Maurice's dick as hard as his, and his mouth watered.

They both leaned down to gently kiss her awake—her neck, her breasts, and Aidan made his way down to her secret spot. Waxed nude, her skin was smooth everywhere.

Separating her petals, he had his first taste of his sweet Vicki. Her scent intoxicating.

She moaned and arched slightly.

He continued to make love to her sex, making sure she was nice and wet, while Maurice caressed her breasts and suckled her nipples.

"So beautiful, Vicki," Maurice whispered.

"Baby, we're sorry to wake you again. We had to have more, we haven't had enough." Slipping two fingers into her channel, he found it already soaking wet. "God, baby. You're ready."

Aidan looked at Maurice, whose eyes brimmed with lust.

"Can you take us again, baby, in your sweet pussy? We're clean, and from now on, we will always take you bareback."

She smiled and nodded. "I'm on the pill."

He knew that.

With both men at her sides, touching her, kissing her, they pulled her legs apart. Maurice shifted and held his dick at her entrance. "My love, I have dreamed about this moment." He pushed inside her, and she bowed off the bed with a moan.

He pumped a few times, as she writhed under their ministrations. Then he pulled out. Aidan shifted next to claim his precious girl, her pretty pussy felt like home.

"Ah," she cried out when he hit the end. He leaned down to kiss her deeply, before shifting for Maurice.

Maurice slid in effortlessly.

"Bend your knees, and bring them up, baby." Aidan's hand rested on her knee.

She did as he asked, opening herself and giving him access to her clit. Aidan's tongue roamed over her clit and over his boyfriend's cock. It was heavenly.

Maurice moaned. "Fuck." He gripped his hair, but Aidan didn't stop. Soon, Vicki was writhing and panting harder. She screamed out her climax, as Maurice released his.

He fell to the side, and Aidan dove in. He pushed and pulled when he felt her pussy muscles grip him. She cried out as another orgasm crashed through her. Aidan released his seed, loving that she now held a bit of both of them deep inside her.

He collapsed to the side, all of them gasping for air while they held hands.

Maurice covered them, and a peacefulness once again filled the room.

This was the beginning of a brand-new chapter in all their lives.

"We should buy a king-sized bed," she murmured.

"Tomorrow," they replied in unison.

She grinned. "Okay." And she flipped over on her stomach, asleep in mere seconds, just as they'd found her hours before.

# Pretty In Purple

# Chapter Nineteen

♥

Mike strolled into his girlfriend Heather's kitchen, eager for a mug to fill with hot black energy. He had an hour before he had to be a work.

"Morning," he greeted Heather's roommate, Jackie.

Jackie glanced up as she broke an egg into a hot skillet. Jackie and Heather were not only roommates but close friends, so naturally Mike and Jackie had become friends. He would occasionally spend the night, and they would talk over dinner or breakfast the following day.

"So, how was your night with Heather? She left so early this morning, I didn't get a chance to ask her."

Mike and Heather had been dating for just over a year. Mike quickly learned that Heather was rather conservative in the bedroom, and he loved bringing her out of her shell. Mike loved Heather—period, and one day he would make her his wife.

"Dinner at La Mans was incredible. But Jack, you know, I don't kiss and tell. Suffice it to say that with my help, Heather is learning all the facets of her sexuality." Mike grinned.

"Lucky you," Jackie murmured.

That stopped Mike dead in his tracks. He spun around, finding Jackie's head down focused on her breakfast preparation. "Did you say 'Lucky you'?"

She worried her lower lip, then after a beat raised her head to meet his stare. "Maybe."

Mike moved in closer. "Jack, let me ask you something. Have you thought about Heather more than as just a roommate?"

"Mike, she's a good friend."

Jackie was holding back something, and Mike had a good idea what it was. "I know that. But that doesn't mean certain thoughts haven't crossed your mind about Heather. Like thoughts of you and her. . ."

Jackie glanced over his shoulder, as if double checking that Heather wasn't around, and leaned in closer to him. "I have thought about her, yes," she said through a tight mouth.

"So, does that mean you're bi?"

She nodded. "You have to swear you won't tell Heather." Her eyes went wide. "She's innocent. She won't get it, and I'm afraid it'll make her uncomfortable. I don't want to risk our friendship."

"Okay. I respect that." Thoughts swirled around in his head, formulating faster than he could find the words to articulate. *Damn! This could be so good for Heather.*

Jackie's eyes narrowed. "What are you thinking about, Mike?"

"What if I gave you the opportunity to be the lucky one?"

Her eyes widened. But slowly, as the thought sunk in, they returned to normal and twinkled at what Mike was proposing. "I would love that. But again, she can't know it's me."

He shook his head. "She'll just know it's a woman."

A puff of breath passed through the circle her lips formed. "Fuck, Mike. That would be phenomenal. I would make it so good for her."

"I know you would. There's only one rule. If she can't handle it, you stop."

"Of course."

He'd give it some thought and figure out the best way to approach Heather with his idea. She might need time to think it over, but he stood a really good chance of letting a woman join them. Jackie was a caring *and* sexy candidate. His cock gave a jump at the idea of watching Heather receive pleasure from someone else. In fact, if he was honest with himself, that person could even be a man.

*Fuck! That could be hot too.*

But they were a long way from that, if at all.

"Okay, let me see what I can do." He spun around, coffee in his hand, letting the idea percolate on the possibility of giving Heather the most erotic night she'd ever had.

***

As Heather and Mike sat on the settee on her balcony, sipping wine, and listening to some French music Mike stumbled onto, he lifted her feet onto his lap.

She smiled, shifting her weight to recline comfortably.

Mike unfastened her straps and slipped off her sandals, then began kneading and massaging her feet. He worked her arches and circled her ankles.

The calm quickly took root, spreading up her legs, allowing her entire body to enjoy what this wonderful man did to her. Mike was always thinking of her. Until she started dating him, she never felt so cherished in a relationship before. Her gut told her, he had the makings of happily ever after.

"So, what would you like to do this weekend?" he asked casually.

She sighed, sinking deeper into a relaxed state. "I'm open. I wouldn't mind seeing the new Tom Cruise movie, but that doesn't have to be this weekend."

"Cool. That sounds good. I had another idea too, maybe for Saturday."

Her eyes stayed closed, but she was listening. "Okay."

"I saw a recipe for a stuffed pork tenderloin I'd like to try. Has bacon in it."

Mike loved experimenting with new recipes, frankly experimenting with lots of new things. "Mmm, sounds great." He was actually turning out to be a great cook.

He shifted and his hands slipped higher up her legs to her calves, massaging her tight muscles.

She moaned.

"Then," he continued, "I have few other ideas for after dinner."

She giggled. He always had "ideas", and she was starting to love his ideas. He was so spontaneous and adventurous, and not just in a sexual way. She had no idea she'd love it so much. "Of course you do."

"Heather."

She opened her eyes to meet his darkening stare.

His hands crept a little higher on her legs. "I was approached by someone. A female."

She tensed. *What the hell?*

"It's not what you think. She's not interested in me." He paused. "She's interested in you."

Heather swallowed hard, trying to wrap her brain around what she was hearing. "She's interested in me? But she knows we're together?"

He nodded. "She knows. She wants to join us—one night."

Heather almost shot out of her seat.

Mike laid a hand on her chest gently between her breasts. "It's okay. Take a breath, baby."

*Holy crap! A woman wants to be with us. With me!*

"Do I know this woman?"

He shook his head. "It doesn't matter. You'll be blindfolded."

She took a gulp of wine, hoping to moisten her dry mouth. "Is she lesbian or bisexual?"

Mike stroked her leg, like he was trying to sooth a scared child. "Don't overthink this, baby. Just know that I will be there, but it's not about me. I won't touch her. It's only about you." He leaned closer, letting his hands slide under her skirt, skimming slowly up and down her thighs. "All you need to think about is what an incredible experience you could have. What it might feel like to have a women's soft lips kiss you, or her tongue lick you?"

Heather gasped. "But . . ." She didn't know if she could say it.

"But what?" he asked, his voice so soothing and reassuring.

"Does that mean I'm gay?" she whispered.

His smile was full of understanding. "No, baby. You would have known before now if you were." He stroked her thighs on the outside, grazing over her hips. "Some people say sex is just sex, passion is just passion. It doesn't matter who gives it."

She nodded slowly.

His hands slid higher, pushing one leg upright against the sofa cushion and tracing the line of her cotton panties.

She didn't stop him. The images in her head frighteningly excited her. She'd never thought about being with a woman before. Ever. She only ever liked men. But now hearing Mike talk about it, tell her this woman wanted to be with her, seemed . . . intriguing, and maybe thrilling.

Mike pulled her panties aside and ran a finger through her slit. "Baby," he whispered, "this idea excites you."

The warmth grew in her face as he continued to play with her wet sex, circling her needy clit.

"Would I have to do anything to her?"

"You don't have to anything you aren't comfortable with. In fact, we can invite her in, but at any point if you change your mind, we stop. We send her on her way. You can trust me."

Mike pushed her skirt a little higher, nearly revealing her sex.

Her eyes darted around. She had neighbors, but none of them were out on their balconies tonight. She would pray they decided not to come out for a while.

As he pulled against her panties more, he slid a finger through her wet core.

Her head fell back as she moaned.

"Think about what it might feel like to have this finger be a female's."

The settee moved, and his hot breath blow over her pussy. "Or what it might feel like to have a female tongue on you." He licked her clit just then and drove in another finger.

She bowed her back, relishing the exquisite feeling, and maybe—God, just maybe—seriously thinking about letting a woman go down on her.

"Can you picture it, baby?" he spoke softly.

"Yes."

"I think it would be beautiful. I think you would love it." He continued his ministrations, quickly bringing her to the brink of ecstasy. Then he stopped.

*Ugh!* She needed release. She needed to come.

"Baby, can I have an answer tonight or do you need more time to think about it?" His fingers twisted inside her channel. The sound of slip-sliding wetness almost as loud as her breathing.

"I think . . ."

He pushed her skirt higher, like he was getting ready to finish her, but was waiting on her answer. "You think what?"

She exhaled. "I think I would like to try that on Saturday night."

He grinned from ear to ear. Then without any hesitation, he yanked her panties harder, ripping them, and lowered his tongue to her clit, laving and sucking her.

Her hands wove through his hair as she flexed her hips to his face.

He pushed a third finger inside as he pressed harder on her clit.

She cried out as her orgasm blossomed, sending waves of sensation throughout her entire body, rocking her like no other orgasm before. When the tremors finally calmed, she relaxed, sinking into the settee, enjoying the after-glow. She licked her lips.

She secretly hoped she'd enjoy Saturday night just as much.

# Chapter Twenty

♥

Saturday couldn't come fast enough. Talking to Heather about Jackie wanting to join them was fucking hot. When Heather had asked if she had to do anything in return, he almost lost his freakin' load right then.

*Fuck!* He hadn't thought about that? What if Heather wanted to try something too? Experiment with a female? This *would* be her chance.

Saturday night had arrived, and as he set the groceries on Heather's kitchen counter, he only prayed she hadn't changed her mind.

He leaned forward and kissed her, sweet and romantic, saving the steamy stuff for later. "Hello, sunshine."

"Hi." She gave him a small smile.

"How are you feeling?" he asked, gauging her mood for the evening.

"I'm . . . good. A little nervous, but excited too."

"Okay, that's good. Remember, I'll be there the whole time."
She nodded.

"So, where's Jack?" he asked for appearance's sake.

"She went out for the night. Probably won't see her 'til morning."

"Okay, great." He turned to unpack the groceries. "I'll leave the leftovers here for her to have some too."

"That's sweet. Thank you."

"Why don't we get dinner underway? Our guest arrives in about two hours."

They cooked together and shared a bottle of wine. Dinner tasted excellent, and he was thankful for Heather's positive outlook on the evening. She squirmed occasionally and had a flush in her cheeks. She was nervous. But knowing her the way he did, Mike was confident once things got started she would love everything Jackie did to her.

After a quick clean-up, he took Heather back to her bedroom. Soon, it would be dark outside, and he bought two candles with him and turned on the bedside lamp. Then he laid the blindfold and some condoms on the nightstand.

"I'm going to take off our shirts, okay? But she wants to take off everything else."

Heather nodded. She was so adorable how tentative she looked.

He laid the shirts over a chair when a knock came at the door.

Her eyes rounded.

"Take a deep breath, okay? Let me slip this over your eyes." He fixed the black fabric in place, double checking any possibility to peek. He gave her a deep tongue kiss, arching her neck so he could take more. "Now lie back and relax. I'll go get our guest."

He was already hard with anticipation. He knew in his gut Heather would enjoy this, and he felt blessed he was the one who got to witness it, experience it with her.

He opened the door for Jackie who wore shorts, a spaghetti strap top, and sandals. "She's ready."

Jackie nodded and smiled.

Mike led the way and leaned down to stroke his fingertips up Heather's arm. Then he took a place up close to Heather's head as she lay crosswise on the bed.

Jackie took a place at Heather's feet.

"Baby," he started, "she doesn't want you to touch her just yet, so I'm going to hold your hands up here. Okay?" Jackie had curly hair and didn't want to leave any clues for Heather.

"Okay," she whispered.

Jackie positioned herself between Heather's legs. One by one, she lifted his girlfriend's leg and removed her shoes. She then stroked her hands over Heather's jean-clad thighs and leaned down placing small kisses over her abdomen.

Heather sighed.

Jackie climbed onto the bed and straddled Heather, moving her kisses up her torso from her satin-covered breasts to her neck. Goosebumps covered Heather's skin. Jackie's fingertips glossed over Heather's lips, until they gently feel apart. Jackie leaned down to claim her prize, softly kissing and nibbling her lips, glossing over her bottom lip with her tongue and driving in to tongue kiss her.

*Fuck me!*

Mike's cock surged against his jeans, and he wondered how long he'd need to go before loosening the denim binding.

Jackie broke the passionate kiss. Heather's lips looked redder and more swollen.

"Baby, you look so fucking beautiful. How did that feel?"

"Good," she breathed out. "Soft."

"Want to keep going?"

Heather nodded.

Jackie continued to kiss her way down to Heather's breasts. She yanked the cup fabric, pulling them down to reveal his girlfriend's gorgeous, full tits. Jackie took a hard nipple in her mouth, and both women moaned. She moved to the other nipple, giving it the same attention.

Heather's back bowed slightly.

Jackie backed away and motioned with her chin toward her bra.

"Baby, she wants me to remove your bra." He reached under and unclipped the garment, pulling it free. He couldn't resist. He leaned over her head and laved at her nipple, sucking and kissing while Jackie stripped from the waist up.

Mike rose as Jackie returned to the bed. With two hands, she cupped Heather's breasts, kissing and sucking them. Heather's breath quickened.

After a moment, Jackie reached for Mike's hands and had him cup Heather's tits, holding them in place. Then she leaned forward, arching her back she lowered herself to rub her breasts against Heather's.

"Geez! That is so hot." He was nearly breathless.

Jackie's nipples peaked rubbing over Heather's.

"Oh God," Heather whispered.

Jackie's breasts swung, tapping the bottom of Heather's chin in the process. Heather's mouth gaped.

Jackie saw it and looked at Mike, who was equally surprised. Jackie moved over her again, this time slower and higher, just glossing a nipple over Heather's lips. Heather's tongue reached forward, barely making contact with her nipple. Jackie shifted to the right slightly, her nipple directly over Heather's mouth. Heather wasted no time. She closed her lips over Jackie's hard nub, drawing it into her mouth.

Jackie moaned, and her eyelids fell closed as his girlfriend brought her pleasure. Jackie shifted, offering her other tit.

"Beautiful, baby. Suck her beautiful boobs." He laced his fingers between hers and enjoyed Heather giving herself over to the pleasure and lust. Releasing her inhibitions to explore her sexuality more.

Jackie pushed back and lowered her mouth to kiss and lick Heather's belly, then to unbutton and unzip her jeans.

Heather rocked her weight giving Jackie access to pull off her jeans. Heather lay before them wearing only her blindfold and satin string panties, in purple, her favorite color. He had no doubt she'd bought them for this special occasion.

Mike slipped off the bed, holding her hands and whispering in her ear. "You look amazing, baby. Your body looks ripe to be fucked."

Heather's breath hitched at the word.

Jackie leaned down, hands on Heather's thighs and inhaled deeply over her pussy. Jackie groaned.

"She can smell you, baby. Can she continue?"

"Yes." Her reply coming between pants.

Mike kissed her, driving his tongue into her mouth, demanding more, taking more. So fucking turned on by his woman about to receive sexual satisfaction from another woman.

Jackie kissed her sex over her panties while her hands roamed freely. When her hands cupped Heather's breasts, he knew it was an offering.

Mike leaned down sucking and toying with Heather's nipples. She writhed under both of their kisses. She whimpered.

He couldn't take the pressure anymore. "Baby, help me with my jeans. I don't have any more room in them." He stood and positioned her hands at his button. She managed to unfasten the jeans and tug his pants and briefs down over his hips. He pushed the fabric the rest of the way and stepped out. Then he took her hands to his dick. "Feel me, baby. Feel what you do to me as I watch you get pleasured from our pretty new friend."

"Yes, baby," she whispered.

Jackie's fingers hooked under Heather's waistband and skated them across her low belly, teasing.

She sucked in at the sensation, and her belly dipped.

With a grip at each hip, Jackie slowly pulled on the fabric, dragging them off her legs and tossing them aside. Jackie's mouth returned to her thigh, licking in long strokes, coming so close to her pussy lips, but not touching. Jackie did the same thing to the other leg, and pushing her legs farther apart. But again, not touching her pussy.

Heather whimpered.

"Baby, you want more don't you?"

"Yes. Yes, please."

"Tell her. Tell her to eat your pussy, baby."

"Please," Heather started. "Please put your mouth on me. Please make me come."

Jackie smiled with utter bliss, no doubt a secret fantasy of hers finally coming true.

Mike watched as her fingers separated Heather's labia and her tongue ran straight up the middle.

Heather arched her back and cried out. "Ah."

"So beautiful, sweetheart."

Jackie's finger pushed into her wet pussy and pulled out, all while circling her tongue on Heather's burgeoning clit.

Heather's breasts called to him as her chest heaved up and down in her fog of passion. He laved and nibbled her breasts, glancing up at Jackie pleasuring his woman.

Heather's moans increased. She was close.

He sucked harder as Jackie dove in with two fingers, pushing and pulling, bringing her to the height of ecstasy. She screamed out as her orgasm crashed through her, panting and writhing on the bed.

After a brief moment, Jackie rose and licked her lips.

Mike kissed Heather's forehead, tasting the salty dew on her skin. "Baby, our friend still has her pants on. I think we should see how this has affected her, don't you?"

"Okay," she whispered back.

Facing Jackie, he said, "Please take off the rest of your clothes and come over here." He pointed to the bed beside Heather.

Jackie was only too happy to comply as she rushed to strip off her shorts and panties. On her knees, she waddled beside Heather.

Mike took Heather's delicate hand and laid it on Jackie's belly. "I'm not going to touch her, baby. You are."

"Oh," was her only response. After a beat, her hand slid along Jackie's flat belly, tentatively exploring. As she went lower, skimming over Jackie's short curls, Jackie moaned and her head fell back.

"That's right, baby," he coaxed.

Heather's finger found its way through Jackie's slit, gliding slowly forward and back. "Oh, gosh."

"She's wet, isn't she?"

"Yes. Soaking." Awe in her voice.

"She's that way because of you, baby."

On her own accord, Heather pushed a finger into Jackie's pussy, and Jackie groaned.

"That's right, baby. She likes it. Her cheeks are pink. Would you like to make her come?"

She licked her lips. "Yes."

Jackie's jaw dropped.

"Excellent. I'm going to position her so you can use both hands." Then looking at Jackie, he said, "Straddle her waist."

Jackie did as he bid, and he placed Heather's hands, one on each of Jackie's thighs, and waited.

Heather's fingers traveled up Jackie's thighs to her sex and burrowed in—one finger over her bulging clit, one into Jackie's channel.

"I want to make you come," she told her friend, unseeing.

Jackie moaned and widened her stance, hovering over her to friend to receive her sensual pleasure.

A drop of Jackie's essence fell on Heather's stomach. She worked faster, her friend moaning behind her clamped lips.

Mike was in blessed heaven, watching his love pleasure Jackie. He knew not to press for anything more. But, fuck, he would keep these images with him for the rest of his life.

Pre-cum slid down his dick that was plastered to his stomach.

Jackie's moans turned higher; she was coming.

Heather knew it. She didn't stop until she was sure her friend was done.

In a beat, Jackie collapsed to the bed beside them.

Mike grabbed her hands, kissing the palms and wrists, licking them clean. "Baby, I'm so proud of you. You were amazing. Your new friend is very sated and satisfied."

The corners of Heather's lips curved up.

"Now, I need your help."

# Chapter Twenty-One

♥

Heather knew Mike would be more than eager to release his load. This had to be as exciting for him as it was for her. "Yes." She smiled, feeling like a woman who'd conquered the world.

His hands on her wrists, he dragged her the short distance to the edge of the bed, allowing just her head to tip off the edge.

She opened her mouth and felt the tip of his cock at her lips. She closed in around his head as he slowly pushed in. She licked, letting her saliva wet him entirely and making his thrusts easy through her mouth.

As he settled into a steady pace, the bed sank near Heather's legs. Her new friend, as Mike had described her.

Soft, warm hands grazed over her stomach. Heather had to admit, she loved the gentle touch of a woman; she'd never imagined something so soft and sensuous in her life. Then a mouth closed in over her nipple—a woman's mouth—and her hands cupped her breasts. A thumb skated over her other nipple.

Heather moaned through her full mouth.

"Baby, you're positively perfect. Your mouth is perfect, and your friend thinks your pussy is perfect too."

The woman's hands had moved to her inner thighs and pushed them up and open, bending Heather's knees close to her breasts. "Um." Heather felt incredibly exposed in this position and fought the urge to straighten her legs.

"Relax, baby," Mike cajoled her.

She took in a breath through her nose, focusing on pleasuring her boyfriend, even as the woman's warm tongue flicked up her clit. "Ah," was the muffled sound coming from her throat.

"I'm going to release soon, on your chest, so you can enjoy another orgasm," Mike said from above.

Yes, good idea, because her mind couldn't focus on Mike while at the same time receiving such exquisite sensations at her sex.

With a grunt, he pulled out and squirted over her abdomen and in her cleavage. Then, the bed dipped beside her as his panting slowly returning to normal. "That was hot."

There was a pause, then the woman pulled Heather back to the center of the bed as Mike supported her head.

Shortly, she felt Mike's warm breath over her mouth moments before he crashed down over her. Pushing through her lips to dance with her tongue.

The woman brought her finger to Heather's pussy, caressing her lips and stroking her core.

"Mmm," Heather breathed out.

The woman added a second finger just as Mike laid claim to her nipples. His mouth on one, laving and sucking, and his fingers on the other, gently twisting and pulling.

The sensation was incredible, receiving pleasure on multiple fronts.

In another beat, the woman slid a wet finger over Heather's tiny rosette. Heather gasped.

Mike cajoled her right away. "Shh, baby. Let her love your gorgeous body. All of it, Heather."

She inhaled deeply, truly wanting to savor the moment.

There seemed to be another pause, as if there was some kind of silent exchange between Mike and Jackie. Mike's hands took her knees, holding her legs in place. It was then that the woman pushed a wet finger through her tight hole.

"Ah," Heather cried out.

"Breathe, baby. Relax."

Oh, God. This was like nothing she'd experienced before.

Her friend pushed further with one finger in her hole and another in her vagina, stroking in and out slowly.

Heather moaned.

Both mouths returned to her body—Mike at her breasts, the woman at her clit.

The exquisite pleasure brought her so much closer to yet another climax.

"Oh, God," she panted out.

As the speed of the pushing and pulling increased, Mike's sucking and nibbling on her nipples also increased. She bowed her back, relishing the unbelievable fireworks bubbling up inside her.

They didn't stop, and Heather's orgasm crashed through her body like an avalanche. She cried out, having zero control of anything at that moment.

Soon, the sensations ceased, and Mike spoke softly as he released her legs. "That was so fucking beautiful, baby."

The bed shifted again as Mike pushed back and the woman came further up her body. She felt the warm breath at her abdomen, then slowly a warm wet tongue trailed through Mike's semen, collecting what she could in one swipe. Then Heather felt warmth near her face and a gentle closed mouth kiss on her lips.

Mike took a hold of her hands, and Heather parted her lips, welcoming the stranger's tongue. So many flavors mingled together as the woman kissed her passionately, cupping the back of her neck to drive in deeper.

Both women moaned.

After a beat, the kiss ended, and Heather knew her interlude was over.

"Baby, our friend has to leave now," he said in a low tone.

Heather swallowed. She gave her something so wonderful, so intimate. Heather was changed forever. They'd shared something she would never forget. "Thank you. That was incredible. I'll never forget this night for as long as I live."

She heard the rustling of clothes, then the bedroom door close gently.

Mike slipped off her mask.

She blinked as her eyes adjusted to the dim light.

"How do you feel?" he asked, lying beside her.

"Incredible. It...I can't explain it. It was hot."

He smiled back at her.

"She was so soft and as much as I love what you and I share, that was also really good."

"I'm glad, baby."

She turned her body into his. "Mike?"

"Yes?"

"I think I would have been okay if you had touched her."

His eyes went wide, and he swallowed. "You *think*?"

"Yes, I mean I would have been okay with it, but I think I would have wanted to watch." Her voice was whisper-soft.

His eyes grew dark. He shifted over her, his hard cock nestled at her entrance. "Baby, that would be incredible. Maybe another time. You know I love you, and everything we share."

She nodded and gasped as Mike drove into her wet channel, his girth pushing against her pussy walls.

"I love you too. Thank you so much for this night." Her arms and legs circled him.

If she married this man, she would have to know he wouldn't stop wanting to experiment. And she was good with that.

He claimed her mouth, joining them further, as he gently rocked them to the heavens.

*Oh, yeah.* More than good with that.

# The Yellow House Next Door

# Chapter Twenty-Two

♥

Tuesday, the fine cougar next door stepped out her front door to water her potted plants. She'd finally gotten rid of the dead weight called a husband about a year ago. But it baffled Chet that he hadn't seen Veronica go out on a date since then.

He figured she had to be prime for some serious TLC.

Right then and there, he made up his mind. He'd patiently waited for just the right time.

He pulled out the junk mail that had arrived last month in his mailbox and headed to the yellow house next door.

"Mrs. Brodowski." It was habit. There was something so damned tempting about an older woman and using her surname.

Chet's parents had moved into the house on Braker Road ten years ago. Chet had been twenty. He'd finished his degree at Brown and started his own internet company out of his apartment. Then two years ago, his parents had called and said they were moving to Florida, and did he want the house? *Hell, yeah.*

"Please call me Veronica."

He grinned. "Here's a piece of your mail."

"Gosh, I really think it's time for our mailman to retire." She glanced down at the inconsequential letter, then met his gaze. "I'm glad you're here, Chet. Could help me with something?"

"Of course." He'd helped her with several things over the past few years—mowing the lawn occasionally, helping move furniture, cutting up a dead tree limb.

He followed the gorgeous, heart-shaped ass into the house and down the hall. "I need to change the filter, but it's stuck."

The six-foot ladder stood beneath an open return air duct with a dirty gray filter wedged in it. He climbed the ladder and tried grabbing a corner of the paper filter. Pieces pulled away, but it didn't budge. "Do you have a flat-head screwdriver?"

"Uh, yeah." She spun around to the kitchen.

He heard her rifling through a drawer, then she returned reaching up to hand it to him. He pried the damn thing lose and stepped down. Resting it against the wall, he leaned down close to her to pick up the new one, intentionally grazing his palm against her naked calf. God bless Texas heat where Veronica wore shorts half the damn year.

She cleared her throat. "Oh, you don't have to do that. I can finish up."

"It's no bother." He popped the pristine white filter in its place and closed the vent cover.

He then stepped off the ladder and folded it against the wall.

He huddled a little close, taking in the floral scent of her shampoo. "Can I wash?"

High color rose in her cheeks. "Sure."

He followed her into the kitchen and washed his hands at the sink.

She held out a hand towel for him.

He stepped very close this time, crowding her against the counter. "At first, I thought you were going to ask for something else, Veronica." He stretched out an arm, resting the towel on the countertop. His other arm caged her in.

She visibly swallowed, and the pink in her cheeks made her look gorgeous.

"I've seen you watching me when I'm outside working in the yard. You know, you're the reason I no longer wear a shirt when I mow the lawn."

"Really?" She squeaked.

He nodded. "I don't know what your asshole husband did, but I have an idea, and he was crazy to let you go."

She glanced down for a moment before meeting his gaze again.

"I know it's probably been a long time since you've been serviced. Properly serviced." He closed the space between them and leaned down. Cupping her jaw, he kissed her cheek. "I'm going to take care of that for you." His kiss trailed down her neck. "I want you to leave your front door unlocked this evening. I'm going to come by and take care of you, if you want," he whispered in her ear.

Her breath hitched.

He kissed her neck one last time, lifted his head, and pushed off the counter. After a glance, he made his way to the front, turned back, and sent her a wink before closing the door behind him.

Oh, yeah, she was ready. He could damn-near smell her. Now, *she* just needed to know she was ready and to trust he could take care of every one of her needs.


Veronica's mouth was as dry as the desert. *Did he just say what I think he said?*

Chet was going to come over that night and…and service her. Holy cannoli!

Did he know she was forty-four? She was old enough to be his aunt.

But God, he smelled so good, and his muscles, the way they flexed when he worked made her practically drool. Chet was a fine specimen of a man. His occasional roommate was too, for that matter.

Jordan was a close friend of Chet's. He'd moved in about a year ago, but he was gone a lot for his job. He was a blond version of Chet—tall, great smile, built, and a voice that made her cream her panties.

She'd had more than one fantasy about her next-door neighbors. Veronica had occasionally seen women come and go. Or sometimes when she couldn't sleep, she'd seen either boy come home late. But nothing that indicated they were serious about any one woman.

But now she had an offer from Chet. The handsome thirty-year-old was going to come into her house tonight, and well, come into her.

She giggled. Oh God, that's insane. She knew his parents, a lovely couple, now retired in Florida. Chet could have any woman he wanted, and he wanted *her*. She licked her lips.

Could she do this?

# Chapter Twenty-Three

♥

Darkness encompassed the bedroom as Veronica stared up into the nothingness from her bed. She squired in her purple teddy as she waited for Chet. Anticipation filled her.

She'd debated leaving the front door unlocked, letting him come in and have his way with her, but God, she wanted it. She hadn't been with a man in so long. Her time with Franklin, her ex, pretty much killed her libido. It was only when Chet had huddled up close to her, exuding his pheromones, did her libido come alive. He had great muscles, an easy smile, and incredible penetrating green eyes. She'd seen him shirtless and couldn't wait to see the rest of him.

She lay in her bed, already wet with the thought of what Chet could do to her.

She heard the door click, then footfalls down the hall. He pushed her bedroom door open.

She could tell it was him by the silhouette filling the doorway—a tall figure with broad shoulders tapering at the waist. Chet did an incredible job of keeping himself in shape. There was hardly an ounce of fat on him.

Silently, he approached her, grabbed the sheet, and pulled it all the way off her.

"Fuck, look at that gorgeous body." He lifted off the T-shirt he wore and tossed it aside, then popped the button on his twill shorts.

She lay stock still, watching him. Her heart raced as he placed a hand at each side of her head, his toes supporting his legs, and lowered his lips to hers.

He nibbled and pecked, and she opened for him. Slowly his tongue entered her, tasting and gliding along hers like he wanted to relish this moment. Their lips were the only point of contact and Veronica was about to combust.

Hovering over her, he whispered. "I'm glad you left the door unlocked." Then he lowered his lips back to hers.

Her hands rose to his chest and shoulders, touching him for the first time. He was warm, and his hard planes made her want to swoon. She crept her hands lower, over the ridges of his abs to the bulge in his shorts.

He groaned. He was bigger than her ex. Oh, God, so wonderfully big. He rose and knelt on the bed, spreading her legs and straddling her right. He reached a single finger to the strap of the teddy and pulled it carefully off her shoulder, revealing her left breast.

His movements, so sure and deliberate, heightened her senses and filled her with eagerness, having her panting before he'd really done anything.

He repeated the motion to the other side, completely exposing her breasts. "They look exactly as I imagined," he caressed and fondled her with his large hands, "full and luscious." He bent over and swiped her nipple with his tongue and sucked on it lightly.

She moaned.

"They taste just as I expected. Delicious."

His hands and mouth tortured her, and her head pushed back into the pillow, savoring the incredible feel of this man bringing out a part of her she thought long gone.

She writhed under his attention, building the incredible ache at her sex. "Chet," she breathed out.

With his mouth still on hers, he grabbed the sides of her lingerie and slid it down her body, stopping at the edge of her mons. His mouth traversed the plane of her torso, kissing and licking. When he arrived at her sex, he simply kissed her over the silky fabric. His lips, his hot breath, tantalized her. Then his tongue licked her slit through the fabric.

"Unh." She bowed off the bed and flexed her hips.

"Ah, you like that, baby." He swiped again. "Let's have a look." He pulled the fabric aside to find her bare sex.

He gasped. "Veronica, did you shave for me?"

"Yes." She'd always done a bikini wax, but after his proposition, she showered and shaved herself clean. It was a spontaneous thing she'd hoped he would like.

"I love it, baby." He licked her denuded sex, circling her hard clit.

God, she was close. *How is that possible?*

As if sensing her impending climax, he stopped and climbed off the bed to strip off his clothes. He unwrapped a condom and covered himself. Then he returned to the bed, pushed her legs apart, and nestled down to feast on her again.

"Unh," she cried out with the soft touch of his tongue. "Oh, God."

He applied pressure and sent her tumbling over the edge of ecstasy.

"Chet," she called out, thrusting her hips off the bed as her orgasm crashed through her.

As she calmed down, he hovered back over, his hips resting against hers. Meeting her eyes, he gently pushed into her swollen, anxious channel. They both moaned at the long-awaited contact.

He leaned down to kiss her, his lips firm and commanding. His kiss was as new and exciting as his cock gently thrusting inside her—pushing and pulling back, each stroke gaining more room inside her.

Her arms circled his neck, holding him as they rocked together.

He tunneled a hand between them to stimulate her clit—rhythmically, gently.

She didn't have the heart to tell him she never climaxed twice.

He pulled off her mouth and claimed a pointed nipple—sucking and laving like it was a sweet treat. This, combined with the delicious friction he'd created with his cock and finger, had her climbing again.

"Oh," she panted

"That's right, baby," he breathed over her breast.

She writhed and pulsed her hips, meeting his thrusts, until the dam of exquisite pleasure broke free. She cried out, digging her fingernails into this back, just as he grunted his own release and collapsed into the mattress.

His arm held some of his weight off her and his breathing slowly steadied.

He covered her in a full mouth kiss before he pulled out and stood. Depositing the condom in the bathroom, he returned to dress.

He met her gaze as he covered his semi-erect cock with his briefs. "I'll be back tomorrow night, Veronica. Are you on the pill?"

She nodded.

"Good. If I decide not to use a condom, you can rest assured I'm clean." His shirt covered his wonderfully etched abs.

"Okay," she murmured, her head still reeling from her two orgasms.

He leaned close to her and caressed her breast. "I want you in a dress or skirt, waiting in the kitchen so I can bend you over the counter and fuck you."

She gasped.

"We have a lot to make up for. And one final thing. In the bedroom, I'm in charge. Can you handle that?"

Her lips parted. There was something so enticing about a man who could take charge in the bedroom *and* know what he was doing. "Yes."

"Good." He pecked her lips one final time before recovering her with the sheet and heading toward the door.

*Wow!* Veronica never felt more alive. As satisfied as she was, laying there, basking in the glow of amazing sex, Chet made her crave more. He was coming back the next night, and she couldn't wait.

Had she ever come twice before in her life?

She had trouble coming just one time. She'd thought it was her, but she realized now maybe it was Franklin. Maybe he hadn't known what the hell he was doing.

She replayed the incredible night, her teddy still bunched below her waist. Chet said something about making up for lost time. What did that mean?

She sighed. Who knew how long this little affair would continue. All she knew was tomorrow night she got to have more of that delicious man again.

# Chapter
# Twenty-Four

♥

Thursday, Chet texted Veronica right after he saw her enter her house coming home from work: *Get your pretty little ass over at 8:30. Don't change out of your work clothes.*

He knew she was an independent woman, not used to taking orders from anyone. That's why Tuesday night he'd laid down that rule right away. He didn't want to take her independence, just her pussy. He wanted to own her body, her pussy, her every climax. She might eventually find a man—not that he was thrilled with the idea—but until then, she was his.

The previous night, as he'd promised, he'd gone back over and fucked her again. She looked so amazing, her skirt over her waist, her blouse and bra laying *somewhere*, and her panties puddling around her ankle and high heel. She looked gorgeous taking in his cock as he pounded her from behind. Her screams were like music to his ears. She clutched the edge of the island with every orgasm and called out his name.

Chet knew she was ready for more.

He might be getting hooked on her, and he sure as shit wanted her hooked on him.

He had things he wanted to do with her, not just in the bedroom. He couldn't define it, but over the past two years, images of them—hang gliding, going down his favorite rapids on Colorado, making love on the beach at sunset—filled his random thoughts. *So many things.* But for right now, the fastest way to winning over his sexy neighbor was with his large cock and talented tongue.

At eight-thirty on the dot, a knock came at the door. He opened it and pulled her inside, laying claim to her lips in an instant. He consumed her mouth, a prelude of what was to come.

Veronica wore the blue V-neck dress from work that day with black high heels. She was curvy and hot as Hades, and now that he knew what a great body hid under those clothes, he needed to have her again.

He released her pretty pink mouth and smiled. "Punctual. I'm glad."

She nibbled her bottom lip. "I wonder if the neighbors saw me."

He hauled her close. "Baby, it doesn't matter what they think." He pecked her one more time, then grabbed her hand, leading her to the kitchen. He poured a glass of white wine for each of them and handed her one. "Cheers."

He needed her relaxed and agreeable. If he timed things right, there was an incredible chance that before things got too far along, Jordan would walk in. Occasionally, he and his best friend would share a woman. Chet could take it or leave it, but this time? This time was for Veronica. She had a lot of lost time to make up for when she was with that dead-beat husband.

"I'm glad you wore that dress."

"You are?" she asked.

"Yup, because I can't wait to see you strip out of it."

Her eyes grew wide, returning to normal quickly. Good, she was getting to know what he liked and what he wanted them to do whenever they were together. He had so many incredible ideas, she was going to need a vacation when he was done.

Weaving his fingers between hers, he guided her to the living room. He left her standing in the center of the room as he pulled the coffee table to the side and shut the blinds. The neighbors weren't getting a free show.

He took a seat in his favorite club chair, which provided a view of the entire room *and* the front door.

"Take another sip of your wine and take off your dress for me, Veronica."

Her mouth gaped.

*You can do this.* He sipped from his glass and waited patiently.

She took a nice gulp and set her glass on the end table. Then she loosened the sash at her waist and pulled apart the dress, sending it down her shoulders to the floor. She stood before him in a pale pink lacy bra and panty set and her high heels.

"You are fucking gorgeous." He made a show of licking his lips. "I've been hard all day thinking about you."

Her C-cup breasts gently rose and fell with the increased breath.

"Now, get down and come over here."

She went to the carpeted floor and crawled on all fours in between his legs.

"Good girl. Loosen my pants and take me out." His commands were all a primer for what he had planned. Soon, he would stretch her boundaries, and she would do whatever he said, without question. The reward would be sweeter than anything she'd ever experienced. He would stake his life on it.

With his fly loose, she opened his jeans further and reached into his briefs to take out his raging cock.

"That's what you do to me, Veronica. I can't count how many times I've frigged myself to the images of you. Images in your bed, by your pool, on the roof of your car."

Her eyebrows rose.

"Now, please suck me off, before I explode."

The corners of her mouth curled, then her precious pink mouth came down, encompassing his head. Her tongue poked his slit and circled him.

"Fuuuck." He barely got the word out. Her mouth was like goddamn heaven.

Her fist worked in concert with her mouth, stroking up and down, sucking the life out of him. He resisted holding her head and fucking her face.

Then, a click came at the door. Her head popped up, and her eyes flew open.

"Don't move," he commanded.

Jordan walked in, looking to the right as he shut the door, seeing the scene before him. "I'm terribly sorry. I didn't mean to interrupt."

Chet held back a grin. "No interruption. Mrs. Brodowski, you remember Jordan, yes?"

Her face was beet red. She looked up at him, then over her shoulder at Jordan. "Hi, Jordan," she said meekly.

"There's wine on the counter if you'd care for some," Chet called to his roommate.

"No thanks, but it's been a long flight. Mind if I chill for a bit?"

"No, we don't mind, do we Veronica?" He pinned her with a look.

Her eyes were nearly dark as night. When she didn't reply. He simply whispered, "Trust me." Then he cupped her jaw, guiding her back to his rock-hard dick. "Keep going."

It was downright adorable how she tried to focus on her blowjob. If he wasn't careful, he'd lose his load right then.

Jordan took the seat opposite Chet with a view of Veronica's ass. His erection already pushing against his pants.

"I can't remember if I told you, but the last two nights, I snuck into Veronica's house to fuck her." He spoke casually, like this was nothing noteworthy.

"Oh, really? I bet that was great. She's got a fine body."

"She does." Chet stroked Veronica's jaw. "Baby, lift up your ass so Jordan can see that beautiful work of art."

She raised off her haunches and shifted her weight to her knees.

He leaned forward and stroked his hand down her back, all while her hot mouth smothered him.

"She does have a really nice ass." Jordan scratched his chin. "She looks like she's having a good time."

They talked over her, like she was a possession. Little did she know just how much she owned *them*.

"Are you, baby? Are you having a good time?"

Her doe eyes lifted to meet his.

He lowered his mouth close to her ear. "Lower your panties, show Jordan how much you're enjoying yourself."

She stopped.

He knew she wasn't used to exposing herself like that. He patiently waited.

Finally, *slowly,* she reached back and lowered the lacy confection over her hips to her knees. *Fucking perfect.*

"Now spread those knees as wide as they'll go."

Her breath caught, but she obeyed.

God, what he wouldn't give for the gorgeous view Jordan was getting.

"Fuck, Chet. Veronica has a beautiful pussy." Jordan rose and strode closer, then bent down behind Veronica. "She smells incredible, and her juices are about to run down her thigh." He leisurely dragged a single finger up the inside of her thigh, stopping short of her sex.

Veronica whimpered around Chet's dick.

"Oh, I'd love to see that." He gently pulled on her hair to lift her off him.

She looked at him questioning.

He stood and as she tried resting back on her calves, he said, "Uh-uh. On your knees."

She knelt upright, his dick a mere inch from her face. "Good girl. Now pull down your bra and show Jordan your beautiful tits."

She pulled down the cups for her bra, with no hesitation this time. She was wonderfully debauched. God, he wanted to drive into her so badly.

Jordan came to her other side, glancing down at her luscious globes.

Chet leaned down and, lifting one knee at a time, he slipped her panties over her knees to her mid-calf.

"Perfect," Chet muttered.

"She is. Smart, pulled-together, successful businesswoman by day. Gorgeous, hot slut by night," Jordan said in awe.

"Jordan, why don't you take my seat for a while?"

Jordan popped his pants button and got comfortable before her.

Chet leaned down to kiss her deeply. Maybe it was a possessive kiss, telling her who she belonged to. It didn't matter. "Now, my gorgeous slut, let's make sure our guest feels right at home. Take out his dick and suck him off, baby."

Her breathing was heavy now. She had to be aching for relief.

She leaned forward, unzipped Jordan's pants, and wasted no time taking him into her mouth.

Both men were well-endowed. They would need to take it easy on his innocent Veronica.

"That's right," Chet praised her, and Jordon groaned.

Then Chet walked behind her, crazing his fingertips down her back.

"Fuck." The liquid heat spilled from Veronica's pussy. It had to be the most gorgeous thing he'd ever seen. "She likes having two men to please."

Jordan pulsed his hips. "Her mouth is incredible."

Chet bent down behind her and pulled her knees further apart. Her panties stretched to the maximum.

Her forearm braced on Jordan's thigh for support. Her other hand and her mouth still working his dick.

"Take it easy on him, baby. He doesn't want to come too soon."

Chet leaned down close to her dripping cunt and blew hot air over her. "She's so wet and swollen, Jordan. I think she's primed for a good fucking."

She mewled over Jordan's cock.

Chet made a simple, soft pass over her clit and pulled back.

"Please," she panted.

"Please what, baby? Tell me." Chet knew he was torturing her.

"Please make me come with your mouth."

*Perfect.* She'd been so perfect tonight, he would give her a quick climax to take the edge off and then build her back up again.

With her legs already apart, he spread her lips with his thumbs and licked her anywhere his tongue reached.

"Ah," she cried out.

He applied pressure to her hot little button while working two fingers into her slick channel.

"Ah," she cried out again, her mouth off Jordan now to take in air. Her muscles clenched around Chet as her clit began to twitch. Soon, her whole body shuttered as her climax took control, sending her heaven.

Her head collapsed onto Jordan's lap as she panted heavily.

He loved to see her like this—completely spent from extreme pleasure.

# Chapter Twenty-Five

♥

Veronica had never come so hard in her life. The orgasm raced through her and rocked her to the core.

"On your knees, precious. We're not done with our gorgeous little slut."

She lifted her head at Chet's voice. He gently pulled her hair, until she was up on her knees. Jordan rose and Chet shifted to her side, but stayed down to run a finger through her slit.

She was on fire.

He licked his finger clean then gripped the back of her neck to give her a deep tongue kiss, the flavors comingling in her mouth. Chet consumed her. She'd never been with a man who wanted her so much, who demanded so much, and at the same time had given her so much.

There stood both men presenting their cocks before her. "We know you're ready to be fucked, but we're going to fuck your pretty face first, baby. Stick out your tongue and clasp your hands behind your back."

She did as he bid, and God if the ache hadn't returned to her pussy. Both men gripped the back of her head, stabilizing her. First, Chet slid his cock into her mouth. She stretched her mouth over him. He pulsed a few times, then pulled out. Jordan gripped her hair, turning her head. She opened for him. He thrust gently.

Chet turned her back to him. He claimed more space, hitting the back of her throat. She was about to gag, but the sensation passed when Jordan's cock replaced Chet's.

The fluid in her mouth gathered so quickly, it started to run out of her mouth.

The men took turns, doing just what they said—fucking her face.

She relaxed as much as she could, taking the soft blows against the back of her throat, drool streaming full force down her chin now.

"God, Veronica, your mouth is exquisite." That was the first time Jordan spoke to her directly. His eyes closed briefly as he thrust into her.

"Look how perfectly debauched she is for us. Our perfect slut, so gorgeous, so eager to please." Chet thrust into her. "Fuck, I'm going to come." He pulled out and shot his sperm over her chest and breasts.

Jordan took her mouth next. She sucked hard, then he pulled out with a grunt and squirt across her chest as well.

The men went down to their knees, panting, but not completely spent. Their hands roamed her body, rubbing in the sperm or toying with her clit.

"Head back, precious."

She dropped her head back and both men lay claim to her nipples, sucking and lapping at them, sending delicious jolts straight to her clit.

Jordan's fingers circled her clit while Chet continued tonguing her nipples. Everything was exquisite but her legs were getting tired holding herself in a semi-straddled state.

Chet seemed to sense her need. "Hang in there, precious. We're almost done with you, then we'll take it nice and slow."

Chet removed his finger, and Jordan pulled back. They helped her to stand. Thank, God. Although it was awkward with her panties around her calves.

"Bend over. Hands on the chair," Chet commanded.

She knew what was next, and she needed it. Her body ached for release.

Chet spread her legs wide again, stretching her panties across her legs. He seemed to have a fascination for her looking disheveled while in the throes of passion.

"I want to see Jordan fuck your pretty little pussy."

She nodded and heard the tear of a condom wrapper.

Jordan took position behind her, wetting himself through her slit.

Chet knelt beside her, brushed her hair to the other side, and kissed her neck.

Jordan gripped her hips and slid into her eager channel, his girth pushing against her walls.

She moaned.

"That's right, gorgeous. Take him. You look so fucking hot." Chet watched the joining, Jordan thrust slowly, as Chet absently stroked her back. With each pass, his hand crept lower. At one point, Jordan pulled out so Chet could slide his finger inside her. Then he dragged his wet finger over her tiny hole. His circular massages were insane.

She mewled.

They repeated the process so he could gather more wetness, and with an easy slide, he pushed passed the tight ring.

Her head flung back, and she moaned at the sensation.

With his free hand, he reached beneath her to toy with her nipples.

"Oh, God," she panted. She was overwhelmed with the pleasure, high on lust.

"That's right, my gorgeous slut. You love letting us take your body anyway we want. You love being our sex slave, don't you?"

The pressure built deep inside, clawing its way to the surface.

Jordan's pace picked up, ramming into the end of her, triggering a cataclysmic orgasm.

She cried out as the explosion went on and on.

Her legs gave way, but Jordan wrapped a strong arm around her as he growled out his own release.

Chet removed his finger, and Jordan lowered her to all fours on the floor.

Her heart raced with exertion.

Chet kissed her shoulder and smoothed her back as she panted. "You were beautiful, baby."

They both helped her upright. Chet's erection was still strong.

Jordan had put himself back together. "Thank you, Veronica. You were amazing. I'll never forget this night." He kissed her sweetly and patted Chet on the shoulder. "Talk to you later, man." Then he grabbed his luggage and went upstairs to his bedroom.

Chet haphazardly pulled her panties up and lifted her in his arms.

Her weak legs and arms instantly went around him as he walked them out of the living room, down the hall, to the master bedroom and en suite bathroom.

He set her standing by the tub and turned the faucet on high. Then he gingerly slipped off her shoes and stripped off her bra and panties. He opened the closet for two fresh towels.

She watched him remove his clothes and reached over to gently fist his erection. "What are we going to do about this?" she asked with a grin.

"Don't worry about it, baby. I'm always hard when you're near."

*Wow!* She'd never had any man talk to her like that. In fact, the whole night was peppered with compliments. Even in Chet's way—telling her her pussy was pretty or that she was a gorgeous slut—Veronica felt special and somehow cherished.

Chet stepped into the filled, oversized tub and offered her a hand.

She sank down into the hot water between his legs and leaned back against his chest, his cock pressed against her low back.

He wetted a washcloth and stroked her torso, washing away the sweat and come that had dried there.

"How are you feeling?" He broke the silence.

"I'm good."

He kissed her head, then moved her hair to the side and kissed her neck. It was like he was slowing everything down and taking care of her now.

She closed her eyes and rested her head on his shoulder, savoring the pampering.

After several minutes, the water had begun to cool. Chet nudged her and helped her rise. He swiftly wrapped a towel around himself, then preceded to towel her off. He patted her back, her arms, gently patted between her legs, until every inch of her she was thoroughly dry.

The motions, so quiet and tender, left her speechless. She knew Chet was a polite and considerate man, but she'd never seen this side of him.

He wrapped the towel around her and dried himself off, dropping his towel to the floor.

Veronica could see his erection hadn't budged.

Stopping at the bed, Chet whipped off the duvet and pulled back the bed linens. The fresh smell of laundry soap flew up from the mattress.

"Lie in the center," he told her.

She climbed to the center of the king-sized bed, her head cradled on a pillow.

He turned to the bathroom, rustled around for something, and switched off the light. The room darkened except for the moonlight shining through the windows. He pushed the bedroom door closed.

Wordlessly, he opened her towel and placed her arms a few inches from her body. Then he popped a lid on a bottle and squirted some liquid into his hands. Starting at her shoulders, he massaged the warm lotion down her arms. He worked his way to her center, circling her breasts and smoothing down her tummy. Slowly up and down he went. His mouth came down to her nipples, causing them to harden.

She sighed.

Dear Lord. She had never felt anything so glorious, so incredibly soothing and yet exhilarating to the same time. Her eyelids closed.

He reapplied liquid and caressed her right leg with the perfect amount of pressure. Long languid strokes lulling her into a kind of erotic peacefulness. He placed her leg wide and repeated the same process with the other. Then his hands stroked up her thighs and his lips kissed her sex.

She bowed off the mattress.

His palm laid over the space between her breasts, signaling to lower herself. "Shh, baby. Relax now." His hot breath caressed her denuded sex. "I'll bring as many orgasms as I can squeeze out of your delicious pussy." His hand stroked her lotion-slick torso. "You'll stay in my bed with me tonight so I can fuck you before work in the morning."

Another gentle kiss and swipe over her clit. His tongue circled slowly. "But tonight, I'll make love to you until you fall asleep."

More licking. So gentle, she wanted to lift her hips for more. But she lay still, letting her body sink into the bed, sink into the exquisite, tender torture from her lover.

The first orgasm snuck up on her, surprising her in its easy yet powerful release.

His tongue never relented, and his hands continued to roam. All she could do was lay there, spread open for him to feast. To bring her joy. A joy she hadn't known in *years*, if ever.

Her panting grew, and she writhed beneath him.

"Breathe, Veronica. Take a nice deep breath, my beautiful woman." His voice carried on a quiet hot breath, coasting over her sex.

She did as he bid and in mere seconds another orgasm rolled through her.

Chet didn't move. His mouth made love to her pussy as his hands caressed her body and toyed with her nipples.

God, how much more could she take?

His hands slid down to her thighs, massaging, and taking her legs a fraction wider.

The subtle stream left her pussy to trail down the edge of ass.

"Chet. Oh, God." Another orgasm climbed higher with his expert ministrations. She moaned long and low, letting the ripples roll through her.

Finally, he rose. She opened her eyes to watch as he licked his lips, wet with her arousal.

He shimmied closer, lifting her hips so his knees could slide underneath her.

His rock-hard erection pressed at her entrance. He leaned down to take her mouth in a deep, consuming kiss. Again, not crazy or wild, but no less passionate.

He cupped the back of her neck, holding her to him as he pushed into her, her pussy muscles clenching around him.

She cried out into his mouth. He stole her every pant, moan, whimper. His thrusts kept pace with his kissing—deep, slow, thorough.

The angle of his cock rubbed her in the most-perfect way. He'd detonated another orgasm, clutching him until they both moaned.

"You're incredible. God, Veronica, how many times have of I thought about this?"

Her jaw dropped. *What?* She had no idea. Sure, he would help sometimes with things in her house, or offer help after her husband had moved out, but she never imagined he had visions of her...like this.

His gentle rocking thrusts continued. "You are the first woman I've brought to my bed. And the first woman I've fucked bareback."

His eyes read a kind of vulnerability, an honesty, she'd never seen before.

"Chet. I had no idea." Her heart swelled in an inexplicable way.

"I know. I knew your husband wouldn't last. He wasn't right for you. All I had to do was wait."

The emotion that welled inside her was overpowering and humbling. She reached her hands to his head, bringing him down for a deep kiss. His arms wrapped around her. Their tongues and bodies tangled in a way she'd never felt.

His back tightened under her hands as he gave a final thrust, releasing into her.

He gingerly pulled out of her, shimmying the towel out from under her. He wiped himself and her, then tossed it to the floor.

He covered them and pulled her into him, cradling her with his strong, warm body.

Their breathing calmed, and suddenly she felt drained. Sleep came quickly and easily.

# Chapter Twenty-Six

In the middle of the night, Chet peppered Veronica's back with butterfly kisses. He damn-near spilled his heart out to her last night. He had to watch it, or he'd scare her off.

She moaned in her sleepy state.

He'd said he would fuck her in the morning, but he couldn't wait. He hadn't budged since they fell asleep after sex, her body wrapped tightly in his arms. It felt so fucking right.

He'd never slept with a woman. He couldn't stand it. The snuggling and cuddling. It was like after sex, he was instantly antsy to get the hell out.

He'd been a bastard. All the women knew he wasn't a commitment kind of guy, but it didn't help. He'd still felt like a bastard.

Veronica was different. He could lounge in bed all day with her. How could he make that happen?

Gently pushing her on her tummy, his kisses traveled south, over her full, round ass. He pushed the sheet away to take in the sight, then he returned his mouth to her naked body.

Carefully lifting her hips, he brought her off the mattress and closer to his face. He laid his entire mouth over her sex.

She moaned into the mattress.

She was already wet for him. God, he loved how her body responded to him.

"Baby, you're so wet."

She gripped the fitted sheet as he slowly made love to her sex, circling her growing clit. Then he lowered her, spread her legs further, and brought himself to her entrance to slide his aching cock into her.

They both moaned at the incredible contact. He kissed her back and neck, pulled out, and lowered his mouth to her sex again. Licking and sucking, then grazing the tip of his tongue over her tight little rosette.

She moaned low and long.

He popped back up and entered her. Slowly claiming more and more space in her sweet pussy, until he felt the end of her.

He pulled out one last time and found she'd raised her hips for him.

*That's my girl.* She was giving herself to him, offering herself.

He licked and toyed with her asshole and moved to her clit. At the first flutter, he knew he'd brought her to orgasm.

She screamed his name, muffling it in the mattress.

When she was done, he entered her the final time, kissing her neck, languishing in the beauty that was beneath him. "Roni, I know this is probably all very sudden for you." More kisses along her shoulder. "But you know you're mine now, right?"

"Yes, Chet."

He smiled, not once stopping his gentle thrusts. "I don't want another woman. I only want you." He wrapped his arms around her and rocked them on the mattress. "And I don't mind telling you that I'm in love with you. I'll wait as long as it takes for you to feel the same way."

Her panting came heavy now. "Oh, God, yes. I love how you love me, Chet. Please don't stop."

"No way, baby. Never. This is the beginning of something amazing. Get ready."

# A Smattering of
# Gray

# Chapter Twenty-Seven

♥

The car trip to Chappaqua, New York went relatively quick.

Victoria looked forward to this trip to the Novak's every year. Pierce Novak, formerly Pierce and Priscilla Novak, hosted a Memorial Day gathering, mostly for the Palencia executives and their families. The festivities lasted all week and ended the following weekend.

Victoria most looked forward to seeing her friend Larissa. She was due up the next day, and Vicki couldn't wait.

The two had become fast friends when Larissa's mother took the position with Palencia as CFO. They'd occasionally gotten to see each over other major holidays, and, of course, kept up on social media. But the week of Memorial Day at the Novak's was what they looked forward to most. Sunbathing, water skiing, eating, drinking, swimming at midnight, just about whatever they wanted.

Vicki and Larissa had talked about what they'd do after graduation and agreed to try and get jobs close to each other. That was two years away now.

Vicki got settled into "her room" at the sprawling house. The decadent house had like twenty bedrooms, thirty bathrooms, a pool and hot tub, and a foyer chandelier mechanized for the housekeepers to clean easily. Any guest would have trouble leaving this mini paradise outside New York City.

With her bikini and cover-up on, she grabbed her sunglasses to meet everyone on the back patio for lunch.

***

Friday night, a spread was laid out by the staff on the back patio—shrimp cocktail, barbeque chicken, grilled salmon, potato salad, garden salad, hot dogs for the little ones ... enough to feed an army. And only half the guests were there. The rest, like Larissa and her family, would arrive tomorrow.

Her brother, Theo, was due Thursday when he could break away from work.

The atmosphere was relaxed and jovial as the grill master lassoed his fire and the drinks flowed.

Her parents chatted it up with several couples at the big table, and Vicki listened to Tamara go on about an incident with her physics TA. Tamara always had the wildest stories. Vicki could listen to her all day.

After some time, several people made their way to the large in-ground pool. Pierce included.

Vicki tried her damnedest not to look at him. For forty-eight, he maintained a good physique. He stripped off his shirt to dive into the pool, and she had to hide her gaping mouth behind her hand. He must have a thousand woman vying for him.

For some reason, Vicki couldn't keep her eyes off the man. He was the most handsome man at the party, regardless of his age. Unlike previous years, she'd glance a time or two, but her lady parts hadn't come alive like now.

He was delicious eye-candy. No doubt about it.

In a bit of contrast ... Johnny, Phyllis Bernhard's son, approached and took the vacant seat beside her. He had the hots for her. Vicki wasn't interested, but he was harmless.

"Vicki, how's it goin'?"

"Hey, Johnny. Good. How are you?"

"Excellent. Where's your swimsuit?"

"I'm good for now. I ate too much so I need to wait. You go ahead, jump in."

"Okay, but don't wait too long." He winked because he thought he was cool, but what Johnny needed was a bookworm-type. Someone who was happy with books, small towns, and routine.

Vicki was the opposite of that.

Johnny couldn't handle a spitfire like Vicki.

She had big dreams of a big city, a high-paying job, and maybe a nice summer fling. She crossed her fingers and grinned into her sangria. Who knew? She might even entertain an older man.

***

Vicki awoke in the middle of the night. With the rare exception of being stressed over a major exam, she'd slept eight hours every night.

*Maybe it's because I'm not in my own bed*, she thought.

She walked to the kitchen to find some chamomile tea or Calm to help her get back to sleep. This was supposed to be her summer vacation—the epitome of R&R. In the fall, her junior year at NYU would begin.

The water boiled, and she poured it over the tea bag in her cup. The house was completely silent. She leaned against the counter and stared out the back window into the dark night. The moonlight reflected off the water in the pool and caught the tips of the evergreens at the property's edge. What a calm, serene view. Sometimes it still amazed Vicki what money could buy.

She wanted this kind of success when she got older. She'd get her bachelor's degree and work her ass off to climb the proverbial corporate ladder. She didn't need a man to provide her with money; she'd make her own.

She heard a noise and turned to see Pierce walking into the kitchen from the hallway. The owner's retreat was downstairs, while most of the other bedrooms were up.

"Hey. Didn't mean to startle you." He was barefoot, wearing only long pajama bottoms.

She swallowed hard at the image. Of course, Vicki had seen his bare chest before, but now when it was just the two of them, in his dark kitchen, her body was "seeing" him a different light.

"Hi. You didn't. I didn't mean to wake you."

"It's okay." He strode closer to her and peered into her cup. "Tea?" Without waiting for an answer, he lifted her hand and the cup to his lips and sipped. "Oh, sugar." He wrinkled his nose.

Vicki and Pierce had never "shared" food before. Ever. Her heartbeat ratcheted higher, and she wasn't sure why.

"You don't like sweetened tea?"

He shook his head. "And you don't need sugar, Victoria. You're sweet enough."

*Wow!* That was a lovely compliment, and surprising.

He moved a little closer, standing behind her, making it impossible to meet his gaze anymore. "Do I scare you?"

She forced in a breath. "No," she whispered. It was the truth. He intrigued her.

"I see you watching me."

*Shit!* He *had* seen her. She couldn't say why, but she couldn't seem to keep her eyes off him—the way he moved, how he carried himself, the twinkle in his eye when he laughed.

"I'm sorry."

"Don't apologize." His voice was low but firm. His arms bracketed her, and the heat from his body flooded her entire backside. "Do you have a boyfriend, Victoria?"

"Um, no." She chuckled lightly. "Your questions make me think of truth or dare."

"I haven't played that game in a long time." He exhaled. "Truth or dare?"

*Crap!* She tried to focus and not act like a bumbling teenager. Those years were behind her. "Truth."

"Have you ever been with an older man?"

"No," she managed to squeak out. She licked her lips. "My turn. Have you ever been with a younger woman?"

"No, not one half my age."

The age-gap was even greater, but she didn't mention that. As long as her parents never found out, she wanted Pierce... Was it possible he wanted her too?

"It's a shame," he breathed close to her ear, "that you have no boyfriend. Your body is meant to be worshipped by a man who knows how to appreciate a woman. Knows how to give her all the pleasure she can take."

*Oh crap!* She wanted that. One hundred percent!

Her heartrate skyrocketed.

"Dare me," she whispered before she changed her mind.

A sharp intake of air sounded at her ear. "Victoria, you don't know what you're asking."

"Maybe, but...but aren't you curious. Just a little." *Touch me.*

Several long moments passed, and Pierce just stood there. Finally, he spoke. "Spread your legs."

She moved her legs, widening her stance.

She could definitely feel the subtle press of his erection against her backside.

He shimmied her T-shirt over her hips, revealing her pink thong. Her *wet*, pink thong.

His fingertips glossed over her thighs and ass. He was either intentionally teasing her or still unsure of his next move.

Her pants came harder.

Then he slid a finger under her satin confection, caressing but not going to the area she needed most desperately.

She felt his other hand, but before she could ask him to touch her, her thong snapped at the seam and slid down her left leg. She was bare to him from the waist down.

Her lungs worked for air.

His hands covered her ass, caressing her and creeping toward her center and lower. Slowly, a single finger skated through her wet slit. He inhaled deeply.

He took his time stroking and discovering her pussy.

The wetness grew, and Pierce smeared it over her clit. She pitched forward over the counter, offering herself to him, eager for completion yet never wanting his touch to disappear.

She climbed quickly, but he didn't let her tip over.

"Do you want more?" he spoke, knowing full well what he was doing.

She nodded feverishly.

He opened a drawer with his free hand and retrieved a pad and pen. "Write your cell number down."

She couldn't focus. The delicious stroking of his fingers in her core and his thumb on her clit made it nearly impossible to concentrate. One number at a time, she carefully wrote.

"Good. If this is what you want," he rammed three fingers into her while covering her squeal with his free hand, "then this is what you'll get. You're mine for the summer."

He stroked, swirled, pressed, and circled.

She was delirious with desire until the lust finally exploded, the euphoria flexing her body then causing her to collapse onto the countertop. She gasped for air.

Vaguely aware, he leaned down and lifted her foot, then replaced it.

"Watch your texts," was all he said, and he was gone.

*Holy shit!* That had to have been the best orgasm she'd ever had.

The pad of paper was gone, and glancing down, so were her panties.

She replayed his words: *You're mine for the summer.*

But how was that going to be possible. The yearly visit was always only a week and two weekends.

Well, she was prone and couldn't take the time to think about his words any longer. She tugged down her T-shirt, poured her cold tea down the drain, and made her way back upstairs quickly.

Something told her, her life was about to jump to a whole new level.

*Holy fuck!* Victoria was hot! He had no idea what had gotten into him.

*Those long, smooth, shapely legs. Mmm.*

He knew she'd had a remote sort of interest in him, looking up to him in a way. But now with the divorce finalized, it was like the quasi-paternal glasses were removed. He could see Victoria in a way he never would have dreamt about before.

She was so eager, so willing. She was putty in his hands, and he fucking loved it. As long as Cary didn't find out, there wouldn't be a problem.

Pierce's head spun with ideas. He paced the bedroom a few times.

He and Priscilla never had kids, and he longed to share his knowledge with the next generation. Victoria would be his little protégé.

By the time, he was done with her this summer, she would feel like a new woman. He wouldn't just dominate her pussy, scrumptious as it was, he would dominate her mind.

This would be the best summer he'd had in a long damn time.

# Chapter Twenty-Eight

♥

Larissa arrived the next morning. Victoria wanted to tell her friend about Pierce. How she was excited and thrilled, and yet scared pea green at the same time, but she couldn't. No one could find out or else her parents would flip out. Dad would likely quit working at Palencia, and there would be a rift between him and Pierce forever more. Vicki couldn't live with that on her heart.

As Larissa stashed away her clothes, Vicki sat on the twin bed she usually slept in. "So, how did it turn out with your big talk with Justin."

Larissa shook her head. "Not very well. We broke up."

"Oh, no. I'm sorry."

"He said he couldn't go monogamous overnight." Larissa snapped her fingers.

"Well, that's what you do when you enter into a relationship."

Larissa nodded. "I'll be okay. Better I know now."

"That's right." Vicki rose and wrapped an arm around her friend. "And this week came just in time."

"Yup," Larissa grinned. "A great way to start forgetting about him. Speaking of which," she gave an exuberant smile, "is your brother here?"

Theo was four years older than Vicki and worked at an architectural firm in New York City.

Vicki grinned. "Not yet. He has work. But he'll be here Thursday."

"Lucky me. Well, we better head down there." Larissa waggled her eyebrows. "I need to work on my tan."

Seemed that both women had their sights set on some men this summer.

***

By dinner that Saturday night, there was a full house. Most of the executives and their families from Palencia and a few close friends of Pierce were in attendance. Pierce had his staff working to keep plates and glasses full. The man could throw a hella party.

This time when she watched him, she saw him in a different light. Before she appreciated his nice physique, his gym-training muscles, his smooth skin, and the smattering of gray at his temples and on his chest. Now she fantasized about running her fingers over his body and savoring all those delicious parts.

God! She was thinking about sleeping with a forty-eight-year-old man. How is this possible?

And Pierce epitomized the self-assured, confident host and executive. No one would even guess he had his CIO's daughter the prior night, or what was to come.

Vicki breathed out and took a sip of her hard lemonade. She'd better keep herself in check in public.

But Pierce seemed to not even notice her.

After a few hours of what seemed like neglect and Vicki wondering if he'd changed his mind, he cornered her outside the bathroom. She walked out of the bathroom and smacked square into his chest.

"Oh, Mr. Novak. I'm sorry."

He flashed his sexy smile, then without warning, he cupped the side of her neck and kissed her lips. His tongue broke passed her lips and tunneled into her mouth, connecting with her.

She pushed onto her toes to take more.

*God! What an incredible kisser.*

He stepped back. "My sweet Victoria. I'll have you tonight, won't I? You'll come to me, won't you?" he whispered. Then he side-stepped her to continue down the hall to his bedroom.

She exhaled and licked her lips.

In half a beat, Phyllis Bernhard turned the corner of the hall, heading in her direction.

"Victoria, dear. How are you finding NYU?"

"I love it, ma'am." She smiled, knowing her face was probably a deep shade of pink.

"Wonderful. My Johnny loved it too." Phyllis ducked into the bathroom, and Vicki headed out back as fast as she could.

"Hey. You okay?" Larissa asked.

"Yeah, maybe time to switch to water. Then let's go in the pool."

Vicki grabbed two water bottles out of the cooler, and the women walked to a chaise and yanked off their beach cover-ups. The water was heavenly as Vicki knew her body's temperature had climbed significantly with that kiss.

Geez! How would she survive this?

***

Vicki glanced at the chime from her phone on the nightstand. Pierce texted her.

*Come to my bedroom now. Naked.*

Vicki turned toward Larissa. She snored lightly, facing the other wall. Larissa was out for the night with all the alcohol she'd consumed.

Pierce wanted Vicki to come to him, just as he said earlier. She'd been waiting all day for his text.

But naked? Was he crazy? There was no way.

She flung back the bed covers and made her way to the door. The hallway was dark except for the illumination from the lamp on a narrow table.

She took a deep breath, closed the door behind her, and quietly headed downstairs to his bedroom.

She rapped lightly, and he opened the door. His gaze assessed her as she walked through.

"I see you have trouble following directions."

"Pierce, I can't walk naked through your house."

He raised an eyebrow. "Can't or won't?"

She swallowed hard, and her face grew warm.

He wore his pajama bottoms again, and his chest was bare. His muscles worked as he walked to the closet. He returned with a washcloth and a red tie.

She wanted to run her hands over the smattering of hair on his chest. An outline of his semi-erect penis showed. He was gorgeous.

"Strip," he told her.

She knew not question. She knew what she wanted and knew he could give it to her. She pulled off her sleepshirt and pushed out of her panties, standing before him naked.

His eyes grew dark as midnight. "Your first lesson is courage."

*Lesson? What does that mean?*

"A lot of courage would be required to walk through my house naked and come into my bedroom so I can fuck you."

He approached her, the skin taut on his face.

Her mouth wet dry at the glorious image.

"Hands out," he commanded.

She stretched out her hands. He wove the tie over and around her wrists, then he led her to the slipper chair at the side of the room.

As quick as a lightning strike, he bent her over the back of the chair and pulled the tie down the front, quickly binding it to a chair leg.

"Hey." She protested.

"Quiet, my sweet. I wanted to fuck you tonight, but it seems you haven't mastered courage yet."

*Oh my.*

"You will have to wait another night for my cock. I will have to be satisfied with disciplining you."

"What?" she almost shrieked.

Leaning over her, he commanded. "Open your mouth and bite down on this towel."

*Oh shit!* He was serious.

She knew what was coming. In retrospect, walking down naked would have been easier.

She opened her mouth wide, and he placed the folded cloth in her mouth, shoving it securely, but not too tight.

"Is this okay? I don't want you uncomfortable, just enough to muffle your screams."

*Oh shit!* She nodded.

"Good."

He pushed her hair to the side and kissed her neck. "You look so fucking gorgeous, Victoria, leaning over my chair, open to my every whim."

He rose, and Vicki could clearly see his erection tenting his pants now.

His hand stroked her naked back, up and down several times, moving toward her ass. He caressed her globes. "So perfect. So creamy. I can't wait to see my hand turn it a sweet cherry red."

She whimpered in anticipation and nervousness. She'd never been spanked before.

*Slap!*

His hand came down, and she squealed into the cloth.

*Slap! Slap!*

His hand came down on the other cheek. He turned on a reading light beside him. "Oh yes. If you could see how pretty pink your ass cheeks are. So beautiful."

*Slap! Slap! Slap!*

His hand covered her ass and her thighs. He leaned over her to whisper close to her ear. "Now, precious, spread your legs."

Her heart pounded in her chest from the rush of adrenaline. Her ass and thighs stung, but there was a yearning she couldn't understand.

She hesitantly separated her legs, leaving herself more vulnerable.

*Slap* on her upper thigh.

"Look at that deliciously wet pussy."

*Slap!* He'd made contact over her pussy lips.

Her scream was muffled by the cloth. The smack sent fire throughout.

His finger slid through her slit. "So fucking wet, Victoria. I can't wait to claim you."

*Slap! Slap!*

More contact over her pussy.

She panted, and the cloth became wet with her saliva and tears. The ache at her pussy was maddening.

"I love how swollen your pussy gets, princess. Swollen and red." His finger toyed over her clit, and she moaned long and low.

Another minute, she would be coming.

*Slap! Slap!*

Her ass screamed with heat.

Then he leaned down, kissing and licking the tender skin. "I wonder. How much more can you take, princess?"

He kicked her legs further apart, slapped her several more times, partially over her pussy.

"Fuck, Victoria. You look so beautiful. You're dripping on my carpet. My dick has never ached so much to be inside a woman until now. Until you." His voice deep and gravelly.

*Yes! Please!*

*Slap! Slap!*

The tears streamed down her cheeks, anxious to put out the fire on her ass *and* in her pussy.

Then he leaned down, blew over her desperate pussy, and licked her.

They both moaned.

He licked her twice more, drove in two fingers, and she came. Long and hard.

He didn't relent, licking her clit, stroking her swollen channel, making love to her pussy.

She climaxed again, as fiercely as the first time. She screamed through the cloth.

She bucked as he continued fucking her with his tongue.

His hands held her apart for him as another two orgasms crashed through her.

She didn't know how much more she could take.

Finally, he rose, panting as heavily as she.

He leaned over her, peppering her with kisses on her damp back. "You're beautiful, Victoria. That was so fucking beautiful," he whispered. "I've never had a woman come on my tongue so many times… I'm as hard as granite, baby." More kisses. "I can't wait to slide deep inside you. Then, you'll be mine. You know that, don't you?"

*Yes, yours!* She nodded.

He walked to the front of the chair, unbound her, and brought her to standing. He removed the cloth and brushed away the stray tears. He stared into her eyes for several long moments, then he leaned down and kissed her. He drew her near, pressed his large erection against her belly, and dove deeply into her mouth.

She forgot about the fire on her ass as he kissed her and caressed her naked body for several long minutes. His hands were like a balm over her heated skin, stroking her, cherishing her.

Finally, he broke the kiss. He reached down and handed her her sleepshirt, but nothing more.

She slipped it over her head.

"Good night, Victoria."

"Good night, Pierce." While she still had the strength, she turned and made her way to the door, closing it quietly behind her.

*Holy shit!*

Pierce strode into the bathroom to relieve the sexual tension that threatened to rip him apart. His dick was an angry red that he hadn't seen before. And larger too.

*Fuck!* She was amazing.

Victoria trusted him. Bound and gagged, she looked positively gorgeous. She took every one of his spankings and nearly creamed herself in the process. It took every ounce of fortitude he could muster not to dive right into her bent over the back of his chair.

Under the spray of the shower, he pulled on his dick to relieve the pressure. Not that it would relax for a while with the memories of his precious Victoria racing through his head.

Yes, he had plans. Exquisite plans for her.

# Chapter Chapter Twenty-Nine

♥

Vicki couldn't sleep in. The memories of the previous night raced through her head, like a song on a loop.

She wanted Pierce. She couldn't deny it.

*Fuck it*, she scolded herself as she quietly threw on shorts and a tank top over her red and white bikini and headed downstairs for coffee, leaving Larissa to sleep in.

She greeted several folks who chatted in the living room and a few in the great room.

"Good morning," she called back to them.

As she prepared her coffee, she saw through the back window Pierce and her father talking on the patio. She couldn't make out what they were saying but her instinct was to find out.

Vicki quietly went out the front door, sipping her coffee, giving the appearance of a morning stroll. She headed around the west side of the house where she knew some large red tip photinia bushes would provide good cover but place her close enough to hear what the men were talking about.

*"He's doing well. The firm keeps him busy, but I'm glad he could at least break away for several days to come up here."* It sounded like Dad might be talking about Theo.

*"And how is Victoria doing?"* Vicki's ears perked up when Pierce asked about her.

*"Vicki's Vicki,"* her father started. *"We haven't really pushed her for a summer job, but we sure would like to see her take the initiative, like Theo did."*

Her jaw gaped. This was news to Vicki. She had no idea her parents expected her to get a summer job. Sure, they provided for everything, but in fairness, Vicki didn't go crazy with her spending, not like a lot of her friends had.

*"Ah. But her grades are good?"*

*"Oh, excellent."*

*See.*

*"I have an idea,"* Pierce continued. *"What if she worked at Palencia for the summer?"* There was a brief pause, but Vicki couldn't see a thing. *"In fact, maybe she can work under me, learn the ropes. Get real business experience firsthand, not just what some author chose to put in a textbook."*

*"Pierce, that's an exceptionally generous offer, but I can't ask that of you. You don't need some intern following you around."* Her father chuckled.

*"You didn't ask, I offered. I can set her up in some projects, like a floater position, in different departments. She works, uses her brain, and earns some money."*

*"You're serious?"*

*"I am."*

Another pause. *"Well, that sounds terrific. I'll ask her."*

*"Excellent."*

Then her dad turned the conversation to some company stuff that made no sense to Vicki.

*Pierce wants me to work for him, beside him.* This was his plan to have her for the summer. Her heart pounded against her rib cage.

*Holy shit!*

Later that night, as everyone went through the buffet line for dinner, Dad pulled her aside. "Vicki, I had a conversation earlier with Mr. Novak. He had an idea about you working for Palencia in a kind of intern role."

"An internship? This summer?" She had to provide some resistance, make it look like she wasn't completely infatuated with the man. She crossed her arms over her chest.

"Yes."

"Will I get paid?" She lifted an eyebrow.

"Yes. I think you'd really like it. And it would be good for you, give you practical experience. Ten times more valuable than just reading the textbooks."

She audibly sighed. "I suppose. I hope the pay is good."

Her father kissed the top of her head.

Inside, she was doing backflips. Wow! She was going to work for Pierce, *real* work. She had no objection to that, despite the ruse she played for her father. But working with Pierce, seeing him every day, she simply couldn't contain herself.

She spun around to find Larissa and share the news.

"You lucky bitch." Larissa punched her upper arm.

Vicki simply grinned.

"He's hot. I'm sure he's got several women warming his bed at night now that Mrs. Novak is gone..." Larissa rattled on.

Vicki's heart sank. Why hadn't she thought of this? Pierce could very well be sleeping with other women *right now*. Being with someone who played the field was *not* Vicki's style.

*Shit!*

She would need to say something. He might be out, and Vicki would be disappointed but so be it. Call her greedy, but she wanted to be the center of his world, if only for three months.

Courage? She had courage. She'd say something that night.

***

The text came through at midnight. Vicki's heart skipped a beat when she read it from Pierce: *Come to my bedroom. Naked!*

Vicki swallowed hard. Geez! There were more people in the house—ten of them were under the age of eighteen, although the chance of them not being glued to their electronics right now was low. Hell, Vicki would normally be on her phone right now, winding down before sleeping.

One last glance to the other bed confirmed Larissa was in a deep sleep.

She stepped out of her clothes. Wetness already gathered at her sex. She quietly opened the bedroom door and peered out. She listened for anything—talking, snoring, laughing. Nothing.

Her heart thumped and vibrated her throat. God, she couldn't believe she was doing this.

The other bedroom doors were closed.

She could do this. She had to do this. She wanted Pierce.

She made her first step, careful to listen for any sign of life. Fourth step. So far so good.

She descended the stairs. Still nothing.

Her heart beat so fast, she felt lightheaded. She gripped the railing and tiptoed downstairs in the dark house.

She made it to the first floor and heard a splash from the pool. She quickly crouched down. Staying below the line of sight from the windows was impossible; they were tall, mostly floor to ceiling.

She strategized about a work-around. If she went through the dining room, that would drop her in the hallway next to the theater room, which would connect her to hallway to the owner's retreat.

*You can do this.*

She crawled away from the staircase to the dining room. She rose and went to the other entrance. Checking for any sign of life, she then cut down and across the theater room. Thank God, no one was watching a movie that night.

Finally, she arrived at the main hall leading to his bedroom, which of course, was at the very end.

She glanced left and right. One. Two. Three.

She took off running down the hall, turned the doorknob, and busted through the door, closing it behind her.

She leaned against the door, panting.


Pierce looked over from his club chair at the beauty clutching the doorknob, chest heaving, with a gorgeous pink glow in her cheeks from her exertion.

He took one last sip then set down his whiskey and rose. *Fuck!* She was breathtaking.

She ran here, either partially or all the way.

He burst with pride over her. He knew she could do it once she set her mind to it.

She tracked him as he moved closer.

Without a word, he cupped her jaw in his hands and crashed his mouth to hers.

She moaned.

He felt her body soften, probably from the relief of having made it without being caught.

Their tongues tangled in her sweet mouth. He wanted to consume every fucking inch of her. He shouldn't. He'd scolded himself a million times for wanting a woman who could be his daughter. But she wanted it too. They were two consenting adults, so what the fuck.

Without breaking the kiss, he lifted her and carried her to the bed to lay her down.

"I'm so proud of you. I knew you could do. Now for your reward." He kissed her one last time and trailed down her neck and clavicle to her full tits, waiting for his mouth.

He laved and sucked in as much as his mouth could take. She was fucking delicious.

She squirmed and whimpered beneath him, weaving her fingers through his hair.

Lust and desire swirled inside him, creating a fire he was desperate to put out.

"Courage, baby," he whispered over her navel as he dipped his tongue. "Congratulations on your first lesson."

That was all the talking they needed to have right then. He moved down her body spreading her legs before claiming her sweet pink pussy.

She was bare of hair. He didn't have an opinion either way about that, but somehow on Victoria, it was fucking perfect.

He licked her and loved on her eager, wet pussy as he divested himself of his shirt and unfastened his trousers.

In no time flat, she came—moaning, writhing, and squirting on his tongue. *Perfect.*

The precise moment she came down, he didn't hesitate. He rose and drove his entire length into her.

She cried out. "Ah!"

"So, fucking tight, Victoria." He panted as he thrust inside the gorgeous, smart, vivacious woman spread out on a cloud of white cotton. He crashed his mouth to hers.

Her legs and arms swung around him, pulling him in.

He broke the kiss to watch her face as they made the most incredible connection together. One that he would repeat many a time during the summer.

She opened her eyes, and their gazes locked. It was as if their bodies had a whole conversation of their own, their brains were simply along for the ride.

"I'm on the pill."

"I'm clean."

The sparkle in her eye stole his breath. "Then, you need to come inside me."

He latched onto her mouth one last time because he knew he couldn't hold out another minute. He dove deep several more times before sending his seed into this perfect being.

He panted into her shoulder, wondering how the hell he got so lucky.

As they calmed, he slipped out and collapsed to the side of the bed. They lay side by side for several beats before she rose on an elbow.

She leaned over him and pecked his lips. "So, I'm working for you this summer?"

He simply smiled. She'd learn soon enough, he always got what he wanted.

"No other women this summer, Pierce. I want all your attention, all your kisses, all your climaxes."

He lifted an eyebrow. He wasn't expecting that. Of course, he knew she would be the only one as long he had her, but she surprised him. In a good way.

She smiled, stood, and slipped on his shirt, buttoning it as she strode to the door. She opened it and walked out, not looking back.

*Holy fuck!*

His little filly had a fire inside her. He might want to tame her, but some parts of her, he absolutely wouldn't touch.

He smiled, watching her walk down the hall of his house.

Did he have to wait a whole day before she'd be back in his bed?

# Chapter Thirty

♥

Vicki replayed the last several days at Pierce's. Everything was amazing, incredible. Even Johnny hitting on her didn't bother her as much this year. She actually laughed him off and offered to bring him a beer when she went inside.

Pierce did an exceptional job paying her little attention when others were around, but when they were alone, he took whatever he could get away with.

He was incredible.

She'd been sneaking down to his bedroom every night so he could fuck her. He'd text her when it seemed the coast was clear, and she'd tiptoe downstairs. She wondered when the man ever slept with these late-night rendezvous. At least she was lucky enough to sleep in some days.

Pierce still worked out of his home office during the week.

*Would he do me in his office downtown? Bend me over his desk?* God, she hoped so.

Thursday night she was exhausted from hours out on the lake. She fell asleep, waiting for Pierce's text.

She had the most splendid dream. Pierce was kissing her tummy and pushing her T-shirt higher to kiss her breasts. He whispered sweet words over her skin. When he lowered his body, she knew what came next. She moaned as he kissed and licked her sex, spreading her legs wider to get to precisely what he wanted.

It felt so real.

Vicki's eyelids lifted slightly as her brain tried to process the incredible sensations. This was no dream.

From the glow off the alarm clock in the room, she could see: Pierce was licking her in her bed.

She pried her eyes open to take in her surroundings. Pierce on her bed, Larissa sleeping on the other twin bed.

*Holy shit!*

She should stop him, she knew she should, but it felt too good. She covered her mouth when an orgasm crashed through her, ricocheting like she hadn't had a hundred orgasms already this week.

Pierce lifted his head and smiled at her. He raised over her, snapped her panties, and tossed them to the floor. Then lowering his sleep pants, his hard cock shown so large, so perfect in the dim light.

He lowered himself to her and claimed her mouth as he effortlessly slid into her pussy.

She tamped down her moan and clung to him, wrapping her arms and legs around him.

"Hi," she whispered after they broke the kiss.

"Hi, beautiful." He kept his gentle thrusts inside her.

"Did you text me?"

He nodded. "Twice."

She furrowed her brow, wondering why she hadn't heard it.

"It's okay. I can come to you," he said in the crux of her neck.

Just then, Larissa rolled over. They froze. In the darkness, she couldn't tell if Larissa's eyes were open or closed. Vicki's heart hammered in her chest.

*Shit! Shit! Shit!*

"What are you two up to?" Her voice tainted with sleepiness.

"I'm sorry, Lar. I didn't mean to wake you."

"Ha," she said. "Mr. N, I'm surprised to see you up here. In Vicki's bed."

The pause in the air was like the silence before the killer in a horror movie struck his next victim.

Then Pierce spoke. "A thousand dollars to forget you ever saw me here."

Larissa thought a few beats. "Three thousand."

"Done," he retorted.

"Shit. I'm rich." Her voice was jovial. She turned the other way, lifted the pillow sham, and sandwiched her ears to drown out their love making.

God, Vicki loved that woman! Absolutely loved her.

Pierce looked back at Vicki, and they chuckled softly as Pierce began to move again.

The connection they shared was glorious. He worshipped her body like he said he would that very first night. She'd climaxed effortlessly with him, as he stroked her deep inside while doing the same outside.

"Pierce." She moaned in his ear, through her second orgasm.

"I love to make you cum, baby." Then he growled into the crux of her neck while he shot his seed deep into her pussy.

He laid there, the glorious weight of him pushing her into the mattress.

After a few long moments, he shifted. She didn't want him to leave, but she knew he had to.

"Until tomorrow night, baby."

"Until tomorrow."

He kissed her one last time, then pushed off the mattress. He pulled up his pants, quietly opened the door and was out.

Vicki sighed. The man was quickly becoming an addiction.

She lay, thoroughly relaxed in the bed, just as he'd left her, fantasizing about the summer. What would it be like working side by side with Pierce? The man was brilliant. This she knew for fact. And she prayed she'd concentrate on learning from him instead of just making love to him.

***

Sunday afternoon Larissa hugged Vicki tight, whispering in her ear, "Lucky bitch."

"I'm lucky? You're three thousand dollars richer and have a date lined up."

They both giggled and held each other for longer than most would think was acceptable. But they didn't care.

"Good luck this summer."

"You know it and good luck with your date."

Larissa had landed herself a date with her brother Theo. The sparkle in her eyes showed just how excited she was.

"Text me. With all the juicy details."

"Maybe."

Larissa smiled as she pushed back from the hug. A minute later, she was settled in her parents' car and heading down the long driveway.

Vicki turned back inside to see her parents saying their goodbyes to Pierce. Everyone else had already gone.

Pierce turned to meet her gaze. "So, I'll see you tomorrow morning?"

"Yes, sir. Can't wait." She tried to hide the excitement bubbling inside, but she didn't know if she succeeded.

"Perfect. I'll see you as well, Cary." He shook her father's hand. "Audrey, always lovely to see you. So glad you could make it up again this year."

"Wouldn't miss it, Pierce." She smiled and hugged him.

Pierce pivoted to the door, as her father lifted their two suitcases and motioned for the ladies to exit. Vicki lifted her suitcase down the front four steps and rolled it to her father's car. As Cary loaded the suitcases in the trunk, Pierce opened the door for her mother.

"Thank you. And thanks again for hosting such a wonderful week."

Pierce smiled, then met Vicki's eyes as she walked toward the passenger door.

"Allow me," he said.

As she stepped closer to the car, Pierce grabbed her ass with his warm hand and squeezed.

Her insides flipped over. How in the world was she supposed to sleep in her own bed tonight without Pierce giving her an orgasm or two? She grinned, sliding into the backseat of her father's luxury import.

"Safe travels." Pierce stepped back and waved.

She looked up at him. Even in shorts and a polo shirt, he was the epitome of confidence, power, and charisma. She smiled and winked before turning to face the front.

The car began to roll forward, away from the house, but closer to her next adventure. For three glorious months.

# Chapter Thirty-One

♥

Vicki arrived at Palencia's offices and took the elevator to the twentieth floor Monday morning where Rhonda, Pierce's admin, greeted her.

She rose from behind her desk located outside Pierce's office. "Excellent. Glad you made it. Right this way, Victoria. Let's get your paperwork started."

Rhonda swung around to head toward the elevator. She wore a navy pant suit that complimented her salt and pepper hair. She stood about five feet tall, and Vicki couldn't help thinking what wonders heels would do for her stature.

"But shouldn't I check in with P— Mr. Novak first?"

Rhonda paused a split second.

*Shit! Vicki, be careful.*

"No. He's on a call. He knows you're here, but he's expecting to see you later, after a trip to HR."

"Yes, of course." Her bag over her shoulder, Vicki followed the woman to the elevator and down to the third floor.

She introduced Vicki to Raymond, the human resources rep who'd handle her paperwork. "I'll see you back in twenty when you're done."

Vicki smiled. "Okay. Thanks."

After an hour, Vicki was nearly cross-eyed with all the forms she had to complete: personal information, employee handbook, medical benefits, and more. Pierce was giving her full benefits, like a regular employee. And the salary to match too. She beamed inside signing that form.

Finally, she rode the elevator back to the executives' floor. Rhonda was on the phone, so she peeked into his office. It was empty.

Vicki took a seat in the waiting area. What should she be doing? Surely, he wasn't paying her to sit around.

In a few short minutes, Pierce arrived, looking incredible in his charcoal suit with red striped tie. Drool worthy!

"Victoria, everything squared away with HR?"

"Yes, sir." She didn't know what she should call him, but somehow it felt right. Definitely better than "Pierce" in his place of work.

His eyes shown a little twinkle. "Excellent. Follow me."

She strode beside him as they walked the long hallway to another bank of elevators.

"This week you'll be with the marketing folks," he said breaking the silence.

"Okay." She didn't know what to say. It was surreal being next to Pierce and not talking like they would have back at his house. She was at odds—standing close to him, knowing all the wonderful things he could do to her, for her. But on the other hand, this was a serious place of business. She couldn't dare let on what they did in their private time.

Going down two floors they arrived at an office with a tall, brunette typing away on her computer keyboard.

"Leah, this is Victoria Atwood, our newest intern and the daughter of one of our execs."

"Hello, Victoria." Leah rose and offered her hand.

Vicki smiled. "Vicki. Nice to meet you."

"Leah is working on an ad campaign for our latest product launch. She can tell you all about it. I'd like you to shadow Leah this week. Soak up all you can."

"Yes, Mr. Novak."

Pierce's eyes sparkled as he looked down at her. The corner of his lips lifted slightly. "Come see me when you're done for the day." He pivoted and left.

"As you may know, Palencia makes chips for gaming, robotics, automotive, and more. We sell B to B."

Leah didn't stop to ask her if she knew that meant "business to business". Vicki liked her in an instant because she didn't talk down to her.

"Our goal to come up with an ad for a trade magazine as well as something we can use to put in our monthly newsletter."

"Okay." Vicki nodded.

Vicki followed her to a round worktable where papers were spread out.

"Have a seat." Leah motioned. "Here are the features of our newest chip from Product Development."

Vicki scanned the documents in front of her. Her pulse kicked up a notch. This was real life. She'd done something like this in school for a fictitious *widget*, but now she got to put her knowledge to use: ad goal, target market, timing, outlets, messaging.

Leah typed out something on her tablet and brought up the beginnings of some ad copy.

Vicki recognized the logo in the corner. "Is that program InDesign?"

Leah smiled. "Yes. Are you familiar with it? We use this a lot in Product Marketing."

Vicki nodded. She hadn't used it yet, but one of her professors spoke highly of the program.

Leah handed her the tablet. "You play around a little with it. I'd like to add this paragraph somewhere in there." Leah pointed to a sheet from the development team. "But I think it needs a little finessing."

"Okay." Vicki read the content and made some mental notes.

"I'm gonna run and get us something to drink. Want anything?"

"Just a water, please."

Leah returned with bottled waters, and Vicki hardly noticed. She'd been so engrossed with the program, she couldn't focus on anything else.

The women worked side by side, occasionally Vicki would ask a question. Then when she felt like she had something good to show, she handed the tablet to Leah. "Um, what about this?"

Leah took the tablet. Her eyebrows lifted. "I like it. We have some more things to do, but how about we break for lunch?"

Vicki looked at her phone: one-thirty. "Oh wow. Sorry."

Leah chuckled and rose. "No worries. I get the same way some days."

The two walked down the street to a deli on the corner. "So, how long have you worked at Palencia?" Vicki started.

Leah filled her in on her adventures of taking a job at a small company after college, and after two years, that company was bought by Palencia, where she'd been for three years.

"That's awesome."

"I love it. And the occasional visit from Pierce Novak doesn't hurt either." She wiggled her eyebrows.

Vicki chuckled.

"My girlfriend has been put on notice that if Pierce ever expressed an interest in me," she placed her hand over her chest, "a younger woman, that I'd have to dump her." The humor in her voice and in her eyes had Vicki giggling.

*Oh, you have no idea.*

Vicki smiled, and the conversation flowed effortlessly.

The day blew by quickly. And by the end, they had a rough draft of an ad for the trade rag and an idea for the email blast.

"Okay, I'm cooking dinner tonight, so I can't drag my ass. I'll see you in the morning."

"Sounds great." Vicki smiled and walked toward Pierce's office while Leah waited for the elevator to take her down.

Vicki was on a high. She loved putting together an ad campaign, working out the particulars and collaborating with Leah. Leah was smart and easy-going. Vicki knew she was going to learn a lot this week.


Victoria peeked her head through the doorway of his office. Rhonda was already gone for the day. He waved her in.

"Okay, Jessica, let's touch base next week. And thanks again."

*"Anytime, Pierce."*

He disconnected the line from his head of HR and looked up at the beaming beauty smiling down at him.

"I take it you had a good day."

"The best. Leah is so nice, and so smart."

He rose to close the door. It was after five, and he didn't want to be interrupted when Victoria told him all about her day.

"We were working so hard, I almost forgot about lunch."

Pierce couldn't help but smile at her vitality, her zest for learning something new and fascinating.

She made a step closer and wrapped her arms around him. "Pierce, thank you so much for this job."

He hugged her back, pulling her easily into him. "This was just the first day. Wait until the end of summer."

"Oh, I know I'll love it all." She looked up at him.

He couldn't resist. He leaned down and claimed her full red lips.

She returned the kiss but all too quickly stopped. She stepped out of his grip and looked at the door. "Mr. Novak, I don't think we should do any … shenanigans in your office."

He closed the gap between them and wrapped one arm around her waist the other hand cupped her jaw. "My precious Miss. Atwood, I'm in charge of this company. I can do whatever I want." He kissed her deeper this time, causing her to moan.

"Oh, but I think this is an HR violation, Mr. Novak." The twinkle in her eye showed how she toyed with him.

He slipped off his jacket and tie, laying them over the back of an armchair. Then, he undid his cufflinks and rolled up his sleeves twice. "Victoria, I think I would know about such things, but more importantly," he walked toward her, backing her up against his desk, "I'm willing to overlook any slight infraction if it means you get to make your boss happy."

She bit on her lower lip.

He stroked a thumb over her lip, pulling it free. "And you do want to make your boss happy, don't you?"

She nodded.

The corner of his lip lifted. He reached for her buttons on her top, noticing the slight acceleration of her breath.

*Fuck!* She was gorgeous in her black bra, looking up at him, open and vulnerable to his wishes.

Reaching behind her, he made quick work of her skirt, sending it to the floor. "Step out."

She kicked her skirt aside. She stood before him in matching bra and panties and high heels.

Pierce knew deep inside, her lingerie was new. She'd bought it for him.

"Spread your legs, Victoria."

She moved her legs and gripped the edge of his desk.

Caressing her upper arm, his free hand slid over her plump breasts, his fingertips dancing over her smooth skin. He casually pushed her bra straps off her shoulders. "Is this new?"

She nodded, her lips gaping slightly.

He pulled more, baring her breasts completely to him. He claimed a nipple instantly with his mouth.

She moaned.

*Fuck!* He loved how she responded to everything he did to her. His erect cock begged to be set free.

His fingertips glossed downward and over her lace thong, stroking the damp fabric. "Fuck, Victoria." He shifted his hand over her throat, tipping her head back.

Holding her this way was a possessive move, he knew it. But something about this vixen brought out the worst in him. Or maybe the best.

As his fingers toyed with her slit, he sucked and kissed her neck, soaking in the scent of her. He might never get enough.

With an easy flick of his wrist, her bra slid down her arms, landing on the carpet.

"Lean back."

She leaned back, arching her back to give him full access to her tits.

Her clit grew under his unceasing touch. "My precious Victoria," he whispered over her tight pink nub, "you need me to fuck you, don't you?"

"Yes," she panted. "Yes."

He laved on the other hard nipple. He knew this had to be torture for her, not giving her what she wanted.

Then, the first tiny tremor shook her legs.

He released her jaw and eased open his fly to release his cock.

Her climax grew as she moaned, trembled against his desk, and flexed her pussy against his fingers.

*Beautiful.*

When she was mostly done, he yanked down her thong, spun her around, aligned his cock, and dove deep into her.

She cried out, and the beginnings of another climax gripped his dick.

He gathered her long brown hair falling around her face and pulled her back, flush against his front. "My precious, how your young pussy grips me. You make your boss very happy." He pumped, holding on to his own explosive orgasm for just another few moments.

Her hands circled behind them, and she grabbed his ass. "Pierce," she breathed out.

As one hand held her close, the other toyed with her sumptuous pink nubs. "You need me to fuck you every day, don't you?"

"Please."

That was the last thing he heard before the blood roared behind his eardrums with the release of his seed inside her.

*Fuck!* He needed her. Every day.

Hands braced on his desk, they both panted wildly, waiting for their heartrates to calm.

He retrieved a handkerchief from his pants pocket, slipped out, and wiped them both as clean as he could. He put himself back in place and spun her around, his lips easily finding hers.

She swung her arms around his neck.

He kissed her like they had hours, when in fact he knew they had to wrap it up.

He broke the kiss and stared into her eyes. "I want you in my bed."

Victoria's eyes widened. "We can't. People will be suspicious if I stay with you."

He shook his head. "Tell them you're staying at your apartment. It's closer to the office. Go home tonight pack for the week. You can get the rest of it this weekend."

She smoothed her lips together.

"The only ones who will see us are my housekeepers, and they know not to say a word."

She nibbled on her plump lower lip.

"Victoria, do we need to review the lesson on courage?"

There was a sharp intake of air. "No. I can do it."

He smiled and caressed the back of her neck. "That's right, baby. Now, let's get out of here before the traffic gets any worse."

She leaned down to retrieve her clothes and dress.

He shut down his PC and locked his desk drawers.

She went to the door and gasped when she pulled it open. "The door wasn't locked," she said with wide eyes.

"So?"

"So, someone could have walked in on us."

He chuckled. She was adorable, no doubt about it. "Victoria, no one would dare enter my office without knocking first. The building could be engulfed in flames, and security knows to wait for my response before laying a finger on that door."

"Oh."

He pushed the door closed and hauled her close. "Baby, I won't put us in jeopardy." He kissed her thoroughly, released her, and glanced out the door to make sure the coast was clear.

# Chapter Thirty-Two

The second week at Palencia had Vicki in the sales department. After seeing the copy generated for the new chip, she had a better understanding of what the sales team would be selling.

"So, I noticed," she started as she looked at Pierce while he drove them into the city, "that I am shadowing yet again another woman."

He didn't bother to glance her way. "Yes?"

"I find that rather interesting. Will it be like this the entire summer?" She lifted an eyebrow, not that he could see.

"Likely." The confidence that oozed from every pore on the man was downright intoxicating.

"Uh-huh. You afraid I'll find some young stud to replace you?"

He turned, and the corners of his lip lifted. "You looking?"

"Not really."

"Then, I'm not worried." He reached across the center, leather console of his German sedan and clasped her hand, bringing it to his lips. "I want to make you happy," he breathed over her skin. "I crave making you happy."

*Wow!* No one had ever spoken to her like that.

"I know what you need, Victoria, and I love to give it to you. If only for the summer. But at least you'll know, when you head back to school, what you want in a man."

His words circled around for a minute. He might be right. Already, she found herself comparing men to Pierce.

"Okay."

His smile grew. He kissed her hand again and held it the remainder of the drive in.

Pulling into the parking garage, they had a routine. He would go in first. People were used to seeing him early in the morning, if they were even in the office at this ungodly hour.

Normally, getting up this early would make Vicki grumpy and ornery. However, Pierce waking her with butterfly kisses over every inch of her body—every inch—made it easy to exist on less sleep. In fact, she felt invigorated, not tired.

Pierce left the car keys with her. She waited several minutes, killing time on her phone. When the coast was clear, she slipped out and headed toward the building's front door, like she'd walked from the train station.

She'd head right to her assigned area, acting as if she hadn't had amazing sex that morning with their boss's boss's boss.

When was the last time he'd felt this way, Pierce couldn't say. Certainly not with Priscilla. She never came apart in his hands like Victoria had. She never eagerly went to her knees to suck him to high heaven the way Victoria had.

*Fuck!* He would miss his little filly when she'd go back to school. But it couldn't be helped.

Getting settled at his desk, he opened email and instantly grimaced at one from his director of sales, Donald Parker. It appears they were late submitting their proposal for a large deal with Ford.

Pierce bit down on the inside of his cheek. He didn't want to lose his cool when there would be more opportunities like this, but he'd need to make sure their sales rep didn't miss any more deadlines like this in the future.

He shot off an email to Stefan, asking him to swing by the office around four. Then, he texted Victoria. This would be a great learning opportunity for her as well.

*Come to my office a little before 4 today.*

She replied quickly. *Yes, sir.*

*Fuck!* He loved when she said that, and he couldn't say why. Hearing it at the office was commonplace but hearing it from his princess brought out the dominant side in him. And in a small way, made him crave her more. But now was not the time. He had a company to run.

At few minutes before four, Victoria arrived at his door.

"Victoria, I'm bringing Stefan in the office to try and get to bottom of a deal that we might have lost."

Her lips formed a perfect O. "He's in the sales department."

"That's right. You can sit here at the conference table. Try and look preoccupied on your phone but take some glances at Stefan. Watch his body language?"

She shifted her weight to one hip. "Is this another lesson?"

"Why, yes, it is."

She grinned and got comfortable at the side of the room.

At four, Stefan knocked on his door.

"Come in," he waved the man in. Stefan was in his mid-thirties, a grad from Harvard Business school, but sometimes flighty when it came to commonsense stuff.

"Hi, Mr. Novak." He walked in, stealing a glance at Victoria.

"Stefan, I think you've met our newest intern, Victoria."

She looked up from her phone and smiled at him.

He took a seat across from Pierce.

"So, I was hoping to get some clarification on the delay with the RFP to Ford."

Stefan glanced down before meeting his eyes. He spoke slowly, careful with his words.

Pierce could tell the man was nervous. He didn't want to grill the man, but he wanted to get to the truth. Unfortunately, the longer Stefan spoke, the more convinced Pierce was he wasn't getting it today.

"Well, thanks for clarifying things for me. Let's just hope for positive feedback." Pierce rose.

"Yes, sir." Stefan shook his hand and left.

Victoria rose and stood next to his desk.

"So, what did you think of that interaction?" he asked his protégé.

"Well, I think he was telling the truth, but he definitely seemed nervous."

Pierce nodded. "Uh-huh. Did you notice when I asked about the delay in the RFP, he looked up and to his right."

"Yeah."

"That's because he was tapping into the right side of his brain. The creative side."

Vicki's eyes rounded. "He was lying about waiting on numbers from finance."

"Bingo."

"Holy cow! That guy literally lied. So, what are you gonna do?"

He flashed his eyebrows. "It's not what I'm gonna. It's you."

Her eyes rounded.

"Tomorrow. You'll go to him, tell him you couldn't help but overhear. That you're there to help, that maybe you could talk to me on his behalf."

She nodded.

"After a few minutes of talking, if he doesn't open up, put your hand on his shoulder and say 'I know how hard this must be for you.' This technique works for men and women. He'll feel like you're really listening and that a burden will be lifted if he tells you the truth." He met her stare for a few beats. "There is a slim chance it could backfire. Do you think you can do that, Victoria?"

She grinned. "Of course, I can."

"That's my girl."

***

The next day, Vicki reported to the sales floor and settled into a temporary desk next to the rep. she was shadowing for the week.

"Hey, Carol."

"Good morning."

"Do we have a minute? I need to do something first."

"Sure."

Vicki made her way to Stefan's cubicle. "Hey, Stefan."

"Hey, Vicki. How're things going?"

"Good. I'm learning tons." She snagged a rolling chair from the empty cube beside him and sat close, but not too close.

"I couldn't help by overhear a little of your conversation yesterday with Mr. Novak."

He glanced down briefly. "Uh-huh."

"Well, I don't mean to pry, but I was sorta feeling like there was more to the story than you could tell him."

Stefan just shrugged.

"I get it. It's hard to be completely honest with someone like Mr. Novak and not feel like the backlash would be huge."

"I guess."

"I was thinking if you wanted to talk to me, I might be able to run interference for you. I know this is on his mind, so you probably don't want him asking a bunch more people about it, right?"

He glanced behind her shoulder, probably checking to see if anyone was near. "It's stupid really, and I doubt Mr. Novak would appreciate hearing it from me."

"What is it, Stefan?" She leaned forward placing a hand on his shoulder. "I bet you feel like the weight of the world is on your shoulders."

He exhaled and slumped forward a bit. "It's just that…"

She leaned closer to hear him.

"My girlfriend thought she was pregnant. She was late, and the test read positive." He looked up at Victoria. "We can't have a baby right now. We can't afford it. I have a huge student loan I need to chip away at first."

She nodded.

"She got her period the next day, but my head wasn't in the game. It was just this one deal, but of course, it's one of the best ones we'll have this year." It was like his entire face drooped.

"Why couldn't you tell this to P—Mr. Novak?"

"I was afraid he'd fire me for incompetence."

She nodded again. "So, you don't think anything else slipped through the cracks?"

"No. I swear. I doubled check everything the next day."

"Okay. Try not to worry, Stefan. Let me see what I can do."

"Vicki, I would really appreciate it."

She sent him a wink, put back the chair, and returned to her cubicle. She quickly shot Pierce a text that she'd see him at the end of the day.

*Poor guy*, she thought. But what would she do if she were pregnant with Pierce's baby? On one hand, she would be thrilled. On the other, holy crap! How would she be able to explain that to her parents? No flippin' way.

***

A little after five, Victoria arrived at his office.

"Have a good day?"

She glanced back, probably seeing Rhonda still at her desk, winding things up for the night.

She pushed the door almost closed. "It was a good day, sir. I'm learning lots." She moved closer. "I also had a conversation with Stefan."

She leaned against the side of his desk, as he'd come to learn was a comfortable position for her. Perhaps sitting in the chair across from him felt too formal. Pierce didn't care. He'd grant her just about anything.

"And what did you learn?"

She sighed. "His girlfriend had a pregnancy scare."

The thought of Victoria swollen with his child instantly flashed in his mind. Beautiful and glowing. But that would create way more problems that couldn't be easily explained or justified. "I see. Well, that really isn't a good reason." He shook his head. "It's a shame, the kid had potential," he murmured and spun back toward his computer.

"Uh, Pierce."

He glanced her way, eyebrows raised. This was the first time she'd used his first name at the office. "Yes?"

"Are you thinking about firing him because you can't. He didn't mean to forget. Life sometimes throws you curve balls. I think he deserves a second chance."

"A second chance?"

She crossed her arms under her delicious breasts. "I think it's only fair."

Ah, fair. The classic motto for Gen Z. He'd recently learned all about "fair" witnessing an interaction with his niece and sister-in-law. His gut told him, if anyone could turn this world around, it would be Gen Z.

Just then Rhonda rang his like. "Pierce, I'm wrapped up here. Need anything else?"

"No, thanks, Rhonda."

"You're welcome. See you tomorrow."

He hung up the phone and met Victoria's defiant gaze. "So, what can you give to me if I give Stefan a second chance?"

The corner of her lip curled upward. She strode to the door, closed it quietly, and walked back his way, unfastening her buttons as she did. "I'm negotiating for Stefan's job, I see. Well, Mr. Novak, I'm up to the task."

Her blouse hit the floor, followed by her skirt. She stood before him in her bra, panties, and heels. Correction—panties and heels as the bra joined the pile. Then she went to her knees.

In no time, she had him out and worshipping him with her delectable mouth.

His head lulled back. "God, Victoria, you'll be the death of me."

# Chapter Thirty-Three

Pierce watched Victoria for several minutes, bathing herself in the sun by the pool. It was a gorgeous Saturday—sunny and warm. A perfect day on the heels of a week full of nonstop rain.

God, even though he'd leisurely made love to her already that morning, he needed her again. He felt like a horny teenager.

Work called to him, but he had a few minutes to spare.

He finished his glass of iced tea and walked out the back door, toward her bikini-clad body. She should sun herself naked. It wasn't like the neighbors' properties were close to his, and the staff had the weekends off, with rare occasion.

His wood was already evident by the time he stood beside her chaise lounge.

"Hey," she said, shading her eyes as she looked up at him.

"Baby, stand up."

She blinked and swung her legs down to stand before him. He wasted no time capturing her lips and consuming her mouth. She kissed him back, taking as much as he gave.

He broke the kiss and stared down at her. "You should sunbathe nude, precious, so I can get my fill of your gorgeous body." His fingers stroked the edge of her bikini top.

Her mouth gaped, and her torso subtly flexed closer into his touch.

He reached behind and pulled the string loose on the fabric. Then, before she could say a word, he flung the fabric up and over her head, tossing it.

Her intake of air was sharp, but she didn't say a word. Pierce always got what he wanted, and Victoria, being a star pupil, knew this fact.

With a hand splayed across her back, he tipped her back, giving him free access to her breasts. They were plump, and her nubs hard for him to suck on. *Perfect.*

In the distance, he heard a truck door close.

*Ah, the landscapers.* With all the rain, they couldn't attend to his lawn this week, as normal. They were here now.

*Well, they're about to get a show.*

He brought Victoria upright. "My precious, I'm going to fuck you in my pool." He pulled off his cotton T-shirt and threw it. "Take off your bikini bottoms, and then my shorts."

She swallowed and glanced around.

He'd give her a moment to gather her strength.

She hooked her thumbs under her bikini and dragged them to the ground.

*Beautiful.*

Then, she unfastened his shorts and slipped them off. His cock ready for her. Only her.

Taking her hand, he led her to the steps. Once they were immersed, he pulled her close and with a free hand, aligned his dick at her entrance and drove home.

"Unh." She clutched his shoulders and arched slightly at the sensation.

"That's my girl. So wet and ready."

"I'm in a pool." Even in the throes of sex, she was still sassy.

He chuckled. She was always ready for him. Her body was learning his, how to respond, and how to accept his worshiping.

The back gate opened. Her eyes went wide.

He shook his head twice and said one simple word, one command. "Mine." Then he plunged his lips to hers, diving deep into the recesses of her mouth like he was learning it for the first time. If he wanted to fuck her in front of his staff, he would. All of them knew not to cross him.

Slowly, he walked them to the pool's edge and went up a step.

She clutched him closer, squishing her breasts to his chest to hide them. Her eyes scanned the perimeter, seeing the three men set out to start their work at the far side.

They might have noticed Pierce with his princess, but whatever. It didn't matter.

With a hand, he unclasped hers, set her bottom on the edge of the pool, and spoke. "Lie back."

"Pierce," she whispered. Her pulse fluttering the spot on her neck. He waited.

Hesitantly, she set her hands down and laid back on the cement.

They were still connected in their intimate, most favorite way.

He leaned over her, kissing her sweet skin. "Mine anytime I want you, precious," he whispered over her breasts. With two hands on her hips, he drove into her harder, punctuating his point.

She shrieked and instantly covered her mouth.

"Arms overhead, precious."

"Oh, God." She pinched her eyes closed. She knew it was useless to fight him.

He would reward her later for her bravery.

He pumped another few times, then pulled out, hoisted her hips up several inches, and claimed her pussy with his mouth.

She moaned, and her eyes fell closed.

*That's my girl.*

He made love to her pussy, easily bringing her to orgasm. She writhed and panted.

Pierce didn't want to leave. He licked and toyed with her bulging clit, acutely aware of the lack of movement by his landscapers.

He worshipped his princess more, bringing her to climax number two. He rose, aligned himself, and drove home.

Victoria cried out.

He pumped into her as he leaned down to love on her breasts.

Lifting up, he watched her beautiful face. She opened her eyes and met his gaze. She didn't look away, only at him.

He whispered. "Mine." His thrusts continued.

Her eyes sparkled. "Yes."

"All mine."

"Yes," she said again.

In a few short moments, he was coming inside her. He groaned and collapsed while regaining his breath.

God, she was so perfect for him.

Slowly, he rose.

The corners of her lips lifted. "You're crazy."

"Crazy for you."

He brought her close, lifted her, and walked out of the pool toward the house. Every worker had his back toward them.

Pierce knew better. They witnessed the whole thing. He knew it, and Victoria knew it.

Fuck, she would give him whatever he wanted. And he loved it. Having her at his house was exactly where she belonged.

Vicki couldn't believe what they did by the pool—with the landscapers watching, no less. She stared at her reflection in the bathroom mirror. She should be beet red. She definitely had a glow, but she couldn't tell if it was of embarrassment, the sun, or the incredible sex.

It had been three weeks since she started working for Palencia, and almost as long living at Pierce's house. She was becoming addicted to him. She knew he felt the same way.

She sighed.

He was taking her out for dinner that night. She found a long, strapless fuchsia dress to wear with black strappy heels.

A knock came at the door. Pierce was such a gentleman. He could walk right in since it was his bathroom. He'd told her to set up in his room. That there was no sense being anywhere else since she would be in his bed every night.

"Come in."

"Hey." Pierce wore a dark suit with a crisp white button-down shirt. "You're wearing that dress I see on the bed?"

She nodded, meeting his gaze in the reflection.

"Perfect." He sidled closer behind her with his hands on her upper arms. "No jewelry or lingerie tonight, Victoria."

*Oh shit!* She nodded, because truly was there any sense in arguing with the man who could have whatever he wanted whenever he wanted it? And frankly, Vicki loved turning her body over to this man. He took her to heights she'd never imagine she could have.

He kissed the top of her shoulder, smiled, and left her to finish getting ready.

Vicki pressed her lips together as Pierce escorted her to a restaurant called Lark outside of town. He greeted the hostess, and a few hushed words were exchanged.

She smiled and spoke, "Follow me, please."

With two menus in her hand, she led them to a dimly lit, private dining room at the far end of the restaurant. "Jazmine will be right with you."

The room had just four round tables, all vacant, clothed, with a single, lit votive candle resting in the center. The best part of this quiet room was its view through the large picture window. A large pond spread out before them on the grounds with a fountain and two ducks taking a swim.

"Wow. This is beautiful."

"It is. I love it here when I need some peace and quiet. At night, the fountain is lit."

He guided her to the table and tucked in her chair. He took the seat beside her. They discussed the menu, both deciding on the sea bass and a bottle of white wine.

"What are you thinking?" Pierce pulled her from her wandering thoughts.

She grinned. "I feel like royalty. You're spoiling me." She motioned to the room. "This is all so incredible."

He lifted her hand, kissing the back. "This is just the beginning."

She lifted an eyebrow, but before she could ask what he had planned, Jazmine brought the bottle of wine and poured them each a serving. She didn't try to engage them in small talk or chatter, and she didn't question Vicki's age. She wondered if he designed it that way.

"A toast."

Vicki smiled and lifted her glass.

"To my princess and the best intern Palencia's ever had."

His words warmed her deep inside. She clinked his glass and took a sip. It went down like butter. "Mmm."

Pierce set down his glass. "Now for your surprises." He reached for her hand.

She couldn't help but smile.

"I was so proud of you today. Giving me what I wanted even with an audience watching."

She licked her lips. She might never forget this day.

From under the table, he lifted a tiny, velvet black box and set it before her.

She glanced down. "Oh wow."

"Open it."

She opened the box to see a silver chain with a perfect diamond sparkling up at her. She gasped.

He lifted the pendant from the box and commanded. "Turn around."

Grasping her long hair, she held it high and pivoted to present her back.

He reached around and clasped the necklace. He kissed her neck.

"It's beautiful. Thank you." She leaned closer and kissed him, loving how amazing and thoughtful he was to her.

He brought his hand up again and placed another tiny black box in front of her.

Her eyes went wide as she looked from the box to him. She didn't wait to be told; she opened the box to find a pair of diamond stud earrings, just as beautiful as the pendant.

"Pierce, this is too much."

"Nonsense." He pushed back from the table. "Come here."

She rose with her box in hand and sat on his lap.

He removed one earring from the box and attached it. When she twisted to present him the other ear, he said, "Uh-uh. Straddle me."

Her breath hitched. He wouldn't try something here, would he?

She hiked up her dress to straddle his lap. She had to lift it higher when he spread his knees farther apart. She clasped his shoulders, and her heartrate ratcheted up.

He set her new diamond stud earring in place, then wove his hand through her hair, drawing her closer to his mouth. "Beautiful and elegant, just like you," he whispered over her neck.

His kissed down her neck, her clavicle, to the top of her breasts. Slowly, his deft fingers inched her dress bodice lower, revealing more skin.

She prayed no one would come in right then.

"Your gorgeous, Victoria. And tonight, I'll fuck you wearing only these diamonds."

The dress was so low, her nipples were almost uncovered.

He toyed with her, his tongue dipping into her cleavage and along the top of the dress.

The wetness gathered at the apex of her thighs. She feared what "mess" might be evident on her dress or his pants.

Then, before she could think anymore, he peeled away the fabric to lick and suck on her nipple. First one, then the other.

She moaned and arched into his warm, expert mouth.

"Victoria, you taste delicious. If I wanted to fuck you right here, you would let me, wouldn't you?" He didn't wait for a reply. He dove a finger into her wet channel, causing her to whimper.

"Victoria."

She opened her eyes and met his gaze. "Yes, I'd let you."

"Tell me," he commanded.

"You'd clear everything off this table in one swift motion, then you'd lift me..." she panted, desperately trying to focus under his incredible ministrations, "onto the table, spread my legs, and have me as an appetizer."

Her head fell back as she felt her impending orgasm climb.

"Then?"

"Then, as you licked my pussy and twisted my nipples, I'd squirt all over. Before I could catch my breath, you'd ram your huge cock into me, making me come again as you rocked me and the table."

"That's right, baby. I wouldn't care if anyone saw because I'd need to be inside you, nothing else would matter. Like today at the pool." His thumb circled her clit as he added a second finger. With the final sucking and gently tugging of her nipples, her climax exploded.

She moaned and writhed on his lap at the glorious, unexpected pleasure Pierce so expertly gave her.

"Beautiful."

She opened her eyes, focusing on his handsome face.

He slid his fingers out and licked them, then plunged his mouth to hers. His kiss was voracious and hungry, tangling with her tongue.

Vicki knew he wanted her then but was holding back.

And it was a good thing.

He'd just broken the kiss and pulled the bodice of her dress over her naked breasts when someone arrived with their dinners.

She grinned at her dinner date, who simply waggled his brows and helped her lower her dress as she moved to her seat.

He said, "Thank you," to the server, who noticeably didn't make eye contact with either of them.

When he left, and the door closed, Vicki looked over at Pierce. "We could have been caught," she said in low tone, like someone could hear. "Will this be a habit?"

He reached for her hand and kissed the back. "Precious, I want what I want. I really don't care who sees." He kissed her again and slid the tip of his tongue between her fingers. "Besides, I know you love it."

Even as her stomach did backflips, she lifted her eyebrows in defiance. "How many women have you had sex with in the open?"

"You're the first."

She was shocked but secretly liked knowing they had shared something special.

"Hm. Well, thank you for taking me out, and thank you for my gifts. I love them."

"They're beautiful on you."

He lifted his fork, and they continued to eat.

They chatted more, and he spoke a little about Priscilla. From what Vicki could gather, she liked Pierce's money more than she liked Pierce.

*Her loss. My gain.* Vicki smiled to herself.

# Chapter Thirty-Four

♥

After several minutes and a nearly empty wine bottle, Jazmine entered the room. "Can I get you all some dessert?"

Pierce knew exactly what he wanted for dessert, but he would order something too. "Yes. How about your decadent chocolate cake and two forks?"

"Very good, sir." Jazmine was doing an excellent job waiting on them. Pierce recognized her from previous visits. She was experienced and took direction well. She'd earned herself an excellent tip.

She returned shortly, setting the dessert in between them. A server followed her, refilling their water glasses.

"Thank you, Jazmine. That will be it for the night."

"Very good, sir. Enjoy."

Victoria furrowed her brow, probably wondering why he was dismissing their waitress since he hadn't yet paid his bill.

*Never mind that, precious.*

Eyeing the scrumptious dessert before her, Victoria lifted her fork. "Uh-uh."

She stopped midway, meeting his gaze.

He took the fork out of her hand and shifted on his seat. "I want what I couldn't finish earlier."

Her delicate throat moved as she swallowed.

He motioned with a finger for her to stand. With his hands on her hips, he drew her close.

Her nipples peeked under the dress, and she looked stunning.

He couldn't resist. He closed his mouth over her nipple covered in fuchsia.

She moaned.

He toyed with her, wetting the area as he took in as much breast as he could.

She gripped his shoulders and dropped her head back, letting him have free reign over her delectable body.

Her breathing increased.

He pulled away to see the evidence of his impetuous action. "Now, take off my jacket."

One arm at a time, she slid the jacket off and hung it off the back of his chair.

"Good." He shifted the cake closer to his right side, within reach. "Now straddle my legs, precious."

She did as he bid, lifting her dress, almost revealing her delicious pussy.

He forked a piece of cake and fed her.

She smiled, and her eyes fluttered closed. "Mmm."

He helped himself to a bite as well. *Nice.*

He fed them each another bite, then commanded, "Open my fly, Victoria, and take me out."

She smoothed her lips together and proceeded to unbuckle and unzip his pants, freeing his hard dick with her soft hand.

That gave him a little relief.

"Good, now hands behind your back."

She was breathtaking—the glow in her cheeks and the sparkle in her eyes. She wanted all he could give her, he knew.

He lowered her dress to her stomach. He heard the soft inhale, but she didn't say a word.

He rewarded her with another piece of cake, then with his index finger, scooped the chocolate frosting. Strategically, he coated one nipple then the other, getting ready for his feast.

He claimed one breast at a time, savoring the sweetness from his sweetness.

She mewled.

He cleaned her pretty pink nipples and spoke, "Now, Victoria stand up."

He pivoted out, and she stood before him, hands still clasped behind her back.

With a hand at each side, he slid the dress down her body, waiting for her to step out.

She glanced at the door but stepped out of her dress.

"Now, on your knees."

The corner of her lip curved. She knelt before him and watched.

He reached for a gob of chocolate frosting and smeared it down his shaft. "Some more dessert, Victoria?"

She smiled and leaned forward, licking him like a popsicle.

"Fuuuck." He watched his precious, her red lips stretched around his dick. "God, you're beautiful, Victoria."

She glanced up, not breaking her flow.

After several more moments of her sucking, he couldn't stand it anymore. He needed to be inside her.

In one smooth move, he hoisted her up, threaded his knees between her legs, and set her down as controlled as he could without hurting her.

She moaned. "Pierce." She breathed out.

He cupped her face, bringing her lips to his. He devoured her soft mouth, tasting the chocolate again. "Ride me, precious."

She gripped his shoulders and moved over him, her breasts bouncing lightly.

He wet his thumb and circled her hard little nub.

She sighed, and her head fell back.

God, she was a sight. He loved seeing Victoria in extreme pleasure. In just a few more minutes, she exploded on him. He could feel her ejaculate on his groin.

He gripped her hips and rammed into the depths of her twice, three times, before releasing all the pent-up lust from the last few hours.

She collapsed on him, and he wrapped her in his arms. *Perfect.*

"I told you I wanted to fuck you in just those diamonds."

She chuckled into the crux of his neck.

After a few minutes, they dressed and Pierce pulled out several hundred-dollar bills, dropping them in the center of the table. It would more than cover the bill, leaving a handsome tip for Jazmine.

Victoria gasped, pulling his attention.

"What's wrong?"

She turned to face him. "My dress has two large wet spots on it."

It was true. Where he'd loved all over her, his saliva wetted her breasts right over the nipples. He wanted to be remorseful for her, but he simply couldn't. He loved claiming her and "shouting" it to the world.

He stepped closer, cupping her cheek. "You look simply beautiful. I can't wait to go home and make love to you again. I don't care what anyone thinks about what I did to your dress. If they were me, they'd do the same thing, given the chance. Now, you do have a choice."

She bit her lip.

"You take off the dress and let it dry while I fuck you up against that window. From behind." He would only mention two because those were the ones that took the most courage. Wearing his jacket would be the easy way out.

She inhaled quickly. "It's still light out."

"Or you can hold your head high and walk out of this restaurant with me now."

She looked at the window, probably accessing who could possibly see her from this location. She bit on her lip again. "Okay," her voice soft, "I'll leave now."

He was so fucking proud of her right then, his heart swelled. He leaned down to kiss her and spoke, "Let's go."

She lifted her purse, pushed her shoulders back, and took the hand he offered her.

Pierce intentionally walked a half-pace slower. A few heads turned, and one bastard's gaze lingered, tracking their movements. His eyes were trained on Victoria's breasts, and the corner of his lip lifted before returning to his meal. He knew.

They passed Jazmine, who had her sight trained on their eyes. "Have a good night, folks."

"Thank you, Jazmine."

When they made it to the car, Victoria let out her breath. He opened the car door and chuckled lightly. She was fierce, that was for sure.

# Chapter Thirty-Five

♥

The weekend was simply incredible. Every weekend, every day, with Pierce was incredible. She was pretty sure she was falling in love with him, but it couldn't be helped. And it felt so damn good, why bother to fight it?

Monday, Vicki wasn't sure where to report, and Pierce had been very hush-hush. She waited a few minutes, then arrived at his office. "Good morning, Mr. Novak," she said for appearances.

"Good morning, Victoria. Please sit."

She did and couldn't stop her smile. He smiled back but quickly refocused. "I want to tell you a story about negotiation. Jon had an old blue 70's Chevy he was looking to sell. Kevin needed a new door for his red 70's Chevy but was having no luck finding one. He saw Jon's listing for the same car as his, and the two agreed to meet."

Vicki didn't know where this was going but she had a feeling it was important.

"Kevin said he wanted to buy the driver's door of Jon's car. Jon said, 'The whole car is what I'm selling.' Kevin said 'Well, I can't pay that much.' Jon said, 'It's a collector's item.' Kevin replied that it wasn't in very good condition, although they both knew the driver's door was in near-perfect condition. 'Collector's will love the car' was Jon's reply.

Kevin tried again, 'Well, the car is the wrong color. I'd have to pay to have it painted.' Jon said, 'Collectors don't mind what color it is.'" He sat back. "What do you think about this scenario?"

Vicki thought for a moment. "It sounds like Kevin is getting frustrated because Jon won't budge on price, but he doesn't seem to be able to find a car door anywhere else, so he's gonna have to pony up if he wants a nice car."

Pierce grinned. "Precisely. And Jon never changed his stance."

"The car is a collectible." She supplied.

He nodded. "Today, you have an appointment."

She furrowed her brows. "Okay."

"This is a chance to work on *your* negotiation skills." He sat back in his leather chair. "You need to appear fair and that your interests are aligned with theirs—you want a product at a fair price. They want to sell the product and make a profit."

"Okay." Her heart beat triple-time.

"In every negotiation, you'll have a minimum and a maximum you will accept." He pushed a paper across the desk. There were two bullets listed—number of art pieces and several thousands of dollars.

"In this case, the negotiation is art for money. These are your limits."

"Art has a question mark."

"Yes, you need to decide what art we need for our lobby. You can get one big piece or several smaller pieces for the front wall."

"Okay." Her palms grew slicker the longer Pierce spoke.

Then, he slid over a business card. A gallery was listed in a cursive font. "Your meeting will be in the lobby at eleven o'clock. You can take a few hours to do some research on this gallery and others in the area."

*Their competition.*

"Come to me after your meeting, and we can discuss it over lunch."

She swallowed hard. "Okay."

She could do this. She wanted to show Pierce she could do this. She could buy some damn good art without spending a crap-ton of money.

***

At eleven, a Justin Crandbrook walked to the reception desk and announced himself. Vicki quickly closed the distance and called to him. "Justin?" She held out a hand and gave her best smile.

*Shit!* He was pretty cute. He wore a dark suit with a white shirt, no tie. He was about six-one with dark blond hair, blue eyes, and friendly crooked smile.

Vicki would typically turn on the charm and maybe even flirt a little, but this time she wanted to win using her head, not her boobs.

He shook her hand.

"Victoria Atwood. Mr. Novak sent me to meet with you today."

"Oh." He seemed a little disappointed.

"Don't worry," she began, "you're not wasting your time. He gave me full authority to make a decision today."

Justin smiled and stood taller. "Excellent. Shall we sit?"

She led him to a sofa on the east side of the lobby, with a good view of the main entrance wall. She lifted her arm a pointed to the wall. "This is the area we're looking to fill."

"Okay. Wow. That's a big space."

It was.

Justin continued. "I estimate it's about fourteen feet wide and probably twelve feet tall, from the reception desk. Although the art doesn't need to necessarily go that high," he said with a smile.

"Right. I'm thinking something contemporary with color, but nothing too whimsical or loud."

The corner of his lip curved upward, and his eyes lit up. He was probably likely somewhat impressed that she had an opinion or an eye for what would work well.

"Very well. Let me show you some pictures of what we have. And of course, we can always commission something."

She nodded, not really interested in waiting for that. Afterall, school started in less than two months.

He flipped open his portfolio, stopping to discuss the piece—the artist, the size—whenever she showed an interest.

Vicki saw a few that she was drawn to. She'd stop occasionally and glance up at the wall, visualizing the product mounted there.

*God, this is so much fun.*

"Justin, these are wonderful." She must have seen forty different pieces. "Let me ask you something." She reached in the pile and retrieved three pictures that she liked the best. "What do you think of these up there?"

He looked at them, shuffled them around, looked at the wall, and his eyebrow rose. "I like it. They all have a similar feel, and the color value and intensity are spot on. We could frame these to have them be the same size. Yea," he dragged out the word, "I really like it. You have a good eye, Victoria." He met her gaze.

"Super. How much?"

He quickly did some math on his calculator and gave her the figure.

*Not bad.* "Is that framed and hung?"

The glimmer in his eye came back. "Well, not exactly, usually that's separate."

She thought about how to play this. "I see. Well, I would love to make a decision today, otherwise, I know Mr. Novak will have me talk to Windsor and Cappelli. And I have too much on my plate to want to bother with that."

His eyes rounded slightly at the mention of his competition in town.

"The figure is within my budget, but then framing and installation would kick me out."

"Sure. Maybe you could pick two of the three to hang."

She wrinkled her nose. "That wouldn't look as good, would it? I mean, for such a big wall."

He shrugged, chewing on the inside of his cheek.

She leaned forward a smidge. "And the thing is, I have a feeling after this, there could be more rooms needing a sprucing up."

"Really?"

"Definitely. Especially on Mahogany Row."

He chuckled at the term for the executive floor. "I'll tell you what, Victoria, since you've been so kind, and we would love to have all your future business, I'll get it approved to have the price include framing and installation."

She gave him an exuberant smile. "That would be wonderful."

He made a few notes, and she pulled out her phone.

"And Jason, is this piece still available?" She held up her phone, showing an oil painting of a naked woman, her back to the artist, sitting on her hunches, stretching before a fire with her fingers in her long hair. It was sensual, seductive, and reminded Vicki of herself—the long hair, the curvy ass, even the hint of boob on the side. She knew Pierce would love it in his bedroom.

Justin looked from the phone to her, holding her gaze for a few beats. "I believe it is."

"Good. I want that too." She'd already seen the price, and she was still within her budget. "And have that one delivered here." She handed him a card with Pierce's home address written on the back. "Please feel to call me to coordinate any of this."

Justin smiled and nodded. "Very well. Excellent choices."

They chatted a bit more. She confirmed a few more details, but then she stood to shake his hand and say goodbye.

Justin held her hand for another moment. "Victoria, you are simply captivating. Would it be unprofessional of me to ask you out for dinner sometime."

She smiled. "Thank you. I'll have to take a raincheck. I'm currently seeing someone."

"Okay. I'll talk to you soon. Thanks again." He gave her a wistful smile and headed for the front doors.

Vicki turned to the elevators. She was on a high, and she couldn't wait to tell Pierce all about it.


Victoria stood in his doorway, a sparkle in her eyes.

Pierce'd much rather hear about her meeting than about a cost analysis from Randolph. "Hey, someone just stepped in my office. Let me get with you later, Randolph."

*"Okay. Thanks."*

He hung up his office phone and sat back in his chair. "I presume you have good news to share."

She grinned and stepped into the office. "Indeed." She handed him her notes.

He lifted an eyebrow. "Three pieces, framed and installed? Nice."

"Yes." She folded her arms and leaned against his desk. She acted a bit cagey, and he didn't know why. "Now, you promised me lunch."

He tipped his head. "I did. Let's go and you can tell me all about it."

He locked his door, and they walked side by side to the parking garage. He knew just where to take her.

After a short trip, they arrived at the Waterhouse Building, and was quickly greeted by a valet.

"Where are we going?" she asked.

"You'll see."

The elevator ride to the top of the high-rise wasn't terribly long, and he was instantly greeted by a hostess who recognized him.

*What was her name? Kimberly? Kathy?*

"Good day, Mr. Novak. A table for two?" she asked with a gracious smile.

"Yes, please. Some place a bit secluded."

"Yes, sir."

Victoria eyed him, and he wanted to chuckle.

They were seated in a high booth in the corner. *Perfect.*

"This is a really nice place." She looked out the window of the high-rise to see more of Lower Manhattan.

"It is. I thought it would be a good place to take you to celebrate."

They ordered an appetizer and iced teas. He was in no rush to get back to the office. He would enjoy this time and celebrate with his sweet.

"So, tell me how it went."

"Well, Justin showed me a lot of nice pieces. Most were too small."

*Justin?* Pierce knew he had a bit of a possessive side to him, and it surprised him when she spoke of him, like they'd become friends.

She opened her phone and turned it his way. She moved closer, flipping through each one.

"I like them."

She beamed. "I'm so glad. Justin will let me know when the framing's done, then they can be installed."

The appetizers were delivered, and they ordered their entrees, but Pierce didn't much care. He wanted to hear more about her meeting.

"Justin, huh?"

She batted her lashes and leaned in even closer, her light floral scent filling his nostrils. "He asked me out on a date."

He raised an eyebrow. "He did, now? And what did you say?"

She whispered in his ear. "I told him I'd love to, but I was currently fucking my boss and he probably wouldn't like it."

He pursed his lips together and met her gaze when she sat back. Pierce knew she was joking but hearing her talk like that made his cock want to stand at attention.

Reaching for a bruschetta, he spoke. "Really? I bet that made him crazy hearing that. I know it would me."

She grinned and took a bite. "How crazy, Mr. Novak? So crazy you'd reach under my skirt to see if I was wearing panties during my meeting?"

He growled.

She was toying with him. At this rate, he wouldn't be able to stand for another hour.

He laid a hand on her thigh, pushing her skirt higher. Accepting her challenge.

Her eyes darted around.

"Victoria, higher."

She smoothed her lips together, then slid the skirt higher, giving him more access.

The tablecloth would hide whatever he did to his precious, but still cozying up close was risky when anyone he knew could walk in.

Hell, having her sit this close was already suspect.

He lifted her leg onto his lap, causing her to gasp.

He stroked her inner thigh, making his way higher and higher. "Precious, you'd better be wearing panties. If I find out you weren't, and you met with *Justin*," he sing-songed the kid's name, "you won't be able to sit down for a week."

Her lips gaped, keeping his eye contact as she was held captive to his desires.

His final pass landed on her center covered in wet, warm panties. "That's my girl." He pulled her panties aside. Then, Pierce caught a glimpse of the waiter coming to their table with their entrees.

He pulled back his hand and gripped her thigh with his left hand. "Don't move."

"Oh, God," she whispered under her breath.

The waiter set down their entrees. "Anything else I can get you?"

He smiled. "No, everything looks excellent."

The waiter spun away, not suspecting a thing. Or if he did, he did a great job hiding it.

Pierce reached for his precious. "Now, where was I?" he whispered as it gently pushed a finger inside Victoria's wet pussy.

*Fuck!* She could be the death of him. She made him want to do things he'd never dream of doing with anyone else.

Her eyelids fluttered closed.

He slowly stroked her core and thumbed her clit. "Precious, for teasing me, I have half a mind to lean you over this table and fuck you."

She squirmed under his touch. She was getting close. Damn!

"This pussy is mine—you are mine—until I say so. You know that, don't you?"

"Yes, sir."

He drove a little deeper, a little harder.

That tipped her over the edge. She gripped the table and held her moans as she squirted on his hand.

Fuck, how he wished he could take her this instant.

After she calmed, he pulled away, kissed her neck, and wiped his hand on his napkin. "Leave that skirt high. It seems things are very wet down there."

She opened her glassy eyes and smirked. She looked around making sure no one was looking their way. She took a moment but then dug into her entree.

After a few bites, she started, "There's another thing I bought."

He side-eyed her. "You did?"

She could have bought whatever she wanted. He was sure he'd love it. He was more alive with Victoria than he'd been his entire life. He'd give her the moon and the stars, if he could.

She lifted her phone, showing him a picture of the painting. A woman bathed in warm firelight sat naked before a fireplace looking fucking sensual and sexy.

"I'm having this delivered to your home. I'll hang it in your bedroom."

He stared into her gorgeous eyes that damn-near glowed. "It's gorgeous. This makes me think of you."

She pecked his cheek and whispered, "It's supposed to." She grinned and went back to her meal.

He smiled. It had to be the best present he'd ever received. And to top it off, he grew harder.

They finished eating, paid the bill, and headed to the car. His jacket strategically covered his hard-on. He needed her. Now.

They got settled in his car, and quickly found a parking garage that was nearly full.

She glanced his way; she knew what he wanted.

The moment they parked, she unfastened her seatbelt while he undid his pants.

She easily maneuvered over him, pulled her panties aside, and sank down.

"Fuck, Victoria. So fucking good." He claimed her mouth like he'd done a thousand times, only somehow it was new. Hot, demanding, and uniting them in the most perfect way.

She knew him, knew what he liked. She unbuttoned her blouse and pulled down the cups of her bra, giving him access to her perfect tits.

He growled.

He didn't have much time. "Cum, baby."

She rode him harder and massaged her clit, exploding and whimpering a moment later.

She was perfect for him. He was madly in lust with her, and with the seven weeks left, he couldn't wait to share every possible experience with her.

# Chapter Thirty-Six

♥

Pierce told Vicki to take the rest of the day off. That her skirt was too wet and noticeable. She hated bailing out of work, but *really* hated the idea of coming back from lunch and people seeing her backside hosting a big wet spot.

She had to chuckle. She got out of the cab Pierce had paid for and went into his house.

She immediately went to the closet to slip on some comfy shorts and a tank top. She knew just what to do with her free time. She had a mental list—register for fall classes, reach out to her best friends, and order some more skirts and tops for work.

The day replayed in her head, including the steaming hot lunch. Pierce was most certainly a risk taker. She didn't know what she would do if her father had walked into the restaurant and saw them canoodling in the corner. Pierce definitely let his guard down more since being with her. And just last week, he'd told her he was sleeping better and longer with her in his bed.

She smiled inside. She slept better too, and waking up to Pierce's kisses was cap. She'd never had so much sex before, and it felt amazing. She sighed and opened her laptop to get to work.

Pierce arrived home just before seven. He didn't usually work that late.

"Hey. How was your day?" she asked from the kitchen table where she'd been working.

Without a word, he crossed to her, dropped his jacket over a chair, and, cupping her jaw, he kissed her. Deeply and thoroughly.

She knew the chef likely witnessed the interaction. Warmth spread to her cheeks.

He broke the kiss and met her gaze.

"Well, hello." That was unexpected.

He waggled his brows and grinned.

"I'll get changed, then we can eat," he said to chef as he made his way to his bedroom.

Pierce returned a few short minutes later as chef was plating the food. He'd made a chicken, quinoa, and vegetable dish that smelled divine.

"Mr. Novak, a chocolate cake is under the cover here." Chef pointed to the triple layer confection. "Will that be all?"

"Yes, thank you. Everything is delicious."

The chef pivoted and made his way out.

For several moments, they ate in silence. Vicki didn't realize how hungry she was.

Pierce set down his fork and lifted his wine glass. "You did well today."

She glanced his way and smiled. "Thanks."

"There's something else I want to mention about negotiation."

She rested her fork on the side of her plate and sat back in her chair.

"When you get out in the corporate world—"

"*If* I go into the corporate world."

"Ah, yes, my Gen Z protégé, Human Resources will often lowball offers for women more than men."

She scrunched her nose. "Why?"

"Because women are more likely to take it. Let's say there's an opening that pays 80K a year. The manager has found the best candidate and turns it over to HR. HR will try and save the company money and offer 60K."

Her jaw dropped.

"The candidate may negotiate and get 65K and think she's won the lotto. HR pats themselves on the back because they saved 15K. Meanwhile, a week later that same HR rep offers a man 70K, he counters with 80K and gets the job or he'll walk away."

"What the hell."

He raised his hand. "It's not right. I've already talked to my HR department and all my hiring managers that we won't play that game. If the candidate is good, pay them what they're worth. But Victoria, I tell you this because you don't have to settle."

"I won't."

"That's my girl."

She couldn't say why but she loved hearing Pierce say that to her. He was ticking so many of her boxes—in bed and in her psyche. She couldn't wait to see how much more he was going to teach her.

After dinner, they shared a slice of cake. Actually, Pierce had a bite, and Victoria had the rest.

"You can leave the dishes. The housekeeper will get it. I have a little work to finish then we can watch a movie."

She beamed. "Sounds great."

Pierce headed to his home office and opened his laptop on his desk. He had a bit more work because of the extended lunch he took with his princess. But he didn't want to share that nugget of information. Victoria would feel bad, and he absolutely refused to have her feel bad about anything they were sharing.

This summer had been and continued to be incredible. Beyond his wildest imagination. Seeing her blossom in a work environment and having her in his bed gave him immense pleasure. She was a smart cookie. She could do anything she set her mind to.

After forty minutes of work, he shut everything down and went in search of his desire.

Victoria sat on his oversized, comfortable leather sofa, the TV on low, her nose in her phone.

"Love, did you find something to watch?"

She looked up and smiled. "No, but I didn't really look."

He snatched the remote off the table, took the seat next to her, and pulled her into his side. As he flipped through his cable stations, he spoke. "I was thinking. One weekend soon, I want to get away. Before school starts."

Her eyebrows rose. "Yeah?"

"I was thinking Martha's Vineyard."

"Oh, Pierce," she flung her arms around him and kissed his cheek, "that would be amazing. I've always wanted to go, but my parents could never seem to find the time."

"Great." He held her chin and drew her close for a kiss. Suddenly, the movie didn't matter. "It's settled then." He set the remote down, swung her legs onto his lap, and let his hands wander under her tank top. "I'll make the arrangements. In the meantime…" He laid claim to her lips, just a few minutes away from laying claim to her pussy.

***

The next morning, Vicki waited her usual fifteen minutes before heading to Pierce's office for her next assignment. "Hey—" She froze two steps passed the threshold.

Cary stood in Pierce's office and spun around when he heard her. "Wow. Hi, pumpkin. It's nice to see you here so bright and early." He reached out an arm for her to step into.

"Hi, Dad." Her heart beat double-time.

Would he notice the new diamond earrings and necklace? Would he suspect anything was going on between them?

"I'm excited to get started on my new assignment." She wrapped her arms around his waist, eyeing Pierce, whose face remained neutral.

He peeled her back and glanced at her face. "Well, you certainly seem happy. How's it going?" He looked from her to Pierce.

"Great. I'm learning tons."

"She is," Pierce chimed in.

Cary nodded and smiled. "I'm so glad. Why don't you come over for dinner this weekend? I know your mom would love to see you."

She swallowed hard. "Um..."

His grin grew. "I knew it. You have a boyfriend. Well, how about Sunday night then? You can spend the night and take the train in if you want."

She kept the smile plastered on her face. "That sounds great. Sunday night."

"Cary, I'm going to get Victoria squared away in Procurement. How about I circle back with you later?"

"Yeah." He met the man's eyes. "Sounds good. Let me know when she's due at MIS." He winked, kissed the top of her head, and made his way back to his office. As CIO, Cary managed the entire MIS department.

Vicki waited, then let out a breath. "Holy shit," she said under her breath.

Pierce grinned. "Follow me, please."

She followed him to the elevator, and when they were alone, she asked, "You found that all very amusing, didn't you?"

"Very."

"He could of—"

Pierce looked over at her. "He could have what? He doesn't suspect a thing. Keep your eye on business, and you'll do fine."

She play-glared at him and met his gaze dead-on. "Says the man who fingered my pussy yesterday at lunch."

His mischievous smile returned. He was playing with fire and loved it.

Damn, she wished she had *half* the confidence he did.

# Chapter Thirty-Seven

As the chef prepared a salmon dinner for them, Pierce approached her in the sunroom.

"When are you leaving for school?"

She hated thinking about that, but it was inevitable. "The twenty-second."

He nodded. "You'll spend the night here the twenty-first?"

"Yes." She thought about all her clothes at his place. "If you can help me take a load of stuff to my apartment."

He grinned. "Certainly. And we'll do something special."

Ah, now she knew why all the questions. They still had two weeks, although it was closing in fast.

Was he planning another trip to Martha's Vineyard?

That had to be one of the best trips she'd ever taken. They'd walked hand-in-hand, strolled in and out of shops, ate some incredible food, and made love for hours.

She smiled. Speaking of something special… "Pierce, do we have the house to ourselves tonight?"

He tilted his head. "Of course. It's Friday."

"Okay." *Perfect.*

"I'll be in my office until dinner."

"Mm-hm." She returned to her texts to Larissa. The woman had to know everything going on. Vicki chuckled to herself. Larissa's phone might be melting.

The minute she knew the coast was clear, she ran to the bedroom and into the closet. She'd recently purchased a long silky, champagne-colored gown, which showed off the bit of sun she'd gotten. It wasn't meant to be worn in public. The gown had spaghetti straps, a V-neckline showing off her cleavage, and a slit up to mid-thigh. She stripped down to nothing and slid the gown over her head. She fluffed her hair, touched up her makeup, and dabbed on a hint of her favorite fragrance.

She then cracked the bedroom door and waited until she heard Pierce and chef talking. The smell of something delicious floated in the air.

She slipped on some high heels with a strap around the ankle and sauntered down the hall to the dining room.

The table was already set. Chef came in and set down two covered plates near each other on the massive table.

He smiled and pivoted back to the kitchen.

Quick as lightning, Vicki reached under the V-neck, toyed with her nipples to make them pointed, not that much attention was needed. She glanced to see her nipples were at attention. Perfect.

Three seconds later, Pierce strolled in. He stopped in his tracks and took in the sight of her.

By God, but he was handsome. His work shirt open, revealing a hint of his muscular chest and the sleeves rolled up showing his strong arms.

The depth of his eyes grew. "Victoria, you look lovely." He stepped closer, caressed a hand down her torso to her hip, and kissed her lips and neck.

"Why, thank you, kind sir."

He drew back, smiled, and dragged her chair out for her. He took his own seat.

Chef arrived carrying two decent chocolate mousse glass bowls for dessert. "Will there be anything else, sir?"

"No, thank you. Everything looks amazing. Have a good weekend."

"Good night," he said to them and left.

She removed the food cover, and Pierce placed a hand on her thigh. "I have half a mind to take you over this table right now."

She gasped. "Sir, please. Can a lady eat her meal without hearing such crude remarks?"

The twinkle in his eye told her everything. He *would* take her on that table. And maybe that's what she'd been hoping for.

Over dinner, they talked about work mostly and all she'd accomplished during her internship. He'd told her several times he was proud of her and said it again.

She enjoyed the summer more than she thought she would. Her friends were a little curious she'd only seen them a half a dozen times, but they also understood. Vicki had a hard time leaving Pierce. He was good to her on so many levels—dominating her when she needed it, stretching her comfort zone, treating her like a princess, all of it.

She couldn't get enough. They had sex every day, several times a day sometimes. He had an incredible sex drive and always made sure she enjoyed herself.

Close to finishing, she asked, "Any chance I would be able to drop by some weekend to see you?"

"After you return to school?"

She nodded.

He raised her hand to his mouth and kissed the inside of her wrist. "Abso-fucking-lutely."

That was all she needed to hear. Who knew if she'd start dating someone, but knowing Pierce was always willing to see her made her heart pitter-patter.

As she sipped the last of her wine, Pierce finished his dinner and blotted his mouth. He rose, pulled over a brass cart, and loaded the dishes onto it.

Her heart turned over. She knew what he wanted.

He moved the silverware, the wine glasses, the dessert, all of it.

"Don't we get to eat our desserts?"

He lifted a brow and yanked her hand gently to come to his lap. "You can have your dessert later. I want mine now." And he claimed her mouth without any further hesitation.

She tasted the wine on his lips and tongue as he gripped the back of her neck, holding her just where he wanted her.

"Princess, I love this." His fingertips slowly roamed her clavicle, her cleavage, and over her hard nubs. Easily he slid off one strap, then the other, letting the fabric flow down to her waist.

Instantly, his mouth was on her chest, sucking in a nipple fiercely.

"Unh," she cried out. But it didn't really matter. Pierce could have what he wanted when he wanted it.

He tortured and worshipped her breasts for several long moments before he spoke. "Stand up, Victoria."

She rose and the gown clung to her hips.

"Arms up."

She lifted her arms and with one fluid movement, he raised the gown up over her head, leaving her in her diamonds and high heels.

"Fuck me." He grabbed her waist, kissing her tummy and breasts. "I will never get enough of this incredible body." He drew back, eyeing her from head to toe. "Something's missing," he said as he stroked a finger between her breasts and straight down to her mound.

Pulling back, he reached into his pocket. Drawing out what looked like a long necklace, she eyed the gold chains with little diamonds dangling from them.

She gasped.

He circled her waist and clasped the gold chain around her waist—actually two chains, a smaller one looped and dangling from the larger one. From each chain hung a mini strand of diamonds, stopping just above her mound.

She glanced down and caressed her fingertips over the jewelry. "Pierce, it's beautiful."

He smiled. "I had it made for you." His hands roamed her body as his kisses peppered her torso.

The wetness gathered quickly, and the ache built at her sex, eager to have him claim her.

He lifted her onto the table and one at a time, placed her feet on the arms of the chair.

She sat before him open wide.

He stood in between her legs, cupped the back of her neck, and devoured her mouth. One hand slid south, playing with her pussy, spreading her essence.

She reached between her legs for his pants, unfastening them and pulling him out. She cupped him and stroked him. God, she would never tire of the feel, the weight, the size of him in her.

He broke the kiss and commanded, "Lie back."

She lay on the hard wood table and instantly felt his mouth on her breasts as his hands stroked her torso, hips, and thighs.

He trailed south and circled her clit with the tip of his tongue.

"Ah." She grabbed the side of his head.

He made love to her pussy in the most exquisite way. With his hands, he pushed against her thighs, spreading her further.

"Ah." She straddled a fine line between pleasure and pain.

He slid two fingers inside her, and in no time her orgasm flew to the surface.

She bowed her back and cried out his name.

Before she fully came down, he dove into her.

"Unh."

"This is what you wanted all night, wasn't it princess?" His deep timbre raced to her core.

"Yes. Yes. Please."

He pumped into her, detonating another orgasm.

She panted and became vaguely aware of his release.

He growled in ear. "Fuck, baby."

She wrapped her arms and legs around him, wishing he was completely naked.

*Soon*, she thought. They would be in his bed replaying their love making again. And she couldn't wait.

# Chapter Thirty-Eight

♥

Vicki's final week at Palencia was here. And that meant her final week with Pierce. She dreaded leaving him. She'd gotten so accustomed to playing house with him. Having him spoon her naked body as she fell asleep in his bed after making love to her. And having him wake her up to fuck her before getting ready for work. He was everything she wanted in a man—generous, caring, commanding, and loving.

Her head knew they couldn't be together, but her heart and body wished there was a way.

Making her way to Pierce's office for a meeting, she ran into Johnny. He looked as surprised as she.

"Hey, stranger. How are you?"

He made a show of scanning her body up and down. "My goodness, don't you look damn fine."

She felt a strange vibe coming off him, but kept it conciliatory, nonetheless. "Thanks. What brings you by?"

He stepped closer, into her personal space.

She glanced around and saw no one nearby. Her heart rate sped.

"I'm running an errand for my mom." Then he leaned down to her ear. "And don't you look incredibly fuckable in that skirt and those heels."

"What?" She pushed back and met his glare. "What the hell, Johnny?"

He closed the space again, backing her up against a cubicle wall. "Vicki, you have the finest ass I have ever seen. Haven't I told you that?" His hand reached around and cupped her ass.

The rage and fear flew to the surface, and she could barely see straight. What happened to harmless Johnny?

*Courage.* It was there, deep inside. She knew it was. Pierce showed her she had courage.

She licked her cool lips.

"Do I?" She used her most seductive voice, then stroked his arm down to the hand on her ass. She pulled it off, smiling, like she had a delicious plan just for him.

And boy, did she.

She grabbed his fingers and bent them back as she braced the arm still with the other hand. "If you ever do anything like that again, I will grab your balls and tie them into a bow for your Christmas present. Are we clear?" She hardly recognized the low, menacing voice coming from her mouth.

The color faded from his face and sweat gathered on his brow. "Okay. Okay. Just let go."

She didn't move.

"Please," he begged.

Pierce stood back in the doorway, peering out just enough to witness what that dickhead was doing to his girl. He was five seconds from pummeling the guy for treating Victoria like a piece of meat and grabbing her ass.

Then Victoria took control of the situation. Johnny looked to be about ready to pee his pants. Pierce couldn't make out exactly what was said, but he scampered away the second she released him.

Pierce came up to her and wrapped his arms around her. To hell with whomever saw them.

"Are you alright?" he whispered in her hair.

He could feel her pounding heart against his chest. He didn't say a word. He led her to his office and loaded his laptop and a few files in his case.

Then he locked his office and told Rhonda he had to leave early. He had to get his girl out of there. She was his priority. He'd deal with Johnny later.

"Where are we going?" she asked. "I'm okay now, Pierce. Just a little shook up."

He reached for her hand and kissed it. "I know, but we don't need to be around here anymore today. Not to mention, if I see the asswipe, I'm liable to rearrange his face."

She chuckled and that made him feel better.

They drove out to a secluded spot by a lake a little farther upstate. Just getting on the highway about four, he called a restaurant nearby and ordered the works, including a blanket to sit on. Then gave them directions on where to meet.

He parked, and they stared at the peaceful water for several moments. He'd always loved this lake. Occasionally, he'd come with a friend or two to fish early in the morning.

Finally, she spoke. "I always thought he was harmless." She shook her head. "I never thought he was secretly a dick."

Pierce nodded. Well, the punk would definitely not be stepping foot on his property again.

"I mean, what if we *weren't* in the office? How far would he have gone if there was no risk of anyone catching him?"

Pierce held her close and kissed her head again. He couldn't stand the thought of something bad happening to Victoria.

"You would have handled him just like you did today. And I'm proud of you." Pierce didn't bother to mention that he would have a little conversation with the punk as well. Pierce would ensure he knew not to treat women like that *ever*.

After some time, a car drove up. A waiter dressed in black and white exited and retrieved two large bags from his back seat. "Mr. Novak?"

Pierce met the young man and took the bags. "Thank you so much, Brett." He read the name tag and handed him several bills, enough to cover dinner and the extra service.

Victoria joined him on the grass and helped him set up their impromptu picnic. "Wow, money really does buy anything."

"Not everything, but almost." He wagged his brows.

The restaurant thought of everything—dishes, cutlery, napkins, glasses for the wine. This was why Pierce rewarded good service and remained loyal to places that treated him well.

"Take off your shoes, get comfortable."

She slipped off her heels and took the plate he offered.

They ate, chatting a bit, but mostly enjoying the incredible peace and the calm, warm breeze.

Victoria's shoulders relaxed, and she was back to her usual self—making wise cracks and laughing at his ridiculous jokes.

He loved to see her happy. He hated the thought of her having to leave, but oddly he was excited to see how she'd flourish at school and in the real world.

As they finished, he piled everything he could in the bags and set them aside. He reclined holding his glass of wine with his free arm out wide. Victoria smiled as she laid beside him, her arm across his torso.

He felt so at ease with her, he knew there was only one emotion that could do this to him.

After a few quiet moments, he worked on his shirt and yanked off his leather belt.

She watched him as he then unbuttoned her blouse and unfastened her skirt.

Wordlessly, she let him strip them down—he in his briefs, her in her white thong.

"Victoria, this summer has been incredible for me." He kissed her lips, diving in, memorizing every nuance about her. He traveled down her neck to her perfect breasts.

"For me too." She moaned when he took her succulent nipples into his mouth one at a time.

"So perfect." He kissed and licked her belly, making her way to her smooth sex. He peeled away the fabric and wasted no time claiming a tiny bundle of nerves.

"Mmm." Her fingers laced through his hair, and he felt her hips lift upward, wanting more.

He gave her just what she wanted. Her first orgasm came easily.

He ripped her panties away, a man driven to want to give his woman everything under the sun. He spread her legs, making more room for his shoulders and claiming her in just the way he knew she liked. He'd learned her body inside and out—every moan, every cry, every flex, every whimper. She was his in every sense of the word.

When he knew she was close, he pulled back. He pulled off his briefs and came back on top of her. He gripped her hands in his and easily slid into her.

"Pierce." Her eyelids fell closed as she savored the contact just as he did. Intimate, soothing, erotic.

"Baby, look at me."

She opened her eyes, glazed with lust.

"You know I love you, don't you?"

Wetness grew in her eyes. "I love you too."

He stroked her methodically. They moved together as if they were meant for each other.

"I'll miss you, but I'm so excited for you to get out there and claim your place in the world."

She smiled even as a tear streaked down into her hair.

He released one hand to reach between them and caress her clit. He kissed her as he slowly made love to her and brought her to orgasm.

She panted in his mouth. He didn't let her go. Claiming her pussy, her mouth, her clit, he persisted until she climaxed again.

God, he loved the feeling of her flexing around him, drawing him in, wanting him to be one with her. Her body's own natural reaction to their joining.

He couldn't hold on any longer. He released inside his love, spurting three, four times. He filled her and loved the connection they had that no one would ever know about.

He collapsed on the blanket and drew her into his side.

"Pierce, this feels so good," she said, mirroring his exact thoughts and how incredible her naked body felt next to his.

She hoisted up on an elbow and looked down at him. "I was thinking. Maybe you should get a place in the city, like for the weekends."

He grinned. "I see. Someplace close to campus?"

She smiled and nodded.

He rolled her on her back and kissed and suckled her neck. "I think I'm ready for round two."

She laughed and wrapped her legs and arms around him. Giving him everything he could want and receiving everything he gave her.

# Plush Pink Lips

# Chapter Thirty-Nine

♥

Lance's doorbell rang at eight that night. He wasn't expecting anyone in particular, especially over the summer when most of the Lakemont students were home for three months. There was one person it could be.

He opened the door to Anabelle, his best friend since elementary school. She was a complete sweetheart and like a little sister to him. "Hey Ana, c'mon in. I'm surprised to see you." He hugged her because, one, she was like family, and two, because her body felt so damn good next to his.

"I hope I'm not bugging you. I was just so bored."

Ana lived in one of the student apartment buildings on campus, which was likely looking like a ghost town now.

Lance lived in an apartment off campus. His job as a teacher assistant and research assistant for the psychology department meant working twelve months a year while getting his master's degree.

He'd been thinking of heading over to Jake's, a friend and fellow research assistant in the Physics department, but this was much better. "No work tonight?"

She shook her head.

"Wanna beer or a glass of wine?"

"White wine would be great."

He went to his fridge. "So, where's the boyfriend?"

She groaned. "A family reunion-trip thing. He's gone for two weeks."

He grimaced. "That sucks."

She took the glass he offered then followed him to the sofa. "Yeah."

"If you can stand it, I'm watching a French movie. There are subtitles though."

"Okay. Sounds cool."

He hit play.

She snuggled in closer to him, something she'd done many times before when hanging at his place. She had a younger sister but had always wanted a brother. He had a younger brother but had always wanted a sister. For years, they filled the "surrogate" roll for one another.

He wrapped an arm around her.

After several minutes, a sex scene came on, and her breathing changed a bit. Or maybe that was his.

Changing the focus, he started, "So, you sorta sighed when I asked about Matt. Is everything all right?"

She let out a nervous little laugh and took a sip of her wine. "I guess I'm questioning why I miss him so much. He makes me laugh and that's a big thing for me."

Lance tilted his head. "But you don't miss other things, like the sex?"

She shrugged. "He definitely plays it safe in that department."

"Have you said anything to him?"

She glanced up at him. "I don't think I can do that. I mean, I'm not sure what to say. And…" She shrugged again.

Lance pursed his lips, both of them still watching the naked action before them.

Lance would bet his last dollar she was too unsure of herself and shy, she would never say anything to Matt. He turned to face her. "An, do you want me to help?"

It was a risky proposition. They were best friends, and if this backfired, he could ruin the best relationship he ever had. But Ana meant the world to him. He had to give it a try.

"Huh?"

"Like I could show you a few things, we can talk about. Maybe you'd feel more confident talking to your man then."

She swallowed. She was sweet and innocent. Discussing sex probably ranked up there with a root canal.

Lance had a suspicion this boyfriend was her first sexual experience.

Her naivete was the main reason her parents pushed her to attend Lakemont, because Lance was there. He could keep an eye on her.

"You mean like sex and stuff."

He tipped his head. "Sorta. Nothing too heavy, but I could sorta walk you through a few things during these few weeks. Then, when he returns, you'll feel more confident to tell him what you like because you'll know. And if he asks about this new approach, tell him you were reading Dr. Ruth."

She laughed.

Lance loved to see her smile. Always had.

"Um, I guess it's okay. We need to go slow. Okay? And I definitely need to keep my privates covered."

He nearly grinned at her choice of words. Instead, he nodded because he could certainly work with that. He knew his skillset. He could work Ana into a frenzy in those two weeks, she'd be like a new woman. A new wanton woman.

"Okay, take a big sip and then hand me the glass."

She drank, and he turned down the TV volume. "We'll talk a little bit as we go about learning what you like."

She nodded. Her pupils were dilated, and he was hard. He'd fantasized about something like this for God knew how long.

"I'll start with some simple things."

"Okay."

He reached behind her head and carefully removed a ponytail holder. Then, he massaged her scalp.

Her eyelids fluttered closed, and he moved in closer, slowly kissing her face, her eyes, her cheeks, and a few pecks on her lips.

"Good, huh?" He knew it was. Her breathing had accelerated. "And yet so simple, right?"

She nodded but didn't open her eyes.

He trailed his kisses down her neck to her clavicle. He continued over her T-shirt, knowing he'd have to amend that situation.

"Now, I'm gonna reach up and pull down your bra straps a little."

The flush on her cheeks was gorgeous.

He slid fingers under the cotton fabric, finding the straps. He pulled down as much as he could. Then he shifted to the floor and in between her legs. He tugged her down a little, so she was in a more reclined position.

Honestly, he loved the idea of being between her legs. He probably shouldn't think about it or want it, but he couldn't stop the desire to want to learn more about what turned his precious friend on.

Returning to her neck, he kissed her soft skin and tongued a little circle over her racing pulse point. He made his way to her upper chest, kissing the covered area, and stopping at the bra line.

Her breathing came heavier now, a hard pant.

*Excellent.*

He kissed her cleavage, following a line down to her stomach. As he kissed, he lifted her shirt to expose her tummy. Her tan just proved she was regularly going to the pool in those little bikini's he loved, even though in his dreams she sunbathed nude.

"How are you feeling?" He lifted his eyes to gaze at her face.

"Um, good."

Her lips gaped, and she looked positively beautiful.

Lance was fairly certain her boyfriend wasn't taking care of her like he should.

"Baby, I want you to do me a favor now. The padding on your bra can block a lot of sensation." He rose upright yet remained on his knees and offered her his hands.

She took them and sat up.

"I'm going to reach behind and unfasten your bra, so you can take it off."

She opened her mouth to speak.

"Your T-shirt will stay on. I'm honoring our agreement."

She licked her lips.

He didn't wait for her acknowledgement. He slid under the fabric to unhook her bra.

She took one strap off at a time and pulled it down her right arm.

Her nipples were at attention. It was one of the most beautiful things he'd ever seen. "That's right. Now you can lie back again."

He went back to kissing a safe zone—her stomach. Slowly, he made his way north. Kissing under her gorgeous C-cups, over to the side, and up the center. Each breast got the same attention.

Then for the *pièce de résistance*. He landed his mouth over her right nipple, and she moaned. God, it was fucking beautiful. He kissed and licked, and when he knew it was safe, he sucked. He punished her with such exquisite torture, by the end of this he'd have her begging for all he had to offer.

He loved on her breasts, kneading them gently, probably making her insanely wet. Her panties were surely wetter than her T-shirt right now.

She moaned again and squirmed some.

He knew she was close to coming. *That's enough for tonight's lesson.*

He rose upright, pulled down her T-shirt, and watched as she opened her eyes.

"What…"

"Precious, let's not do too much the first night. I want you to go home and think about tonight, especially what you were feeling, what you liked and didn't like. Come back tomorrow night, and we can talk about it some more. Okay?"

She nodded, her pretty doe eyes looking up at him with eager anticipation.

"Why don't you go to the bathroom and get dressed." He stood and helped her upright.

When she was behind closed doors, he pulled out a notepad and made her a shopping list. This would be good for her, and hella fun for him.

She came out a few minutes later and stood at his side.

"You did great tonight."

"Thank you."

"Here is a shopping list. These are things we will need for the next two weeks. And maybe beyond." He grinned. "The starred items are what you will wear tomorrow. Okay?"

She nodded and took the folded paper and the three bills he put inside.

She gasped. "Three hundred dollars! I can't take this."

He drew her close and pecked her lips. "Shh, princess. Do as I say, and you will enjoy your lessons. And your boyfriend will never want to leave you alone for this long again."

Her smile blossomed. She clearly loved the idea, and Lance felt his stomach turn.

She pecked his lips, shoved the paper in her purse, and headed out to her car.

Lance watched her through the front window.

*Fuck me!*

# Chapter Forty

❤

Ana made it to her campus apartment building still panting. What the hell was that? Her best friend, whom she'd forced herself to think of as only platonically, offered his help in learning more about sex. The goal being to have more fun and get closer to Matt.

She locked the door behind her, dropped her purse on the side table, and immediately went to turn down the air conditioning. Her temperature must have risen to two hundred degrees.

She plopped down on a chair and retrieved his list.

4 pairs of white cotton thongs *

1 lacy black thong

1 lacy thong in your favorite color

3 mini thongs, different colors

1 see-through bra

1 see-through T-shirt

2 underboob T-shirts

1 deep V-neck, loose tank top

4 flowing short skirts (that can be worn in public)*

Wow! This was quite a list. She wasn't so sure about some of these things—they were definitely risqué but she had to trust him. She didn't have much choice if she wanted his help.

Now, where to find this stuff.

*Damn! Why was it so hot?*

Ana stripped out of her T-shirt and shorts, then opened the laptop her parents gave her freshman year.

She looked, read, clicked, and searched some more. Okay, she had most everything picked out, *and* they offer expedited shipping. She had to buy the white cotton thongs and the skirts locally because Lance said he wanted her to wear them for tomorrow.

She checked out and exhaled.

Wow! What a night. What a truly amazing night.

Her smokin' hot friend was teaching her about sex.

For the longest time, Ana secretly had a crush on Lance. He was kind, funny, and so good looking. Her girlfriends had always wanted to hang with her in the hopes of seeing him. They constantly called her lucky.

Ha! If only they knew what she was up to now.

Tonight, she'd vacillated about his offer. They grew up together and were like brother and sister, *and* she had a boyfriend. But maybe because they were so close, it didn't count as cheating. Plus, she'd told him her privates had to be covered. She was proud of herself for adding that little piece in there.

But laying on his sofa, receiving all those incredible kisses, she was so turned on. She'd hoped he might help her to come, but no such luck. Her face got warm at the thought.

*Where is this coming from?*

Licking her lips, she checked beneath her panties. She was wet.

Gosh!

She turned off the lights, grabbed a glass of water, and headed for her bedroom. She needed to put out this fire. Hopefully, tomorrow he could find a way to do it.

***

At eight o'clock, Ana rang Lance's doorbell and shook out her hands. She was nervous, but she didn't need to be.

He greeted her with a smile. "Hi, pumpkin. Come on in. Want something to drink?"

"How about some water." Her voice sounded timid, even to her.

He smiled, brought both waters to the living room, and sat beside her. "How're you doing? How're you feeling?"

She swallowed some water and met his big blue eyes. "I feel good."

"How did it go last night after you left here?"

"Um..."

He seemed to be waiting.

*Do I actually have to say it?*

"Yes?"

"I, um, was still turned on."

"And what did you do about it?"

She felt the warmth rise in her cheeks. "I masturbated."

He lifted her chin to face him. "That's good. How did that feel?"

"Good. Um..." She couldn't say it.

"Go 'head, baby. What else?"

"I was going to say that I wanted you to do that."

He met her gaze, penetrating her with those intoxicating eyes. "Okay, baby. That's some good stuff. How did you do with the list?"

"I got most of it online, but it should be here soon."

He nodded, then reached to cup her jaw. He placed little butterfly kisses on her face again like the previous night. She never realized how much she liked that.

He landed his lips on hers, giving her gentle, slow kisses. She didn't know if she should open her mouth, but she did a little. He licked her bottom lip.

Oh God, it was so good. She wanted more. She opened her mouth more and held her tongue close to the front for him. Then, she felt it—his warm wet tongue gliding into her mouth.

Oh, how many times had she thought about this? Her heartrate ratcheted higher, and she was very aware of her nipples peaking under her bra.

He wrapped his arms around her, brought her snug against his hard body, and probed the recesses of her mouth more deeply. He was such an incredible kisser, she didn't want it to end.

Unfortunately, it did.

He stopped. Without saying a word, he met her gaze and reached under her T-shirt.

She knew what he was planning to do.

"Baby, when you're with a man, you don't have to rush things. I think in this case, since you'll be keeping your shirt on, it would okay to remove your bra now."

She nodded and helped him slip off the garment. There was something sexy about wearing only a T-shirt for Lance.

He stared at her chest a moment, then reclined her as he'd done the night before.

"I'm going to do a lot of what I did last night, but I'm going to go below your waist too. Okay? I'll make sure you stay covered."

She nodded. A thrill raced through her. It was funny, but when she was with Lance, she didn't really think about Matt. At all. But maybe it didn't matter if ultimately this was all to help her relationship with Matt.

Lance kissed her neck and pulled against the fabric to kiss and lick her chest.

In hindsight, the crew neck T-shirt was probably not the best choice. She would remember that for future lessons.

His kisses traveled to her upper breasts. He went excruciatingly slow.

Ana loved his kisses, and how he treated her. He took his time, and as much as it drove her crazy, she positively loved it. Maybe it was because he was her best friend, whom she already adored, but she hoped like crazy Matt could make her feel just as good.

Like before, he avoided kissing *all* of her breast, instead he lifted her shirt, higher this time, and kissed the exposed skin. He even pulled against the waistline of her skirt to expose more of her stomach. Ana couldn't help but squirm a little. It all felt so good, she wanted more. She licked her lips, but her mouth was too dry.

When Lance had covered her entire tummy with kisses, he moved up to the underneath of her breasts.

*Wow!* She laced her fingers through his brown hair and savored the sweetness.

Shortly, he started kissing and licking her right nipple, then her left. She bowed her back, but he didn't seem to mind.

She was trembling. She could actually feel her body trembling, but she wasn't cold. She tried taking a few deep breaths, but it didn't seem to help.

Lance looked up at her. "It's okay, baby. It's because your body is turned on. You don't have to worry that something's wrong." He gave her a small smile, and she smiled back.

That was reassuring.

"How about I move my kisses to another location now. Are you ready?"

She nodded.

"If at any time, you need me to stop, just let me know. Also, like when you touched my hair, you're welcome to touch any part of me. You don't need permission."

She smushed her lips together and nodded again. *Please just keep me covered.*

She wasn't a cheater. Letting her bestie help her was okay. If it got too intimate, she'd never forgive herself.

Gently, his hands slid under her skirt over her thighs. With each pass, her skirt came higher. She wanted this. She wanted his kisses on her sex. Matt didn't do a lot of that, but maybe it was because she needed to tell him how she liked it. How it would make her cum. Lance could help her learn how best to make her cum in this position.

Her white panties came into view, and then he bunched her skirt on her stomach. Her heart beat like crazy.

The wet spot on his princess's white panties was evident instantly. God, how he loved turning Ana on.

When she'd said she'd wished he was the one to give her her orgasm, he knew he was golden. He could give her an orgasm every night until the two weeks was up. He wanted her so addicted to his orgasms, she'd not want to go back to her boyfriend.

Where did that thought come from?

But seriously, Matt was a stupid ass! You don't leave a woman like Ana—sweet, kind, book smart, with a deliciously hot body—alone for two fucking weeks.

He started in a safe area, kissing her thighs and her lower belly. When he knew she ached for relief, he moved his mouth to the fabric-covered areas, making his way to her covered mound. Slowly, he headed south. He pushed her legs a little wider and held them there. His gut told him he could give her more than one orgasm.

He covered the entire area with kisses and a few licks. She tasted and smelled of ambrosia. She no doubt would have her panties entirely soaked before she left his place.

He took long sweeping licks, starting low and working to her clit. There, he circled a bit and started the process again.

She moaned when he made love to her pussy. She writhed under his attention, and her fingers threaded through his hair.

He loved the feel of her touch, and he couldn't wait for her to want to discover more. He had at least prepared himself and wore loose shorts for tonight's "lesson."

Now, to tip her over the edge. He held her legs firmer and focused all his attention on her clit. Even with the fabric in the way, he knew he could give her just what she wanted.

She moaned and at the first twitch of her clit, her cries grew louder.

*Fuck!* How he wanted to slide in a finger or two. He could make it so much more powerful with internal stimulation too.

He didn't stop.

She squirmed and panted. "Lance," came out on a breath.

He glanced up at her face to make sure it wasn't something other than being filled with lust.

She likely experienced the intensity of that orgasm, but he wasn't finished.

"Precious, some women have an easier time having another orgasm close to the first one."

Her lips gaped, and she tracked his movements as he went back to making love to her sweet clit.

In the span of a few short minutes, he had her cumming twice more.

Her panties were soaked, and she slumped on his sofa.

She looked freshly fucked, even though this was just the beginning.

He rose to the sofa, sat next to her, and kissed her damp forehead. "I'm so proud of you."

She chuckled even as she panted.

"You did great tonight." He kissed her hair a few more times and held her into his side.

He must have held her for five minutes, when she lifted off the back of the sofa and met his gaze.

"Thank you for everything." Her doe eyes had him melting again.

"You're welcome."

She glanced down, a clear show of the evidence of his arousal. "You're turned on too."

He nodded. "You don't have to worry about that, precious." *Those lessons can wait.*

She looked down again, bit her lip, and reached her fingertips for his hard length trapped in shorts and briefs. Her jaw hung open. She no doubt discovered the size of him.

*Don't worry about that, princess.*

She pulled back her hand, blinked, and grasped her glass of water. "Okay, I better head out now."

Probably a good idea. This was only their second lesson. There was time to teach his beautiful girl how, with trust, she could lower her guard and soak up all the pleasure a man could give her.

# Chapter Forty-One

♥

*H*oly guacamole! Lance had made her cum three times tonight. She felt so pleasantly relaxed, she couldn't describe the euphoric feeling.

And then, she felt his erection. Wow! He was so big. She didn't know how big, but it was bigger than Matt's penis.

She thought about the night over and over, until she dozed off.

When she slept, she dreamt of Lance. He had taken her to some nature area and had her up against a tree. He was removing her clothes and somehow, she knew to let him. Then, he whispered, *I want you naked so I can kiss your entire body.*

Oh, it'd felt so real. So good.

It was Monday, and she had to work that day. Oh crap, she needed to remember to tell him: she worked late twice this week. Did that mean they couldn't do their lessons?

Her heart sank.

Prying herself from her comfortable bed, she went to make tea, and the idea hit her. She thought of something she could wear for her lesson tonight.

Lance had told her the same as before—white panties and a flowing skirt. But he didn't specify the top.

She had the perfect idea, but she only had two hours before work.

***

At eight o'clock, Lance opened the door to his princess, and fuck!

She'd worn a skirt as he told her to, but her top was a crop top. Not just any crop top. One with four snaps which held her perfect boobs in place. It was pink—her favorite color. She had the top snap undone. From the looks of her protruding nipples, she'd skipped the bra.

He took her hand, led her inside, and slammed his lips to her mouth. He devoured her, his half-mast cock going to full mast. He broke the kiss. "I love this top. I love how you took the initiative. Some things on your list, you will learn, not only make you feel sexy, but look good to a man. If your man gets turned on visually, he will want to do wonderful things to you." He smiled.

Her cheeks turned pink.

He brought her to the sofa, ice water already waiting. "Is there anything from yesterday's lesson you want to review or discuss?"

"I, um … I liked everything."

"Great. Anything that could be changed?"

She shook her head.

He already knew that answer, but he had to ask to make sure his precious stayed comfortable through the entire process.

Their mothers were practically sisters. Lance and Ana had known each other and been friends since he was eight and she was five. They were practically brother and sister. And that fact could bubble up at any point and rapidly put out her fire. If he was to get his holy grail, he had to ease her into it.

He nodded. "Today, we'll expand the lesson again. I want to put some pillows behind you to support your back more."

"Okay."

He placed the pillows, and caging her in, he brushed her hair aside and kissed her exposed skin. His lips and tongue worked their way over her delicate neck, her clavicle, down her cleavage.

"Ana, this shirt is so perfect because today's lesson will be more ... tactile."

She'd opened her eyes to his words. "Oh, okay."

He knew she wasn't entirely sure what he meant, but she would soon find out.

He reached his hands to her shirt and danced his fingertips over her full tits and then slid down the sides of her torso. He didn't stop his kissing, and after a few moments, his hands skated upward, blatantly over her breasts.

She moaned, and her eyelids fluttered.

He cautiously released all the snaps, allowing more of her beautiful breasts open to his mouth and his hands.

He kissed and licked her lower as his hands gently pressed her tits toward the center.

*Fuck!* In this position, a little areola escaped from behind the pink fabric. He moved only his thumbs to dance over her nipples.

She mewled, and it was music to his ears.

He asked against her skin, "Can you tell the difference in my thumbs today compared to my mouth the other times?"

She nodded quickly.

He chuckled. What he wouldn't give to be able to take her bare nipples into his mouth. How good he could make her feel. Instead, he settled for capturing her precious nubs over the shirt.

She moaned.

With his mouth, he toyed with her nipples, one at a time, as his thumb caressed the neglected side. A synchronization of pleasure was sure to take his princess higher.

He didn't let up on loving her tits. Over the fabric or on her soft skin, he kissed and loved her the way she deserved. The way, Lance suspected, her boyfriend wasn't even coming close to giving this incredible woman.

She panted hard and writhed beneath his ministrations. She was ready for more.

He slid his right hand down her torso, searching for the hem of her skirt. He slipped beneath the fabric, massaging her thigh as he made his way north. When his hand felt the wet cotton, it took all his strength not to pull the confection aside and finger-fuck her.

*No,* he reprimanded himself, *it's too early for that.*

He settled for creating soft circles over her clit, working in long strokes down her covered slit.

Her hips flexed into his hand.

*Good girl.* She was getting ready to peak.

Was it his imagination or was she cumming quicker and quicker every time?

That might require another lesson—edging.

She exploded and moaned, but of course, he didn't let up. Her hard nub was like a precious magic button with the touch of his finger.

Lance loved learning how to please her. Recently, he'd lain in bed, dreaming of the many ways to please her, the many ways to show her what it could be like to not only be in touch with her sexuality, but to embrace it. And most importantly, by the end of their time together, to scrutinize whom she allowed to experience and share that sexuality with.

Men were simple beings, not much was required to bring them to completion. Lance never really allowed himself to think about Ana that way, but now he wanted to share any lesson he possibly could with her.

His precious exploded again, and moaned, "Lance."

God, he loved to hear his name fall from her lips while high on passion.

His finger didn't stop but he lessened the pressure. Meanwhile, her shirt had big round wet spots over her nipples from his tongue stimulating her.

He gave her another two orgasms and sensed she was done for the night. That was probably for the best so that he could go into his bedroom and relieve his excruciating ache.

He held her close, kissed her damp forehead, and whispered, "You did great, baby. You're letting your body take in the sensation and awaken the passion and lust that lays deep inside."

Her breathing returned to normal, and she looked up at him. "Lance." She glanced down at his crotch and back at him.

He wanted to chuckle. He cupped her jaw and pecked her lips. "Baby, I want you to use your words."

She licked her lips. "You're still hard."

"And?"

"And I don't think that's fair."

He nodded and let her work out a solution she was comfortable with. She might be ready to hold him in her hand, but it had to be her decision. He already told her she didn't need permission.

Pulling her hand from beside her body, she gently reached over and cupped his erection through his shorts.

He growled and let his eyes close. He wanted her to see for herself the power she had within to please a man. A man of her choosing.

She stroked him up and down, and he cursed the layers of fabric between them.

Again, all in good time.

She added more pressure, and he convulsed. "God, Ana, your hand feels so good."

In another few short moments, he came. It was probably an insane mess in there, but nothing he couldn't clean up.

He opened his eyes and met her gaze. "Thank you, baby. That was perfect."

She smiled.

He kissed her, then stood and took her hand.

"Oh, I have to work late Thursday and Saturday this week."

*Fuck!* Of course, she did. He kept a poker face. "That's okay. We have the rest of this week and then Friday."

The sparkle in her eyes dimmed.

As much as it hurt him to see her disappointment, it spoke volumes about how much she valued their time together. Truly, they'd been friends, close friends growing up. That friendship wasn't going any-where. Now, adding this new dimension to their relationship—one that she was becoming addicted to—was all he could ask and hope for. He kissed her on her forehead and watched her go to her car.

The glow inside for his lovely girl had never been stronger.

Now, to clean up his pants.

# Chapter Forty-Two

A na scolded herself. Why was she disappointed about not seeing Lance Thursday or Saturday? He was just her bestie, helping her out. It's not like she wouldn't be seeing him again.

*Besides, what were you expecting? To go over there at midnight.* He probably had to work Friday morning. He wouldn't want to be up late.

She sighed. She had to accept whatever he could give her. She was already learning so much about herself and what she liked. She hoped Matt was receptive to her new requests. Because, really, his style was a bit more rushed than Lance's.

God, just the thought of him had her getting wet.

*Is that okay?* Should she be feeling that way about her best friend?

God, she was a jumble of mixed emotions.

Tuesday morning, she received Lance's text.

*Good morning, precious. Tonight please wear one of your underboob shirts and lacy panties. You can change here.*

She swallowed hard and a thrill raced through her. She had to work this afternoon, but damn, she couldn't wait until tonight.

✳✳✳

At seven-fifty that night, his doorbell rang. Lance chuckled. His eager princess was early.

"Hey."

"Hey." She wore jeans, T-shirt, and a baseball cap. "Can I get ready in the bathroom?"

"Be my guest." He waved his arm in the direction.

A few moments later, she came out and walked to the sofa. She had on a pale blue shirt with her black lace thong, no bra or ballcap. Her hair cascaded over her shoulders.

*Fuck!*

He rose to greet her. He knew he'd pushed the limits asking for the underboob shirts, but if he could keep her nipples covered, he had to believe she'd grow more comfortable.

"Baby, you look so good." *So fuckable.* He kissed her plush pink lips. "Come over here." He led her to the wall, facing it. "Hands right here." He lifted her hands up the wall, over her head. "Good. Now, hold them here."

"Okay," she breathed out.

God, her round, heart-shaped ass called to him. He cupped her glorious globes and massaged them. His dick grew harder.

She mewled.

"As you're learning, a woman's physiology is more complex than a man's. You have several erogenous zones." He preferred to do this exercise on the bed, but he feared it would freak her out.

He moved her shiny brown hair to the side and continued his gentle massages while kissing her neck. Her pants came quicker. He would dare to say his princess's body was becoming accustomed to his kisses, his touch, and could quickly ready itself for him.

His dick was hard as fucking granite.

He stroked his hands down the shirt, and back up underneath it, stroking and caressing. Then he slid to her tummy and moved upward.

She tensed.

"Take it easy, baby. I know where not to go." *For now.*

His hands stroked her front to the underside of her boobs. Her shirt was really more like a crop top, but for these purposes it was loose and that was all that mattered.

His hand glossed up the side and over, avoiding her nipples, which he suspected were diamond-hard.

His hands went back to her round ass, and she whimpered.

He played a little, even massaging over her thong along her crack.

Her legs shifted wider.

*That's my girl.*

"Now, baby, I want you to feel stimulation on ass as well as your torso."

"Okay," she said hesitantly.

"So, I'm going to have part of me caress you, with my clothes on, so I can continue to kiss and caress your body with my hands."

"Okay."

He was sure she was nervous but also trusted him enough to safely go to the next level. Especially after what they shared the prior night.

Lance undid his button and fly on his shorts, pushing them to the floor.

She glanced down to see the garment but didn't say a word.

*Perfect.* One step closer.

"Now, I'm going to slide your thong down a bit, but I know not to uncover your sacred entrance."

He could see the glow tinting her cheeks.

She nodded.

With deft fingers, he took the lacy confection down to beneath her ass cheeks.

*God bless America.*

The lace panties stretched wonderfully over her hips. She was gorgeous, and he couldn't wait to bring his cock in contact with her luscious bottom.

Moving his hands up and down her body again, he stepped closer, letting his cock nestle into her crack.

*Holy fuck!*

Her breath hitched.

He waited for an objection, but it never came. He started to grind gently over her and continued kissing her neck and back as his hands roamed her torso.

Then he squatted down, kissing and licking her along the way. With a silent command, he moved her legs wider.

*Fuck!* She was so perfect. Perfect for him. And her scent was about to drive him bloody insane.

He rose back up, and with his hands on her hips, he angled her ass closer to him and in perfect alignment with his dick.

*Oh yes, precious. This is called dry-humping, and you will love it.*

She let him take his liberties, but he knew she would feel good with whatever he did for her.

He stroked his cock through her ass crack, simulating fucking, and his hands caressed her back and ribcage. Now, the final ask for the night.

Stroking her back, his hands went down and when he came back up, pushed her shirt fabric up. He'd successfully bared her gorgeous full breasts. Unfortunately, he didn't get much of a view. That would be frowned on.

"Ah," she sighed. Her body was climbing.

The key here was to make her feel sexy. That sexy didn't always mean sex. They were skirting the edge, yet she was still on top of the world.

He held her shirt high as he kissed her, then reached down with his right hand to gloss a finger over the front of her black panties. They were warm and wet.

The fabric was a little loose, as he had designed it, but still he knew he had to keep her covered. For now.

He made three or four circles over her hard nub, and she came, calling out his name.

He didn't let up—his hands, his kisses, and his thrusts.

After another two minutes, she came again. This time, she squirted. Some escaped her binding and ran down the inside of her thighs.

God, she was amazing.

Again, he didn't stop. As much as he wanted to cum, he had to give it a few more minutes.

After another two orgasms for his princess, he came himself. He gripped her hips, adding exquisite pressure from her ass, he released an insane about of cum into his briefs.

They both rested, panting, heads dropped—hers against the wall.

"You're amazing, baby. I hope you feel amazing."

She sighed. "I do."

"Good." He pecked her back and fixed her clothes. "You can get cleaned up, okay?"

As she went to the bathroom, he hustled to his bedroom, stripped off his briefs, and grabbed a washcloth, wiping clean his semi-hard dick.

Suddenly, he saw a movement out of the corner of his eye.

Ana stood at the doorway, her jaw slack, watching him work.

His cock reawakened. And he didn't hide it. He met her gaze as he continued to wipe, although it was clean now. He'd let her get her fill.

"I'm sorry." She didn't turn away. "I was wondering if I could get a washcloth and maybe a plastic bag for my panties?"

He took the cloth away and tossed in the hamper.

She was still watching him.

*Good.*

"Sure, no problem." He acted like it was no big deal for her to see him naked.

He strode past her to retrieve fresh boxers from his drawer and pulled them on. Then he grabbed a cloth from the closet and left to the kitchen where he fished out a plastic bag. "Here ya' go."

Her face was a beautiful pink, her eyes were glassy, and her nipples peeked.

If he wasn't a gentleman, he'd take her to his bedroom and start another lesson.

Silently, she turned, went to the bathroom, and closed the door.

*My sweet got an eyeful today.*

# Chapter Forty-Three

Ana was sure she'd never seen a man's penis so large. *How is that even possible?*

Her mind still whirled as she made it to her apartment.

Matt wasn't that big. Matt's size was nice and comfortable. *That's right.*

She should be grateful for what she had. Matt was very satisfying on many levels.

Her lips pulled into a small smile as she set about getting ready for bed. Unfortunately, the unsettled feeling stayed with her as she tossed and turned during the night.

In the morning, she read a text that came from Lance.

*Morning, sunshine. Tonight wear your see-through shirt and white cotton thong. You can change here.*

Her tummy did a flip. When the shipment with the shirt came in, she'd tried on everything right away. The shirt was unbelievably see-though, like an iridescent pinkish-beige color. It was sexy, but more importantly, it made her look sexy.

She smiled as a little surprise crossed her mind.

***

Ana knew she was a little early, but she couldn't help herself. She was so excited about her surprise, she couldn't wait to see the look on her best friend's face.

And the ... well ... exposure probably wasn't so far out of line considering what *she'd* seen the prior day.

Gees! Heat rushed to her face. Lance was certainly well-built. He no doubt made his girlfriends very happy.

After parking, Ana took a quick glance around. No one nearby. She slipped a bra strap through her right arm, then did the same on the left.

Her heart raced in her chest.

She hustled out of the car and made a beeline to his apartment door.

He opened the door, and his jaw dropped. "Holy fuck," came out on a whisper.

He pulled her inside, backed her up against the wall, and kissed her madly.

She moaned into his mouth. Lance was a good kisser. Matt wasn't as good, and she'd wondered if there was something she could do to help him in that area.

After he devoured her mouth, his kisses ventured down her throat and over the shirt to her chest.

She knew he would go to her nipples, of course she knew, otherwise she shouldn't have purchased that top.

He kissed and licked all around, not stopping at her nipples.

She whimpered and begged, "Lance, please."

He stopped and rose to standing. "Baby, you look amazing. This is very sexy. I want to see more. Do you have on panties?"

She nodded.

"Then, I'm going to take off your skirt."

*Oh, yes!* She nodded again.

He pulled on the zipper and pushed the garment downward.

She stepped out. She stood, her back to the wall, in a see-through top without a bra, a white thong, and high heeled wedges.

He stepped back. "Baby, you are a feast for the eyes."

She could see the evidence under his jeans that he liked how she looked. She wanted to preen.

"A goddess." He whispered as he stepped closer, placing his mouth on her neck and his hands on her hips. "A goddess I will now worship."

That was the last thing he said for quite a while.

She panted when his lips and tongue trailed hot, wet kisses over her breasts and nipples. She squirmed and laced her fingers through his hair.

He could send her to Cloud 9 with just his mouth. But then his hands joined in, lifting her shirt off her tummy and then fondling her breasts.

She was in heaven. Her breathing came faster, and she couldn't slow it down.

He moved to her exposed skin on her stomach while a finger gently toyed over her swollen clit.

"Oh, God." She pinched her eyes closed and savored his caressing. In a minute flat, she came.

*Dang!* She'd never cum so quickly or had as many orgasms with other boyfriends. Not that she'd had many boyfriends. And not that Lance was a *boyfriend*.

She'd been incredibly shy growing up. Her parents did all they could to encourage her to make friends and get out more, to no avail. Consequently, she had just a handful of close friends, and not many boyfriends.

Lance went down on his knees and moved his kisses to her mound.

It felt somehow right for her to spread her stance a little. But she knew she could trust him with the boundaries.

He growled low, and she heard it.

Soon, he kissed lower, over her panties, and licked her clit as he'd done times before.

God, it felt so good. So incredible. Even over the fabric.

He replaced his tongue with his finger. He stroked her clit while his hot mouth licked and kissed her tummy, hips, and thighs.

"Baby."

She looked down at him.

"I'm going to shift your panties just a bit, but I'll keep you covered."

She swallowed.

With a hand at each hip, he tugged on the waistband, dragging the fabric lower, then lower still, and stopped.

Gees! He stopped right at the very top of her slit. Her slit was completely covered, but just barely.

She felt the fabric hang loose between her legs, and the air cooled the area wet from her arousal.

God, she felt so sexy like this—perched against the wall with a handsome man at her feet, wanting to please her, but taking no more than allowed.

She glanced down to see how his tongue traced a line along the edge of panties. So hot!

His hands reached behind to cup her ass.

She was thankful she had everything down there waxed. This wouldn't be so sexy otherwise.

His tongue returned to her clit, this time almost teasing her. So light. Too light.

Warmth grew in her face and spread to her entire body. She needed to cum again, but he wasn't going fast enough or giving her enough pressure.

"Lance," she pleaded, but that didn't seem to make a difference. It was pure torture.

He braced a forearm over her stomach, probably to hold her down from her writhing.

Finally, after long minutes, her body had managed to adjust to Lance's barely there stimulation and the first hint of an orgasm started.

She found her voice. "Don't stop."

She flexed her pelvis, but he wouldn't have it.

He braced her harder against the wall and lessened the pressure still.

*Ah!* She couldn't move. She barely breathed. She was afraid any movement would break the precious connection she needed to find her climax.

Her orgasm built, slowly, steadily, from deep inside. It had never been like this—so excruciatingly drawn out. But when the full explosion happened—wow! Incredible.

She screamed out his name, her head tossed from side to side, and her hips flexed into his face.

Then, she collapsed. Thank God, Lance caught her.

She went limp in his arms and was vaguely aware of him carrying her. To the sofa? Maybe the bed. It didn't matter.

She sunk down into the plush surface, felt his arms wrap around her, and that was the last thing she remembered.

*Fuck!* Ana looked so amazing, so sexy. She probably didn't know how sexy she truly was.

When Lance'd given her the shopping list, he thought for sure he would get push-back, especially on the see-through top. But then tonight she showed up, early, wearing that without a bra. The hint of dusty pink was no longer a hint. The flesh tone top barely concealed a thing. She was sexy as fuck. No two ways about it.

Her succulent nipples called to him. This was the closest thing to having her naked as he would likely get, and it felt amazing.

He could tell—the high heels, the sheer top, how she stood when he answered the door—she felt sexy too.

And now, she lay on his bed, snoozing from the insane climax he'd given her. He'd strung it out, intentionally, to show her how crazy-good it could be.

He'd been hard the entire time, still was, but that didn't matter. What mattered was helping his sunshine bloom and come into her own.

She turned in his arms and snuggled into him. She sighed and mumbled what sounded like "Lance."

He kissed the top of her head. Ana was so precious; he knew in his gut her boyfriend didn't have a clue. Not a clue about how sweet she was or a clue how to turn her on.

Lance didn't know how this would pan out in the end, but one thing he knew for sure. Ana would be stronger for it. She could grab her love life by the horns and take it where she wanted it to go.

# Chapter Forty-Four

♥

Thursday night had been good, even though he hadn't seen sexy Ana. Lance had gone to the bar with his bros, and of course, they'd harassed him. *Where have you been hiding? Why don't you go out anymore? Are you cheating on us?*

Lance had told them he had to coach a student taking a summer class, but after a few weeks, his schedule would loosen up.

At those words, bile rose up. After these two weeks, his relationship with his sweet "sister" would go back to normal.

Maybe there was something he could do.

***

Friday morning, he sent a text to Ana.

*Morning sunshine! Tonight let's go out for dinner. My treat.*

She replied a few minutes later. She must still be waking up.

*You mean like a date?*

He grinned.

*Sure. An opportunity for another lesson. Pick u up at 7.*

Lance had a busy day and finally left the office at six. He had just enough time to shower and get over to Ana's.

She greeted him at the door wearing a pale pink knit top, one of her new skirts, and high heeled sandals. She'd been getting a little more sun during the day, and she looked incredible.

"Hey, pumpkin." He wrapped an arm around her and kissed her forehead. "Ready?"

"Yes, I'm starving."

She locked up and when they arrived at his car, he held open the door for her. Her eyes twinkled with surprise. She might not have been used to that.

He drove them a few minutes out of town. Really, he wanted to be away from prying eyes. Maybe tonight he could be in more of a boyfriend role than a friend role.

They were seated in a booth in the corner, as he'd requested. The restaurant had been around for years. It wasn't a five-star, but still had clothed tables with votive candles and a waitstaff dressed in black and white.

He ordered a bottle of white wine which arrived as they made final entrée decisions.

He held up his glass. "A toast to my star pupal." He sipped.

Ana blushed in that sweet way she had and smiled. "Thank you. And thank you for being such an excellent teacher." She glanced down. "But considering this is a supposed to be like a date."

"Ah, yes." He slid closer to her, laced his fingers through hers, and kissed the back of her hand. He whispered over her sweet skin, "To the most beautiful woman in the room." He kissed her hand again and slipped his tongue in between her fingers, slowly, sensually.

Her precious full lips gaped slightly at the intimate sensation.

Nonchalantly, he took another sip of his wine and smiled. "So, it's almost been a full week of lessons, what are your thoughts?"

She drank a long sip from her wine before answering. "Um, I like what I'm learning." She blinked and shook her head. She met his eyes now. "I like what you're showing me...what you're doing to me." Her voice was soft. "I like learning how, um, my body responds."

He nodded. "That's good. Do you think you can take your new experiences back to Matt and implement them?"

She licked her lips. "I hope so."

With her hand still in his, he kissed it one last time, then rested it on her lap. Reaching to the back of her neck, he drew her close and breathed over her lips, "I know you can, baby. Make him give you exactly what you want. What you deserve."

He pecked her lips and drew back for more wine.

She took another big sip, and he wanted to chuckle. She was probably getting turned on by these easy things he was doing.

"I learned something else too."

He glanced her way. "Oh?"

She smoothed her lips. "I learned that you can still have fun without having intercourse." She swallowed. "Without penetration."

*Wow!* He knew that had to be hard for her articulate. God bless wine for allowing her to loosen up.

He leaned in close. "That's right, baby, because the sexiest organ is the one right between the ears." He tongue-kissed her but didn't linger. Just enough to get the juices going.

She stared for a moment, then smiled and said, "Says the psychology major."

He laughed. It was true.

The rest of the dinner went smoothly, chatting and laughing, as they often had, but now it had a sexy undertone. This was a great idea, but he had a feeling she wouldn't be too thrilled with the outcome.

They wrapped up dinner, and he held her hand as they walked to his car. He opened the door for her, and she climbed in.

As they got closer to campus, she looked his way in question. They were heading back to her place.

She didn't say a word. She likely didn't know what to think since every lesson was at his place. He parked and strode around the front of the car to open her door.

Silently, they held hands and went to her apartment. She unlocked the door, took a step, and turned around, realizing he wasn't following. "You aren't coming in?" Her eyebrows pinched together.

He stepped forward and cupped her jaw. "Not tonight, baby."

"But I don't understand."

"Just a little time to review your lessons, sorta think on what you'd like going forward."

Her jawed dropped. "Wait. You're ending our lessons."

The shocked look on her face ripped his heart in half, but it had to be done this way.

"No, baby, just a little break. A little breather to think about how you'd like to proceed with Matt in light of all that you've learned thus far."

Her lips formed an O, but he could tell she still wasn't happy. "But there will be no lesson tomorrow."

*Halleluiah*. He had to believe the disappointment was because she wanted her time with him. Not because she wanted to be ready for the boyfriend to return.

He pursed his lips. "Ah, that's right. Okay, I have an idea. Since we can both sleep in Sunday, how about you come over after work? Do you think you'd be up for that?"

She nodded several times.

"Maybe even bring some things to crash the night," he held up a hand, "if you want." He wanted her in his bed, even if platonic, it was a start.

"Okay," she replied quickly, the sparkle back in her eyes.

Then, he stepped close, wrapped an arm around her waist, and said, "Goodnight my sweet girl. Sweet dreams." And finished with a deep diving French kiss. One, he hoped, she'd never forget.

"Goodnight. Thanks for dinner."

He left her grinning from ear to ear. His goal to have her need and want him was working. At least it seemed to. He had to take it a step at a time.

***

Ana awoke to find texts on her phone—one from Matt, one from Lance.

She opened Lance's first, maybe out of habit.

*Morning, sunshine! Tonight after work come over. Wear an underboob shirt and micro-thong.*

Her heart skipped a beat. Holy crap! That sounded hot. And her second underboob shirt was shorter than the first. She would have a lot of skin exposed. Not that that really mattered. She trusted him.

She flipped over to Matt's text.

*Hey Ana! How are you? I've been busy with family stuff, but this cruise is a blast. Hope ur not too bored. Miss you! See you soon!*

*Soon? A week is an eternity.* Well, still it was nice of him to text when he's so busy and likely has spotty cell service.

She sighed.

She didn't take too much time ruminating over it. She had a busy day. She had to pack, clean her place, work for six hours, then, head to Lance's place.

She couldn't wait. Maybe her boss would let her leave early if they were slow.

*****

Ana arrived just before midnight. Lance'd been fucking anxious all day. But he had to play it cool.

He switched off the overhead light, leaving only a table lamp on in the living room, and answered the door.

"Hey, pumpkin. C'mon in. Wanna drink?"

She followed him into the kitchen. "Sure, some wine would be great."

He poured them each a glass. He'd already had two beers, trying to calm the lust flowing through him.

"How was work?" he asked as he met her on the sofa. The sight of her large canvas bag a welcome site.

"Good, we were busy."

He sipped from his glass. "I hope you get a lot of tips."

She took another drink of wine, set down her glass, and smiled. She lifted her bag and went to the bathroom.

His heart beat double-time.

She came back in just two minutes, but it seemed like two hours.

*Holy fuck!* She looked so hot. Lance licked his lips. He wanted to attack her but that wouldn't get him anywhere.

"Geezus, Ana. You look incredible."

She wore a pale pink short T-shirt with the pillow of her tits peeking out beneath and matching micro-panties. The panties maybe covered two square inches. Just enough to hide her slit and lips.

She was gorgeous.

There were no words to describe the excruciating pain in his dick at this point.

She approached him, and instantly he wrapped his hands around her hips and kissed her naked belly. So warm and soft, just like her whole body.

She ran her fingers through his hair in that way which always sent delicious tingles everywhere.

He kissed her torso and hips as he caressed her bare ass. She felt like a million bucks.

Then he made his way to the breasts that played peek-a-boo, daring him to satisfy her. He kissed and licked the bare skin, working his way to her covered nipples.

She moaned instantly, and her subtle scent filled the air.

*Oh baby, you have no idea how incredibly desirable you are.*

He made love to her breasts, teasing the area he knew gave her the most sensation. Squatting lower, he kissed her lower belly, her hips, her upper thighs, and her mound. Again, he toyed with her, tormenting her.

She sighed and spread her legs wide. An offering.

He returned his mouth to her perfect mound, then licked her center over her new virginal white panties.

She moaned, and her head dropped back.

He held onto her hips firmly as he loved on her precious pussy, her delicate nub pressing against the fabric.

Ana wavered slightly, then took the step to the sofa and sat.

He knelt before her, hands on her thighs, when she raised a palm to his chest, stopping him.

He met her gaze as she slowly lifted her arms over her head resting them against the wall.

*Holy fuck!* Her tits were entirely bared to him.

Her glassy eyes beamed. He knew he had permission to feast.

He wasted no time laying claim to her bare nipples. God, she tasted like a warm dessert he wanted every night after dinner. They both moaned.

God, this woman was going to be the death of him. If she didn't want him at the end of this, he didn't know what he was going to do.

He whispered over her skin—so sweet, so precious, so beautiful—over and over. He couldn't get enough of her.

She purposefully reached for the hem of the shirt, folded it above her breasts, then reached for his cock. Her hand caressed the front of him, and nearly unmanned him.

He gave her just one minute of stroking, then pulled back. He couldn't go down like this.

Pulling out of her grip, he ventured further south to her precious swollen clit, waiting for his attention.

He kissed her sex several times, then looked up. "Baby, I'd like to shift this fabric, just a little bit. See if I could caress your clitoris a little more directly. I won't expose your sacred part."

Her lips gaped, then she chewed on her bottom lip.

He'd wait for her okay. He had to believe she'd give it to him.

She nodded. "Okay," she whispered.

*Fuckin-A!*

The fabric didn't have far to go to lay her clit open for him, but he had to be incredibly careful. As he kissed and licked her mound, he carefully pulled her tiny panties down, allowing her clit to be exposed.

*Perfect!*

She moaned the instant his tongue came into contact with her bare nubble.

God, she was so sweet, so delicious.

She came in a flash, and he knew there was more to come.

As he made love to her newly exposed clit, he reached up with both hands and toyed with her turgid nipples.

She came again, gripping the fabric of his sofa.

He lifted his head. "You're doing great, baby. I think the panties are getting a little loose. Do you want me to stop?"

Her eyes went wide.

*Please tell me to take them off.*

"Um…"

When he knew he wasn't going to be able to push anymore tonight, he went to plan B.

He lifted his right hand and bent his fingers, showing her his knuckle. "How about I use this, and only this, to put the fabric in a bit more securely. Would that work?"

She licked her lips.

He kept his eyes trained on her but went back to scattering kisses on her soft mound. He slowly pulled his hand back, lined up the fabric to her hole and gently pushed.

Her eyes fluttered closed, and she sighed.

He claimed her clit once again, then pushed the fabric a little deeper.

"Ah, God, Lance." She panted, and her hips flexed toward his mouth.

*I got you, sugar.*

As she climbed on her fourth climax, he pressed a little more with his knuckle, then pulled back. Oh so carefully, he stimulated just the very entrance of her pussy.

Her syrup flowed and flowed.

She came again on the heels of climax number four.

How many could he give her?

He loved to make her happy. He would spend the rest of his life doing just that, if she'd let him.

After her ninth orgasm, she pushed against his shoulders. Panting vigorously, she pleaded, "No more, please. I can't take anymore." Her eyelids gently closed, and her chest rose and fell.

He stood, adjusted his raging hard-on, fixed her clothes, and lifted her in his arms, taking her to his dark bedroom. He set her on the bed, removed her T-shirt and tugged on one of his. Then, he swung her legs around, tucked her in, and whispered, "Sleep, baby," as he pecked her head and cheek.

God, she was so amazing tonight. So open, so giving, so willing.

He only prayed in the light of the day, she wouldn't regret giving him such latitude.

Lance turned off all the lights and headed to the bathroom to try and put out the fire from his angry cock. *Sorry buddy, no action for you yet.*

# Chapter Forty-Five

♥

Ana awoke and stretched on the mattress, her muscles reminding her of the delicious night she had.

God, she slept like the dead. The best sleep she'd had in a long time. Actually, come to think of it, since starting her lessons with Lance, she'd slept very well.

*Must be all the orgasms.* She sighed.

She turned, expecting to see him. Instead, she found a note.

*Good morning, precious. Ran out to grab us some breakfast.*

She smiled. *Yay! Yum!*

She pushed up and grabbed her bag, so she could shower and get ready for work. It was a shame she couldn't spend the day with him, but hopefully she could see him tonight.

*Dang!* She scolded herself. He was her best friend and supposed to be helping her with her relationship with Matt. If she wasn't careful, she could lose that friendship she'd cherished for so long.

He arrived just as she'd finished dressing and combing out her long, wet hair. She could do her makeup after breakfast. She was famished.

"Morning, sunshine. How'd you sleep?"

"Great, actually." She smiled and helped him unpack the bags of pancakes, eggs, and bacon, helping herself to a coffee.

"Good. Me too. So, what's the plan today? What's your schedule like?"

They sat at his round little kitchen table. "I work from eleven to four. But I'm free tonight."

"Super. Come over when you can. I'll go grocery shopping and cook us some dinner beforehand."

They both knew what "beforehand" meant, and her anxious little sex clenched at the thought. *Oh boy.*

His plan to woo his best friend chugged along nicely. Maybe even ahead of schedule.

He texted her as she finished her shift.

*Hope you had a good day. Now, let's have a good night. Wear your V-neck shirt and thong panties.*

She replied seconds later. *OK.*

He loved how she looked forward to spending her nights with him. They hardly talked about her boyfriend at all. *Did Matt call her? Did he even miss her?*

***

At five that evening, Ana rang his bell. She wore cut-off jean shorts, a tie-dye fitted tee, white chucks, and her hair in a ponytail. Ana was what people referred to as a natural beauty. It had always been there, but people couldn't always appreciate it since she was so shy and preferred to stay inside, reading. He could chuckle.

The older she got, Lance slowly exposed her to new things, new interests, slowly bringing her out of her cocoon. Ana had so much to give. She was funny, bright, and had a magnetic personality that made people want to be around her. Maybe if she wasn't an only child that might have changed things.

At any rate, here she was, smiling up at him, ready for her next lesson.

"C'mon in. You can help with dinner." He closed the door behind her.

"Great." She set her bag on the sofa. "What are we having?"

"Spaghetti."

"Seriously?"

"It's not what you think. No jarred sauce for my girl. We are making it from scratch."

"Okay. Wow."

He showed her the recipe, and as he diced onions, she diced the tomatoes. Over the dinner prep, he asked her, "How was your day?"

"Good. Busy again at work."

"And how is Matt? Have you heard from him?"

She tilted her head his way. "Yes. The reception is spotty on the cruise ship, but he texts me."

She didn't seem to be overflowing with a "Matt report." Secretly, Lance was happy. Deep inside, he knew he could give Ana way more than Matt could. Last week, when Ana'd told him she thought their sex life was lacking, that told Lance instantly the man didn't know what he had. That he was likely out for himself and his satisfaction. Ana deserved better than that.

"Well, as you recount what you're learning here, think about the ways you can communicate this to him to show him what you like. It doesn't always need to be in words. Sometimes, it could as simple as moving his hand. Make sense?"

She had a slight tinge of pink in her cheeks, and she nodded.

He knew the feeling. Just discussing this made Lance hard.

Over dinner, she asked about his working toward his master's degree.

He had a handful of clients to see, work that his advisor might give him, and his own studies and papers to write. He kept busy, but his time with Ana was sacred. He wouldn't trade it for the world.

Cleanup took no time at all, and when they were done, without a word, she took her bag to the bathroom to change.

Lance had the bedroom ready. Those blackout drapes were worth every penny.

He leaned against the wall outside the bathroom, and then Ana came out.

Just as he'd asked, she wore a sexy deep V-neck shirt with large armhole cutouts. She knotted it at her hip showing off her pretty thong.

She was stunning.

He clasped her jaw and leaned in to kiss her plump lips. "Precious, tonight we're going to be in my bedroom."

She glanced that way and took the hand he offered.

He sat her on the bed. "I wanted it dark so it makes it harder to see. That engages the other senses more acutely."

Her lips formed an O. He closed the bedroom door, drowning out most of the light.

He crawled on the bed behind her and began massaging her scalp.

She dropped her head back and moaned.

His hands continued as his lips dropped to her neck and shoulder. He kissed, suckled, and licked her warm soft skin. Reaching around, he untied the knot in her shirt, loosening the fabric. With his teeth, he pulled the fabric to the edge of her shoulder, giving him access to more beautiful skin.

He pushed her long hair aside, tugged the shirt, exposing most of her back to his kisses.

She pitched forward and curved her back like a cat.

As he kissed her, he stroked his hands over her back and worked his way to the sides of her torso. Wrapping his fingers around her ribcage, he skimmed the edge of her breasts, and she sighed.

Letting her passion build, he stayed behind her for another few minutes. "How do you feel, baby?"

"Good," she whispered.

*So good,* she thought.

Then the bed shifted, and she felt Lance at the side of her, and his breath on her neck.

He kissed her neck, and she let her head fall back. Slowly, he pulled the shirt from the hem, dragging them across her breasts, igniting her nipples.

She moaned; she couldn't help herself.

He went to the exposed skin on her chest, and she leaned back, bracing herself with her arms. The fabric shifted again, this time exposing the sides of her breasts.

His mouth did wonderful things to her body, lighting up every nerve ending.

On its own, her body flexed, arching into the exquisite sensations.

"Ah," she let out, eager to feel his mouth take her nipple.

Instead, his kisses traveled lower, and his hand slid along her thigh.

He overwhelmed her with sensation, and the wetness at the apex of her thighs grew. He pulled against one thigh, and the other seemed to spread wide all on its own.

"That's right, baby," he whispered low against her tummy.

He teased the area with his kisses, making her completely insane.

"Lance." She begged.

Thankfully, he didn't keep her waiting long.

"Oh, God."

He hit the spot so perfectly, her orgasm started building within seconds.

"Ah," she moaned as her climax hit her full force.

She panted and felt Lance's kisses over her tummy. And again, the T-shirt fabric shifted over her nipples.

His mouth headed north, claiming every inch of her bare skin, shifting the shirt this way and that slowly exposing her to his mouth.

When his fingers glossed down her slit over her panties, she bowed her back off the bed. His tongue had wiggled a way under the shirt to her hardened nipple.

"Oh, God."

He seemed to love torturing her—his mouth, his fingers, all bringing her to the brink of ecstasy again.

She couldn't help but want to touch him too, to feel what this was doing to him. She reached in the dark for his leg and felt her way for the inside of his thigh. Slowly, she crept upward for her prize. His incredibly hard erection.

He groaned over her breast.

He wore simple, nylon workout shorts, so caressing his length was easy. Hearing him pant as heavily as her felt heady. She loved that she could do something wonderful for him. He deserved it, and it was the least she could do.

"God, Ana." His ministrations never stopped, and neither did hers.

Her climax climbed again, but she didn't want to release. Not until he was satisfied too.

She moaned. "Lance."

"God, Ana, don't stop."

And then it happened. Just as she felt her climax burst to the top, his erection pulsed under her touch. She caressed the length of him, over his shorts, praying he felt at least some of the exquisiteness he was giving to her.

She cried out, and he growled into her shoulder.

Then he collapsed to the side of her, panting as he pulled her close.

They lay together in the quiet dark for several long minutes. She didn't want to move. Or leave.

But she had no choice. She wasn't his girlfriend. And he wasn't her boyfriend.

She sighed and curled into him further. If only things were a little different...

# Chapter Forty-Six

F uck, Ana was driving him insane. On one hand, he was ecstatic she was getting more and more comfortable with all they were sharing. On the other hand, he craved her, all of her so desperately, no words could do it justice.

Deep down inside, he could have guessed *she* was all he ever wanted. His relationships with women all his life had been lackluster compared to what he had with Ana, even before all the sex play. He'd never had anything long-term or of any depth. And none of them made him feel the way Ana did.

This week, she had to close at work three nights. So, that gave him three remaining chances to try and take this escapade to the next level. He had planned another big obstacle for her to cross. He only prayed she wouldn't pull back.

***

At eight at night, mid-way through their second week of lessons, Ana rang his doorbell.

He had texted her earlier that she could wear whatever she wanted. And there she stood, wearing a pink floral summer dress that fell barely halfway down her thighs. Her smooth, tan thighs.

"Hey, princess. Come in. Don't you look nice. Very summery." He kissed her cheek.

She giggled, and damn if he didn't love to hear her laugh.

"Thanks. I wasn't sure what you had planned, so…" She shrugged her shoulders.

"C'mere." He took her hand and led her to their perch on the sofa, two ice waters waiting.

He craved kissing her, so he didn't hold back. He gave her a peck on her cheek, then her neck and smoothed the rest of her hair down her back. "How are you feeling? Anything you want to discuss?"

That was the forty-thousand-dollar question. She took in some air. It might be embarrassing, but she had to talk it out with her bestie. She looked up from her lap. "I love what we're doing, what I'm learning. I'm just a little nervous about trying to get Matt to understand."

"Okay. How so?"

"I mean, I like how you take your time, kissing me and stuff. Matt doesn't really do that. He's so anxious to get right to the sex part."

Lance nodded slowly.

"I mean, I like that he's excited to be with me, but…"

"But that's not all of it, is it?"

She shook her head.

"It will take time, but you can make him understand that women are more complex than men. And what works one day may not work that next."

*Exactly.*

Lance continued. "The good news is you still have some time to think about how you can approach him. I suggest you take it in steps, sorta like what we're doing here. Ease him into this new way of intimacy."

That sounded good.

He leaned in and kissed her neck again. God, she loved how he positively drenched her body in kisses.

He took her hand and kissed the inside of her wrist. "Baby, tonight, we're trying something new. Instead of me touching you with my hands, you will touch yourself."

Her eyebrows shot up. *What?!*

He lifted a red tie off the corner of the coffee table. "To make sure you're comfortable, you're going to tie my hands behind my back. I only get to use my mouth." He grinned that terribly cute, boyish grin he had. His entire face lit up.

She couldn't help her smile, but still, could she do this? She swallowed but her mouth was too dry. Her heart pounded in her chest.

He pivoted in his seat, presenting her with his back and his hands laced together.

She managed to speak. "I don't think this is necessary."

"Maybe, but let's give it a try, babe."

She smoothed her lips and wove the tie around the right wrist, then his left, and tied the ends together securely.

He turned around, smiling. "Perfect. Now where was I?" He leaned in to return to loving her neck and across the top of her chest.

So, if she was the only one with the use of their hands, she would need to move or remove clothing if she wanted what Lance could give her.

Her heartrate kicked up, but she knew she was in the driver's seat here. She reached to the back and pulled against the dress zipper.

As the spaghetti strap loosened, he bit on the fabric and pulled it off her shoulder, causing the bodice to dip and expose more skin to kiss.

He growled as he shifted in his seat.

Ana glanced down and noticed the bulge in his shorts. She wanted to touch it again.

His mouth skated across the terrain of her chest, not venturing south. She knew she'd have to give him permission.

She slid the other strap off her shoulder and pulled her arms through, allowing the dress to fall to her waist.

He groaned as he claimed her nipple.

"Oh, God." She clutched his shoulders as she arched into his expert mouth.

God, she never knew how much she loved having her nipples kissed.

He paid excellent attention to her breasts, and the wetness grew at her sex. She needed more. Lifting her hips enough, she shimmied the dress off her waist and down her legs.

Lance's kisses and licking traveled south.

*Oh yes.* She was ready for him. Ready to feel him bring her amazing pleasure.

Before he got to her mound, he slid off the sofa to kneel between her legs. "So beautiful." Then he leaned down and kissed her sex and her inner thighs over the white lacy thong she wore.

His tongue toyed and circled her clit, bringing her body alive.

"Mmm." She gripped his head, holding him where she wanted him. In mere minutes, she came, detonating the fireworks deep inside.

She panted wildly, not realizing he'd lifted his head to watch her.

She blushed under his scrutiny.

"Baby, that was beautiful. Now, bring your hand down here. You'll help me for the next one."

She swallowed hard. Help him? Did he want her to masturbate?

"You can do this. Show me. Show me what you like."

Slowly, she slid her right hand down and under her panties. Her heart beat staccato in her chest. Her fingers grazed over her clit, through her slit, and back again.

"That's right, baby." He kissed her low belly. "So good."

Her core temperature rose. This had to be the most erotic thing she'd ever done. She didn't stop. With Lance's kisses and sucking her skin and nipples, she came again.

God. She sank further into the sofa cushions.

"Babe, you're beautiful when you come. Do you want another one like this, or would you like to take off these panties for the next one?"

*Holy cow!* Could she? Could she be completely naked?

This was why he had her tie his hands. He could only use his mouth—that incredibly wonderful mouth.

She trusted him. She hooked her thumbs under the waistband, lifted her butt, pulling off the confection.

Oh God, she was naked—completely naked—for the first time in front of her best friend.

And his eyes were so deep, she'd never seen them so dark. She couldn't steal away. Instead, she brought her right hand back to her pussy, stroking the way she knew she needed to orgasm.

Lance's jaw hung ajar, watching her every move. "Shit, Ana. That's the hottest thing I've ever seen."

She didn't stop. His lust fueled her passion, rocketing her climax to the surface in no time. Her hand went lax.

He leaned down before she'd entirely calmed down and kissed her sex—the crux at her thighs, her lips, her mound.

When he nuzzled her fingers gently as his tongue sought out her clit, she was lost to him.

She sighed. "Oh, God, Lance."

*Yes. Please.*

Instead of pulling her hand away, she added the second. She separated her lips, making him room for his tongue.

He growled and continued his licks with gusto—each pass of his tongue fluid and confident. His tongue dipped lower before circling her clit. Practiced beyond his years, he knew how to tease and please her.

Her body burned. It was pure madness. Beautiful, insane madness.

She came hard, harder than the first two times, causing spots to appear before her eyes. She cried out his name.

He pecked her mound lovingly and laid his head on her thigh. He was so good to her, she thought she could cry.

It was then the realization hit her. They might have crossed over the point where they couldn't return to just friends.

She couldn't think about that right then. Most of the pleasure was one-sided. Something needed to be done to make this endeavor fair. She might not be an expert, but she had to try.

Stroking his hair, she spoke softly, "Lance, can you sit up here?"

He lifted his head, leveraged his body and sat beside her. "How do you feel?"

She smiled. "I feel good." Then, she leaned in and kissed him as she stroked his muscular chest, and slowly made her way to the hardness in his pants.

He moaned into her mouth.

She loved knowing she could please him, at least to some extent. She unfastened his shorts and crept her hand inside, cupping his glorious erection.

She broke the kiss because she had to see. Pulling more of the fabric out of the way, she could see the outline of his bulge through his underwear.

She bit her lip.

"Baby."

She looked up at him.

"You never need to ask."

She licked her lips, and with two hands pulled against the last layer covering his manhood and peeled it down.

He shifted on his hips to help.

God, he was glorious. An Adonis.

She lowered her mouth and poked the slit before taking a long, sweeping lick up with length.

He groaned, and his head fell back.

She circled around the very tip and then sunk him into her mouth. Her lips stretched around him, going further down with each pass.

"Fuck, Ana."

She did it again, feeling emboldened by his positive affirmations. She repeated her sequence—sinking down and sucking on the way up. She added her hand, stroking him in concert with her mouth.

"God, Ana, I'm going to cum. You should pull back."

*Pull back?* She didn't want to. She loved bringing him this pleasure. She loved knowing she could return some of what he'd given her, even though he certainly didn't need a *lesson*.

She sucked harder and went faster, bobbing up and down.

His cock twitched in her mouth, and then she felt it.

He growled long and low, flexing his hips, as he came in her mouth.

She swallowed his load and licked his tip clean. She rose to see his eyes closed, his head back, and chest rising and falling.

He opened his glassy eyes to meet her gaze. "That was fucking incredible," he breathed out.

She smiled. She made him happy, and for that, she glowed inside.

She covered his privates, wiggled her hands behind him, and untied his hands.

His arms instantly wrapped around her.

Unthinking, she swung a leg over his lap to circle her arms around him too. The fact that her naked sex was one thin layer of fabric away from his wasn't lost on her. But just then, she didn't care, couldn't care. They held each other close for several long minutes, savoring his embrace.

At that moment, she'd felt closer to her best friend than she ever had her entire life.

# Chapter Forty-Seven

♥

Lance woke up hard. And with only one woman on his mind. A woman he'd once considered his little sister. Ana.

Had this incredible feeling for her been there the entire time he'd known her? Maybe just buried deep inside, waiting for a reason to come forward?

She no doubt had become the center of his world, and he needed to keep it that way.

He wouldn't see her that night, but maybe that was good. She would probably have some shopping to do for their next lesson.

He reached for his phone and typed out a text.

*Good morning, sunshine. You may have some shopping to do. Tomorrow you need to bring a working vibrator to your lesson. Wear a lacy thong.*

That would likely freak her out at first, but she'd come to embrace her shopping trip. He had to believe that.

***

Ana wiped her palms down her skirt as she rang Lance's bell. The vibrator she bought was buried in the bottom of her bag. She could only guess what he'd do. Would he make her use it on herself?

He opened the door wearing a white T-shirt and blue jeans with bare feet. God, there was something so appealing about seeing him like this. The fabric stretched over his muscles made her want to run her hands all over him.

"Hey, sunshine. Come in." He pecked her cheek. He seemed so carefree and confident when her stomach had a squillion butterflies running lose.

Over the last two weeks, Lance had slowly made her see what sexy things she could do with Matt without actually having sex. And showed her how to be proud of her body and be open to express the sexuality she had deep inside.

He led her to the sofa. "How are you feeling? How did you feel after Wednesday night?"

"I feel good. And Wednesday was incredible." Her voice was too soft. *Dammit*! She sat taller. "I felt great knowing I could pleasure myself in front of you."

His eyes sparkled when he smiled. "I'm proud of you." He gave her a chaste kiss. "I know that took a lot."

She nodded.

"Did you bring a vibrator?"

She felt the heat fill her cheeks. "Yes." She reached into her bag and set it on the table.

"Good. Tonight, baby, you don't have to use it on yourself, although you can always do that at home whenever you want."

She blushed again.

"I'll use it on you, if you'd like."

Her sex clenched. *Oh dear.*

He slid closer and brought her legs across his lap. Then, he cupped her neck and kissed the sensitive spot, working his way to her cheek. "Tonight, I'd like to take off these clothes and worship you," he whispered.

*Oh my!*

He made his way to her lips, and she opened for him. He dove in, toying with her tongue in the most sensual way. When he broke the kiss, he asked, "Have you ever used a vibe before?"

"No," she managed to squeak out.

His hand loosened her shirt buttons. "You're going to love it. This can be just another way to have an orgasm."

His kisses traveled down her chest, and he pealed her shirt out of the way, exposing more skin. He kissed, licked, and sucked, making his way to her already hard nipples.

She sighed and pushed herself into his mouth, eager for more.

He didn't stop as he pulled off her shirt, one arm at a time. Then he slid off her bra straps.

"Ah."

His mouth on her felt divine. God, how in the world would she be able to get these same feelings and sensations with Matt?

His hands roamed her body, then clutched her torso. With his right hand, he shoved a pillow behind her back and tugged her forward, toward the edge of the sofa. Her skirt slid higher too.

He went to his knees before her. "So beautiful, Ana," he whispered over her skin.

She snaked her fingers through his hair, forgetting about everything else in the world except for Lance and his incredible mouth.

His hands caressed up and down her thighs and under her skirt, slowly pushing it higher and higher. He didn't wait another second before claiming her sex.

"Unh."

His tongue played with her clit over the lace fabric, pushing her closer and closer to the edge. Gripping her thighs with his strong hands, he didn't relent.

Her orgasm flew to the surface and with little time to come down, Lance added more pressure and gave her another orgasm almost immediately.

"Lance," she cried.

Her eyes closed and her heart raced. She lay sprawled out on his sofa gasping for air.

She heard the vibrator turn on. She opened her eyes to see him trail it over each nipple, toying and teasing her, having her climb closer to ecstasy again.

"Oh."

His eyes were trained on hers. Her mouth gaped. She'd never felt a sensation like this before.

Then, with the same thoughtfulness and desire to please he'd used these entire couple of weeks, he moved the vibe to her mound.

Her heartrate climbed as he carefully skated it over the area, avoiding her needy clit.

Slowly, he slid it over her clit, and the sensation shot out everywhere.

"Unh."

The vibe was on low, but the sensation was electrifying. Lance lightly circled over her tiny bundle of nerves and at the same time leaned down to suck her nipple into his mouth.

"Oh, God." She was steadily climbing to the top again. She writhed and clutched his shoulders as the climax overtook her thought and reason. She screamed.

He pulled back the vibe and turned it off, pecking her moist cheeks and neck. "So fucking beautiful, Ana."

Slowly, she opened her eyes. "Holy cannoli."

He smiled. "Baby, I'm not done with you yet." He claimed her mouth in a passionate kiss.

Ana knew, this turned him on as much as it did her.

"Baby," he met her gaze, "if you want, I want you to slide your panties to the side and let me use this inside you while my mouth is on you."

Her heart skipped a beat. *Holy crap!*

They had been hovering very close to the line she didn't want to cross. Technically, they hadn't crossed the line, and this implement *was* plastic, not flesh.

She moved her hand, and biting on her lip, she pulled her panties to the side, exposing her naked sex to him.

His eyes grew darker. "God, Ana," he slid a finger through her slit, "so wet. So incredible."

The vibe poised at her entrance, he slowly pushed it inside.

"Unh." She arched her back at the exquisite sensation. "God, Lance."

He dragged it back and pushed again.

Her eyelids fluttered closed as she lay before him, completely at his mercy.

Then she felt his warm mouth, and his tongue claimed her clit. She tugged the fabric and unknowingly spread her legs wider, giving him complete access to her.

Her heart threatened to leap from her chest. The sensations overwhelmed her, and there was no holding back. Another climax crashed through her, leaving her boneless.

Lance pecked and kissed her down there. She should have been embarrassed, but she only loved him more, and God help her, wanted him more.

He glanced up at her, meeting her gaze, and as if he could read her mind, he started again.

"Oh, God."

He licked her as the vibe moved in and out of her.

She couldn't pull her eyes away. It was so hot watching him make love to her pussy like this. She wanted to rip the fabric out of the way.

God, he was so incredible to her.

"Lance," she moaned, feeling the impending orgasm build from deep inside.

Then it hit with full force, bursting to every corner of her body.

She panted and collapsed into the sofa.

He pulled out the vibe and laid it on her bag. Again, he took care of her. It was always about her.

She mustered her strength, slid to the floor before him and kissed him madly, tasting her essence on him.

He circled his arms around her and pulled her closer into him. His erection dug into her.

She broke the kiss. "Please stand."

He paused a brief moment before he rose before her.

She worked free his jeans and set him free. She looked up at him as her lips closed over his purple tip.

He clutched her shoulders. "Fuck, Ana."

She didn't want to wait another minute to return the pleasure he'd given her. Her mouth swallowed him as much as possible before her gag reflex hit. She sucked on the way up and sank back down, fisting him at the same time. She worked him up and down, not stopping until he could release.

"Ana ... you have to ... stop now."

*No way!* She could take it, wanted to take it all.

And she felt the first twitch of him on her tongue. Then, he released, filling her mouth. She swallowed and sucked more.

"Fuck," he cried.

When he was sucked dry, he collapsed to the sofa, panting with his eyes closed.

"God, Ana, you are so good at that."

She beamed at his compliment. She would give him anything. Anything he wanted. She would... If she could.

Technically, she still had a boyfriend. A boyfriend she'd told she loved.

A few weeks ago, she'd known what she wanted.

Well, now her vision was rather blurry.

# Chapter Forty-Eight

♥

Ana rolled over, away from the sunshine trying to wake her.

She sighed. She was wet and she knew why. Lance.

Images of the incredible dream she had of her best friend making love to her replayed in her mind. He'd whispered compliments and kissed her in a thousand places before he slid inside her, causing her to climax. A climax so strong, it woke her.

It seemed so real, and a melancholy shadow fell over her. Over these two weeks, he'd taught her so much about herself and her body. He showed her how much he loved her and once again proved how he'd always been there for her. Just as he had when she been nervous about starting a new school year. Or when he'd punched Bobby Jenkins in the mouth for lifting up her dress. Or a thousand other things he did for her.

Today would be their last night together. Their last lesson.

She had mixed emotions about it. Matt would return the next day, and she was excited, but she knew she'd also miss Lance. Of course, they would still be friends, but it would be different. They would go back to the way it was before the lessons.

She sighed again and blinked away the wetness that gathered in her eyes.

She would soldier on. This all happened to help with her relationship with Matt. She needed to keep that in mind.


This was it. Their last night together. Fuck, his heart already ached for her. Ana didn't belong with Matt. She belonged with him. Lance knew it like he knew her favorite ice cream flavor, or how she liked to arrange her drawers, or how to coax her out of the corner when she wanted to hide in a crowded room. He knew her better than anyone. And he loved her better than anyone.

When his doorbell rang, he was already hard with wanting her. He gave her no instruction on what to wear. He simply wanted her comfortable.

He pulled her in and instantly laid claim to those plush pink lips. Would he ever get tired of kissing her? Not in this lifetime.

He broke the long kiss and smiled.

"Well, that was a lovely greeting." She smiled back at him.

She wore a pale blue floral summer dress with spaghetti straps and white kitten heels.

"You look beautiful," he said as he covered her neck with kisses.

She moaned, and it was music to his ears.

"Baby, I want to take you into my bedroom tonight, so you can lay down and be comfortable."

She nodded. "I trust you."

He needed to remember that. He didn't want to do anything to betray that trust, but tonight he could skirt the edge. He wanted her to leave here wanting him, aching for his orgasms and his kisses. Not Matt's.

He led her to the dimly lit room. He didn't turn on a light but left the drapes open a few inches.

He drew her into his arms. "These few weeks with you have been incredible. I hope you've enjoyed them as much as I."

"I have." Her eyes sparkled.

He kissed her neck, her cheeks, and finally stopped on her lips.

She opened for him. He loved how she was so open, so trusting of him. She would always be his, regardless of who she dated.

Then, she broke the kiss and stepped back. She kicked off her heels. Meeting his gaze, she reached for the hem of her dress, drew it up, and flung it off to the side. She stood before him naked.

"Fuck, Ana. You look amazing."

"Lance," she whispered, then pecked his lips before sliding onto the center of the bed.

He knew this was his chance to be skin to skin with his love.

She kept her eyes trained on him, so he slowly undressed for her. He took his time in case she wanted to change her mind; she could tell him to stop.

He got down to his boxer briefs and paused a long moment for her. Then with his thumbs under the waistband, he drew the briefs to the floor.

He stood before her, letting her take in the sight of his cock, hard for her.

He climbed on all fours over her. He kissed her deeply, soaking in the taste and feel of her.

"Baby, you're going to feel me against you. On you, but not in you. Okay?"

She nodded. "Yes, Lance. I want to feel you."

Fuck, her words sent a thrill through him. He wanted to give her everything. But it had to be in her time, under her terms.

He lowered himself, letting his cock slide against her thigh just before he sucked her delicious nipple into his mouth.

Her hands skated over his arms, shoulders, and against his back. Her hands were as soft as velvet.

Leveraging himself over her, he slid his cock along her stomach. Her fingertips stroked him, and he almost lost it right then.

He switched over to her other breast to give it equal attention while he reached down to caress a finger over her budding clit.

"So beautiful, Ana," he whispered over her smooth skin.

"Oh, God, Lance. So good."

To his surprise, her climax took only another minute. She bowed off the bed and moaned aloud.

His dick wept. He wanted them closer. He had to believe she wanted to feel the connection as badly as he did.

He slid a hand to her thigh and pulled up her bent leg. Shifting in between her legs, he bent her other leg.

"Lance—"

"I know, baby. I won't enter. I promise."

She nodded.

With a finger, he gathered her slickness and smeared it along the underside of his length.

Watching him, her jaw hung open.

He repeated the task a few more times until he was slick enough. Then he aligned his dick over her slit.

"Oh, God." Her eyelids fell closed.

She could feel it too. Just this simple connection—so close and yet so far—held so much emotion in it.

He gripped her hands, laced his fingers in between hers, and held them over her head. Then he moved his hips. With his gaze meeting hers, he slowly stroked his cock up the center of her slit and over her clit.

Shit, she felt incredible.

"Oh my gosh, Lance." Her face flushed with warmth.

He laid claimed to her mouth as he pressed her hands into the mattress and stroked her bare sex with his hard length. It was the closest thing to making love they could share.

Back and forth, slowly he moved. "Baby, you feel so incredible. You know I love you, right? I've always loved you."

He didn't know if she knew the true meaning of his words. It was more than as a surrogate baby sister. Maybe it had always been there, and he was only now realizing it.

"I know. I love you too, Lance."

He kissed her again, feeling her tiny bud twitch under his cock. It was the best feeling in the world.

She came and cried out into his mouth.

He released at the same time, knowing he could keep going. He might never get enough of his precious Ana. The cum shot onto her stomach, but he didn't let her free.

His hardness only gathered more of her essence, letting him glide over her.

He loved moving like this between her legs. He wanted a greater connection, but the fact that she would give him this, made his heart full.

He didn't stop. He held her hands as he kissed her warm swollen lips and mimicking fucking this most perfect, beautiful woman on his bed. The *only* woman he wanted on his bed.

She climaxed again, and he drank it up.

"That's my baby. I want all your orgasms. You deserve to feel good all the time, baby."

Her body writhed under his, her breasts scraping against his chest. "Lance."

"Let it go, baby. Don't hold back."

Her head arched back as another orgasm claimed her. She panted, but he couldn't stop.

He continued the act of fucking her, his thrusts not going too fast or too slow. Occasionally, he dragged his cock lower to smear her lubricant along his length.

It was so fucking beautiful. So fucking perfect.

He would make sure she'd never forget this night. Or these past few weeks.

Sweat gathered along his brow. He didn't know how much longer he could hold out, but he wanted this night to last forever.

Ana was his. Always had been.

As another orgasm took over, he knew he could release again. He growled out her name before he collapsed to her side and pulled her into his embrace. Exactly where she belonged.


Ana lay in his bed with his arms wrapped around her, cradling her as he slept. She'd dozed off shortly after that incredible make out session.

Geez! Who was she kidding? They nearly made love. If she'd given Lance the go-ahead, he would have done it.

*Oh, God.* It would have been amazing. Equally as amazing as his words: *I love you.*

For a fraction of a second, she thought he meant it as something beyond their lifelong friendship. For just that brief second, his words had reached deep into her core and made her believe Lance could be her happily ever after.

What if she was with the wrong man? What if she was supposed to be with Lance?

She felt the tears threaten.

But how could that be possible? Lance had always thought of her as a friend, his best friend. And she, for the most part, always thought of him the same way. Of course, she loved him. But now, she knew, she was *in love* with him.

How in the world was she supposed to go back to Matt after these two incredible weeks with her best friend?

On the same token, how could she leave Matt for a chance with Lance, only to be rejected because he didn't see her that way?

She clasped harder to the warm strong arms wrapped around her and let the tears fall.

# Chapter Forty-Nine

♥

Lance dragged himself out of bed and to the shower. He felt like shit, but he had two patients to see that day and a mound of paperwork.

That day. Ana's boyfriend would return from his trip. He'd probably head right over to see Ana. That's what Lance would do, assuming he'd leave Ana for two weeks, which he wouldn't.

Ana was probably excited to see him, especially with all her new-found confidence. She probably couldn't wait to experiment with her boyfriend. And the thought made Lance sick to his stomach.

*Why didn't I do something sooner?*

He scolded himself repeatedly, but it did no good. He'd had his chance. He loved Ana and maybe that's why he never made a move. He didn't want to ruin a good thing. But now he had a taste of just how good they could be together, and it killed him that she wasn't his.

After the second nick from his razor, he drew in a deep breath and told himself to focus.

Once done, he threw on some fresh clothes and headed to the kitchen for coffee and a protein shake he could take with him.

One thing he knew for sure—he couldn't be alone that night. No fucking way. He sent a text and waited for a reply.

***

Ana took the whole day off. Matt wouldn't arrive until four, but she wanted to be ready. She exfoliated, shaved, moisturized, and perfumed—all to impress and woo her boyfriend. She wore one of her new skirts, a sleeveless button-down blouse, heels, and her new lacy thong with matching bra.

A knock came at her door. Her heart kicked over. Matt walked through her apartment door, scooped her up, and swung her around.

"Baby, I missed you," he said right before he kissed her. He took over her mouth in a way she wasn't expecting.

She tried to adjust her kiss like she had with Lance, but his wide, flat tongue refused to glide along hers. It more dominated hers. She had to break the kiss. She clutched him close. "I missed you too."

He smiled and brought her to the sofa. His cologne seemed stronger than usual, but he was handsome as ever, especially with his glowing tan. "I have a present for you."

He pulled a wrapped box from his back pocket and presented it to her.

"Oh wow." She pulled off the wrapping and opened the box. There laid a pretty gold dolphin pendant on a gold chain.

"I swam with the dolphins and saw this and thought you might like it."

She smiled. She couldn't tell him she preferred silver. She always wore silver. She thought he knew that. "Thank you so much. It's beautiful."

"It's beautiful like you, baby."

She had a weird tick race up her spine hearing him call her *baby*. It sounded different than when Lance would say it. "So, tell me all about your trip."

"Oh, that can wait." He leaned in to kiss her neck, leaving it wet. "I need to be with my boo," he whispered into the crux of her neck and started unfastening her buttons and pulling the shirt from her waistband. Then he found the zipper to her skirt, and he unzipped and yanked it off her legs in no time.

"Whoa, Matt—"

"Oh, baby. Are these new? These are wonderful." He went down to his knees, gripped her thighs apart, and laid claim to her sex over her panties.

Images of Lance instantly popped in her head. She moaned, the wetness grew with each passing second. But before she could lie back and enjoy his tongue kisses, Matt reached up with both hands and pulled her panties over her hips.

"Matt," she exclaimed.

His eyes rounded. "What, baby? I need you now."

"I don't wanna go so fast."

"Oh, baby." He leaned forward cupped the back of her neck to kiss her, and with his other hand, pulled her right hand to cup his erection. "See what you do to me? I can't go slow."

She sighed as he stood and stripped out of his clothes just as quickly.

"Matt, please. Can you go back to kissing my body like you did before?"

He stopped right before he got to his briefs and pulled his eyebrows together.

"Ana, what's going on?"

She suddenly felt incredibly exposed. She looked down at her hands on her lap, the shyness coming on full force. "I, um, I just..." She thought about Lance, always asking her how she felt. Her back straightened. "I got to do some soul-searching while you were away, and I want to slow down and take our time." She met his gaze. "I don't want to rush. I like it when you touch and kiss my body before...you know."

"You want to go slow?"

She nodded.

"Okay, we can do that." He leaned in pecked her lips, taking his kisses across her jaw to her neck, then down her chest. He pulled on her bra straps and massaged her breasts as he sucked on her nipples. Her wetness grew. She closed her eyes and savored the sensations. Although it felt different from Lance, it was still nice.

He reached behind to unclasp the bra, then yanked it from her arms and sent it flying.

He kissed, licked, and sucked on her hard nipples while his right caressed the side of her body down to her thigh. He made his way to her center, sliding a finger through her wet slit. He growled over her skin and drove two fingers into her core. He pumped with force. "Oh, baby."

She jumped at the suddenness.

She pushed against his hand. "Easy. Go slow."

"Oh, baby. So hot." He pulled back her hand, and she exhaled.

Then it all happened so fast. He pulled down his briefs, came upright on his knees, pulled her hips to him, and rammed his penis into her.

He groaned, and she yelped.

He pumped into her feverishly as he claimed her mouth again.

In another ten seconds, he came, growling and panting into her neck.

She lay there stunned. She wanted to cry. Her first attempt to better her sex life with her boyfriend, and she'd failed. She didn't even come. She felt like a hole for him.

"Baby, you are so fucking hot." Matt pulled out and smiled at her. "Let's take this into the bedroom."

"Um." She couldn't say why, but she didn't want that. The emotion bubbling inside overwhelmed her. "I need to use the bathroom."

"Okay."

She all but ran to the bathroom. She shut the door and sank to the toilet. This wasn't what she wanted. She didn't want to go fast. Lance showed her that she loved the build-up. He showed her she could come multiple times that way.

She tried not to cry, but it was useless. Silently, the tears fell, and Ana knew it wasn't just for what happened with Matt. It was for missing what she had with Lance.

He knew her better than anyone. He knew how to please her and worship her, as he'd said. But she didn't know if he saw her as more than her best friend. What if he wanted to date another woman, or women? What if he had no interest in a love relationship because he liked it the way it was?

She swallowed hard. She had to face the music. Even if she couldn't have Lance, she didn't want Matt. She'd convinced herself that she loved him, but that was far from the truth. She loved Lance. He was her rock. Always had been.

She opened the door to find Matt naked on the bed, his erection out in the open.

He smiled at her and waved her close.

She grabbed her robe off the hook on the bathroom and tied it closed before she sat on the bed beside him. "Matt, we need to talk."

"Okay, baby." He leaned up, pushed her hair aside, and kissed her neck.

"Please, Matt."

"Ana, what's going on? Something's obviously wrong."

She sighed. "It occurred to me that maybe we aren't as compatible as I thought."

He furrowed his brows. "Is this about the sex?"

"Yes. No. I mean, it's more than that. I was lying to you. And to myself."

He pushed back and shifted more upright, his lips thinning. "What?"

She rested her hand over his. "I'd convinced myself that I loved you, but not in a way you deserve." She shook her head. "I sorry, Matt. I can't be with you anymore."

His jaw dropped, and the silence between them dragged. "I guess I knew that deep down. That I wasn't what you wanted."

"I don't doubt that you will find the right woman. Someone very compatible with you." She smiled, wishing only the best for him.

He nodded. After another moment passed, he rose and went to the living room to get dressed.

She followed him. Lifting the jewelry box, she offered it to him. "Here. I don't feel right keeping this."

He closed her hand over it. "No, I want you to keep it. And I hope you find the right man for you."

Without another word, he kissed her forehead, spun toward the door, and left.

Ana stared at the door for moment. She felt sadness at the broken relationship, but also relief that something she knew she should have done months ago went so smoothly. That Matt took it so well. He was free to find the right woman, and she was free to find the right man.

The thing is, she'd already found him.

She knew what she had to do next. She had to put on her big-girl panties and tell the man she loved that she loved him.

After a shower and some freshening up, she headed to Lance's apartment. It was nearly six o'clock. He'd be home from work soon.

She rang his bell, and no surprise, there was no answer. She sat at the stoop outside his place and waited. And waited. People had passed her, saying *excuse me*, but still no sign of Lance.

The knot in her stomach grew. The visions of him with another woman, maybe out on a date, took root in her head.

Was she making a fool of herself? How long should she sit there, waiting for him?

More time passed and darkness slowly settled.

Ana wanted to cry. He wasn't missing her at all. He'd moved on. What they shared was nothing special to him. Simply a teacher and a student.

She swiped stray tears that had escaped. It was time to throw in the towel. She bent to grab her bag and rose. When she looked up, there stood Lance, still dressed from work, his computer bag slung over his shoulder.

"Ana? I wasn't expecting you." He came closer. "Shit, Ana, what's wrong? C'mon inside."

He wrapped an arm around her and led her inside.

God, it felt like heaven—safe, warm, loving. More tears streamed.

He closed the door behind them, then took his bag and hers, setting them on the floor. He instantly held her in an embrace. "I hate seeing you like this. What happened? Did Matt hurt you?"

She shook her head. "Lance, I'm so glad to see you."

# Chapter Fifty

♥

Her words were surprising. Lance hated to see her in pain, but glad that she was there, looking for comfort.

She drew closer, wrapping her arms around him tighter.

He clung to her, giving her the time she needed to tell him what was wrong.

Instead of speaking, she rose to her tiptoes and kissed him. She glazed her lips over his and kissed him more.

He was confused but he opened for her, and she dove in. He moaned, or maybe it was her.

She kissed him like her life depended on it.

Then he felt the wetness from her tears. He broke the kiss. "Ana, I won't take advantage of you like this. I can see your heart is broken, but I can't."

She smiled and shook her head. "No, I miss you. I love you. It's not about Matt. I'm so glad to be back in your arms."

She loved him. He'd heard that before, but something told him this was different. This was what he'd been wanting all along. "You love me?"

"Yes. I'm not supposed to be with Matt." She relaxed her grip on his. "I only hope you'll have me." Her voice was timid and unsure.

*Have me?* The smile tugged at his lips. "God, yes. I love you too."

The tears started anew, streaming down her cheeks. "I couldn't be with Matt. I don't love him like I love you. You are my whole world, and it wasn't until recently did I realize that." She crashed her mouth to his.

He kissed her back with the same ferocity that she gave. He broke the kiss. "God, Ana, I thought I lost you. I craved being with you, and not just in a sexual way."

"Although that was good."

"Amazing," he chuckled.

"I want that again, Lance. I want it all the time, but only with you."

*Fuck!* Music to his ears.

"Wait a second." He released her, retrieved his bag, then lifted her and the bag, and walked to his bedroom.

She giggled and kissed his neck, driving him crazy.

He set her by the bed, whipped off his shirt, and then hers. He went to his knees kissing and caressing her soft body. Her skirt hit the floor, then her bra and panties. He suckled her nipples causing her to moan.

She was so gorgeous. And she was his.

He guided her to sit on the bed.

She spread her knees wide for him.

"Oh, baby." He leaned down, claiming her sweet pussy.

"Unh." Her hips flexed toward his mouth.

He loved on her until she came.

She cried out his name, but he wasn't done.

He rose and stripped off his remaining clothes. Then rifled through his bag.

She slid to the center of the bed, probably thinking they'd finally make love. But not yet.

"Ana, you mean the world to me." He kissed her as he hovered over her. "I didn't want to ruin the friendship we had, but these last two weeks showed me we can have the friendship and more."

A tear streaked to the mattress.

He kissed her perfect naked body again, heading to her pussy. He laid claim to her. He reached for her nipples and toyed with them as he licked her.

She mewled. "Lance," she begged.

He didn't let up until she came on his tongue.

"Ah," she cried out, gripping his hair.

He rose up, positioning himself over her, his cock posed at her entrance. He kissed her lips one more time. "But baby, know that you are mine now." He gripped her hands, laying them flat on the bed.

She nodded.

"Say it."

"I'm yours now."

"And forever more."

More tears released. "Forever more. I'm yours forever more. Please, Lance, please."

Getting ready, he gripped the ring sliding it down her finger on her left hand just as he entered her for the first time.

"Ah." She bowed her back, and he growled.

"Mine, baby." He claimed her lips and pumped into her, letting his seed go deep into a place that would one day hold his child. He didn't stop, he couldn't stop. He was as madly in lust with Ana as he was in love with her. She was his world. Life was dull without her.

He continued pumping until she came around him, gripping him, drawing him in.

They whispered over and over *I love you*, kissing their bodies anywhere they could reach.

He came again inside her, smiling inside to know he could send his seed into her now and forever.

She pulled her hands, and he released them. Then she wrapped her arms and legs around him. "Fuck me, Lance. Please. Make me yours."

He pushed onto his hands, meeting her gaze. He thrust harder and more deeply. "I love you, Ana." His thrusts didn't cease. He needed to hold on until she came again.

In a few short moments, she screamed—the loudest he'd ever heard—clutching his dick detonating his own climax.

He collapsed to her side and pulled her body into his. They held each other while the panting slowly subsided.

Finally, he had the strength to speak. "Do you like your ring?"

"Yes." She smiled against his chest.

"Did you even look at it?"

"No. But I don't need to." She looked up at him. "It's from you, so I know I'll love it. And it means I'll be your wife." She cupped his jaw. "Lance, you give me a love and peace that only you can give. I want you for the rest of my life."

Well, she could look at the ring later. She would love it, he knew.

But in the meantime, he'd somehow recuperated in record time, so he rolled her onto her back and smoothly entered her, moaning like it was the first time. "God, Ana, I love you."

"I love you, Lance."

"You're mine."

"I was always yours."

# Lush Lavender

# Chapter Fifty-One

♥

Roger glanced up as Paige entered his office. She'd dressed for work in a straight navy skirt, ivory blouse, navy heels, and a long camel coat. She practically oozed style.

*Gorgeous.*

She smiled as she greeted his receptionist, Sarah. His long-time, incredibly loyal receptionist-slash-office manager, honestly his life manager. Whenever she decided to retire, Roger was screwed.

Dr. Roger Winslow had been an obstetrician-gynecologist for over a decade. He'd always known that would be his specialty because he got to help happy mothers grow happy babies.

It wasn't *always* that simple, but for him it was fulfilling and rewarding. And as a long-time bachelor who had been left without a mother since age six, this filled a void and need on many levels.

He watched on the closed-circuit TV as Paige chatted with Sarah. It afforded him a moment to watch her graceful moves, her womanly curves, the smile that lit up her entire face.

The first moment he'd laid eyes on her, he knew he had to have her.

Of course, she'd been married then.

Roger rose one last time to double check the exam room.

Slightly warmer temperature.

Check.

Soft blanket on the table.

Check.

He adjusted the lighting down. Perfect.

As he exited the room, he saw Sarah showing Paige into Room 1, the exam room he primarily used to see patients. Room 2 was for overflow or for Nasy, his assistant, to take vitals when Room 1 was in use.

"Sarah, I'll take Ms. Simmons in Room 2."

Paige looked from Sarah to him and back again.

"Oh, okay. I'll send Nasy right in."

"That won't be necessary." He didn't wait for the piercing look he was sure to get from his diligent manager. Instead, he waved a hand, directed Paige inside, and smiled. "Right this way."

She walked through the doorway and set her purse and coat on the side chair.

"Please, Ms. Simmons, have a seat."

She lifted an eyebrow, then turned to scan the room. "This isn't the usual room I'm in."

"No. I thought we'd spend more time on your exam today." He flipped open his tablet cover to review her updated information. "Here we'll be away from the hubbub." The corners of his lips lifted.

He'd been blessed with two symmetrical dimples he knew women loved. Today, he would use that to his advantage.

"Okay."

"So, let's review your notes. Your labs look good from last month." He scrolled as he read. "Vitals are excellent." He met her gaze. "You work out."

She lifted an eyebrow.

"It shows." He pointed to the tablet.

She grinned, and her face beamed like a Christmas tree.

Roger couldn't pinpoint one thing he'd liked about Paige because really his infatuation grew over time. "Any changes in your medical history since your visit last year?"

Her lips pursed, even as her eyes still held their twinkle. "No."

"Any health concerns?"

She tipped her head briefly. "No."

"Are you still on the pill?"

She laughed and instantly covered her mouth with her hand. "Yes."

"Okay, I'll make sure to send over a refill to your pharmacy once we're done here."

He lowered his voice. "Any residual stress from your divorce? Stress can wreak havoc on the body. More than people often realize."

She shook her head. "No, everything went surprisingly smoothly. I feel pretty good."

"Good. Glad to hear it. So, like I said, I'd like to take a little more time with you today. More than just the pap smear, pelvic exam, and breast exam. I often find for many women, I am their primary doctor."

"Okay." Her brows pinched together slightly.

"When was the last time you saw a dermatologist?" His fingers hovered over the keys.

She tilted her head. "Um, I don't know exactly. I guess three or four years."

He typed. Not that her answer mattered. "Okay." He closed the tablet. "You know the routine. I'll leave you to undress. You can wrap in this blanket. Opening in the back."

She rose and ran her hand down the plush lavender blanket draped on the table. "This is a nice touch."

"I thought you'd like that, especially on such a cold day." He grinned and exited to give her a moment to strip. But fuck, how he'd love to stay in that room and watch. He'd seen everything before, of course. But he'd never tire of the sight of that gorgeous body—kissable lips, plump breasts, and lean legs. Her husband was a dumbass to dump her for someone younger. Not that there was much difference between thirty and forty. Roger shook his head.

After a few minutes, he rapped on the door and entered.

Paige sat on the table, the blanket wrapped around her like strapless dress. A *bulky* strapless dress.

He grinned and adjusted the lights lower. "Sometimes, these florescent lights can be so harsh."

She nibbled on her lower lip.

He started his exam in a rather benign way: checking her ears, nose, and throat. He especially lingered his fingertips on that delicate neck of hers, the softest skin he had ever touched.

"Excellent."

He slipped the stethoscope into place, separated the loose blanket in the back to listen to her lungs. Then, to the front, he started high and gently tugged the blanket to listen to her heart. He moved from the sternum slowly to beneath her left breast.

Her breathing changed slightly, and he might have heard her swallow.

God, she was so enticing. His dick flexed behind his trousers.

"Excellent. Now I'll check for any unusual moles and spots." He removed the penlight from his lab coat pocket to do an inspection of her skin along her hairline. He inspected down her neck, over her shoulder, and down her arm. He repeated the sequence to her left side. "Great. Would you mind standing and turning around for a moment. I'll scan the back as well."

"Sure." She slid off the table and turned, clutching the blanket over her ass.

*Oh precious, that's useless.*

He brushed her hair to the side, leaning in close as he searched and glided his fingertips over her skin. He roamed from her shoulder blades, scanning slowly to her lumbar.

She broke out in goosebumps.

Then he tugged the blanket from her left hand, revealing her butt cheek. He scanned all the way down to her foot, taking his sweet time, being thorough.

Precisely why he'd blocked out an hour for her, so he could take his sweet time savoring her lush, ripe body. She needed a man like Roger; he knew it as sure as he knew Michael Jordan was the greatest of all time.

Gently, he tugged free the blanket from her right hand. She didn't recover her left side, leaving her entire backslide open for his perusal. He took that as a very good sign.

He continued his scan. The increased movement of her back from her breathing did not go unnoticed. He knew she had to be reacting to his touches, warming slowly to his seduction.

Her heart-shaped ass called to him. If he didn't do something fast, he'd grab those globes and kiss and fondle them before taking over the rest of her body.

He cleared his throat and stood. "Now, you can hop back on the table and lie down. I can help cover you."

He'd purchased a soft, terry cloth table covering for her visit. Clinical paper was *not* the feel he was going for that day.

There she was, stretched out before him, a warm blanket draped over her naked body, without another soul in sight to witness what was about to transpire.

Unveiling one leg at a time, he did a thorough visual scan of each outstretched leg, gently sliding his fingertips along the route.

Recovering her leg, he went to her torso. Looking as professional and unaffected as possible, he pulled the blanket aside, giving him half her torso to inspect.

She sucked in a breath when his fingertips skated along her breast.

He repeated the treatment to the opposite side, then without covering her, he stuck the light in his pocket and spoke. "Excellent. Good job wearing sunscreen." He smiled.

With his left hand, he lifted her arm over her head. His right hand stayed on her breast, gently massaging in small, circular movements. Of course, he took extra time with Paige and allowed his thumb to graze over her nipple, back and forth, bringing it to a nice hard peak. *Gorgeous.*

Lifting her other arm overhead to join the first, he repeated the same actions to the neglected breast, checking for any abnormalities. How he loved the subtle way he was turning her on. He could see a soft pink hue filling her cheeks.

As much as he hated to move on, he recovered her breasts, just barely, and turned to grab his roller stool.

She hadn't moved her arms down. Maybe because he hadn't told her she could or maybe because she loved the idea of being laid out for him. He hoped for the latter.

Now for the grand prize.

He took in several breaths discreetly in an attempt to calm his racing heart.

*Here goes.*

♥

# Chapter Fifty-Two

R oger pulled out the stirrups and situated them wider than normal, then one at a time, he placed Paige's feet in them. He pushed in the table extension and peeled back the blanket, showing her perfect pussy. "Please scoot closer to the end of the table." He placed his bare hands on her ass, letting the tips of his thumbs touch her pussy lips, as he guided her to the edge.

She moved closer, and he caught a whiff of her scent. Pure heaven.

"Perfect. Now, try and relax. Closing your eyes may help."

She met his gaze, then closed her eyes.

He flipped on his floor light and pulled it closer, focusing solely between her legs. *Ah, yes.* The sheen of lubrication began to show between her bare nether lips. Just as he'd suspected.

He gently separated her knees farther and pushed the blanket clear of her mons and abdomen as much as possible while keeping the visual barrier with it draped over her knees.

He moved the light in closer to warm her gorgeous pussy. How he loved that sight. His dick grew in his pants, aching to be set free. His closed lab coat would hide that bulge.

In medical school, his class had a jokester and self-professed adventurer named Gilbert. Gilbert had all kinds of weird thoughts and ideas.

One had been he knew how close one could get the light to the skin to warm it, without burning it. Gilbert didn't end up finishing the program; instead, he went to work at his dad's company. But Roger never forgot the weird things that came out of his mouth.

Buying some more warming time, he stood, walked to the head of the table, and said softly, "I'll lower this to make you more comfortable."

He didn't bother to ask if it would indeed make her more comfortable. He lowered the angled table, bringing her head to a flat, level position.

"Thanks," she murmured.

Resuming his seated position between her legs, he pulled back the light just enough to give him room to work. First, he started by snapping latex gloves. The sound that would normally be heard if he'd pulled them on. But of course, he wanted his hands and fingers bare, able to feel—really feel—as much of the beauty on the table as possible.

He lubed the warm vaginal speculum, separating her labia, and sliding the implement in. He adjusted the tool to give himself good access to her cervix. He swabbed, again touching and smoothing her thigh to her mons, resting his thumb over her burgeoning clitoris.

He fucking loved seeing her body respond to him, to his touches. And her scent was damn-near clouding his thinking. His dick grew in the tight confines of his pants even more.

He finished his swabbing and carefully sealed the tubes for the lab. After releasing the speculum, he moved the light back in closer. He rose and asked, "How are you doing with your Kegel exercises?"

She opened her eyes and paused a moment to focus. "Um, I do them occasionally, I guess."

He nodded. "Kegel exercises can prevent or control urinary incontinence and other pelvic floor problems. They strengthen the pelvic floor muscles, which support the uterus, bladder, small intestine, and rectum. And some women report stronger orgasms when they regularly do these exercises."

She nodded. "Oh."

Roger noted how the color had grown in her cheeks, and her lips gaped ever so slightly. She was the epitome of a relaxed woman, possibly open to a more thorough exam.

Switching off the light, he slid in two bare fingers into her wet channel and almost growled out loud.

She was so silky smooth, so swollen and puffy, it made Roger's heart sing. She was ready for a man to enter her. Her cunt was so perfect, it took his breath away.

With his left hand, he felt around her abdomen around for anything unusual. "Let me know if you feel any pain."

"Okay," she said, her tone breathier. Her eyes remained closed.

Of course, he didn't feel anything unusual, but he didn't stop his ministrations. He pushed gently with his left hand as his right fingers stroked her wet channel slightly. His thumb glossed over her clitoris, loving how it continued to grow.

His mouth watered. He had to taste her. One little taste.

Carefully and quietly, he sat and ducked his head down low, not stopping the exam with his hands. Then, leaning close, with the tip of his tongue, he licked her tiny nub.

She might question what she was truly feeling, as the area was very warm from his light.

He couldn't stop. He circled her little bud a few more times, wishing he could stay there all afternoon.

A tiny mewl escaped her mouth.

*Oh, yeah!*

He slid his left hand to her right thigh. He didn't want to take his hands off her now that he'd started.

Quietly, he spoke. "Now, let's work those pelvic floor muscles a bit. Squeeze my fingers and release."

She licked her glossed lips and paused a moment. He had to believe she wanted to continue.

Finally, she did as he bid. She had great muscle tone, and he would ensure they stayed that way.

He moved in and out, more obviously now, stimulating the area, bringing her to new heights.

"Excellent." He praised her while continuing the stroking of his fingers and added a gentle rub of her clit.

Her pants were more apparent. He knew he could bring her orgasm if he wanted to.

And he wanted to.

With his left hand, he pulled the blanket off her breasts, dragging it slowly over her nipples. Her dark pink nipples were hard.

What he wouldn't give to have his mouth there right now, tasting and laving them.

He swallowed hard and spoke again. "Many women report that the sensitivity of their nipples can heighten and enhance the sensation down below. Do you think you experience that?" He didn't wait for an answer. "I'll do some light massages there. I want you to continue your exercises at the same time."

"Okay," she said on an exhale.

*Oh, yeah.* She needed an orgasm now. Probably more than one.

He stroked her precious core, feeling her arousal slide down his fingers as he stroked and caressed her perfect nipples with his other hand.

She moaned.

*That's right, precious. Let Dr. Winslow take good care of you.*

Just another minute of him stroking her channel, rotating her clit, and toying and pinching her nipples she came. She sucked in air and bowed off the table.

It was the most beautiful sight.

Roger worked fast. While she was momentarily unconscious in her climax, he reached under his lab coat and lowered his pants' zipper.

"Very good. Your muscle strength is fine." It was better than "fine", but she didn't need to know that now. "I'd like to try that again. Please continue your muscle flexing and releasing, but now I want you to do some tightening of your gluteal muscles as well. Would you try that now?"

"Um, I don't know if..."

He tilted his head. "Know what?"

She looked from the door to him. "What if someone hears?"

"You let me worry about that."

She nodded as her beautiful mouth gaped for air and clenched around his two fingers.

"Good. And don't be afraid to let your hips rise off the table."

"Okay." Then she closed her eyes again, he stroked her core, and she flexed her muscles.

She was the picture of perfection.

He toyed with her nipples and watched the lust rise again in her body—her flushed cheeks, her peeked nipples, her slick pussy—everything he'd hope to see in her today. Everything he'd dreamt about.

Now, he focused his sight in between her legs. He wanted more from her; he had to have more from this fine woman stretched out on his table.

"This time, really clench your muscles and lift your bottom off the table."

She did as he asked.

"Good. Now hold it there." He stroked her core, twisting his fingers inside her. Then he pressed against her G-spot. "Feel that? Feels a little like you need to use the bathroom, right?"

"Yes," she breathed out.

He never stopped stroking her slick core. "You can investigate this yourself at home, but it's the area right past the wrinkled patch." He worked his fingers in her and on her breasts. *Come, baby.*

She pulsed her hips, accepting all he'd been giving her, when the climax took her over. She cried out, and it was pure music to his ears.

He removed his fingers, discreetly licking the nectar that had coated them. He stood, rested both hands on her thighs, and waited for her to open her eyes.

She finally met his gaze, her eyes slightly glassy.

"That was excellent. I'd like to try one more exercise if you think you're up for it." He didn't wait for an answer. He squatted before his cabinet and rustled some things, but that was mere distraction. He freed his eager, weeping cock from his briefs. He stood, of course his waist was completely out of her view.

He returned his hands to her thighs, gently spoke, "I'd like to try something to provide a bit more resistance against your pelvic floor muscles, then we can give them a break."

"Okay." She met his gaze.

"It will be a bit thicker than my fingers, but it won't hurt in the least."

"Oh, okay."

"Great. Close your eyes again and take a nice deep breath."

She nodded, and as she inhaled, he slid his thick cock into her dripping wet cunt. All the way in.

She moaned, and her back bowed off the table.

*Good girl.*

He squeezed his muscles fiercely to stave off his climax. He inhaled slowly and evenly, then he moved.

"How do you feel? Is the tool comfortable?"

"Yes. Yes."

"Okay, I'll move it some more. You continue squeezing and releasing your muscles."

She nodded several times, no doubt savoring the tool in her channel, working to please her.

With his hands free, he reached up to both breasts to play, toy, and twist her nipples.

She gripped the edge of the table overhead. The glow in her cheeks blossomed to a rosy red.

He moved a little faster. "That's right. Keep working those muscles." He praised her as he spoke, using every ounce of strength to control the lust in his voice, when really he felt like an animal finally able to breed his most prefect complement.

When he felt a flutter deep inside her, he gripped her hips and hammered into her hard and fast.

She cried out louder than before, throwing her head back. There was a high probability that his staff heard that one.

As she slowly calmed from her explosive climax, he quickly pulled out, released on the hard-surface floor, and tucked his semi away as fast as possible. His lab coat would hide his open fly.

Slowly, she opened her eyes.

He slid the blanket down over her knees, regrettably covering her pussy once again from his view.

"Wow," escaped past her full, red lips.

"You did very well today," he said with the upmost professionalism he could muster, knowing full-well that he'd acted the complete opposite.

He set her legs down, collapsed the stirrups, and checked that her footstool was still in place. "I'll give you a few moments to dress, and I'll make excuses to the staff."

She bit her lips between her teeth.

He exited and closed the door behind him. He righted his clothes and took several deep breaths.

*Fuck!* She was hot as fuck! That was everything he'd hoped for and more.

She might have been embarrassed, but it didn't matter. She took in what he'd offered, savored it, and let the pleasure send her on waves of delicious ecstasy.

He'd planned for both of them to savor the incredible lust, and it worked. It worked perfectly.

He strode to the reception desk.

Sarah turned in her chair to look at him with a raised eyebrow. "That sounded interesting."

He handed her his tablet. "She's fine. Just something took her by surprise."

"Uh-huh." Sarah pursed her lips and spun back around.

He loved that woman. Maybe he should think about upping her year-end bonus.

He sauntered back to exam Room 2, rapped on the door, and waited for a reply before he entered.

Paige draped her coat over her arm and looped her purse over her shoulder.

Roger would love to linger longer with his most favorite patient, but he had two more to go before he could call it a day. And nothing, absolutely nothing, would replace the amazing time he'd just spent with Paige.

"Well, keep up the good work," he said with a smile.

A gorgeous glow still graced her face. "Thank you," and she shook the hand he offered.

He watched as she turned out of the room and strolled down the hall toward reception. After a beat, he closed the door and inhaled the scent floating in the air. The scent of Paige and of sex. But he had work to do. First, he pushed his chair out of the way from the mess he'd left on the floor. He reached for paper towels and the bottle of spray cleaner. Easy peasy. The cleaning crew could disinfect overnight. Next, he washed his hands and walked across the hall to review the records of his next patient. With a few minutes to spare, he reclined and closed his eyes, resting his head back against his chair, savoring the afterglow of an amazing fuck.

He replayed everything that had just transpired. Paige was incredible, laying herself open and vulnerable, but trusting him, nevertheless. He would savor his time with her until his last days.

His phone buzzed. He opened his desk drawer to retrieve it. A text.

*That had to be the most erotic thing I have ever experienced!! When you get here tonight, your favorite dinner will be waiting. And me, on my knees.*

*P xx*

He grinned. God help him. He loved that woman. Someday very soon, he'd make Paige his wife. No doubt about it.

# Scarlet Silk

# Chapter Fifty-Three

♥

Today was the day.

Micaela had been on the job for one month and quickly gotten into a comfortable routine with her boss, Neil Ross. But Micaela wasn't interested in comfortable.

She had a ladder to climb. In a male-dominated world, where women made seventy-eight percent of what men made, no thank you. Micaela had her sights set high.

Despite the economy, Micaela was determined to create her own success, her own wealth. Sure, her grades from Lakemont U were good, but she wasn't banking on that. She was banking on her *other* assets.

She strolled into the office, stashed her purse, and hung her suit jacket on the back of her chair, then strode into Mr. Ross's office.

"Good morning, sir. Can I get you a cup of coffee?" she asked with a smile.

He glanced up from readying his desk for the day. It took several seconds for him to speak. "G'morning. Yes, that would be great."

She nodded and smiled to herself. *Oh yeah. He noticed.*

That morning Micaela dressed in a scarlet red silk blouse, black skirt, and black heels. Her lips and fingernails matched her shirt. Perfectly festive for the Christmas holidays only four weeks away.

One thing she didn't wear—a bra.

And the cold silk made her nipples perkier.

Phyllis, another assistant, passed her leaving the breakroom and did a doubletake.

"Good morning, Phyllis."

"Good morning, Micaela."

Micaela kept walking. She had success on her mind, even if the first step was as simple as getting her boss coffee. The goal was making him happy.

She returned to find him furrowing his brow at something on his computer. He was a mostly handsome man in his mid-forties, single—although it appeared he'd had a girlfriend—with a respectful management style and a good sense of humor.

She remembered their interview barely two months ago, how at ease he made her feel. She was lucky to have him as a boss.

The question though, did he feel lucky having her as his admin? Time would soon tell.

She set down the coffee and took a sip of her own.

He shifted his sight to the cup, then to her. He reached for the cup.

She could hear him inhale and exhale.

"Miss Summer, you look very nice today."

"Thanks. I think I'm getting into the Christmas spirit."

He smiled.

"So, what's on the agenda for today?"

He nodded, absently. "How about you get settled, and I'll buzz you in a bit?" He motioned to the email awaiting his attention.

"Sounds good." She pivoted away to get her day organized. She had emails to go through and decide which were important enough for Mr. Ross to respond to. She had voicemails to retrieve, reports to file, and meetings to set up that Mr. Ross gave her last Friday.

She hoped he watched her walk away. She needed him drawn to her for her plan to work, otherwise… Well, she'd hate to leave this amazing company with great pay, but she would. She'd look for another job where she could fast-track her career. Experts in finance were needed everywhere.

She had a plan, and she'd let nothing get in the way. She didn't have boyfriends; she had fuck buddies. She had planned dinners with her family every Sunday. And she spent time with her friends, mostly on the weekends, when it didn't interfere with work.

Well, it wasn't just work and sleep. Micaela worked hard to look good. She worked out at the gym, got facials, scheduled mani-pedis regularly, and ate right. Again, any and everything to help propel her career forward.

Sure, it was a single-minded focus, but wasn't that exactly how they described most successful people, usually men, in the world? Determined, singular in focus?

So, if that's what it took, she was all in.


Day One of her fast-track plan had gone well. The remainder of the week, Micaela had the same plan: braless with a hip hugging skirt and heels. She would work in some snug sweaters in lieu of button-down blouses.

As she got more money, she had some purchases to make: back-seam stockings, lacy undergarments for days when she didn't go braless, and a garter or two that would be evident under a smooth, straight skirt. That should get Mr. Ross's attention.

Also, on her To-Do list this week? Change out the buttons on the cream blouse.

She'd wear that next week in the hopes a button or two would give way.

***

Neil greeted Micaela with a smile, his eyes dropping to her chest.

*Fuck! Stop that!*

He couldn't help where his sight drifted; Micaela hadn't worn a bra for the past seven working days.

Her gorgeous breasts faintly hidden behind a thin layer of silk, highlighting her plump globes and delicate nipples.

He didn't know if it was work appropriate, but he wasn't about to say something. Would a man's nipple show through their dress shirt? It could happen. And no one would say a word.

The difference was Neil's dick had flexed behind his pants at the delicious sight. He'd been curious about the sudden change, but that might be something he would never know.

"Good morning."

"Morning. Lots to do to wrap up year end."

She nodded, her pretty, long hair wrapped in a bun on top of her head. "Yup. I'm on it." She pivoted away, her ass sashaying to her cubicle outside his office.

Close to the end of day, Neil spoke over the intercom. "Micaela, Randy brought up the end of year statements, and they're ready to go. Would you have them interofficed out?"

"Sure. Be right there."

She entered and scanned the files stacked on his desk.

"Any questions?"

"Nope, looks clearly labeled." She hoisted the first stack in her right arm, then the second stack in her left hand. Everything went smoothly until...

"Um, Micaela, a button came loose." He casually pointed.

She looked down, files in both hands resting on her hips. "Oh." She smushed her lips together and made a step closer in his direction. "Do you think you could help me?" Pleading with her eyes as she looked like she had no intention of relieving herself of the files.

He pushed back from his desk and straightened in his chair, throwing a quick glance to the door.

She stepped between his spread legs and waited.

He licked his lips and inhaled her light floral scent. He reached for her blouse, trying to reign in the adrenaline coursing through his veins.

Before he could fasten the offending button, another one popped free. With both sides of her shirt in his hands, he examined the garment. His brows pulled together. "It looks like the buttons may be too small for the buttonholes."

"Oh," she breathed out, but didn't move as muscle, even as her shirt was in worse condition than when she'd walked in.

His heart hammered in his chest at how fucking close her naked breasts were to his face. He glanced one last time toward the door. No one was there, not that he was expecting anyone.

Slowly, he grazed the fabric over her breasts, causing her nipples to poke against the delicate fabric. He swallowed hard, admiring the view of some more creamy skin.

He glanced up at her; her dark eyes accepting whatever he wanted from her.

The back of his finger skated between her tits over her softness.

One little brush to the left or right and he could have his fill of this beauty, seemingly offering herself to him.

*No. This isn't right.*

He pulled back and let out an expletive. "You better take it from here." He rose and headed to the executive washroom as fast as lightning, hoping his jacket covered his raging hard-on.

*Fuck!* He was her boss. They couldn't be carrying on like this. She was young and impressionable, and he was sixteen years her senior.

*Fuck!*

Something was different with his assistant, and he needed to get to the bottom of this. Soon. Right now, he needed to think of the difference between the Unit of Product Method and the Straight-Line Depreciation Method for a depreciating asset to get the rock in his pants under control.

He splashed water on his face and sucked in several deep breaths. He glanced at his watch. Two hours until quitting time. He'd table the discussion until tomorrow, if he could get through the rest of the day.

# Chapter Fifty-Four

♥

Neil was certain of one thing. His twenty-four-year-old assistant wanted to have an affair, a relationship of some sort with him. The question was why? She could have any guy her own age. She was smart, vivacious, had a pretty face, and a rockin' body.

So why him?

As he got ready for work, the conclusion became clear and simple. If she came in again without wearing a bra, he would have to ask her. She clearly had a motive that wouldn't go away, so he'd just need to get to the root of the issue and tell her it wasn't possible. No relationship other than that of boss-employee was permitted.

Not to mention, he was dating someone. He wasn't a cheater, even though he was quite certain Nisha was sleeping around on him. The four-year relationship had probably run its course, and he was being lazy in not bringing it to an end. Nisha wanted to get married, and Neil wasn't particularly interested in marriage. Or in having kids for that matter.

He sighed as he wiped the condensation off the bathroom mirror. The faster he reigned in this little filly, the better.

At the office, an hour later, his gutsy, braless admin set a cup of hot coffee on his desk. He knew he had to say something. He asked, "Micaela, can you stay for a little bit after work today?"

She tipped her head, and her hair fell over her shoulder. "Of course. Anything you need." Then, she pivoted on her heel and headed back to her desk.

Shortly, after five, Micaela strode into his office.

"Please close the door."

She did as he asked.

He inhaled fully and motioned to the chair in front of his desk. "I know it hasn't been two months yet, but how are you liking the job so far."

The corners of her full pink lips lifted. "I like it a lot."

He nodded. "I ask because I'm of the impression that maybe you want more."

Her eyes didn't divert. "That's right."

*Okay, now we're getting somewhere.* "Would you care to tell me more about that?"

"As I mentioned in my interview, I want to build a career with Mathison. I want to use my finance degree to get ahead and earn money so I'm not relying on support from anyone else."

That was admirable. He nodded.

She licked her lips and rose, slowly rounding his desk.

He spun to face her, pushing back from the desk, opting not to stand. At six-two, he knew he intimidated people sometimes. In this case, he needed Micaela comfortable enough to trust him with the truth.

"You, naturally, are in a position to help me get those promotions I long for." She scooted in closer and sat across his lap.

He hid his surprise but didn't push her away.

"Quite simply," her voice dipped, "I know that pleasing you is paramount to fast-tracking my career. Honestly, I'm willing to do whatever it takes."

He swallowed hard. There it was. Her confession. And damn if any man on the planet wouldn't love to hear those words: *pleasing you*.

All the words he had rehearsed that morning were lost in the ether. Absently, he held onto her hips. "Um, Micaela, I don't think that's possible. People could find out."

"They will only find out if we want them to."

This fine woman before him offered herself to him, and he had a hard time thinking of a reason why they couldn't do what she wanted. He would help her get promoted regardless, but his dick thought this option was the best.

"Don't you have a boyfriend?"

She shook her head. "I don't do boyfriends. I have friends..."

He knew that was code for fuck buddies.

"But I'm putting my career first. And frankly, the marriage and kids thing doesn't appeal to me, despite my mother's wishes." She grinned.

He appreciated her directness and honesty. Would she leave if he didn't give her what she wanted?

Before he could ask the question, she put her hands to her blouse buttons to unfasten them. "Would you like to try a redo of yesterday?"

He grabbed her right hand.

Her deep eyes widened.

Before he thought better of it, he gripped her hand behind her back and lifted his free hand to her delicate neck, stroking and feeling her rapid pulse under his fingertips. He grazed his fingertips down her cleavage and undid the first available button. Then another and another.

He stroked back up, bringing goosebumps to her smooth skin.

With his index finger and middle finger, he dragged her lapel to the side, exposing her left breast. He repeated the motion to her right breast.

Her chest rose and fell rapidly, and her delicate pink nipples pinched to hard points.

He teased her skin with the slightest touch.

Her mouth gaped and lust brewed in her eyes as she watched his face.

"Your breasts are beautiful. I will admit. And having you come into the office without a bra on has been the highlight of my days."

He cupped her tit and brushed his thumb over her nipple.

She let out a low moan, and her eyes fluttered closed.

He needed a taste. He lifted her to standing as he separated his legs for her to stand in front of him.

Keeping his gaze trained on her, he glossed both hands up the sides of her tits, fondling the pillowy flesh.

His dick ached for relief, but he hadn't made up his mind yet. Once they fucked, there would be no turning back.

"You are so fucking enticing, Micaela." He leaned forward to claim her nipple, laving and sucking on her deliciousness.

"Ahh." Her head fell back.

He worshiped her tits for several moments and knew he had to stop. He couldn't take it any further.

He straightened and dropped his hands to his lap. "Micaela, I will consider your offer. Thank you. I'll see you tomorrow."

Her eyes sparkled, and her cheeks were pink with excitement. "Thank you." She buttoned her blouse, smiled, and spun away.

His hard-on expected him to lunge after her, but he would have to wait. Neil couldn't make some rash decision based on what his dick wanted.

Micaela slid into the front seat of her car in the parking garage. The wetness between her legs sliding between her lips.

*Holy shit!* That was one of the hottest things she'd ever done. Truly, when Mr. Ross said he'd wanted to see her after work, she panicked. She feared he'd write her up or worse, fire her. And frankly, spending more time with him, she really wanted to have sex with him, not just for her career.

Then she took the brazen move to sit on his lap, and it blossomed into something wonderful. She half-expected he'd lean her over the desk right then and take her fast and hard. She knew his cock wanted to come out and play.

Damn, that was incredible!

Now, she didn't have a firm answer, but at least she made her wishes known. Some feminists would likely scream at her, saying she'd sent the movement back decades. Micaela wasn't anti-feminist. She'd simply decided the fastest way to achieve her goals and gain financial independence would be to use all the tools at her disposal.

And based on earlier, Mr. Ross might just be on board.

Micaela tried to focus on her workout, then cooking dinner. She was so tempted to call one of her *friends* for relief. Instead, she planned her outfit for the next day—a body-con pink sweater, *sans* bra, a navy pencil skirt, and a sexy lace thong. In case he got to take a peek.

In bed, she reached for her vibe to put out the flaming fire he lit in her.

# Chapter Fifty-Five

♥

Neil awoke rock-hard with Micaela on his mind. Which was both a blessing and a curse. He looked forward to seeing her, working side-by-side with her. But on the same token, she'd want his answer and he didn't have one yet.

Well, first things first: Nisha. He shot her a text, asking if she could break away for lunch. Instead of waiting for her reply he jumped in the shower, taking care of his woody was priority.

As he snapped on the lid to his insulated coffee cup, her reply finally came through.

*Can't today. How about tomorrow?*

Really, anyone could ask, were they even a couple? Where was she and what was she doing? Well, none of that mattered now.

He stared at his phone. How bad would it be to break it off via text? He shook his head. That would be an asshole move after four years.

But fuck! That meant one more day of putting off the incredible, sensuous Micaela.

The notion stopped him dead in his tracks. The fact that he was mad he had to wait to break it off with Nisha before getting to fuck

Micaela told him the answer. He wanted Micaela. He wanted what she was offering and was confident he could return the favor.

The day went as could be expected, perhaps more paperwork than usual for end of year. And Micaela was on the edge of her seat, anxious to hear Mr. Ross's answer, partly for her career, and partly for her body.

As five o'clock approached, Mr. Ross called out. "When you get a moment, Micaela, would you come in here?"

Her tummy flipped. "Sure." She tried to sound unaffected, but the little interlude from the prior day had her ready for more. If Mr. Ross told her *no*, she'd have some hard choices to make.

She shut down her PC and strode through the doorway.

"Please close the door."

Her heart rate sped.

He pushed back and motioned her to stand in front of him. He made a show of scanning her body, likely seeing her nipples peek under his scrutiny.

"When you left here yesterday did you masturbate?"

She sucked in air. "Yes."

"How?"

"I, um, used my vibrator."

He nodded. His gaze was locked on hers; she didn't dare look away, but damn if she didn't want to see if he was hard.

"Do you always use a vibrator?"

She shook her head.

He grinned, and the depth in his eyes grew. "Good. I'd like to see that."

*What?*

His large, warm hands gripped her hips. Without a word, his fingertips skated over the straps of her garter, no doubt curious to know more. He slid under her sweater and caressed her torso, making his way north, when he cupped her breasts and toyed with her nipples.

She nearly panted at the slow erotic seduction. How she wished he'd just pull up her skirt and spread her legs over his lap.

"So lovely, Micaela." He lifted her sweater above her breasts and claimed her. One at a time, he licked and sucked her nipples. The sensation was out of this world. This man had an incredible mouth and knew how to use it. She gripped his arms for stability.

He pulled back and spoke. "Come to the sofa."

*Oh, yes.*

As she sat, he shoved a pillow behind her back and pulled on her legs, forcing her into a slouched position. He adjusted the sweater, making sure her breasts were on display. Then, he walked to the door and locked it. Grabbing his chair, he placed it in front of her with a clear view of her body.

He cleared his throat and spoke four simple words. "Let me watch you."

She licked her lips. She'd never masturbated for a man before. As much as she needed release, could she do this? Would she even cum with an audience?

She shimmied her skirt higher. The temperature of her body rapidly rising.

He sucked in air when her thong, garter belt, and stockings came into view. He was about to get his very own, private peep show. And based on the bulge behind his zipper, he liked what he saw so far.

When her skirt was completely bunched at her waist, she skated her hand over her tummy down to her mound.

He tracked her movements, like a lion stalking his prey.

She ran a hand over her sex, but quickly dipped her fingers under her panties to circle her needy, eager clit. She sighed at the impending relief.

Mr. Ross rose, and she stopped.

"Don't stop," he commanded.

When she resumed her self-pleasure, he reached for her panties at each hip and yanked them down to mid-thigh. Pushing her legs farther apart, the fabric stretched, cutting into her skin.

With her free hand, she caressed and fondled her breast and nipples. All for Mr. Ross.

"Fuck, precious. That has to be the sexiest thing I've ever seen."

She was debauched and wanton, just the way he wanted her. Her liquid heat slid onto her nether lips. Micaela made a pass spreading the slickness over her clit. She moaned. Her climax grew easily under his watchful, eager eyes.

Then, he pitched forward, bracing himself on the sofa, and leaned down to claim a nipple in his mouth.

She bowed her back. "Mmm."

"So fucking beautiful. Don't stop frickin' yourself." He claimed the other nipple.

She wanted to beg for him, beg for more. But she was close. Her orgasm was a whisper away.

Then, he sucked in her left nipple, hard.

"Ah." She arched her back as her orgasm exploded to the surface, going on and on as his mouth made love to her breasts.

Finally, her body returned to earth. She opened her glassy eyes to focus on the man in front of her.

He stared, his breathing as heavy as hers.

Carefully, he lowered her sweater and lifted her panties back in place. He lifted her right hand and drew her finger through his wet warm mouth.

Her breath stalled.

"That was the fucking hottest thing I've ever seen," he whispered. Then he pushed back to his desk.

She lowered her skirt and sat upright, getting her bearings.

"Miss Summer, I can't tell you how much I appreciate you staying after like this. Have a great night. I'll see you tomorrow."

"You too, Mr. Ross."

They gave each other cordial, secretive smiles as she made her way to the door. She left it wide open as she lifted her jacket and purse to head out. Hoping once again he'd watch her backside, with appreciation.

Neil stared at the perfection that was his sexy, seductive assistant as she walked out the door.

The idea to have her put on a show for him came to him at the last minute. He was certain she'd balk. Instead, she'd taken his challenge and gave him the most incredible show of his life.

The look of sheer pleasure and satisfaction on her face when she came was splendid. He had to see that look again. He had to give her that himself.

His dick had hardened to the point of pain. She looked so gorgeous, so sexy and debauched, laid out before him. He had to have her. There was no turning back now. But he wasn't a cheat. He needed to break things off with Nisha first, then he could sink into his precious assistant and give her what she wanted. What they both needed.

# Chapter Fifty-Six

♥

Nisha loved to keep people waiting for her. Neil knew this and for some reason had accepted it.

Once, he was in lust with her, wanted to give her the moon. She had incredible womanly wiles and knew how to flaunt them.

Now, as she sauntered through the restaurant toward him, he wondered what he'd even seen in her.

"Neil, love. How are you? I'm so sorry I've been busy lately."

He rose and kissed her cheek.

If she expected more, she didn't show it.

"I understand." *I understand you're spending time in another man's bed.*

She slid into the booth across from him. "Well, I'm really glad you called. I've been meaning to reach out so we could have a chat."

Ah, she wanted to chat.

The waitress approached. "Nisha, do you know what you want?"

She ordered a salad with dressing on the side.

He ordered a club on rye.

He continued because now his curiosity was spiked. "You were saying."

"Yes," she sipped her iced water. "I'm glad we have a chance to talk because I've been thinking about us a lot lately."

He might not need to say a word if he was reading the situation right. He clasped his hands together and waited.

"You know I really want to get married."

He nodded.

"And I know that's not what you want."

He nodded again.

"Well, then I guess I'm questioning what kind of a future we have together."

*And there it is.*

"I see." He looked down trying to appear conciliatory and pensive, when in fact, she was totally letting him off the hook. He smiled inside.

She reached over, placed a hand over his, and spoke. "I'm sorry, Neil. I'm breaking up with you, but I have no doubt you will find someone who will make you incredibly happy."

*Like you already have.* He nodded.

She rambled on a few more minutes when the food arrived. And what a blessing. It might be childish, but he didn't have to stay. Nor did he want to. She'd said her peace, and he had nothing he needed to say.

"Can I please get this to go?" He lifted the plate to the waitress, who smiled and carried it away.

Neil looked back at Nisha as her eyes rounded. "Nisha, I appreciate you letting me down gently. I too have no doubt you will find someone who will make you happy. It's clear we just weren't meant to be, and I wish you the very best."

Her lips gaped, and he was sure he shocked the hell out of her. Like she expected him to fight for her, to profess his love, and change his mind on marrying her.

It wasn't gonna happen. He'd been upfront from Day One about not wanting to get married.

The waitress arrived and set his bagged sandwich on the table.

He flipped open his wallet and left several bills on the table. "Thanks so much for meeting with me. Enjoy your lunch." With that, he stood and headed for the door. That went so much better than he'd expected. He thought there'd be tears and drama.

Turned out she already had one foot out the door.

Better for him. Now to return to the office, his lovely assistant, and some discussion of her very provocative offer.


The mail clerk pushed his cart through the floor, weaving in and out of offices and cubicles. He stopped at everyone's cube.

Micaela thought that was curious since he rarely needed to stop at *every* cube.

Finally, he came to her cube and handed her the mail. A few interoffice envelopes for Mr. Ross and one white, business envelope addressed to her.

"Thanks," she called after the guy.

She ripped open the seal and inside laid a check for two-thousand dollars. The stub attached read *Year-End Bonus*.

Her mouth gaped. She'd never had a year-end bonus before.

The volume on the floor rose as chatter and giggling ensued.

Micaela tucked away her check and walked to Barb's cubicle, the assistant next to Mr. Ross's office.

"Hey, Micaela. Isn't this great? We weren't expecting a bonus this year." She grinned and as she laid down the check and crumpled up the envelope for recycling.

"Wow. How exciting." She couldn't help but glance down at Barb's check. *$500.*

She leaned in conspiratorially. "And five-hundred dollars will be perfect during this time of year." Barb got five-hundred dollars.

"I agree." She smiled big and waved as she went to the break-room. More people had gathered there, smiling and gushing over their five-hundred-dollar bonuses. She reached for her bottled water in the fridge, smiled back at everyone, and headed back to her cube.

Mr. Ross gave her a bigger bonus. Four times bigger!

She had to thank him, but he had a lunch appointment. She was so giddy, so excited, she didn't know if she could wait.


Forty minutes later, Mr. Ross strode past her cube carrying a bag that looked like lunch. "Hey, Micaela. Did I miss anything?"

He didn't wait for a reply and kept walking.

Good because she wanted to thank him in the privacy of his office.

She gathered his two messages and his mail she'd already sorted. Then she undid an extra two buttons, covering herself with the documents because, of course, she wore no bra.

She strode into his office and pushed the door closed.

He stood behind his desk, flipped on his PC, and looked up as she walked in. If he was surprised she'd closed the door during working hours, he didn't show it.

"Sir," she rarely called him that but loved the ring to it, "I have some mail for you."

The corner of his mouth lifted.

"And two calls for you to return." She stacked the papers in the center of his desk and closed the distance between them.

His eyes dropped to her blouse opened in a deep V.

"Mr. Ross, they distributed year-end bonuses today."

The depth in his eyes grew, but he didn't move a muscle.

"I wanted to thank you." She swung her arms around his neck and kissed his cheek. "I heard everyone else got five-hundred dollars. You are very generous." She whispered in his ear.

One arm snaked around her waist while his free hand snuck between them, sliding under her shirt easily to caress her breast.

"Miss Summer," he kissed her neck as he whispered, "I appreciate your hard work, dedication, and your generosity as well." He twisted and toyed with her nipple, sending glorious waves of energy to her sex.

"Ah," she breathed out.

"And I would very much like to discuss your future with Mathison. Would you be able to stay a little later tonight?" He kissed her neck again as he massaged her other breast.

She was so wet and turned on, she wanted to hop on his desk and spread her legs for him.

His glorious erection pressed against her body, tempting her.

She slid a hand down to cup and stroke him over his wool trousers. "Mr. Ross, I would love to stay after for that discussion. For however long you need me."

He lifted his head and reached for her hands kissing the palms. "Very good then." He smiled.

She stepped back to fix her blouse and circled back to her cubicle, eager for five o'clock to come.


Micaela was a fireball. No doubt about it. It surprised Neil she had no boyfriend. Although he could understand it. And the longer he thought about how their arrangement could pan out, the more he liked it.

He didn't like relationships where marriage was expected. He could commit, but the idea of needing an official paper to tell two people they were committed to each other seemed ludicrous. Then, there was buying property together, having kids, mounting debt, and so on.

He simply wasn't a fan. He liked a certain amount of independence, and it seemed Micaela did too. And fucking her whenever he wanted had a vast amount of appeal to him.

At five, she strolled into his office with her purse and jacket, laid them on an armchair, and pushed the door closed.

He swung away from the desk, waiting for her to come to him.

*Fuck!* He might never get used to seeing her in her lovely blouses without a bra on. Her nipples poking through made his mouth water with wanting.

He sat tall and rested his hands on her hips. "Miss Summer, I've given your offer much consideration, and I accept."

The corners of her pink lips lifted.

"We just need to be very careful. If it got out that we had more than a business relationship, we could lose our jobs."

She nodded. "I'm good with that."

He scratched his five o'clock shadow. "Micaela, this is a business relationship. Nothing more."

"Agreed. You help me get ahead. I do whatever you ask to help make that happen." She held out her hand.

He grinned and shook it, not letting go. Instead, he separated his knees giving her room to step closer.

"Miss Summer," his hands slid over her thighs and hips, "I can't tell you how much I appreciate all that you've done in the short time you've worked for me." He met her gaze. "And I truly appreciate how very generous you are with sharing your gifts with me."

He glossed his hands over her stomach and up her torso, searching for the first button to undo. "I'm glad you like your bonus; you've earned it." Another button gave way. "And I have another bonus, just for you." Two more buttons undone.

Her chest rose and fell as she let him have free reign over her gorgeous body. "Yes, sir. Thank you."

His fingers slid under the fabric of her shirt, spreading it wide to reveal her perfect full tits for him. "These are so incredibly succulent."

He wasted no time closing his mouth over her nipple. He loved on her precious pink fruit as his hands caressed her warm soft skin, slowly loosening her top from the skirt's waistband.

"Ah, Mr. Ross." She begged him for more. He knew the sound of a plea.

But this was their first time. He would not rush it.

He reached behind, feeling for her zipper and sent her skirt to the floor.

She stood before him in black heels and a black thong, and as the last button gave way, he pushed her blouse to the floor, leaving her topless.

He returned to kissing and sucking her breasts. "And I love that I get complete and sole access to this incredible body." He glanced up at her. "Please know that I will be fucking no one else while we have this arrangement."

He saw a slight surprise in her eyes.

"Mr. Ross, I appreciate that. And I will follow those same rules. Also, I'm on the pill and I've been tested."

"Perfect." He slid a hand south, skating over her lace-covered mound. "And I shall get tested too because the thought of fucking you and not feeling that juicy, wet pussy tears me apart."

Her head fell back as he massaged her precious nub. "Unh."

Then, he grabbed her panties at the sides and slid them down a few inches. His finger slid through her wet slit.

She was more than ready for his length.

He rose, pushing his chair back to give them room. "Miss Summer, please help me with my pants."

She reached for his belt and unfastened his pants, pushing them to the floor. Her hands trembled with lust. Then, she dipped her fingertips under his boxer briefs, pulling them over his raging hard dick and dragging them down.

Her gaze stayed glued to his cock. "I think that's a very good enticement with this deal."

"I'm glad you like what you see. Now, open that drawer."

She opened the drawer that was right at her hip. Seeing the box of condoms, she pulled out one, ripped it open, and rolled it onto his length.

"Excellent." He had to be inside her. Another moment couldn't pass.

He lifted her up and out of her skirt, set her on his desk, and tore the panties from her body. In an instant, his mouth laid claim to her pussy as he held her legs apart.

She shrieked and covered her mouth with her hand.

He groaned at the first taste of his precious, giving assistant.

Her first orgasm flew to the surface in no-time.

He persisted, laving at her ripe cherry, laid out only for him.

She writhed as the passion built inside, ready to explode.

And explode she did. Again, covering her mouth, she cried out, and Neil fucking loved it.

He loved knowing he was the one to bring her such pleasure.

He wasted not another second. He rose and licked her essence covering his mouth. Then, he pulled her to the edge of the desk. With his dick aligned at her dripping wet cunt, he pushed all the way in as he covered her mouth with his, swallowing her scream. She felt warm and tight, and he couldn't wait to have her raw.

Her legs wrapped around him, and her hips flexed as he thrust into her.

Neil latched onto her mouth, claiming that precious tongue while he rocked her gorgeous naked body on his desk.

He'd never look at this desk the same again.

He broke the kiss for only a moment. "You are a fucking dream come true." Then, he covered her mouth one last time to pound into her and release all the incredible lust built up inside him from the last few weeks.

Micaela was a godsend to him. Precisely, what Neil needed. And as her last orgasm crashed through her, it was precisely what she might have needed as well.

# Chapter Fifty-Seven

♥

Micaela's new arrangement with her boss was incredibly perfect for her. Only occasionally did she find herself distracted with thoughts of their sexcapes. But for the most part it was a well-oiled machine.

For the past two months, she continued to go braless, occasionally panty-less, and every workday they had sex. Either on his desk or his leather sofa. He also had her sitting on his lap more when going over work things.

If anyone in the office knew, no one was saying a word.

She signed off her computer around quitting time, and when the coast was clear, she took her jacket and purse into his office. She closed and locked the door for privacy. They had to stay quiet if the managers with offices to the right and left were still in. But it wasn't too hard. First, Mr. Harris was old and had bad hearing, according to Mr. Ross. And next, Mrs. Fletcher traveled a fair amount for the company.

Micaela loved calling him *Mr. Ross* or *sir*. And he seemed to love calling her Miss Summer, but when others were around it was *Mi-*

*caela*. He seemed to love the idea of the boss/secretary dynamic, sneaking gropes and fucks where they could.

Saturday after her workout, Micaela planted herself in front of her computer. She had more clothes she wanted to buy to tempt Mr. Ross. Of course, the others on the fourth floor could see she went braless—a few times she'd received appreciative glances—but all she cared about was Mr. Ross. Making him happy. Giving him whatever he wanted so she got what she wanted.

*Ooh!* On one site, she found a longish, straight pencil skirt with a high slit in the back. Like *really* high. Just a few short inches from the bottom of the zipper. It had an overlapping pleat that gradually fanned open. Nothing would come into view until she bent over.

*Perfect.* She selected her size in both black and taupe and added it to the cart. She could already imagine Mr. Ross's appreciation when she wore those.

Next, she found a lacy bra for days when she'd wear one.

And then, oh yeah, she found a white top so sheer hints of areola would show through. The site had models, with and without bras, showing the effect of the light delicate fabric. The white color was still obvious, but the sheerness would cause one to do a doubletake.

Micaela giggled inside.

That one might be best worn with a jacket, except when she was alone with Mr. Ross.

She checked out, then made her way to the shower. She had her weekly mani-pedi, then the girls were going out for dinner. Micaela would fantasize about herself and Mr. Ross doing dinner out sometime, just the two of them. But she had the feeling he wouldn't want that. Too much mixing of business and personal. Like sex was okay because it was performed in the office.

She snorted to herself and smiled.

Whatever he wanted she was good. She didn't need the complications of a relationship. She *wanted* great sex. And that's precisely what she was getting.

Neil could pinch himself at how perfect his life was. Nisha was a distant memory. Business was good; therefore his job was good, and he had a smokin' hot assistant who begged him to fuck her. Micaela was so fucking delicious, he was hard all the time.

It might take a minute, but he would have her in his bed too. Twenty minutes in his office five days a week wasn't gonna cut it.

When he had interviewed her, he knew she was overqualified. But the job market wasn't the best for employers just then, so he decided to snatch up the smart, ambitious woman for a job that was beneath her. He got the highest level of salary approved by his boss he could. Not that it mattered. His own P&L was *his* responsibility.

The bottom line, he was the lucky bastard to have her lay her cards on the table. She had goals; she wanted more. She didn't want to stay in that position forever. And she was banking on him helping her to succeed at that.

He was all too happy to comply, and her bonus had been the first step. He got it approved because Neil told his boss she was working hard and wanted to be promoted, and again, it fit into his budget.

His boss agreed and disclosed that Neil was also getting a bump in his annual bonus as well.

The only downside to all of this—someday, probably soon, he'd have to hire a new assistant.

Neil had already had a conversation with Luis, their head of finance, about Micaela. He told Luis that she was a hard worker and whenever he had an opening, he wanted the man to interview Micaela first.

Luis eagerly agreed, probably liking her new choice of attire to the office. Scratching his jaw, he spoke, "In fact, how about you have her come by next Monday. We can review some things, and I can see where she's at. I have a financial analyst getting ready to move over to training once three is done with the remodel."

The Third Floor was where all training and human resource functions were held. The owners were remodeling the five-story building, one floor at a time, to be energy efficient and conducive for collaborative business. Three was supposed to be completed in two months. If Micaela could be promoted at that time, she would love it.

A smile pulled at his mouth. Making Micaela happy put Neil on a high. One step in the right direction for her.

***

Micaela was so ready for work, so ready for Mr. Ross to see her new skirt, she could hardly concentrate.

Friday, she walked into the office, dropped her things, and greeted him in her usual manner. "G'morning, sir. Can I get you some coffee?"

His smile was exuberant as his sight combed the length of her.

It never got old the way he appreciated her.

"New skirt, Miss Summer?"

She stepped into a long pivot, showing him her backside. "Yes," she turned back around.

His eyes were liquid heat. "Very nice. Yes, a cup of coffee, then let's meet for a few minutes before we get too far along on the day."

She smiled and left to retrieve his coffee.

To keep appearances, she grabbed her pad and pen when she walked back to his office and pushed the door closed. She took a seat and waited for him to finish typing.

He pushed away and smiled. "So, a few things."

She nodded.

"I have a quick trip to make to the Tallahassee plant next month. I need a flight and hotel, two nights and three days."

Her smile fell. He had to leave?

She quickly recovered because she didn't want him to think she was getting attached. He couldn't think she would miss him. He'd been very clear it was a business relationship.

"Okay." She scribbled notes on her pad.

"Miss Summer, please come here."

She lifted her head to meet his gaze, then without delay she rose and took her place on his lap.

He wrapped an arm around her back and kissed her neck. "Miss Summer, if it's any consolation, I'll miss you too. I've gotten rather addicted to you coming into my office without undergarments on. Or your lovely, toned body laid out like a five-star meal I can take an entire evening to enjoy."

"You will?"

He kissed and licked her. "Yes," he whispered.

He lifted his head. "But I have good news."

She grinned.

"Monday, you're going to meet with the head of finance, Luis Greenwood. He thinks he'll have an opening in two months for an analyst."

Her heart turned over. *Yes!*

He smiled back at her, then stroked the back of his index finger down her cleavage. "Miss Summer."

"Yes, sir."

"He'll ask you some questions, may have you review a few numbers with him. And if you wore something like this, I'm sure he'd appreciate it."

She chuckled lightly.

He winked. "He may be married, but he's not dead. It would likely make his whole month spending a few hours working beside you."

Whatever Mr. Ross told her to do, she would do. She knew he was upholding his end of the agreement: to get her promoted.

The promise of more great things was on the horizon, and Micaela was eager and willing.


That evening Micaela walked in as she'd done for the past few months. He was already hard for her. She rested her things on the chair, then quietly locked the door.

"Good. I'm glad you're here."

"Sir."

He loved hearing her call her that. "Yes, Miss Summer. I need help. It seems I've lost my car keys. If you could, check around in the sofa and underneath maybe, that would be great. I'll check my desk area."

He had to see that gorgeous ass in the air for him. Had to see how high that slit would go.

"Certainly, sir."

She went down to her knees and scanned under the armchairs. Then, she crawled toward the sofa.

Neil could already see some creamy globe peeking through.

She crawled across then turned her backside in his direction.

"Fuck," flew out of his mouth in a silent rush of air. The most incredible sight of her bare-naked pussy struck him between the eyes. "Um, Miss Summer?"

She swung her hair over one shoulder and glanced back at him. "Yes, sir."

"It seems you're not wearing any panties."

"Oh," she feigned surprise. "I guess I forgot them."

"Forgot them?"

"Yes, sir."

He exhaled and knelt down on one knee closer to her. He rested a hand on her lower back. "I understand. These things can happen. We're all human."

She nodded, still keeping his gaze.

"I'm not mad. It's just that... seeing you in this incredibly prone position caught me off guard and now my dick is very hard. Painfully so."

She glanced at his pants' front and back at him. "Oh."

"So, I'm thinking, if it's not too much trouble, I'd like to enter your creamy pussy for just a quick moment, see if that doesn't help curb my ache."

"Oh, sure. I guess that's okay. I mean, I'll keep looking for your keys." She moved her right knee to the right, getting closer to him, taking her legs wider.

Another expletive flew out of his mouth.

He slid two hands up her toned thighs, over her ass, pushing the skirt completely out of the way.

Her puffy lips with the pink center and her tiny, puckered hole were on display for him. Only him.

Her cream had accumulated. She wanted this as much as he.

"Miss Summer," he worked to free his pants, then caressed her smooth skin, admiring the view one last time. "You are simply exquisite." He pushed in as far as he could go.

They both muffled their moans.

He leaned over her, whispering in her ear. "Fuck, Miss Summer, your cunt is so delicious and inviting, I fear that this is not enough. I'm going to have to fuck you."

"But Mr. Ross—"

"Miss Summer, you want to please your boss, don't you?"

"Yes, definitely."

"Well, this would definitely please me."

"Okay. If you think it's okay." She played.

"I do." He began to move in her. "I really do."

He grabbed her shoulders, bringing her flush to his front. He worked free her shirt buttons. One short minute of toying with her nipples, and she came.

Arching her back, she reached behind and grabbed his ass as he pumped into her.

He kissed and suckled her neck. "Your pussy needs me, doesn't it, Miss Summer? It's made for me, isn't it?"

"Yes, Mr. Ross. I want nothing more than to make you happy. Please fuck me. Please."

He gained speed, pumping into her and covering her mouth as a precaution.

Her muffled shriek told him she was cumming again. He released into her at the same time. The sole center of his happiness lately. He wanted no other woman. Micaela filled his needs several times over. If she ever wanted to end this arrangement, he wasn't sure he'd find anyone as well-equipped to meet his needs as her.

# Chapter Fifty-Eight

♥

Part of Micaela looked forward to having Mr. Ross miss her while he was away. Another part didn't. She'd gotten so used to seeing him every day, laughing, making love, and playing their games.

The prior week, he'd tried something new.

Micaela'd walked into his office at quitting time, dropped her jacket and bag on the chair as she had done many times before.

Mr. Ross had on his suit jacket, tie, and reading glasses and worked at his computer.

She'd never seen him wear glasses before.

She locked the door, and he looked her way with an eyebrow raised. Normally, he'd swing around and greet her as she came to him.

Micaela panicked for a moment that he didn't want her that day. She smoothed her lips together and pressed on.

"Miss Summer, is there something you need?"

"Mr. Ross, I just wanted to check on you. Make sure you didn't need anything before I left. Anything at all."

"Nah," he sighed. "Just need to finish this and get home to the wife and kids."

*A-ha!* He was playing the married man. Maybe this "married man" would like a quick romp with his secretary.

Even though Micaela never messed with married men, a little thrill raced through her at the naughtiness.

"I understand, but Mr. Ross, I'm concerned you work too much." She moved behind him to rub his shoulders. "This stress is gonna kill you."

He stopped typing and groaned as her thumbs dug into the hard muscle.

"Let's take a few minutes here to help you unwind before you head home." She grabbed his jacket lapels.

"Uh, okay."

She pulled off the jacket, then slipped off his tie. She dropped the items off to the side and resumed her massage.

"That does feel good." His eyes closed.

"Precisely." She unfastened a few buttons, shifted to his side, and worked his right shoulder under his shirt. After a few minutes, she moved to his other side, massaging his bare left shoulder.

Working a little longer, she spoke. "Mr. Ross, I think this is having a positive impact. I think it may be lowering your blood pressure too. But this is awkward, let's have you lay on the sofa, and I can get better leverage."

"Well, okay. Just for a few minutes." He slipped off his glasses and followed her to the sofa, lying on his back.

She instantly slipped off his shoes and worked free several of his shirt buttons.

"Um, Miss Summer—"

"Mr. Ross, it's just a relaxation massage for a few minutes. I've been working for you for *years*. I think it's safe to say that we can trust each other."

He smiled. "I suppose you're right." He closed his eyes again.

She pushed the fabric off to expose his muscular chest to her and hiked up her skirt to straddle his lap. Discreetly, she worked free two of her blouse buttons as well.

After a few beats, she shifted down his legs to massage his thighs. He didn't say anything.

"These are in the way," she mumbled like a disappointed school marm and unbuckled his belt.

He opened his eyes which instantly rounded to saucers. "Um, I think I'm good now, Miss Summer." He tried to sit up.

She pushed on his chest. "No, please sir. We can take another few minutes for relaxation. I mean, this is enjoyable, right?"

He nodded.

"Okay, let me do my job then."

He grinned and closed his eyes.

She successfully slipped off his pants to see the outline of his incredible bulge. Her hands worked his strong thighs and calves.

He groaned.

When she couldn't stand it any longer, she massaged his hip, pulling the waistband of his navy briefs lower.

Staring down at this peaceful man, she craved kissing him. Instead of kissing his lips, she moved to his chest, kissing and licking his nipples.

"Miss Summer, really?"

"Please, Mr. Ross, try and enjoy your massage."

"I do, maybe too much. I fear we've crossed a line."

She shook her head, her hair falling onto his chest. "I think this is really good for you, and no one has to know about this massage."

Her hand slid over his full erection now and stroked it over his underwear.

He grabbed her upper arms but didn't pull her off.

"And this is only natural. Tension can build here just like it does in your neck and shoulders. It's my job and my pleasure to help relief some of the tension."

She kept her eyes trained on his as she slid her hand under the waistband to massage his glorious cock.

"Fuck, Miss Summer." His eyes pinched closed, and he gripped her arms tighter.

As she teased him with her delicate stroking, her chest kisses resumed and headed south. She kissed him over the fabric, and he jolted.

"Try and relax. Massages are supposed to be relaxing, and it pleases me when I can help you with your work stress."

She peeled away his briefs enough to kiss his hard length. She swiped the precum off the tip.

"Ah, Miss Summer, I don't know."

"No one has to know about your special massage, Mr. Ross. And think of this, you'll be so relaxed and content when you get home, that makes you a better husband and father."

He groaned when she pulled back more fabric and sank her mouth over him.

"Fuck," he whispered again.

She pulled his briefs down farther as she shimmied up toward his crotch. She stroked him, wishing she'd gone without panties that day.

His hands released her arms to claim her breasts. "Miss Summer, you are so very enticing. I must confess, I've thought about your sexy body a million times."

She smiled. "I'm glad. Again, I just want to please you, sir."

She shifted so the apex of her thighs hovered directly over his cock. She reached underneath and pulled her panties aside, aligning her wet slit perfectly with his veiny perfection.

"Miss Summer. Fuck! What are you doing to me?" he lifted her skirt to watch the incredible rocking of her pussy over him.

"Mr. Ross, I'm going to help release this tension now." She rose on her knees as she straightened his cock. "Remember, no one has to know about your simple little massage here. They'll just know how happy you seem."

She lowered herself onto him, letting him sink into her channel completely.

He cupped the back of her neck and brought her to his mouth to dive in. "Fuck, Miss Summer, you're the best assistant I've ever had." He flexed into her. "I can't tell you how much I appreciate you taking care of me at work."

"Of course, sir." She lifted her hips to bop up and down on his shaft. "I'm here to assist in any work functions, including relieving work stress," she panted.

He kissed her again. Her climax drew near.

"Oh, God, your perfect little pussy is just what I needed."

She moved faster until the tension broke free. She burrowed into his shoulder to muffle her cry.

Neil released at the same time, growling in her ear.

She collapsed onto his chest, panting and listening to his heart race in his chest.

His arms circled around her, and he kissed her hair. "Baby, that was so fucking perfect. Thank you."

Micaela's heart nearly stopped. He called her *Baby*. It was like sweet music.

She smiled. "You're welcome."

***

The morning of the Tallahassee trip, she backed into Neil's driveaway, as he'd requested that she take him. His house was well-maintained in a quaint old, restored community not far from downtown. He came out a moment later dressed in a navy suit, white shirt, and red tie. He was handsome as sin.

She got out and circled to the passenger side. She already knew why she was driving him to the airport and was not in the least bit surprised.

He loaded his suitcase into the trunk, slid into the driver's side, adjusted the seat, and pulled out into the road. "Good morning."

"G'morning. Got everything?" She felt a compulsion to want to kiss him but fought it. They weren't an item, even if some days felt that way.

He nodded. Then he reviewed a few items for her to accomplish during the next three days. Most of this he'd reviewed with her already.

"Mr. Ross, I occurred to me that you'll be gone for quite a while." She shifted to face him wholly.

He glanced her way and nodded.

"I bring that up because I want to make sure you don't forget about our agreement while you're away."

"Our agreement?" He tipped his head as he played at forgetting. He was the kind of man who forgot nothing.

She leaned closer and reached a hand to his thigh to stroke it. "The one where I do certain things to help you while at the same time you help me."

"Ah. That does sound vaguely familiar."

"Uh-huh. Well, I could probably remind you," she skated her fingers over his erection, "since we have some time on the road."

"That's an excellent idea, Miss Summer." He grinned.

She unloosed the seatbelt from her shoulder and leaned across to slowly work on unfastening his pants.

His hand slid along her back to her ass, resting it there as she made room to free his erection.

Lightly, she stroked him with her fingertips and licked the tip.

He groaned.

She loved hearing his sighs of satisfaction. She licked his entire length and soon worked him with her fist too. "Does any of this ring a bell?" She glanced up at him.

"Yes," he panted out. "This seems very familiar."

She swallowed as much of him as she could.

His fingers gripped the flesh of her ass as his hips flexed. "Fuck, Miss Summer. That's so perfect."

She continued the torture, licking and sucking as her fist stroked him up and down, twisting.

In several short minutes, he growled. "Fuucckk," and he released in her mouth.

She swallowed him and smiled.

Carefully, she put his clothes back together, tucking him in safely. When he was back to rights, she sat upright and pulled her seatbelt across her chest.

He reached for hand and kissed the back. "I do recall our agreement. How could I forget it?" He kissed the back of her hand again and returned it to her lap.

When they pulled in front of the airport, he put the car in park and grabbed the back of her neck, drawing her near. "That mouth of yours is fucking amazing." And he crashed his mouth to hers, kissing her like a soldier getting ready to leave for a tour of duty.

She unclipped her seatbelt and leaned into their kiss more.

He devoured her mouth with his tongue, and wetness gathered at her sex unbidden. Neil did that to her. Turned her on with his simple words and kisses.

He pulled back and smiled. "See you Friday."

He opened the car door, retrieved his luggage, and without looking back, strode into the airport.

He was so damn perfect for her. How did she get so lucky?

Now for work. She had a ladder to climb, and the sooner the better.

# Chapter Fifty-Nine

♥

On the morning of his last day in Florida, Neil called the office.

"Miss Summer since I've been gone for a while, I think it would be best if we could arrange to meet over the weekend and catch up. I'd really like to stay on top of all my matters."

"Yes, of course, sir. I have no plans, so I'm at your disposal."

"Perfect. Let's start with you picking me up from the airport. We can get to it tonight. And please bring an overnight bag; I have a guestroom. I'd feel better not having you drive home alone late at night."

"Certainly, sir. I'll be outside baggage claim later this afternoon."

Micaela parked her car along the curb ten minutes before Neil's plane was to land. Her tummy was a bucket of butterflies. She had an overnight bag packed for the weekend; she didn't know how long he'd want her to stay. A thrill raced through her thinking about sleeping in Neil's bed with him. She dressed in her cream blouse with the too-small buttons and her navy skirt with the high slit up the back.

Neil seemed to love assessing her attire every day when she came into the office.

Of course, while he was gone, she wore a bra. Really, *he* was her only reason for going braless. That treat was strictly for him unless he had arranged a meeting for her with another department head. He'd told her getting her promoted in the organization would be a culmination of input from several managers and directors, not just him.

And Mr. Ross certainly knew what he was doing. Last month, she'd met with Luis Greenwood and was able to talk about her skills and education. They chatted about the financial markets, and he'd asked her about her accounting and financial modeling skills. The conversation went well. The next day, Mr. Ross told her to return to Greenwood's office for an offer.

She was to start her new job as a financial analyst next month. She knew the job would entail long hours, but she didn't mind paying her dues to get ahead. In Micaela's mind, it was all part of getting ahead.

And that evening after work, Neil'd shared his enthusiasm and excitement with her, over and over.

Wetness gathered as she sat in her car thinking about how many times he'd made her cum: on his desk with his mouth, on the sofa, on the floor. The man had so many incredible talents, Micaela lost count.

The only downside to the promotion—not seeing Mr. Ross as much. Not seeing his smile, not sitting on his lap, and maybe not as much sex. She didn't know about the last part; they hadn't specifically discussed it.

She prayed he didn't think they were through. Her stomach seized up at the thought. Surely, he could continue to help her get ahead. He was a manager with Mathison and had created great relationships with the other managers. Certainly, he was still an influential force in her career. She crossed her fingers, praying she was right.

Mr. Ross stepped out of the airport, tugging his rolling luggage behind him.

She hopped out of the car and popped the trunk lid. "Mr. Ross, welcome back. I hope it was a good trip."

He smiled and heaved his luggage into her car. "Miss Summer, it was a good trip, but I missed getting on top of my other obligations."

She loved his innuendo. "Yes, sir."

He directed her to his house, so she could bypass the GPS. They chatted about what happened the past three days in the office. Nothing too urgent or surprising, and of course, most of it he knew since they'd spoken every day.

As they pulled into his driveway, he said, "Well, Miss Summer, I can't tell you how much I appreciate your holding down the fort as well as coming to my house and bringing me back up...to speed."

She grinned. "No problem at all. I'm happy to do it. Especially since you said you'll be feeding me."

"Oh, yes. I'll be feeding you. Would do me no good to have a starving assistant."

Walking through the entryway, he left his luggage at the bottom of the stairs. "You can drop your bag here. I'll carry it up later."

Then he strode into the kitchen. He'd done a wonderful job with the new quartz countertops, painted cabinetry that almost touched the high ceiling, and the six-burner, chef-grade range.

He reached into the fridge for a bottle of white wine and retrieved two stemmed glasses. "Please have a seat. We can decide on dinner later and have it delivered. In the meantime, I want you to relax and share some wine with me."

She clinked his glass and took a sip. She slid onto a stool at the island and noticed he hadn't sat down yet. "I love the renovations. I like how the quartz looks like marble. Very nice."

"Thank you." He walked up behind her. "I'm pretty pleased with the outcome." He rested his hands on her shoulders, starting to massage them. "I'd like to add some kind of covering for the back patio next."

She nodded, closing her eyes and embracing the luxury of her mini-massage.

"Do you get many massages, Miss Summer?"

"Not really."

"I can tell. You have quite a few knots." He continued, digging into her trouble spots. "You don't mind me doing this, do you?"

Her head lulled slightly. "No. Thank you. It feels good."

His hands massaged out to the end of her shoulders and back in several times. The last time his fingertips reached below her clavicle.

She moaned, and he added more pressure on her pecs. His ministrations accidentally pulled free one of her shirt buttons.

He shifted his hands under the loose fabric to have more contact with her skin. His hands went wide to the left and right, avoiding her breasts. Another two buttons gave way, exposing her breasts.

"Oh, Miss Summer. It seems some buttons came loose, and your breasts are exposed. Should I stop?"

She cleared her throat to speak. "No, sir, that's fine. I'm sure it's just because I changed them all out to smaller ones, and they don't hold as well."

She heard the grunt of his smirk, and that made her smile.

"I see. Well, I can massage your beautiful mammaries as well." He wasn't asking permission, and he didn't need it.

His big, warm hands slid south, caressing and fondling her breasts.

She moaned as her head fell back.

He stepped closer, pressing his hardness into her back. His hands roamed, caressing every inch of her front, popping loose the last button on her top.

He pushed the fabric off her shoulders, making every move a glide over her skin, bringing her body alive and eager for more.

She arched into his hands.

Mr. Ross leaned down and held her throat as he kissed along the side of her neck. He never stopped the incredible caressing. "I love giving extra special attention to these luscious nipples, Miss Summer," he whispered in her ear.

She moaned as the wetness gathered at the apex of her thighs; she felt her spine turning to jelly. She was putty in his hands.

"Miss Summer," he whispered in between his neck kisses, "I'm concerned that I may have put you in an uncomfortable position. Do you need some relief?"

"Yes, Mr. Ross, please," she said on a breath.

He stood and clasped her hand. He led her to his bedroom, not bothering with the lights. He reached for her silk top that hung around her waist, slipped it the rest of the way off, and laid the blouse on an upholstered slipper chair. Then he went to a knee before her, and one at a time, removed her high heels.

His hands skated up and down her legs. "Miss Summer, perhaps you'd like to lie on my bed and give yourself a little release."

"Yes, sir." She wanted *him* to give her the release.

They had all night, and she knew how much he enjoyed watching her masturbate. Plus, him watching her turned her on.

He unzipped her skirt and laid it on the chair, then he flung back the bedspread.

Completely naked, she climbed onto his bed and lay on her back, spreading her legs.

God, Micaela was so fucking hot, lying on his bed, languidly pleasuring herself.

He leisurely removed his tie and unfastened his shirt buttons.

She watched him as he watched her.

Next, his shoes, socks, pants, and briefs hit the floor.

He'd gone three days without being inside his precious Micaela, and it felt like three years.

He kneeled on the bed, planting kisses on her legs. Her sweet aroma grew the closer he got to her pussy.

She glistened. He knew she would have come by now, but she wanted to wait. Wait for him to give her an orgasm.

He kissed and licked her denuded mound. "So beautiful, Miss Summer."

"Thank you, sir. I like to keep it nice for you."

He grunted, then pulled her hand away and blew a warm breath over her swollen, wet sex.

She whimpered.

With the lightest touch, the very tip of his tongue glossed over her protruding clit.

She reached for his head, wanting more. He grabbed her hands and pinned them while his forearms pushed against her thighs.

"So sweet, Miss Summer." Another few gentle licks. He loved keeping her on the edge and watching her sweet cream flow.

"Mr. Ross." She begged.

"Miss Summer, did you miss me while I was gone?" Gentle circles over her aching nub.

"Yes, sir. Very much."

He couldn't say why it pleased him to hear her proclamation. He didn't need any deep, meaningful professions of love. But he did want to know that she craved him on a primal level. That he could fill her sexual needs to the point where she didn't need any other *friends.*

He added more pressure and tipped her over the precipice.

She arched her back and screamed as she tried to squirm beneath him.

He didn't stop until he knew her orgasm was complete.

She was beautiful lying on his bed in pure ecstasy.

He raised up as she opened her glassy eyes. Her cheeks flushed a pretty pink.

"Miss Summer, you are a man's wet dream." He lowered himself to her and aligned his cock. He claimed her mouth at the exact moment he pushed into her warm honeypot.

She moaned into his mouth and swung her arms around his neck, diving into his mouth farther.

He stroked her core for as long as he could but needed to release the build-up of lust at not having access to his lovely assistant in this most hot and intimate way.

At the first flex of her pussy muscles, he let go, a perfect culmination of their joining.

He growled and then collapsed, panting into her shoulder. Both of them gasping for air from the coupling. One of many this weekend, if he had any say in it.

***

That morning, Neil woke her in the most delicious way, making her wet with his tongue before sliding into her.

He was a wonderful lover. It almost unnerved her at how perfect he was.

He told her to take her time. That he'd make breakfast then they had shopping to do.

She showered, wrapped herself and her hair in bath towels, and went to the kitchen in search of coffee. He stood at the stove making scrambled eggs.

"So, you mentioned something about shopping." She instantly thought about stuff for the house, like he wanted a woman's opinion, but she wasn't sure.

"Yes. We're going shopping for you."

She looked up from her coffee and met his gaze. "Me?"

He nodded. He pushed the skillet off the burner, turned off the stove, and wrapped his arms around her waist. He pecked her lips. "Miss Summer, you buy so many wonderful things, and I know it's to please me. I'd like to buy you some things this time."

She smiled. "Anything in particular?"

He shook his head. "Let's see where the day takes us. I just need to be back by five for a family obligation."

She was okay with not seeing him that night. She was fairly certain he wouldn't want to see her two nights in a row.

A few hours later, they were in a unique, high-end ladies' boutique. He had her trying on pencil skirts and silk blouses. She'd worn a bra since they were out in public, but after the third blouse, he motioned her to where he sat.

"Miss Summer, I'd like to see these blouses how you wear them for me."

Heat flew to her cheeks, which surprised her since she'd been going braless for months now. "Yes, sir."

She came out of the dressing room wearing a pale pink blouse, *sans* bra.

He rose and stepped in front of her. "I love this." Discreetly, the backs of his hands glossed over her breasts, causing her nipples to harden. "So perfect, Miss Summer. As your boss, I approve of this."

In a bold move, she reached a hand down the front of him and caressed his erection. "I'm glad you like it. My goal is always to please you."

He must have read the sincerity in her eyes because he stared for a moment, then cupped her jaw and brought her to him for a deep, tongue kiss.

She clutched his shoulders, leaned into him, letting the passion and energy build between them. Although Micaela had great non-committal assignations before, nothing felt this good, this in-sync before. She hoped she'd met Neil's expectations because he more than fulfilled hers.

By the end of the shopping trip, he bought her several skirts, a few shorter than usual, and some silk blouses. At a lingerie shop, he'd purchased thigh highs, stockings, thongs, and several front-closure bras.

They both knew when she moved to Luis Greenwood's department, she'd need to wear a bra. She didn't mind. This shopping trip alone told her Neil wanted to continue with their arrangement. Her stomach fluttered at the thought of continuing their affair—good for her career, and good for her pussy.

# Chapter Sixty

❤

Micaela had been a financial analyst for two years now. She'd received several raises and great reviews from Mr. Greenwood, *and* she continued her agreement with Mr. Ross.

Their rendezvous hadn't always been in the office. Neil would invite her to his house, sometimes to spend the night. Especially if either of them had a busy week, he had to travel, or they hadn't had sex as much as they'd like that week, he'd have her stay the weekend.

Sometimes they'd cook, but usually they'd order in. In the mornings, he'd always awaken her, slowly making her wet so they could have some fantastic morning sex.

The relationship they'd cultivated was like no other. They'd talk, laugh, and have sex when they were together. And yet still felt comfortable in their alone-time.

She'd fallen in love with him some time ago, but of course never told him.

She suspected he felt the same way by the things he'd say to her: *I love how generous you are, Miss Summer*, or *I love how you cum around me*, or *I love waking up with you in my bed.*

They loved to roleplay—boss and assistant mostly, but sometimes other characters. Once they'd played at being married. They play-fought over chores or money and had hours of make-up sex afterward.

One time he'd played the boyfriend, or at least it seemed that way.

They were sharing a deluxe large pizza and a bottle of chianti when he started. "So, tell me about your friends with benefits."

She grinned as she looked over at him. "That was a long time ago."

"I know. I'm curious."

She nodded. "My first friend was in college. Gio. We studied together regularly. One night, he asked me if I had a boyfriend. I said 'No.' He said he wanted to go down on me."

Neil's eyebrows rose. "Just like that."

"Mmhmm. So, I decided to take him up on that offer. I texted my roommate, asking for a few minutes of privacy. Then, I stripped for him. He made me cum twice. He was happy, I was happy." She shrugged. "The next day he asked if I would consider more, but we didn't need anything serious." She sipped from her glass. "I think by then I had already decided I wasn't interested in having a boyfriend, but I liked sex."

He gave her a knowing smile.

"That continued for a few years." She smirked.

"What?"

"He actually introduced me to another friend."

Neil raised an eyebrow. He was so stinkin' cute when he did that.

"We were in his apartment and *thought* his roommate was in class. We were naked, fucking on the sofa when the roommate walked in. He apologized but kept watching. We were both too hot to care. Later, he came to me and asked if we could go out sometime. That he really liked me and knew I wasn't interested in having a boyfriend. It worked out well because Gio was graduating."

"Wow."

She nodded. "I had one other friend after graduating. Each relationship worked well. We knew the other wasn't looking for anything serious, and that it was simply about mutual satisfaction."

"I see."

She took another bite of pizza. "So, what's your story?"

He wiped his hands on the napkin. "I'd been with Nisha for a while. We were dating when you came to work for me."

She nodded. She knew he'd been dating someone and thought it could have been serious.

"She wanted to get married, even though I told her from the beginning it wasn't for me. Anyway, I think she was cheating so the breakup was easy and mutual."

"Interesting."

"So, Miss Summer, have you ever made an offer to a boss, like you have to me?"

She could see the heat grow in his eyes. "No. You were the first."

He rose behind her and kissed her neck. "And if I hadn't accepted, would you have left?" He started working to free her blouse.

She reached behind and stroked his legs.

"That was my plan," she said with a smile, "but I found myself really wanting to have a boss-with-benefits, so I don't know for sure."

She felt him smile as he continued kissing and licking, sending delightful shivers down her spine. "In that case, I'm really glad I took you up on your offer."

He pushed the dishes aside and helped her to stand. He gathered her skirt over her hips, then pulled off her blouse, dropping it to the floor.

She heard his belt buckle and zipper as he freed his cock. In mere seconds, he pushed her over the counter and entered her from behind, like he'd done many times in his office. They both groaned at the exquisite contact.

The sex quantity might have dissipated some, but the quality only got better. She couldn't have asked for anything more—in her work life or her personal life.

***

As Neil wrapped up his Thursday, Luis knocked at his door.

He smiled. "Come in." He motioned toward a chair.

Luis closed the door and that had Neil curious. He'd known Luis for years. Never once had the man closed the door when they'd met.

Neil pushed aside the folder he had open and gave his full attention to the man. Inside, he prayed nothing was wrong with Micaela's performance. "Seems like you have something on your mind."

He nodded. "First, it's not about Micaela exactly. She's doing a great job."

Neil smiled inside with pride. *That's good news.*

"In fact, I have an opportunity to promote her."

That got his attention.

"Franklin just informed me that he'll be retiring soon."

He nodded, wondering where this was going.

Luis picked some lint off his trousers. "So, I have two good candidates I can promote to manager to backfill Franklin. Micaela is one of them."

He nodded again.

Luis licked his lips and met his gaze head-on. "The thing is I know there's something going on between you and Micaela."

Neil lifted his brows, and before he could try and deny it, Luis lifted a hand.

"I've seen it. Your door closed after hours, but both your cars are still in the garage. She didn't wear bras when she worked for you, now she does most days. A few other things I've picked up on." He waved his hand nonchalantly.

"Luis—"

"I don't care, Neil. You know I don't. Except there's one thing you can do for me."

"For you?"

Luis nodded.

"Something that would help you make a decision to promote Micaela." It wasn't a question.

"That's right."

Neil sat back in his plush chair and crossed his arms. "What is it?"

"Neil, you know I'm happily married. I'd never do anything to break those vows."

His heartrate ratcheted higher.

"But a man has fantasies."

*Fuck! What did he want?* "Spit it out, Luis."

"I want to watch. One time."

Neil's jaw dropped. Maybe he should be happy about the request because it could have been much worse.

"You wanna watch?"

Luis leaned forward resting his elbows on his knees. "You can blindfold her. She'll never know I'm there. I'll watch for a few minutes and go home a happy man."

He paused for a moment. "And if I agree, how many more times will you be coming back to me with a request?" *Blackmail, really.*

Luis shook his head repeatedly. "It's not like that. I adore the girl. I want her to succeed, but thinking about what went on behind closed doors in this very office. Well, like I said, a man has fantasies."

He exhaled. "One time. No more requests. When Franklin leaves, she gets that job."

Luis nodded.

*Fuck me!* "Let me sleep on it."

"Okay." Luis rose and pivoted to leave.

*What the actual fuck?!*

Luis just put him in the most compromising position. He couldn't tell Micaela about this crazy request. It was one thing to make an agreement with your boss. There'd been no contingency for "other." So, that meant going behind her back. Which he fucking hated.

Sure, she'd said she'd do whatever to get ahead, but Neil's gut told him being watched, by her current boss, might be taking it too far. If she said *No*, and thought she couldn't get ahead without following through, she might leave.

And if he didn't give Luis what he wanted, she wouldn't get promoted. It wouldn't take too long before she saw people getting promoted instead of her, and she'd leave. She'd leave him.

He rubbed a hand over his brow. *What the hell!*

***

Micaela told Neil she had a lot on her plate lately. He knew she'd been putting in a lot of overtime hours, consequently, they'd been spending more time together on the weekends, and Neil was good with that. Micaela in his bed suited him just fine.

He texted her Friday, telling her to come to his office at six. He knew what he had to do: ultimately, what Micaela wanted. A promotion.

He'd spoken to Luis several days ago, telling him when to come and what to do.

At that time of night, Neil could be sure everyone in his side of the building would be gone. He had his plan, done some shopping, and damn if he wasn't rock-hard thinking about it.

At six on the dot, she showed up and closed and locked the door behind her.

"Miss Summer, thanks so much for taking time out of your busy schedule." He approached her and instantly claimed that delicious mouth he hadn't tasted since Wednesday.

When he broke the kiss, she smiled. "Mr. Ross, you know I'm only too happy to assist in any way you need me."

He nodded thoughtfully. "Well, I have a little surprise. Several actually."

Her eyebrows lifted. "Oh?"

He retrieved a black satin blindfold from his pocket. "I'm going to have a feast on you, then we'll feast on dinner. I'm having it brought in so you can go back to your office if you need to."

Her eyes sparkled at him. "I'd like that."

He wasted no time and secured the blindfold around her, cutting off her sight. "Give me a minute to set up the room." He moved some furniture, quietly unlocked the door, and positioned a chair for Luis.

He returned to her and kissed her sweet lips. His lips trailed down her cheek and neck. "Miss Summer, my sweet, you work so hard. Tireless hours," he whispered, clutching the other side of her head and covering her right ear. "I want to reward you. In a manner that I hope is pleasing to you."

He slid his free hand down her chest, running a thumb over the nipple pebbling behind her blouse and bra.

She gripped his upper arms for stability.

One by one, he released her shirt buttons. Luis poked his head inside the door and waited for a moment to enter.

Neil caressed her jaw and neck down to her chest where he pushed off her top and bra straps. "So beautiful." He stroked his thumbs over her nipples then twisted them gently between his fingers.

"Mmm."

He unclasped her bra and instantly caught her heavy breasts to bring them to his mouth, one at time.

She released her grip on him long enough to let her bra fall.

Luis stepped into the room completely, his mouth agape.

"Mr. Ross." Her fingertips dug into his upper arms.

As he loved on her breasts, he reached behind to unfasten her skirt. He bent down to help her out of the garment.

She stood before him naked save for a tiny black thong, black high heels, and a black blindfold. Luis was probably beside himself at the vision of loveliness.

He stroked and kissed her thighs. "Miss Summer, seeing you like this," he skated his fingertips under her waistband, "has brought about an excruciating ache. I think I need a little relief."

He rose, cupped her jaw, and whispered in her ear, "Go down on your knees."

He took her left hand as she held onto the desk with her right.

She lowered herself to her knees and began to work free his pants. She didn't need her sight for this. She pushed his pants and briefs to the floor and glossed her hands up his thighs, reaching for his hardness.

He groaned.

She smiled, the little vixen, as she worked his length with her hand. Finally, she leaned in and closed her mouth over him.

"Fuuucckk." He gripped her head over her ears, pulsing lightly into her perfect, warm mouth.

Luis took his cue to close the door and take a seat. The hardness evident behind his pants.

Neil savored his former assistant's wonderful torture for several more beats until he couldn't take anymore, then he pulled back.

"Very well done. Always a hard-working assistant." He gripped her shoulders, lifting her, and guided her to the plush, fur-like white rug he'd bought just for the occasion.

This would really make Luis crazy.

"To the floor, baby."

She squatted down and smiled as the rug caressed her skin.

"Now, lie back and spread those gorgeous legs."

She did as he bid, bending her legs like a centerfold posing for the camera.

He removed the rest of his clothes, then went to his knees between her spread legs. "Miss Summer, you look like a gorgeous centerfold. And my job today is to make you scream."

Her full mouth gaped.

He knew she was likely surprised by his words as they'd always tried to keep the noise down, never knowing who could hear. On a Friday night, after he'd already made one pass on the floor, he knew the coast was clear. The only person who would hear them sat in the room. His eyes glued on near-naked beauty about to achieve sexual ecstasy.

Neil stroked her legs, her inner thighs, up her torso to her perfect tits. He whispered over her lips, "Perfect," then claimed her mouth, diving deep, claiming as much of her as possible. Wanting to build the ache for her... and for their audience.

His kisses traveled languidly, loving on her nipples, dipping into her navel, licking the sensitive area at her upper thighs. He ignored her sex. He kissed, nibbled, and caressed.

Her moans grew, and she clutched his head, silently begging for more.

"Miss Summer, are you needing more?"

"Yes. Yes, Mr. Ross. Please."

He kissed her inner thighs a few more beats, her exotic aroma calling to him. Slowly, teasingly, he lowered her thong, pulling it down her legs and over her heels.

Luis's jaw dropped at the gorgeous sight. The telltale circle of wetness showed on the front of his pants.

Neil laid her legs wide and made long strokes up and down as he blew a warm breath over her sex.

She bowed her back, and the fur of the rug poked up in between her fingers as she gripped the covering for purchase.

Finally, he licked her swollen clit and lips.

She moaned loudly.

*That's right, baby.*

He used a miniscule of pressure, keeping her on the edge. He reached to fondle her nipples at the same time.

Her lips flexed, trying to reach for his mouth, desperate to relieve the ache inside.

He pulled back.

"Ah," she cried out, knowing he wouldn't give her what she needed. Not just yet.

"Miss Summer." He slid a finger through her incredibly wet slit. He loved her like this, open and eager for him to fill her. "You seem so anxious to get this over with."

While his finger danced over her sex, he lovingly nibbled on her delicious tits.

A lightly sheen broke out over her upper lip. "Mr. Ross, please."

He pushed a finger in through her incredible liquid heat, slowly pushing and pulling, letting the tension build further.

She writhed on the luxurious rug, gripping it for life as pink filled her cheeks. She was a goddess.

Neil's cock ached to cum, to dive into this beauty from now to eternity. He'd never been more sure of anything in his life—she was made for him, and he was made for her.

He pushed back on his haunches to love on her pussy with his tongue and added another finger.

She moaned.

He had to wait for just the right time.

Slowly, he built the pressure and speed. At the first contraction with her pussy muscles, he pulled his fingers out, took her hips in his hands, and yanked her up his thighs onto his rod, hitting clear to the end.

She screamed, and her pussy gripped his dick like never before. He released the pressure cooker of lust building inside for who knows how long.

He pounded into her, and her breasts juggled with his every thrust of his still-raging hard dick. Another climax crashed through her. She cried out again, bowed her head back, and panted for air.

It was the most beautiful sight he'd ever seen.

He collapsed down over her, drawing her near as he panted into her neck.

Several moments later, he peered up to see Luis gone and the door closed.

Neil pushed off the blindfold, and Micaela blinked to gain her focus. She leisurely glanced at the door, then the chair.

His heart stopped.

"Baby, how are you?" was all he could think of saying right then.

She met his gaze. "How did we do?" she whispered.

His eyes rounded, and his dick started coming back to life inside her.

He paused, debating if he should lie or tell the truth. "How did you know?"

The corners of her lips lifted. "Franklin's retiring, and Luis never came to tell me about the vacancy. All this could have been done at home." She motioned with a hand over the rug, and then shrugged. "I wondered if he already knew."

He nodded thoughtfully. "I knew what you wanted."

"The job."

He nodded again. "Are you mad at me?"

She smiled and caressed the side of her cheek. "I know why you did this. Because you love me."

His jaw went lax. The truth had always been there. "Yes."

He confirmed it, praying she wouldn't get ideas about needing to get married. He hated the thought of ruining what they had.

She nodded. "And I love you. More than I thought I could love another person." She smoothed her lips together. "I know you would do whatever you thought was best for me, and I trust you with that."

He smiled. His heart so incredibly full, he had no words to describe it.

She pecked his lips and held him close to whisper, "Honestly, I was so fucking turned on with the thought of someone watching us."

He pushed back a few inches. "Really?"

She grinned, then brought him in close for a deep, sensual tongue-kiss, rising to meet his thrusts.

Micaela became the center of his world, and he'd never felt so fulfilled in his life.

More slowly this time, he moved in her again, with her. Gently rocking them to another orgasm, basking in the new dimension their relationship had entered.

Best fucking move he'd ever made was hiring this smart, over-qualified firecracker to be his assistant.

Thank you for reading this steamy hot novella. The Epilogue can be found here: https://bookhip.com/QPXFRVK

# That Stormy Obsidian Night

# Chapter Sixty-One

♥

C rystal felt the panic pulsing through her veins, and her heart raced. She was two minutes away from a full-flown anxiety attack.

"Dammit!" She smacked the printer, and finally, the thing began to work. "Please. Please. Please."

Thunder clapped, and the lightning flashed in the sky.

"Oh, dear lord. Please let me print this before the power goes out."

The printer spit out the fourteen-page document, and she lifted one page at a time, inspecting it closely. Normally, she'd simply upload her work of art, but she didn't have that luxury now.

She neatly slid the argumentative essay on pollution due to urbanization into a large manilla envelope, grabbed her raincoat, and headed out of her dorm room door.

Crystal stepped outside the building and tucked the envelope under her coat just as the rain started to downpour.

She dashed inside the back seat of the Uber.

God, it was late, but she simply had no choice. This was her final paper for English Lit, and it counted for forty percent of her grade this semester. It was due that day. No *ifs*, *ands*, or *buts*, according to the cantankerous Professor Pearson. And as much as she hated showing up at the doorstep of his private residence at ten o'clock on a Friday night...

*Oh, God. What if he isn't home?*

"Please, please, please, be home."

The man was hard as nails on his students. Apparently, always had been. But he was handsome as sin.

She figured he was early to mid-forties, six-one, maybe six-two, with amazing brown hair she'd love to run her fingers through.

More than once she'd fantasized about him during his lectures, despite his brash personality. She knew she likely wasn't the only student either. And it didn't help that he wore no ring on his left hand. So, he was single.

Fifteen minutes later in the pouring down rain, the car pulled up in front of her professor's house.

"Can you wait a minute? I just need to drop this off, then we can go back?"

The driver grunted, and she didn't know if that was agreement or not.

She peered out the car window one last time, pulled her coat in tighter, and opened the door.

Rain pummeled her as she ran in her ballet flats up his walkway and ducked under his front porch roof.

"Here goes." She rang the doorbell.

The door opened after a minute and there stood Professor Pearson in a button-down shirt with the sleeves rolled up, dark slacks, and bare feet.

His eyebrows pulled together. "Crystal, what are you doing here?" He glanced over her shoulder. "And in this weather?"

"I went by your office." Not that that was much of an explanation. And of course, she hadn't. She didn't need to know he wouldn't have been there.

"How did you get my address?" His hand rested on his hip, the way she'd seen a million times in class. When he was displeased.

She swallowed. "The internet," she said sheepishly.

Just then, a man she recognized as Professor McCabe, a stats teacher on campus, stood next to Professor Pearson.

McCabe opened the door wider, and his eyes widened. "Don't leave her in the rain, Evan. Do come in," he directed the last part to her.

"Thanks." She looked back to see her ride drive away. *Just great*.

She stepped into the foyer, dripping on the dark hardwood floors.

"Let me get you a towel." McCabe spun away and returned a moment later with a large bath towel.

She took the towel, and he helped her with her coat. Holding her essay, one arm at a time, the coat came off.

Not taking his eyes off her, Pearson spoke, "Is that your final essay?"

"Yes, sir."

"And why is it late?"

She lifted her chin to meet his gaze. She might have a battle on her hands, and that meant no more being intimidated by this man. "I had a family emergency."

"A family emergency?"

"My grandmother was admitted to the hospital. We thought we were going to lose her."

He nodded.

"Come in, Crystal. Dry off." McCabe broke the silence.

She met his gaze and let him lead her into the living room where it appeared the men had been drinking some wine. A few lit candles scattered the room, no doubt in preparation for the inevitable power outage.

"Please take a seat, and I'll pour you some wine." McCabe poured her some wine in a stemless glass as she sat on the sofa.

"What happened to your grandmother?" Pearson now stood with his arms crossed, glaring down at her.

"Her heart stopped. They restarted it, and she's stable now. They're running some tests to find out what happened."

Pearson nodded.

McCabe sat next to her, reaching for her free hand. "Crystal, I'm glad she's alright." Then, he looked up at Pearson and back to her. "When was the paper due?"

"Well, today."

"Oh, then it's not really late." He glanced at his wristwatch. "Still an hour and a half remaining. So, you visit with us for a bit, dry off, and then you can get your ride back."

Professor McCabe was being so nice to her. A stark contrast to Professor Pearson who took a seat in the club chair diagonally across from them.

Maybe she had a crush on the wrong guy. She laughed inside. McCabe was just as gorgeous as Pearson after all, just a little leaner with lighter brown hair.

"Crystal."

She turned her attention to McCabe.

"I'm going to let you in on a little secret. Evan isn't really a sonuvabitch."

Her eyes widened at the use of the word and referring to him by his first name.

She glanced Evan's way, but his expression remained neutral.

"No. It's all really just an act."

Her eyebrows pulled together. *An act?*

He tended toward her. "I mean, just look at him. Women fall for him constantly, make advances and all that. He decided years ago, acting like an asshole kept all of that at bay."

"Oh." She sipped from her glass.

"Wouldn't you agree he's handsome?"

She glanced his way, her face on fire, and swallowed hard. "Yes," she said meekly.

She didn't know why they would be having such a personal conversation, but she relaxed now that her paper was accepted and could maybe unwind a little.

"Exactly." McCabe reached his fingers to her chin, directing her attention back his way. "In fact, we have often spoken about you in a similar vain. Several times."

At his words, she blushed all over again.

"Please don't be embarrassed. Surely, your boyfriend tells you you're beautiful."

She shook her head. "I don't have a boyfriend."

"Oh, that's a shame. You need a man in your life. A man who'd worship you."

She glanced back at Pearson who simply sat back, legs crossed, watching them as he sipped his wine.

Suddenly, a loud crack of lightning reverberated the house, and the lights went out.

She shrieked in surprise.

McCabe gripped her hand tighter. "It's okay. We were expecting this. I'm sure once the storm passes, the lights will be back on."

"Okay." Her words came out a little breathy, and she wasn't sure why.

He stroked the back of her hand with his thumb. "Take another sip, Crystal. I have another question for you."

She more than sipped. She gulped most of it down. Something in the air had shifted, and it wasn't just the fact that they had instantly been plunged into near darkness.

He scooted closer to her, his thigh now touching hers. "It's ironic because we had just been talking about you before you arrived."

"Really?" Her voice just barely above a whisper.

"I hope I'm not making you uncomfortable."

She shook her head.

"Like I said, we both think you're beautiful, and although we'd never done anything with a student before, you would be the one person we'd break our rule for."

"Oh." She swallowed the last of her wine. The temperature in her body rising. She shifted in her seat.

"Do I make you uncomfortable with my confession?"

She shook her head. "Professor—"

"Here you can call me Connor."

"Okay. Connor, I'm not sure we should be talking like this."

He smoothed his thumb over her hand again. "You let us worry about that. Whatever we share needs to stay in the confides of these walls, and no one need know about it."

She bit on her lip. Nervous energy pulsed through her.

"With all this rather intimate conversation, what do you suspect the statistical probability is that Evan is hard over there?"

*Oh gees!* Were they wanting something to happen with her? Now? Here?

"I— I don't know. Eighty percent."

"Eighty? That's it?"

She shrugged.

"Maybe we should ask him to uncross his legs so we can see?"

Her mouth was parched. Crystal couldn't think. She couldn't speak. An energy flowed through her she hadn't felt in months. Her priority had been school—not a boyfriend and not much of a social life. Now, it seemed she had an opportunity presented to her for more. "Okay."

McCabe looked at Evan. "You heard the lady, Evan."

"Connor." It sounded like a warning, but there was no heat in his eyes. Crystal knew the angry, frustrated professor, and this wasn't it.

Conner merely held his gaze, and finally, Evan uncrossed his legs.

*Damn!* His impressive erection pressed against his pants, and suddenly, her mouth watered.

"Wow, Crystal. What do you think about that? One hundred percent probability."

She nodded, unable to take her eyes off her professor. The wetness gathered at the apex of her thighs, and there wasn't a thing she could do about it.

"What do you think about that?" Connor said softly.

"I think it's wonderful. I— I never saw a man hard for me like that without even touching me or kissing me." She looked to the man at her side.

"That's right, baby. Next question, what's the probability that I might seduce you tonight? We might seduce you?"

Her jaw dropped. She didn't know what to say to that. Sure, she'd had her fantasies, but that was just it, they were fantasies. They were never *supposed* to come true.

"Think about it a moment. Think about how you're feeling at this moment." He leaned in closer, placed a tiny kiss below her ear and whispered. "Think about what I said about you being the one student we would ever cross the line for."

Her throat worked for saliva. "One hundred percent."

# Chapter Sixty-Two

♥

*F*<sup>uck, yes!</sup>

This precious co-ed before them, squirming in her seat and her nipples peeking against her thin sweater, knew they wanted her, *and* they would have her tonight.

Connor glanced at Evan, who expertly held his surprise. He was always the better poker player.

When Crystal had showed up at his door, looking so adorable soaking wet, Connor was surprised, to say the least. He knew this was a gift from the heavens. Evan knew it too.

Hell, it wasn't thirty minutes prior that her name came up. They just figured she had a boyfriend. She was easy on the eyes and the stuff of fantasies. She looked older than her eighteen years and carried herself as such. It was hard to look at her as a student. She was smart, personable, and beautiful. A trifecta.

He lifted her hand to his mouth and peppered little kisses along the back.

Her eyelids fluttered, and she exhaled.

*Oh yeah.* This woman was long overdue for some TLC.

He didn't want to shock this precious creature, but his gut told him bold, direct moves were what this woman needed.

He lowered her hand to his thigh, and with his gaze trained on her face, he dragged her hand to his raging hard-on.

She watched their hands, and her full lips formed an O.

He dragged her hand back and forth over him twice. "This is what you do to me just sitting close to me, Crystal."

She met his gaze. Her lips parted.

With his free hand, he cupped her jaw and leaned in to peck those perfect lips of hers. When she opened, he dove in.

God, she tasted sweet. Connor wanted to consume every inch of her.

After several long moments feasting on her, he broke the kiss. "Crystal, your mouth is perfect. As is your whole body."

He glanced Evan's way, his eyes almost solid black. "Your professor has fantasized about you. Maybe we should give him a little taste of what might have been running through his mind."

She turned to look at Evan.

Connor whispered in her ear. "Why don't you slip off that sweater?"

She worked her throat, then watching Evan, she pulled the garment up and over her head.

Her full breasts were covered in a pink lace and satin bra. The nipples hard as diamonds poking against the restraint.

Evan's mouth gaped.

"So beautiful, Crystal. Don't you think so, Evan?"

"Yes," Evan said on a breath.

"Would you stand, baby?"

She sat down her empty glass and rose, likely knowing what was coming next.

He gently pulled her before him, between his knees and facing Evan. He stroked her abs and spoke. "He loves women who are fit because he keeps himself fit. Have you ever noticed that, Crystal?"

"Yes."

He felt for her pants button and unfastened them.

The rain pummeling the windows and occasional thunder and lightning did nothing to dampen the mood inside. He loved hearing her accelerated breathing, knowing lust coursed through her delectable body.

He folded her jeans down a few inches, letting her pink panties come into view. Then, he peppered her back with kisses while he continued to caress her.

"Crystal," he whispered. "Do you think your professor deserves to see a little more?"

"Okay." She hooked her thumbs under her pants waistband when he stopped her.

"First, let me ask you. Do you think by stripping for him, he'll give you a better grade on your paper?"

She looked over her shoulder at him. "No. I'm already getting a good grade because it's an excellent paper."

The corner of Evan's lips rose.

Connor knew it was the truth. Crystal was a good student.

"Okay, then step over there." He pointed a few feet in front of where Evan sat. "Don't forget to turn around when you pull off your jeans to give him a view of that absolutely perfect ass."

She bit on her bottom lip and did as he bid. She started shimmying her jeans over her ample, round ass and bent over for Evan to see the saturated scrap of fabric covering her delicate nether lips. She kicked the pants and shoes to the side.

Evan couldn't take his eyes off her.

She rose and turned to face his best friend.

"She's beautiful. Don't you think, Evan?"

"Very."

Connor rose and stood next to her. He glided his knuckles down the side of her face, then he leaned down to kiss her. He had to consume this woman. She brought a passion out in him that he thought was long gone. Dormant.

Sure, he'd had dates and trysts, but no woman had reached so deeply into his core, igniting a fire that he thought had burned out when Anabelle left him years ago.

He knew this thing couldn't last, but they had tonight, and he would take full advantage of every single minute.

He broke the kiss, nearly panting himself. He moved behind his angel, making sure she faced his friend, who was likely about to explode, exactly as he was.

Connor kissed and licked her neck and shoulder, caressing up and down her soft arms.

He continued to love on her as he found her bra straps and slowly pulled them off her shoulders.

The rise and fall of her breasts increased. Her lush globes spilled free from the fabric. She was absolutely perfection.

His hands slid around to cup her, causing her to moan. Pure music to his ears.

Then he toyed with her pointed nipples, and her head fell back against him.

She reached behind, cupping his ass and likely feeling the dig of his cock into her lower back. "Connor," she breathed out.

"Your nipples are sensitive, aren't they, baby?"

"Yes."

"Good, we're going to love on them all night." He trailed kisses up her neck. "We're going to love *you* all night, Crystal. Do you accept that?"

"Yes. Yes, please."

"I have another question. What do you think Evan would do if I stripped you naked, laid you on his coffee table, and fucked your delectable body? Your pretty pink pussy?"

She gasped. "I— I don't know."

He kissed some more. "Well, I want to find out."

Without needing her permission, he unlatched the bra strap and let the confection fall to the floor. Then he slid a hand down her abdomen to her satin-covered mons and slid a finger underneath.

Her clit was wonderfully engorged. She moaned as he skated over the little nub then dipped lower to feel an abundance of sweet cream.

"Fuck, baby. You're so wet."

Her eyelids dropped closed, and she moaned as he caressed her, having full access to her gorgeous, ripe body.

She was climbing; he could hear it in her accelerated breathing.

"Baby, are you on the pill?"

She nodded without opening her eyes.

He pulled out his finger and squatted down to slide off her panties, leaving her completely naked before them. For them.

"Beautiful." Evan stared at her naked mons, then looked back at her flushed face.

Connor reached between them and quickly freed his dick from his pants. He didn't have time to get naked. He needed to be inside her now.

How many times had he fantasized about this woman? *This* woman. No one else.

Coaxing her, they took the two steps to Evan's solid wood coffee table, and he laid her down.

Her eyes widened at the beast jutting from his body.

"Don't worry, baby. I'll go slow."

He aligned himself at her slick entrance, wove his fingers with hers and pulled them over head. Then, inch by inch, he breached her warm, wet entrance. He groaned at her incredibly tight pussy.

Her back arched, thrusting her breasts higher. She moaned, and her eyelids fell closed as he began to move inside her.

With a mere four strokes, she came, pulling on him like a fucking dream. She cried out, and he didn't stop. He only slowed his pace a bit more. Sweat gathering across his brow as he held back his own release. *Just a moment longer*, he told himself.

When she came down, he spoke. "Baby."

She opened her eyes.

"Do you think Evan watching me fuck your gorgeous pussy is turning him on?"

She glanced at Evan and nodded.

"Maybe we should see for sure. Maybe we should see if his cock is weeping for you."

She swallowed and spoke, "Yes."

"Evan, the lady wants to see how excited you are to see her naked before you."

Without much hesitation, Evan shifted in his chair, unfastened his pants, and pulled the fabric down over his dick, letting it stand at attention.

"Oh, God."

Connor looked at Crystal. "What, baby?"

"It's beautiful, like yours."

The precum slid down the purple head and continued. Connor knew Evan couldn't hold it together much longer.

Connor latched his mouth to Crystal's, still holding her hands over her head, and pummeled her warm, wet channel.

In no time, she came again. He swallowed her cries and released inside her as she milked him with her incredible pussy. What an amazingly overwhelming and yet relieving sensation pulsing through his body. Unlike anything he'd ever experienced before.

## Chapter Sixty-Three

♥

Evan watched Crystal and Connor collapse on his coffee table and panting, like he wasn't sitting there about to go out of his mind for wanting.

Crystal at his front door had been the last person he'd expected to see that night. She was a good student and worked hard for every A she got. He hadn't realized she had not sent in her essay.

He and Connor had been casually talking about her, many things actually, after a steak dinner. Connor had considered wrapping it up until the rain came down like the heavens opened up over head. Evan offered his spare bed. It wasn't the first time, and it wouldn't be the last he'd slept over.

And neither would be sharing a woman. They'd done that several times.

He and Connor had known each other since attending Vanderbilt together. That was years ago, and they remained best friends ever since. More than one occasion had they had shared a woman. It was fun, fulfilling, and only for a night. Connor was the orchestrator and Evan had always let him.

Now, he wanted to throw the man off the beauty before him.

How many idle hours had he spent dreaming about Crystal—her bright smile, her sparkling eyes, her curvy backside, her lush breasts? She was everything Evan wanted in a bed partner. But she was hands off because she was his student.

Only an hour or two earlier Connor had said, *I don't care. If an opportunity presents itself, I'm taking it.*

They both figured it was all talk, so no harm, no foul.

But now here she was, sprawled out before him.

Quietly, he rose and stripped out of his clothes.

Connor looked up, pecked her lips, and carefully pulled out of their affection.

She slowly opened her glassy eyes and peered up at him. Her gaze combed him from top to bottom. Then, fuck him, she licked her lips.

His dick wept with need.

She pushed to sitting and wordlessly she reached for him.

He made a half-step closer and gave her free reign.

Wrapping a hand around his girth, she wasted no time taking him into her mouth.

He groaned at the exquisite feel.

She worked him up and down—her lips, tongue, and fist nearly driving him out of his mind.

But this wasn't what he wanted. She was on the pill, and he'd never had a woman bareback. This would be a first. The first time he came would be deep inside her.

He pulled out of her mouth with a pop.

"Miss. Sumner, your mouth is perfect. And now I need to taste you. Please lie back. I don't think I can wait another second."

She smiled and did as he asked.

He went to his knees, then lifted her legs, bending them at the knees and placing them on the table wide. He guided a finger through the wetness, seeing Connor's semen and her love juice slowly drip from her. He circled over her hard clit, fascinated at her response.

As he toyed with her nub, he leaned down to capture a nipple in his mouth.

She gasped as he sucked and laved her hard nub.

He moved to the other breast then slid two fingers into her wet channel. His kisses traveled down her delicious skin to her perfect, nude pussy.

Her clit beckoned him.

He tested her delicate nub, and her eyelids fell closed as she moaned. He licked the bundle of nerves, wanting to feel it twitch under his tongue from the orgasm he gave her.

He laved and circled as his fingers gently stroked her core.

She gripped his head, keeping him right where she wanted him.

"Please. Please."

He loved to hear her beg. And he sensed she was close.

In just a few short moments, she came, arching her back and crying out.

Before she fully came down, he rose upright, gripped her hips, and aligned his aching cock. Meeting her gaze, he dove into the woman he'd kept his distance from all semester.

She cried out as another climax detonated deep inside. She was pure perfection.

He pumped into her, feeling her body arch up to meet his every stroke. He held tight to his own release. He didn't want this night to end. He'd chastise himself in the morning. For now, she was all theirs.

Unable to hold back any longer, he exploded, releasing the pent-up energy this precious woman brought out of him.

He grunted and collapsed over her, panting into the crux of her neck.

After a moment, he lifted his head.

She reached for him and pulled him down, devouring his mouth. Their tongues tangled and danced, and he was certain he'd never have another woman like Crystal in his life again.

***

Crystal rolled over, sighing at the delicious soreness she felt.

The night's events came rushing back to her.

Her professors had seduced her when she showed up only to drop off her final essay for class. She'd thought her biggest obstacle would be getting Evan to accept it well-past class time.

Instead, they'd thrown her for a loop. It was surprising and amazingly good.

She smiled in the darkness and was vaguely aware that she was in the big bed alone. She heard voices in the distance. The men were likely back in the living room, recuperating from their sexcapades.

She stretched like a cat. *Oh yeah.*

After Evan had taken her on the coffee table, Connor lifted her and carried her back to Evan's bed. He'd kissed her and whispered how he desperately needed to be inside her again.

They'd each shared her another time, until she was too spent to carry on. She fell asleep cuddled in between her men.

She smiled to herself. *Her men.*

She didn't know what time it was, but the storm had settled down and only a light rain could be heard.

It was time to go find them. See if she could convince them the night wasn't over yet. And if she had her way, really she had her whole time at college ahead of her.

She slipped out of bed and pulled on Evan's button-down shirt that laid on the pile on the floor.

Tiptoeing down the hall, she heard their voices, sounding distressed. She paused for a moment.

"If this got out," Evan said.

"I know. I know. I lost my mind. I mean, she was right here. At your front door." Connor sighed, and it sounded like someone flopped down onto a chair or sofa.

They were beating themselves up over what happened. She would put an end to that.

She turned the corner to see both men on the sofa—Connor leaning back, staring up at the ceiling, and Evan with his face in his hands as his elbows rested on his knees.

"I sense some distress from you two," she spoke as she walked toward them.

They looked up, meeting her gaze. Evan's color was faded.

"We took advantage of you," Connor spoke first.

"Really? Or was it *I* who took advantage of *you*?"

They both looked at her with blank stares on their faces.

"Do you think you're the only men to want me? The only ones to make a pass at me? To want to take me to bed?"

They looked at each other. Evan's jaw hung open.

"Do you think I can't say *No*?"

Evan shook his head. "It wasn't right. I'm your teacher," pleading for understanding. Pleading for a way to rewind the clock, she'd bet.

"Well, not for long."

His eyebrows furrowed.

"I need to move my schedule around for next semester. If you'll sign off, I'd like to switch to Professor Stranch's class."

"Okay. She's following the same curriculum. But why?"

"I'm going to need to help out with my grandma."

He stared for a moment, perhaps gauging if he should believe her.

She went to her knees before him, scooching in between his legs. "Evan, you won't be my professor anymore."

She stroked her hands up and down his thighs, and he let her. The color in his face slowly returned.

"I don't know." Evan said the words but wasn't making a move to have her stop the caressing.

Her hands crept higher.

Connor watched without saying a word. "How many times I've thought about you." She glossed her fingertips over his growing erection.

"Crystal."

She wasn't sure if he was pleading with her to stop or to keep going. A glance at the sparkle in her men's eyes told her they didn't want her to stop.

Both hands covered and caressed Evan's hard length. His eyelids fluttered closed. He was at full length now.

She squirmed a hand under the band of his briefs and wrapped her fingers around him.

He groaned, and in a sudden move, he cupped her jawline and crashed his mouth onto hers.

The kiss tasted of passion and longing. It was new and exciting, and at the same time, as if they'd always been together. She was made for him, he for her. Actually, them.

Without breaking the kiss, she slid her hand over Connor's thigh, up to easily find him hard and ready for her.

How incredible the feeling. These smart, intelligent, handsome men, who could have any woman they wanted, wanted her. Grew hard for her. Eager to be inside her.

And she felt just as eager.

She maneuvered her hand into Connor's briefs and stroked him as she stroked Evan.

She finally broke the kiss with Evan, both of them panting. "Move your underwear out of the way."

They made room for her to have complete access to their glorious cocks. She leaned down to take Evan in her mouth.

"Fuck, baby." He growled.

After several moments, she shifted to Connor's cock, licking his precum and poking his slit before taking all she could in her mouth.

"Fuck."

After a few short moments sucking both her men, they tore her away from them. "Stand, baby," Connor commanded with a deep gravel in his voice.

She rose, and the men stood too—one in front of her, one behind.

They worked her shirt free after they stepped out of their briefs.

She continued stroking them.

Evan cupped her breasts to suckle and lave at her nipples. Connor pulled her hair, gently tilting her head back. He dove his commanding tongue into her mouth, consuming her wholly.

She moaned into his mouth.

Then, Connor's fingers toyed with her slick slit and dove in. Evan ran circles over her clit.

She pulled back, gasping for air. The sensations engulfed her, raising her heart rate and body temperature.

"Crystal, you are so enticing," Connor whispered.

"Impossible to say No to." Evan persisted on her nipples.

Connor slid in one finger then two. When he pulled back, grazing over her tiny rosette, she gasped. "Easy, baby."

Before she realized what was happening, a finger broke through her little barrier while another finger slid into her pussy.

"Oh, God." Her head fell back against his shoulder, relishing the incredible gift they were giving her.

She knew enough to know that he was prepping her to be able to take both of them. "Yes. Please, yes." She called out over and over.

Connor repeated his ministrations, wetting a finger to add to the others, slowly stretching her to make room for his cock.

He pulled in and out, driving her mad. She had no idea something like this could feel this amazing. Her orgasm climbed with a force of a tornado and crashed through her, sending fireworks to every square inch of her body.

"That's right, baby."

Her men leaned her forward, and Connor removed his fingers from her backside. His cock was poised to enter. Slowly, he pushed in. He was larger than the fingers.

"Oh, God." She panted feverishly.

He paused, giving her a moment, then he pushed in farther. Finally, he'd entered her completely.

They brought her upright, and Evan aligned his cock at her channel. Carefully, he pushed in.

She was light-headed. "Oh, God," she repeated over and over. She exploded, crying out as she clutched to his shoulders, nearly collapsing.

Her men held onto her. Evan kissed her cheeks and lips. "So beautiful, baby."

"I—I never knew it could—it could be like this.

Stroking her core, another orgasm flew through her. Drips slid down the inside of her thighs.

The men kissed and caressed her as they moved inside her. The joining sent her to a place she'd never been before, like she was outside of herself.

"You're incredible, baby," Connor whispered. "Do you want us to make love to you like this again?"

"Yes. Yes. Yes, Connor please. Evan please. Love me like this for as long as we're all here."

She felt another orgasm rocket to the surface. "Ah."

As she came, so did her men, shooting hot liquid deep inside her and growling into her neck, praising her through their pants.

Then, Connor slid out of her, and Evan lifted her. Her legs instantly went around his waist as he carried her to the bedroom.

They lay down on the bed and Connor wrapped his arms around her from behind.

Evan rested on his elbow. "Crystal, is this what you want?"

She stroked a hand down his jaw. "Yes." She glanced over her shoulder at Connor. "This is exactly what I want. We don't have to tell anyone, but I want this again. I never knew it could be like this."

Evan's lips pulled upward. "Neither did we."

When morning came, Crystal knew she was a changed woman. Her men shared her one more time, but no double penetration so she could give her booty time to recover.

Each of them staring into her eyes and whispering words like, *Your ours now,* and *You'll all we want, baby.* They kissed her lips, her body, making her cum several more times.

Something incredible happened here. Something unplanned and unexpected. When she wasn't looking, she might have found love. She knew this couldn't last forever, but she'd keep it for as long as she could.

# Brown Box Delivery

# Chapter Sixty-Four

♥

F riday. Franco looked forward to this day all week. He glanced down at the manifest on his tablet, and confirmed, he'd be seeing Jordan today. His dick jumped.

He needed to get laid. Funny thing was though, he had no interest in anyone but Jordan. It was like once he learned about her divorce, his body went into overdrive. Craving her in ways he hardly recognized. And going seven months without sex? That was unheard of in Franco's world.

He slammed the door and started the van. He would see her in about six hours and all he had to do was keep it together until then.

Franco set down the heavy box on Jordan's porch and rang the bell. The door opened and Jordan's smiling face beamed at him.

"Hi, Franco." She wore casual shorts and a white scoop neck T-shirt, showing hints of cleavage that made him drool.

"Hey, Jordan. I got a heavy one today."

She looked down at the large box at his feet and frowned. "Oh, okay. Would you mind bringing it inside?"

*Hell no!* He set his tablet on the box and lifted it. This kind of thing was against company policy, but for Jordan, he'd take his chances.

She stepped back for him to enter and pushed the door closed.

"It's pretty heavy. Do you want it here or someplace else, like an office?"

"Oh, um, sure. This way." She pivoted away and farther into the house.

Her shorts hugged her ass, making him itch to touch her. *Incredible.*

She pushed open one of the French doors leading to her office. Inside sat stacks of literature and boxes of pharmaceutical samples everywhere—every corner and even up the wall in places. Her desk was neat and tidy, but everything else was organized chaos.

"You can just set it here, Franco."

As he set the box in front of her desk, she shifted and rammed her shin into the corner of the heavy box.

"Ow," she called out, clutching the desk behind her.

*Shit!* He dropped the box the final few inches and knelt before her, reaching for her calf. Unthinking, he rubbed the area and met her gaze. "I'm sorry. Are you okay?" He didn't wait for an answer as his gaze dropped to the scrape. "There's no blood, but it might bruise."

He continued to rub and looked up at her face.

Her jaw agape, and she stared like she was at a loss for words.

He loved having his hands wrapped around her calf, but was this going too far?

He continued caressing her leg, and the energy between them shifted. "I hope you don't have a big date tonight this would put a damper on."

She bit her lip between her teeth and shook her head. "No. No date."

He shifted closer and set her bare foot on his thigh. He caressed more, slowly moving higher, over the knee to her lower thigh and back down. Lust ruled his hands. "Is this helping?" His voice was soft, warm, and he prayed she wouldn't tell him to stop.

His hands on this woman was simply incredible, a dream come true. He'd lusted after her for years, and only fantasized about being able to touch her like this.

She nodded and bit her lip harder.

The chemistry between them had changed, and hopefully she felt it too. God, how he wanted more. How he wanted to make this beautiful woman feel like a million bucks. Make her feel beautiful and cherished like she deserved. Especially after her divorce from a prick who didn't know a good thing when he had it.

His heart pounded wildly in his chest.

On the next pass, he kept his left hand massaging her calf as his right crept higher up her thigh, his fingertips skirting the edge of her shorts, as he caressed her soft skin.

Her legs were smooth, like she'd just shaven.

Her chest moved up and down with her breath as her hands gripped the edge of the desk.

"Your skin is so soft. So smooth."

"Thank you," she whispered back.

The phone rang. She startled, dropping her leg and twisting behind her to silence it.

He inhaled and stood.

She spun back to face him.

The spell was broken.

"Sorry, again. You sure you're okay?" he asked.

"Yes. Thanks. It's no big deal. Thanks for carrying this in. I guess I'll see you next week."

Damn, a whole week.

He smiled and made his way to the door, tablet held over the front of his pants.

Fuck, they were having the most incredible moment, and it popped in an instant.

He glanced back one last time at the beauty at the door.


Jordan closed the door behind him, getting one last look at those incredibly tight buns.

*Holy cow! What was that?*

She leaned against the door and placed her hand over her beating heart. He'd caressed her leg, and she let him. His hands had crept higher, and *again* she let him!

How far would he have gone?

She'd secretly lusted for Franco since she'd first laid eyes on him. Her marriage had already started to disintegrate, despite her best efforts. She'd allowed their little conversations, their occasional flirting, and her private little fantasizes about the strong, yet gentle man she'd seen nearly every week for the last three years.

She exhaled. She had to get ready for her conference call. She'd have to assess what just happened later. She had a week to decide what to do next. Would there even be a *next*?

# Chapter Sixty-Five

♥

J ordan kept Friday as an office day, as usual. She had her sales team call first thing in the morning, then she followed up with the many emails she owed doctors from a week of visits.

She'd dressed in shorts and a tank top because she didn't want the air conditioning blasting, making her cold, and running up her electric bill. Since the divorce, she'd gotten more frugal. The money didn't stretch like it used to, and with the downturn in the market, she had to put more in savings. She didn't want to work forever. She dreamt of traveling; she had a whole list of countries she wanted to visit.

After a full day, she was ready for a glass of wine. She closed her laptop cover and headed to the kitchen when her bell rang. Her heart skipped a beat. It was later than usual, but maybe...

Franco stood at her door, smiling. She hadn't expected him this late.

She opened her door. "Hi. I didn't think I'd see you." She smiled, and the vision of what happened the previous week flooded her mind and brought heat to her cheeks.

He smiled back and handed her the tablet to sign. "Hey. Not as big today." He motioned to the brown box in his hands. "I can carry it in."

She pulled back the door, and without asking he carried it to her office.

Jordan was surprised, but at the same time pleased he felt comfortable entering her house.

She met him outside her office and handed him back his tablet. "I was just about to pour some wine. Can I offer you some?"

The corner of his lip quirked up. "I wish I could."

He followed her the short distance to the kitchen. "How's your leg?"

She glanced down. "Better. I'm rubbing arnica on it."

In that instant, he'd bent down, taking her leg, and resting her foot on his bare leg. He'd worn shorts that day, and the light dusting of leg hair tickled the bottom of her foot. Her heart rate kicked up.

His hand stroked her calf, one grazing higher, like before. "It does look good. Only a little bruise. That's good. These legs are too beautiful."

Did he just say that?

He rose to his full six-foot plus height. "Jordan, maybe after my shift, I could swing by for that drink?"

She didn't have any plans that night. And damn if she didn't want to see him again. "Yea, sounds good."

"I'll be by around six. Okay?"

She nodded.

He smiled, lifted his tablet, and headed toward the door. "Great. See ya' then."


*Does this count as a date?*

Definitely. He definitely had a date, a wine date, with Jordan. Wine wasn't his drink of preference, but for Jordan, he'd happily partake. The only downside to his "date" was he had nothing to change into. He'd have to show up in his uniform, and today in the heat, it was shorts and a short sleeve button-down.

Oh well. He had the week to think about it. If he played his cards right, he'd have an official date set up before the day was through.

Franco finished his deliveries without too much trouble. His foot tapped the floorboard in his truck as he sat in traffic trying to make it back to Jordan's house.

He parked his extended-cab pickup at the curb in front and looked at her house. He'd always loved her house—warm and inviting with shrubs and flowers in the expansive front beds, a wreath on the door she'd changed for every holiday, and a front porch that made you want to relax after a long day.

He rang the bell, and she greeted him as she always had—with a magnetic smile and ocean blue eyes that sparkled. She still had on her shorts and tank top from earlier, and damn if he didn't love looking at her legs. Looking and touching.

"Hey, Franco. Done for the day?"

The door opened wide, and he strode in. "Yea, sorry about the attire. And I apologize for any smell."

She grinned and pushed the door closed. She mumbled something which might have been "I like your smell," but he couldn't be sure.

He followed her into the kitchen, and if he wasn't mistaken, was her ass getting rounder? Tighter?

"I hope you like chardonnay?"

He nodded. *That's a white wine, right?*

She pulled off the cork and poured them each a glass.

He took in her kitchen. Again, that inviting feeling wrapped around him. When she was married, he didn't see much past the foyer.

She had a large, 6-burner range and light countertops with an island in a dark espresso color. He liked the contrast.

"I have some cheese too." She lifted a small, wooden cutting board with three different cheeses on it.

"Thanks. This is good," he said lifting his wine glass.

She smiled. "Glad you like it."

He wanted to know more about Jordan. All about her. But he hadn't dated much and really had no good idea of how to get to know a woman. His previous experience with women was small talk and flattery. He hated to admit it, but it was true. Most of his life, he needed one thing to feel fulfilled. Now, as he was getting older, Franco realized dying alone sounded like shit.

"Mind if I ask you about your ex?"

*Shit! That's not a good opener.*

She glanced down briefly and shrugged. "Sure. It's pretty simple really. We grew apart. I like variety and adventure. Trying new things, going to new places. Tim was more of a homebody." She reached up in a cabinet and pulled down a box of crackers, pouring some in a bowl. "It hadn't always been that way." She offered him a cracker.

"Thanks. How so?"

"Well, we'd been married sixteen years and it looked like we both wanted the same things—no kids, maybe a dog or two, but lots of opportunity to travel."

He nodded. "I agree. I like to travel too."

She motioned to a barstool at the island and sat in one herself.

He stayed leaning against the counter. "I'm good. Thanks. So, where have you been and where would you like to go?"

She played with the stem of her wineglass. "I've only been to Mexico, but I want to go to Greece, France, Thailand, Australia maybe. So many places." She grinned.

He nodded. He could imagine going to all those places with her. "I was just reading about a special, a cruise, I think, to the Greek Isles."

Her eyes rounded. "That sounds like fun. I mean—" Her cheeks turned pink.

He knew what she meant, but he wanted to go on that trip with *her*. Lounge around the pool deck on a cruise liner, explore villages during the day, and make love in a large king-size bed every night.

"So, I couldn't help but notice," he moved closer to her and reached for cheese and a cracker, "it seems like you've been working out lately."

Her face practically glowed now. "I...um...I have been. I used to work out in my twenties like a fiend, but I've gotten away from it."

"It shows. You have great legs."

She smiled, making her eyes sparkle. One of her many outstanding features, in addition to her toned legs, her shapely ass, her perfect breasts.

Franco had been in lust with this woman for longer than he could remember. It was taking all his strength not to pull her into his arms and ravage her. He wanted to kiss her from head to toe, making sure to return to any areas that needed *extra* special attention.

"Thank you. I made myself a promise to get back to me." She twirled her wine. "For too long, I'd been focused on Tim and forgot about me... What mattered to me. Ya' know?"

He nodded.

"I'm forty now, and I've decided to be smart from now on. No more compromising myself."

God, this woman was incredible. He could hear the determination and fortitude in her voice. Nothing sexier than a woman with a back-bone.

"So, enough about me. I know very little about you. Do you work out?"

"Does this job count?"

She grinned.

"Actually, I used to be an accountant. Stuck behind a desk all day."

Her head tipped to the side. "Really?"

"Yup."

"I just can't picture it." Her eyes scanned him, and he had to admit he loved her admiring gaze.

"Well, it's true. I was getting a soft belly."

In a brazen move, he stepped closer, reached for her hand, and rested it on his hard-earned six-pack.

Her eyebrows lifted. "Wow." She stroked her fingertips crosswise before pulling back her hand. The pink tinting her cheeks was adorable.

"So, I figured a job like this would keep me in shape, plus I get to meet a lot of interesting people."

"Really?"

He sipped his wine and nodded. "Yup. Last week I had a delivery to an art gallery. The box was a bit large and thin, but I seriously doubt it had any valuable art in it. Anyway, I was greeted by this guy who seemed to be running the show. I walked in as he was directing people with art pieces everywhere, talking about what color and lighting would be best. It was completely over my head. Then he saw me. He floated over, instantly wrapped his hand around my bicep and said, 'Oh, honey, tell me you're my art display, and the box is delivering you.'"

She chuckled.

He grinned. "He was flamboyant and confident. I just laughed. 'Sorry, not this time.' He told me where to put the box and asked if I could move something for him. I said, 'Sure.' It was a heavy box, but it wasn't much trouble."

He sipped from his wineglass. "Anyway, he invited me back that evening for some kind of event. Told me I'd be his guest, so I didn't need a ticket. He knew I was straight, even told me to bring my girlfriend."

She nodded. "Sounds like you *do* get to meet some interesting people." She smiled, then said, "So did you go back, with your girlfriend?"

He loved the question. This was a great place to let her know just where he was coming from. He set down his wineglass and closed the distance between them. "No girlfriend. There's someone I've been interested in, but I've been too chicken to make a move."

She swallowed. "And now?" she whispered.

He shook his head. "Not so chicken." He cupped her jaw, stroking a thumb along her cheek. "I've been wanting to kiss you for the longest time."

"Since last week?"

He shook his head. "For the past three years."

He took the chance while he had it. He leaned down pecking her sweet warm lips, and as she opened for him, he dove in. Without breaking the kiss, he helped her stand and pulled her to him with an arm. He tilted her head with his free hand and took the kiss deeper, eager to taste this woman who had haunted his dreams for years. The kiss was hungry and all-consuming.

It was out of control.

He broke the kiss and dropped his hands, clasping hers. His breath rapid, like hers.

"Jordan, I want to take you out. For dinner. Are you free tomorrow night?" Did he sound too eager, asking her out for the following night? He didn't care. He didn't want to leave this place without securing a date.

"I'm free."

He nodded, then smiled. "I'm going now. I need to get cleaned up. Tomorrow, I'll pick you up around six." He wanted to stay, but he didn't trust himself to not lose his self-control. Taking it too far too soon.

"Okay."

She walked him to the door, and he pivoted before heading to his truck. "Thanks for the wine."

She sent him one of her million-dollar smiles. The kind that would hopefully carry him through for the next twenty-four hours.


*Holy crap!*

That was hot as Hades. Franco was hot as Hades.

She'd touched his stomach, run her fingers over his incredible abs. The man was tall, dark, and handsome. When he smiled, his dimples showed. He had great muscles and was an amazing kisser.

She had to be dreaming.

She sank back down onto the stool.

He'd complimented her. He'd noticed her toned muscles.

She breathed in deeply to calm her breath.

How many times had he filled her fantasies? Holy cow!

And now they were going out on a date. She'd need to get ready. Dating at forty was quite a bit different than in your teens or twenties.

A smile pulled at her lips unbidden.

# Chapter Sixty-Six

♥

F ranco waited only for a brief moment before Jordan opened her front door.

"Wow." Did he say that out loud or just think it? "Jordan, you look incredible." He leaned down and kissed her cheek, wishing for a kiss like the day before.

He stepped back. The scarlet knit dress clung to her like it was custom-made. Snug in all the right places, showing a bit of cleavage and a lot of leg. She was a knockout.

"Thanks," she said with a gorgeous smile on her glowing face. "You ready?"

Her purse strap was draped over her shoulder, and he took the cue she didn't want to linger at the house. Franco didn't care either way. As long as he was with Jordan, that was all that mattered.

He rested a hand on the small of her back and led her to his pickup. He grimaced when she climbed in. He figured she was maybe five-seven, but still it couldn't be easy to climb into his extended cab. How he wanted to give her boost up...

He'd been on a waiting list for reservations at a highly rated place named Quincy's. His sister had told him about it. Again, Franco hadn't done much dating. His experience was limited to sports bars and a few clubs. When the restaurant called, saying they'd had a cancelation, Franco took that as a good sign.

Quincy's was all he'd expected. Elegant, dark, and cozy. Perfect for wanting to get to know this woman who had intrigued him for years.

They were seated at a cozy table, and he couldn't miss how her hand skated across her ass to smooth her dress as she sat.

Her ass was perfect.

He swore to himself he wouldn't make any big moves. He didn't want to blow it. Going too far was too risky.

"Mmm." She hummed as she perused the menu.

"See something you like?" He set his menu down and watched her sparkling eyes as they danced over the selections.

"I think I'll have steak tonight."

He ordered the New York strip, and she had the filet. They split two vegetable sides, and he asked her to pick a bottle of red. Again, Franco's expertise was in IPA, not cabernet.

Something he'd have to brush up on if he wanted a chance at a relationship with Jordan.

The cabernet was poured, and he had questions. So much he wanted to learn about this woman, that frankly had nothing to do with her ex.

"So, how long have you been in medical sales?"

"Gees," she looked off to the side. "About nineteen years."

His eyebrows lifted. "That's great."

She nodded. "A few times Tim asked me to quit, saying we should start a family." She sipped from her glass.

He waited. He suspected she needed to get some of this off her chest, so he'd listen.

"We'd always agreed we didn't want kids, so why he changed his mind, I'll never know." She exhaled.

Her ex had changed his mind about wanting kids, there was no dog, and the only place she'd traveled to was Mexico. *That guy clearly wasn't right for her. Sold her a bill of goods.*

"You have any kids, Franco?" She broke his stream of thought.

He shook his head. "I'm more uncle material." He grinned thinking of his six nieces and nephews.

"Exactly. My brother has two kids, and my sister has one with another on the way. I love being Aunt Jo-Jo."

His smile met hers. "That's a great name."

The entrees were served, and his mouth instantly watered at the aroma.

They both tasted a bite.

"Mmm. Perfect. How many do you have?" She referred to his nieces and nephews.

"Six."

"And how often do you get to see them?"

"Fairly often. They don't live far." The image of last weekend's car wash came to mind. "Last weekend, my nephew's soccer team was hosting a carwash to raise money. I drove by early, before heading to the gym, thinking I'd get a wash. Well, everyone was in a panic. The key to turn on the water at the school didn't work, and I guess they couldn't get a hold of anyone who had the right key. I called a buddy of mine who owns a warehouse not far from the school and asked if he could help out."

"And did he?"

"Yup. Two parents stayed behind with signs redirecting people to the new location. Someone thought it was actually a bigger turnout than previous years, probably because there was a grocery store right across the street."

She smiled. "Nice."

He nodded and bit into a roasted potato.

The conversation flowed, and he grew more impressed with how smart and perceptive Jordan was. All the more reason he had to date this woman. He had to have her.

Franco had never been in a rush to settle down. But now, he could imagine that with one woman. The woman across from him who's eyes lit up when she smiled and used her hands when she talked.

When they were nearly done, he asked, "Jordan, I noticed a chocolate lava cake on the menu. Wanna split it with me?"

She wiggled her eyebrows. "Oh, yeah."


Jordan sat back and licked her lips of all traces of the chocolate cake. "That was delicious."

He nodded and dropped his napkin onto his lap.

The conversation had been great and so was the food. Franco was an incredibly decent guy. And evidently full of business savvy as he'd run an accounting firm for several years and sold it to make a handsome profit. It was almost like working delivery was just something to do to pass the time and keep active.

More than once she'd caught herself comparing him to Tim and how Tim had always fallen short.

She tipped her head to the side.

His eyebrow lifted. "What? Something on my face?" Then he sent her a self-deprecating grin.

"I was just thinking. You're too perfect. What's wrong with you?"

His eyes rounded to saucers. "I'm not perfect."

"Okay, so what's wrong with you?"

He licked his lips. "I backed into the garage door once."

She shrugged. "Accident."

"Hm. I get up at five a.m. every morning, whether I need to or not."

*Interesting.* "I love sleep. So, no morning sex?" She couldn't believe the words flew out of her mouth. Warmth crept into her cheeks.

Before she could clarify, he gave her one of his sexy grins. The kind that melted her insides. "If there is morning sex, then I just get up." He winked at her.

She laughed. It might have been the wine because the banter and flirting were effortless.

"That's it? No flaws?"

He glanced down a second. "Okay, I got one. I don't share."

"Really?"

"Always been that way."

She found his minor faults, and ability to face them head on, admirable. "Good thing I didn't wanna try your steak."

"Indeed."

"Hm. I have to give that some thought." She stopped herself from saying *I'll have to decide if I can live with that.*

She couldn't explain the instant chemistry she had with Franco. Maybe it had been there the whole time, and she never allowed herself to think they could ever be together. Really together. She'd been married, and she'd suspected he had at least had a serious girlfriend. He was a catch, after all.

Sure, she'd had her little fantasies, but now, she could act on them. And the thrill of it set butterflies loose in her tummy.


After their two-hour dinner, Franco drove a scenic route home, past the lake and a farmhouse where deer seemed to congregate for no particular reason.

"Wow. Look at them all." Jordan said in awe, watching the deer graze.

"Cool, huh?"

She smiled at him.

He was starting to love that smile. Correction- he already loved it. He hadn't seen it enough in the last year, maybe because she'd been dealing with her ex and the end of their marriage. If Franco had his way, he'd put that smile on her face every day.

Without asking, he reached across the cabin and laced his fingers through hers. He brought them to his lips, laying a kiss over them. Keeping a hold, he continued to drive down the single-lane road, making it to her house fifteen minutes later.

"Thank you for a wonderful night." She faced him.

No one seemed anxious to end the date.

He shut off the engine. "You're welcome." He glanced down at her hand in his, stroking a thumb across the back.

He'd had no expectations for the night, but if he had, they would have been surpassed. He leaned over to kiss her cheek, her subtle floral scent filling his senses. He lingered as he whispered, "And thank you. I had a great time." His kiss trailed to her lips, and she opened for him.

He dove his tongue in to find hers waiting, caressing in return.

Without breaking the kiss, she wrapped her arms around his neck and leaned into the kiss.

Fuck, how he loved kissing her.

He couldn't say how long they carried on, but the urgency grew below his belt, and he knew he had to stop, or he'd do something he'd regret. Jumping in, giving into the lust, was not in his plans for that night.

He broke the kiss and rested his forehead against hers, both of them panting.

"Jordan, I should walk you to your door. I promised myself I would be a gentleman."

She pulled back and met his gaze in the pale light. "Sure."

He should reach for the door but somehow couldn't.

She unbuckled her seatbelt, then his, and shimmied onto the bench, hiking up her skirt to throw a leg over his lap.

*Whoa!* He hid his surprise and reached for the lever to push the steering wheel away from them, giving her room.

The warmth of her body permeated through his clothes. He rested his hands on her hips, and she cupped his jaw. "In a minute, okay?"

He nodded. He'd give this woman whatever she wanted right then.

She tilted her head to kiss him. She dove in, and he could feel the hunger in her kiss.

He cupped her perfectly rounded ass cheeks and pulled her into him, into the hardness that was there because of her. Only for her.

She whimpered into his mouth and rocked herself against his covered cock.

He broke the kiss, panting and meeting her gaze. Holding her, he slouched a little more for her.

Her eyelids fluttered closed as the apex of her thighs made full contact with his cock. She rode him gently.

"God, Jordan. You're so beautiful."

Seeming to have a mind of their own, his hands slid up her arms and shoulders to her delicate neck. Slipping his fingers under the neckline, the stretchy material gave way as he pushed it aside to reveal her smooth satin bra underneath.

Gauging her expression, he slipped the bra cups over and down to expose the most perfect breasts he'd ever seen. He wasted no time claiming her peeked nipple, gently sucking it into his mouth.

She whimpered.

He didn't want to stop. Maybe her nipples were sensitive. Maybe this brought her closer to orgasm. He would stop only if she told him to, and he prayed she wouldn't.

"Franco," she breathed out as her hands gripped his shoulders while still rocking over his erection. She didn't move to unfasten his pants.

They were in this perfect erotic bubble, and nothing could make it pop.

She panted harder and moaned.

Clasping the back of her neck, he brought her full lips down to his, tasting her, feeling the desperation for her climax in her kiss. That same desperation he felt.

And then she exploded. She broke the kiss, her head fell back, and she cried out.

Pure music to his ears.

Hearing her in ecstasy set off his own release, not caring one iota what mess he created in his briefs. He held her firmly, wrapping his fingers around her torso. Her elbow hit the horn, but she didn't seem to notice.

God, she was perfect.

As her breathing slowed, she lifted her head to meet his gaze. Her beautiful eyes were glassy, and her cheeks glowed. "Wow," she whispered.

That was an understatement. Franco could only imagine how explosive they would be naked.

That was one of the sexiest things he'd ever experienced.

He pecked her forehead. "Jordan, you're amazing." Their panting in sync.

After a moment passed, she pulled back, and he helped her fix her dress.

Wordlessly, she crawled back to her side of his truck as he climbed out of the cab, situated himself, and rounded the truck to open her door. He held her hand as they walked to the door.

It had been the most perfect night, and he hated that it had to end.

She turned to meet his gaze. "Thank you, Franco. It was a wonderful evening." Her cheeks colored as she gave him a shy smile.

He cupped her cheeks. "It was absolutely perfect." He claimed her mouth. One last kiss for the night, probably for a week.

She then reached for his hand, shoving a small piece of paper in it. He knew what it was.

He smiled and stepped off her porch, commanding his body to listen to his brain.

She slipped in her house key, opened the door, and lifted her hand to wave him goodnight.

Jordan closed the door, locked it, and leaned back, exhaling. *Holy crap!*

It was a great date. Ten out of ten. Conversation, food, kissing. They exchanged cell numbers. All good things for a first date. So how could she explain straddling his lap and riding him?! She couldn't. There was no explanation. She was out of her mind.

And it was so incredible. His warm hardness beneath her, his thick muscled legs, all had sent her to the stratosphere.

*Oh, what he must think of me.*

She slipped off her shoes and pushed off the wall. Heading to the kitchen for a glass of water, she couldn't stop smiling. She would have to face her embarrassment in the morning, but for now, she was on a high. And nothing could pull her down.

# Chapter Sixty-Seven

♥

Franco had gotten only five hours of sleep. He knew thoughts of Jordan filled his mind, his body.

Their date the prior night was nothing short of amazing. Her graceful moves, her smile, her sexy body. And they'd made-out in his truck, like teenagers. He chuckled softly.

He rolled to the side and reached for his phone on the nightstand. He'd already programmed her number in there, and of course, he had her address. Now, what flowers to send?

He called a local florist whom he knew would answer at this hour. The florist assured him she had the perfect arrangement in mind. He told her what to put on the card and paid for the arrangement. He had a busy day, working on the house, food shopping, and running errands. Most of the shit he couldn't get done during the week because of work. Not that he minded. Getting out from behind a desk was the best move he'd ever made. And the money from the sale of his business sat in a brokerage account, growing, as he considered what to do with it.

He was starting to get an idea of what to do with it...

As he threw on some old clothes and put on a pot of coffee, he knew Jordan would be on his mind the whole day, just like the week leading up to their date. This woman had occupied his thoughts, and now he was one step closer to having her occupy his bed.

Jordan was folding her clean laundry when her doorbell rang. Her heart flipped.

She opened the door to the most beautiful floral arrangement she'd ever seen. So wonderfully arranged, she inhaled the scents of rose, lily of the valley, lisianthus, and what she thought were called saffron crocus. It must have cost a fortune.

She set the vase on the table and slid the card from the envelope.

*Can't stop thinking about last night. Would you please go out with me this Saturday night?*

Franco wanted to see her again.

She smiled and internally breathed a sigh of relief. She didn't know what he'd thought about their prior night together.

She grabbed her phone and texted him she was free Saturday and would love to go out with him.

Picturing his devilish grin, butterflies let loose in her belly. After the tailspin of a divorce, Jordan had questioned if she'd date again. Have another first kiss. Feel the tender touch of a man desperate with need for her.

She grinned at nothing, just thinking about what was to come Saturday.

She strode into her office. Until then, she had a mound of paper-work and a week full of meetings.

***

Franco had a Thursday delivery for Jordan. He doubled checked, triple checked his tablet, and his dick flexed.

*Settle down boy.*

He would be seeing Jordan today. Sure, it was only two days before their second date, but truly, once a week with a woman like Jordan wasn't enough.

That said, he did think it strange considering all her deliveries were set for Friday. Some time ago, she'd told him that the company she worked to try and minimize boxes, disruption to their sales force, and delivery trips by scheduling all deliveries on Friday.

He slammed the door closed and started the van. Anticipation pulsed through his veins. All he had to do was keep it together for a few hours.

Six hours later, Franco stood at her front door, ringing the bell.

No answer.

He rang again.

She probably wasn't home. Since all her deliveries were set for Friday, on a Thursday, she wouldn't necessarily be expecting him. She could be meeting with doctors.

Suddenly, the door cracked open, and Jordan angled her head, and a shoulder came into view.

Her cheeks were flushed, and by the looks of it, she wore a black satin robe.

"Hey, Franco. I wasn't expecting you."

No, of course not, not dressed like that. Was she expecting someone else?

"Hi, Jordan. I got a delivery." He stated the obvious.

She glanced down. "Okay." She stepped back, giving him room to carry in the oversized brown box.

Her silky black robe stopped mid-thigh. She was stunning, even with no makeup on.

Jordan bent to investigate the label. Her brows lowered. "This didn't need to come today."

He swallowed hard at the incredible view of her cleavage as she leaned over the box.

She rose.

He met her gaze.

Her cheeks tinted pink, perhaps realizing he watched her.

"I'm sorry I'm disturbing you. Do you have a date?" The question came out before he could catch it. "Scratch that. I shouldn't have asked."

She waved her hand in the air. "No, no date. Just a long day and needed a shower."

He scanned her body again from head to toe. A shower? Did that mean she was naked under that robe. "Nice robe."

She blushed again. "Thanks."

That silky black robe that showed her shapely legs—Franco groaned inside.

She clutched her robe loosely in front of her chest.

He took a half-step closer. "You don't have to do that. You look incredible."

She swiped her tongue over her lips. "Thanks."

The woman before him was gorgeous. "At first, I thought I...interrupted you."

There was a slight pause, then her mouth gaped. God, she was adorable.

Finally, she found her voice. "I, um, no. Nothing like that."

He nodded slowly. "That's a shame." When had he gotten so brazen? "I mean, how gorgeous that would have been." His dick strained behind his shorts, just thinking about her spread out on her bed. "I'm sorry. That's inapp—"

She cut him off. "Oh. Thank you," she said, biting on her bottom lip.

"You're welcome." He shifted closer to her. "Maybe I shouldn't say this, but I've pictured you. That way."

Her breath hitched. "You have?"

*Fuck!* This woman was going to drive him insane. He nodded. "Your legs spread. Your fingers glistening as they move over your hot button."

He detected a subtle change in her breathing, the way her chest rose and fell. Her nipples peaked.

Her deep eyes met his gaze. "And when you picture this, are you standing over me, watching?"

His cock grew another inch, threatening to rip the zipper of his shorts apart. "Definitely watching. You like me to watch, but I can't touch you."

She shook her head. "That's right, no touching," she said as they wove their fantasy.

The corner of his lip lifted. "But I don't care. I don't care how badly I'm aching. Watching you is worth it." He moved closer still, leaving only a few inches between them.

She stepped back, and his breath stalled. He'd gone too far.

She did it again, and the fire in her deep eyes still raged.

Then, he knew what she was doing. *Fuck!*

She hoisted herself to the second stair and reached back for another, planting her ass on the fourth step.

His jaw hung open, but he didn't care. He prayed she was giving him his fantasy.

She momentarily lost her mind. That had to be it. Because she was wearing nothing underneath her robe. *Naked.*

She had happy hour with the girls that night and hadn't had a break to shower. She'd been toweling off when she heard the bell ring. She hesitated, wanting to blow it off. She hadn't expected Franco. But she'd caved and scrambled to grab her robe.

And now he was here.

His words had enticed her—hell, his *presence* enticed her—and her guard came crashing down.

*What is it about this man?*

Now, here she sat on her front staircase, wetness gathered at the apex of her thighs, needing to put out an ache that had blossomed just being close to this gorgeous hunk of muscle.

Slowly, as he tracked her every move, she separated her bent legs.

Then, she untied her robe, pulling the garment to reveal her breasts.

Maybe she'd rationalized it because after the heavy make-out session the past weekend, he'd seen just about everything.

Franco's eyes grew to a deep chocolate brown as he scanned her body from head to toe. The impressive bulge in his pants telling her he loved everything she was about to do.

God, it felt so good, knowing she could turn him on, with her very private, seductive show.

She slid a hand down her belly to her pussy, feeling the incredible amount of slickness there. With her free hand, she dragged the robe away. Her naked body on full display.

"Fuck," he muttered.

She gathered some wetness, then circled over her clit. She watched him watch her, but she couldn't keep her eyes open one more second. Her eyelids fell closed, and she moaned.

God, how it would feel having Franco do this to her.

Her breath grew more rapid. She wanted to cum, but maybe...she could have more.

She stopped.

His gaze met hers.

"Franco, you're not gonna let me do this alone, are you?" She praised herself for her quick thinking.

She glanced down at his package then back up to his face.

He was a smart man. He shook his head as he worked on freeing his cock from his shorts and briefs. "No, ma'am."

It was a magnificent sight—just the right length and thickness. He pulled his shirt up, revealing his ab muscles, then he stroked his length with his fist.

She began to move her fingers again. They trained their sights on each other as they pleasured themselves. Each sharing this incredible, otherwise individual experience.

He groaned.

She closed her eyes as her climax grew. "Fuck," she muttered. She was close and wanted nothing more than to have this moment with Franco.

His fist worked his length, sometimes covering the purple head. It was hot and thrilling and erotic.

She couldn't hold on any longer as the climax grew to the surface, eager for release, eager to show Franco what he did to her.

"Ah," she cried out as her head fell back and her orgasm exploded.

Franco growled.

She opened her eyes long enough to see him pinch his eyes closed and grip the purple head to catch the semen that shot from his body.

The muscles in his face pulled taught, then relaxed. Slowly, he opened his glassy eyes. "Wow."

She grinned, then added, "Bathroom's right around the corner on the right."

He gripped his shorts and briefs that had threatened to fall to the ground with his free hand and made his way down the hall.

After a few short minutes, she had put herself back together, and Franco had returned. His smile soft and full of some emotion she couldn't quite make out.

He stepped close to her, cupping her cheek, a thumb glazed over her lower lip. "Wow," he said again.

They stood close, not needing to escalate the moment but instead savor it for what it was.

"That was incredible. The most erotic thing I've ever done." Then before she could respond, he crashed his lips over hers, claiming her mouth, delving deep in that sensual way he had.

He broke the kiss, both of them breathless.

"Thank you," she whispered.

He pulled back to meet her gaze and grinned. "Thank you."

They both took steps toward the door, and with her hand on the doorknob she said, "Franco, thank you so much for that delivery."

"You're quite welcome, Ms. Ruiz. We appreciate your business."

She opened the door, and he sent her his adorable, devilish grin before making his way to the truck as if nothing unusual happened.

# Chapter Sixty-Eight

♥

Franco awoke Saturday morning like he could run a marathon. He felt refreshed and invigorated.

The time he'd spent with Jordan two days prior was incredible. Out of this world. Watching her play with her gorgeous body like it was a Stradivarius took his breath away. She'd opened herself to him, masturbated for him, came with him.

The trust she showed him made him want to be with her even more, learn all about her, what drove her, what made her laugh, and what made her cry.

This woman living rent-free in his mind for the past three years was becoming a reality in his life.

He'd texted her the prior day, telling her how much he enjoyed their time together and couldn't wait for their date Saturday.

And Saturday was here.

He had reservations for dinner at a quaint restaurant on Silvercrest Lake, just outside of town. Then, he'd invite her back to his place.

Chugging the last of his coffee, he made a plan to clean his place top to bottom. Then his truck would get a bath.

Everything was coming together. Today would be one step closer to fulfilling a longtime dream and excitement coursed through his veins.

Franco could admit it, he was nervous. He wanted to impress Jordan, more than he'd wanted to impress any other woman before.

And then she answered the door.

She wore a staggeringly gorgeous dress—black with red flowers that hugged her body in all the right ways.

"Hello, beautiful."

"Hi, handsome."

He stepped close, cupped her cheeks, and kissed her. A consuming kiss, letting her know she was all he'd been thinking about since the very moment he woke up.

She swung her arms around his neck, and her body pressed against his, fitting so perfectly as she stood in her high heels.

Their tongues tangled and caressed. His dick came alive holding her in his arms. This woman could light him up faster than anyone.

He pulled back, breaking the kiss, trying to regain his breath. "Shit, Jordan."

She let out a breathy chuckle. "Come in. Have a little wine with me."

He liked the sound of that. He pushed the door closed and turned to catch a glimpse of her fine ass beckoning him to follow.

She lifted the white wine, poured it, and handed him a glass. "What should we toast to?"

"That's easy. To an unforgettable night that'll only be one of many."

She smiled, clinked his glass, and pressed her lips to the glass for a sip.

Franco couldn't take his eyes off her.

She swallowed and met his gaze straight-on. "What?"

The corners of his lips pulled upward. "I can't believe I'm finally here." He shook his head. "You look amazing and being here with you now, like this, is a dream come true."

Her eyebrows lifted. "Really?"

"Yes, really."

"And Thursday?"

How could he *ever* forget what they shared—her on the staircase, him witnessing the most amazing thing he'd ever seen. "Out of this world."

She grinned and stepped closer. She met his gaze straight on as a hand stroked down his chest. "I thought so too. I can't believe what I did. Not that I regret it, I just—"

"It was beautiful."

The corners of her lips curved. She leaned in and planted a soft kiss on his lips, nibbling lightly.

*Fuck*. This woman could drive him crazy.

He set his glass on the counter and cupped her jaw as his other arm drew her close, giving her a taste of just what she did to him.

She gasped, and he dove into that precious mouth of hers.

Her arms swung around his neck.

His tongue tangled with hers while his hand caressed her back down to her ass. He cupped her full globe, then drew her bent leg up the side of his thigh.

But his lust was getting the better of him. He wanted to treat this woman the way she deserved, to be wined and dined, and put on a pedestal.

He broke the kiss and rested his forehead against hers. "Shit, Jordan. Your mouth is incredible, but I fear if we continue, we won't make it to dinner."

She pulled back to meet his gaze, biting on her bottom lip. "I'm not hungry for dinner."

She backed away another two steps and crocked her index finger to follow him. Then, she pivoted and walked toward the staircase.

That vixen! Damn was she hot as fuck!

Franco threw back the last of his wine and followed her up the stairs.

Watching her and that perfect heart-shaped ass, Jordan reached down for the hem of her dress and drew it overhead. She tossed it back.

Fuck! She wore a tiny black lacy thong and matching bra.

He wanted to chase her, grab that delectable body, but he was enjoying the show too damn much.

Next, her shoes. She stepped out of them one at a time.

He collected the litter that trailed behind her. And growled.

She glanced back at the noise and grinned. As she made it to the top, she spun around, unhooked her bra, and flung it at him.

His dick grew to its maximum extent and threatened to rip the stitches of his slacks.

"That's it." He took the last steps two at a time and chased her down the hall to the bedroom.

She laughed and spun around when she made it to the bed, panting and smiling at him.

"You think you can tease me like that and not have consequences." He played, making his way closer like a jaguar about to strike its prey, unbuttoning his shirt at the same time.

"Well, Mr. Tough Guy, what precisely are you going to do about it?"

With his shirt loose, he whipped it off, adding it to the impromptu pile on the floor. Then, he grabbed her upper arms, gently but quickly bringing her to him for a searing kiss. He had to have this woman. He craved her more than air right then.

He lowered her to the bed, then laid her down. And fast as lightning, he whipped off her panties and threw them. His mouth was on her pussy before she had time to gasp at the delicious torment he'd been so eager to rain down on her.

She reached her hands to his head, weaving her fingers through his hair. "Franco," she moaned.

Holding onto her thighs, he licked her hot button and poked into her wet channel. He didn't want to stop until she came all over him.

Her hips pulsed, reaching up for more. He persisted, never ceasing from stimulating her clit.

She moaned again, just before she exploded. Gripping his head, she flexed her entire body and cried out from the pleasure.

He rose when she'd come down and loosened his pants.

She opened her hazy eyes to watch.

He reached into his back pocket for a condom and rolled it on. Bracing himself, he leaned down and pecked her kiss-swollen lips. "I've waited years for this night. I want it to last."

Her rosy face glowed, then she wiggled her hand between them, grasping his length and aligning him with her center.

When he pushed in, her eyelids fell closed, her back arched and she moaned.

He growled but didn't move.

"More, Franco. Please."

His eyes were pinched closed. "Just a second. Damn, Jordan. I should have known you would feel this good."

She gripped his jaw, drawing him near to kiss him.

He dove into her mouth and slowly started a pace inside her precious pussy.

Jordan was like no other woman he'd been with. He wanted to savor everything—every stroke, every kiss, every moan.

His kisses traveled down her delicate neck to her succulent nipples.

It was pure heaven. Jordan couldn't describe the incredible sensation of Franco filling her, moving inside her, laving at her breasts. But God, it was more than a physical thing. She knew it in her heart. This man was different, and he made her feel special.

She moaned at the incredible build of another orgasm. She could never orgasm more than once with Tim, and sometimes not at all.

Now in the arms of this fine hunk of muscle, so strong but gentle, he ravaged her.

If he didn't want to date her long-term, she knew for a fact, she was ruined for all other men.

In fact, her heart had likely already fallen. She hated facing that fact. Grown women didn't fall in love on a whim. But somehow this was different. Franco was different.

He lifted his head to look down at their joining. "God, Jordan. This is incredible."

He reached for her right hand and wrapped it around him as he pulled back. "Feel that."

He was slick with her essence, and it coated her fingers the more he moved in and out of her.

"Oh, God," she breathed out.

Grabbing her hand, he sucked a finger into his mouth and at the same time lowered to kiss her. She could taste herself.

As he gained speed, he glossed a finger over her clit.

"Ah." In a few short moments, she toppled over the edge.

Her climax was powerful, it felt like none she'd ever experienced before. "Franco," she cried out.

Then he growled out his orgasm as he rammed into the end of her before collapsing to the side, holding her and panting with her.

"Incredible," he muttered.

She merely smiled and held him closer. *Yes, it was.*

# Chapter Sixty-Nine

♥

Jordan made the short walk to her mailbox at the street curb and was greeted by her next-door neighbor, Dalynn. The woman was a shameless flirt whose marriage of convenience was well-known by anyone in a fifty-mile radius. There were also rumors that she had more than one "boyfriend."

"Hi, Jordan. How are you? You adjusting to divorced life?" Dalynn's snide smile made Jordan's skin crawl. The woman secretly loved the idea that others were miserable and hated if people were happy. Well, unless they were happy for her.

"Hi, Dalynn. I'm doing exceptionally well." The smile came naturally as she thought of her revitalized love life, and her new affection, Franco.

She retrieved her mail to find Dalynn had stepped even closer. "Well, good to hear. We were all pretty worried there for a moment when we heard Tim had left you."

Sure, *everyone* was worried.

"Uh-huh." Jordan didn't have time for this. She had a few more things she wanted to do before her date with Franco.

A delivery truck drove by, not Franco's company. She looked up at Dalynn, who had another large smile pasted across her face. "Mmm. Too bad that Franco doesn't work on Saturdays. He is one fine *hunk* of a man." She waggled her overly plucked brows.

*You have no idea.* Jordan merely flashed a closed mouth smile and rifled through her mail for a brief moment, wondering when she could ditch the nosy neighbor and head back inside.

Dalynn stepped a little closer. "He accidentally dropped a box and hit my leg. He was so sweet, down on one knee, massaging it for me."

*What?* Jordan's head flew up and her heart skipped a beat. "He did?" That was precisely what happened to Jordan weeks ago.

"Mmm. Next time it happens, I'll be sure to let him know my entire leg aches. All the way up." Dalynn strung out the last sentence with a shit-eating grin on her face. Then, she spun around. "Well, I need to get out of this sun. It causes wrinkles. Talk to ya later, Jordan." She waved her hand backward as she sauntered back to her house.

*What the hell? That couldn't be right.*

Jordan's stomach suddenly felt like lead and sinking farther down.

Was Franco hitting on Dalynn too? Likely, Dalynn gave him subtle hints that she would be open to sharing a romantic interlude...or many. And he might be testing the waters, thinking of accepting her offer.

She licked her lips repeatedly.

Jordan felt betrayed, and she didn't know if she even had the right to. They hadn't been dating very long. They never even talked about being exclusive.

But still, she'd let her guard down... She'd planned to ask him to spend the night with her.

She wanted to cry. She sank down into a kitchen chair and covered her face with her hands. In these few short weeks, Franco was coming to mean something to her, and she knew it was more than lust. Did he not feel the same way? Clearly, he'd rather play the field than stick with one woman.

Well, that wasn't gonna work for her.

The text hit Franco's phone several hours before he had to leave for his date with Jordan.

A smile pulled at his lips.

He opened the text and read it.

*Franco, change of plans. I can't go out with you tonight. Try Dalynn. She seems interested.*

*What the fuck!* What did Dalynn have to do with anything? That woman was bad news. He'd limited his face-to-face time with her to when he absolutely needed a signature for shipments for her husband.

He punched the call button, but it rolled to voicemail immediately. Jordan was ignoring him.

*What the actual fuck!*

Franco grabbed his keys off the front table and headed to his truck. His heart hammered in his chest. He'd get to the bottom of this, if it was the last thing he did.

After a quick drive and a few broken traffic laws, Franco pulled into Jordan's driveway just in time to see her backing out of her garage in her silver sedan.

He put the truck in park and strode to her side of the car.

She lowered her window. "Franco, I'm leaving. Please move your truck."

"Not yet, you're not. Not until you tell me what's going on."

Her eyes darted to Dalynn's house, then back at him. "Whatever. You're not the guy I thought you were." The hurt in her eyes made him want to rip the door off the car and pull her into his arms.

He questioned again what the hell happened and wondered if he'd ever be able to salvage it.

The knot in his stomach grew. "Jordan, I'm exactly who you think I am."

She shook her head but didn't say a word, like speaking was difficult just then.

"What did Dalynn tell you?" He dropped his voice and leaned in closer. "I have no interest in her."

Jordan looked forward, then speared him with a look. "She said you dropped a box on her and knelt down to massage her leg for her."

His mouth dropped open. That was precisely what happened to Jordan weeks ago. Only that's *not* what happened to Dalynn...exactly.

He shook his head, feeling the heat flood his face and neck. "That is not what happened." He reached for the door handle, but the door was locked. "Open the door, Jordan."

"No. I'm leaving."

"Okay. After you hear the *real* story, if you still don't like it, then you can leave."

She pursed her lips together and glanced at his truck in the rearview mirror. She was blocked in.

She put the car in park and opened the door.

He took her hand and walked with purpose across the lawn to Dalynn's front porch. With a free hand, he knocked and swore the door rattled on its hinges. He sucked in a slow, deep breath. It would be best to remember that she was still a customer of his and embarrassing her to the point of calling his boss would not be good.

Dalynn opened the door and instantly her eyes rounded. "Franco. Jordan." Her voice went up an octave.

"Hi, Dalynn. Jordan just wanted to stop by and see how your toe was."

Everyone looked down at Dalynn's bare feet and her bruised big toe. In her shorts, he knew Jordan could see the woman's legs. Legs that had zero bruises from a supposed box collision.

"Um, it's fine."

"Good," he rushed on. "It looks like the ice I got you has kept the swelling down nicely. And if you keep taking the arnica, that bruise should be gone in a day or two."

"Yeah, thanks."

"Oh, you're welcome. Well, take care." Then, he lifted Jordan's hand, kissed the back, and faced her to say, "So, babe, I want to try that new sushi place downtown for dinner. You up for sushi?"

Jordan simply stared at him, speechless. "Um, sure. That sounds good." Probably not even sure what she agreed to.

"Perfect." He gave her his biggest million-dollar smile, and without a glance Dalynn's way, he walked Jordan back to her house.

He could practically feel Dalynn boring a hole into his back.

Stopping at Jordan's car, he opened the driver's door, started the car, and pulled it back into the garage where it damn-well belonged.

Jordan's precious mouth hung open as she watched him.

He clasped her hand, closed the garage door behind them, and led her into the house.

Stepping closer, he rubbed her upper arms. "Do you believe that nothing happened between us? Do you believe that all I did was bring her ice?" he spoke softly.

Jordan smoothed her lips together. Then after a moment, she nodded.

He pulled her closer. "Do you believe you're the only one I want to be with?"

A sheen came across her eyes, and she nodded again.

"Good."

That was the last word spoken when he pulled her close for a passionate kiss. One laced with a hint of desperation. He consumed her like he wanted to show her she was all that mattered to him. That he *only* had eyes for her.

She swung her arms around his neck, clinging to him.

His arms circled around her, pulling her into him. The slight dig of his erection showed her how *she* turned him on. Not Dalynn. Not anyone else.

She pulled back enough to speak. "Franco, I'm sorry."

A tear escaped and ran down her cheek. He swiped it away with his thumb. "No need to be. Right now, I need to show you just what you mean to me." His hands slid under her top, caressing her abdomen as his fingertips slid under her waistband.

"Yes. Please." She craved his touch.

He latched his mouth to hers once again, and in an unexpected move, he lifted her, carrying her to her bedroom.

She wrapped her arms and legs around him.

Setting her down, he stripped off her tank top and pulled her bra straps down to give his mouth access to her nipples.

"Ah." She gripped his shoulders, and her head fell back as he made love to her breasts.

He lifted his head. "Beautiful."

The heat in his eyes she was coming to recognize meant he wanted to devour her.

As he unfastened her shorts, she unclipped her bra and dropped it to the floor.

He went to his knees and instantly mouthed her pussy over her lace panties.

"Oh, God, Franco. So good. So good." The man's mouth was pure talent.

He slid the confection down her legs, and she stepped out, leaving her naked to him. Only for him.

He cupped her face, kissing her fiercely. After several moments with the slickness gathering at the apex of her thighs, he spun her around, resting her hands on the mattress.

He stroked his hands up her thighs to her ass. "Jordan, I've lusted for you for the past three years. Now, that has grown into something more."

Aligning himself, he gripped her hair, gently pulling her head back and pushed effortlessly into her channel.

She moaned as he pushed against her pussy walls.

"Oh, God."

"Oh, God what?" He brought her upright, and she reached behind to grip his ass. Then his fingers came up to toy with her peaked nipples.

"Don't stop."

"Don't stop what?"

She struggled to find her words as his cock rode her G-spot and the exquisite sensation from her nipples shot straight down. "Don't stop fucking me."

"What else?"

"Franco."

He was waiting for something, something more. Did she dare say it?

"Jordan."

"God, Franco, don't stop loving me."

"I won't, baby." His tone softer. "No broken promises, no cheating, nothing but worshipping you the way you deserve."

He pulsed inside her, driving her out of her ever-loving mind.

"Franco." She cried out and gripped his bare ass as her climax crashed through her forcefully.

He drove into her two, three more times and released.

She couldn't even remember hearing the condom wrapper, but she trusted him. She knew it the whole time, and letting Dalynn get into her head was a moment of weakness.

They collapsed onto the bed. He slid out of her and pulled her into him, face to face.

After a few moments of catching their breath, he spoke. "Jordan, I'm not your ex. I'm not a liar or a cheater. I've fallen in love with you. Tell me you know that."

Her sight turned slightly hazy. She nodded. "Yes. And I've fallen in love with you too."

He smiled broadly, and breaking their sex-filled haze, his stomach rumbled.

She chuckled. "Need some food?"

"Yes, please. I need to feed the beast."

She rose and slid on her panties.

He pulled up his briefs and retrieved her bra.

Then, she stood. "Well, I have some incredible beef stew I can heat up, but you'll need to convince me to share."

The smile on his lips faded, but the heat in his stare grew.

She'd just poked the bear.

She spun around and ran down the hall, his footsteps right behind her.

She laughed, and he called out just as he caught her arm, "Not so fast, you little vixen." He swung her around and into his arms. "Let me try and convince you to share with me."

# Afterword

Thank you so much for reading the Kaleidoscope Series!

If you enjoyed this story, please consider posting a review at one or more of your favorite retailers, as well as Goodreads. Even a short review, one or two lines, can be a tremendous help and encouragement to the authors. Your review is also a gift to other readers who may be searching for just this sort of story and will be grateful you helped them find it.

# Other Books by Mia London

Virgo (Zodiac Heat, 1)
Scorpio (Zodiac Heat, 2)

Kaleidoscope Series:
Black Tie
Blue-Eyed Devil
Firecracker Red
Angel In White
The Yellow House Next Door
Pretty in Purple
A Smattering of Gray
Plush Pink Lips
Lush Lavender
Scarlet Silk
Brown Box Delivery
That Stormy Obsidian Night

Second Chance at Love (Chance at Love, 1)

Only Chance at Love (Chance at Love, 2)

Honeymoon Hideaway

Runaway (Cascade Mountain Manhunt, 1)
Renegade (Cascade Mountain Manhunt, 2)

Accidental Tryst

Dry Spell (Sweet Escape, 1)
Hot Spell (Sweet Escape, 2)
Cold Spell (Sweet Escape, 3)

Undeniable Fate (Undeniable, 1)
Undeniable Love (Undeniable, 2)

Life To The Max
Wanton Angel, Prequel to Life To The Max

Perfect Seduction (Perfect, 1)
Perfect Surrender (Perfect, 2)

Beyond Lace (Hard Men of the Rockies, 4)

# About the Author

Mia London loves to write.

After reading fiction for years, she decided it was finally time to put those images and scenes floating around in her head down on paper.

She is a huge fan of romance, highly optimistic, and wildly faithful to the HEA (happily ever after). Her goal is to create a fantasy you will enjoy with characters you could love.

She lives in Texas with her attentive, loving, super-model husband, and perfectly behaved, brilliant children. Her produce never wilts, there are no weeds in her flowerbeds and chocolate is her favorite food group.

Facebook

Twitter

Instagram

Goodreads

www.mialondon.com

Email: mia@mialondon.com